until i found you

until i found you

Victoria Bylin

BETHANYHOUSE
a division of Baker Publishing Group
Minneapolis, Minnesota

© 2014 by Vicki Scheibel

Published by Bethany House Publishers
11400 Hampshire Avenue South
Bloomington, Minnesota 55438
www.bethanyhouse.com

Bethany House Publishers is a division of
Baker Publishing Group, Grand Rapids, Michigan

Printed in the United States of America

All rights reserved. No part of this publication may be reproduced, stored in a retrieval system, or transmitted in any form or by any means—for example, electronic, photocopy, recording—without the prior written permission of the publisher. The only exception is brief quotations in printed reviews.

Library of Congress Cataloging-in-Publication Data
Bylin, Victoria.
    Until I found you / Victoria Bylin.
        pages cm.
    Summary: "Nick Sheridan has made a vow: no dating for a year. And he's keeping it just fine—until Kate Darby turns his world upside down"— Provided by publisher.
    ISBN 978-0-7642-1152-2 (pbk.)
    1. Dating—Fiction. 2. Caregivers—Fiction. I. Title.
PS3602.Y56U56 2014
813'.6—dc23   2013047201

Scripture quotations are from the New American Standard Bible®, copyright © 1960, 1962, 1963, 1968, 1971, 1972, 1973, 1975, 1977, 1995 by The Lockman Foundation. Used by permission.

This is a work of fiction. Names, characters, incidents, and dialogues are products of the author's imagination and are not to be construed as real. Any resemblance to actual events or persons, living or dead, is entirely coincidental.

Cover design by Paul Higdon with Andrea Gjeldum

Author is represented by The Steele-Perkins Literary Agency

14 15 16 17 18 19 20   8 7 6 5 4 3 2

To Sara Mitchell

Beloved friend
Gifted author
Esteemed mentor
Lover of adjectives
Dear sister in Christ

Play the tape!

Loose yourself from the chains around your neck,

O captive daughter of Zion.

Isaiah 52:2 NASB

Prologue

the august sky radiated a perfect blue as Leona Darby carried her morning coffee out to the deck surrounding her log home in Meadows, a small community in the Southern California mountains. The blue jays wanted their daily peanuts, and she needed her moment of quiet. Never mind a nagging headache and the stiffness of old age. For the past twenty-two years, most of them with her husband, Alex, she had started the day by lifting her eyes to Mount Abel, the balding peak behind the house they had built together.

Alex was gone now, but Leona still ran the *Clarion*, the newspaper they started when Alex sold his photography business. Their only son, Peter, had died long before her husband had, and Peter's wife died of cancer several years later. Only Leona's granddaughter was left to carry on the Darby family traditions.

Beautiful Kate.

Troubled Kate.

Leona curled her gnarled fingers around the steaming cup, closed her eyes, and prayed the prayer she had murmured every day since Kate was born twenty-nine years ago. "Protect her, Lord. Be with her . . ." Tears welled in her faded eyes, because Kate was lost—seeking without finding, knocking on doors that led to empty rooms, and asking for things she didn't need.

"I'd do anything for her, Lord," Leona prayed.

The dull ache in her head expanded like a balloon, pressing and pushing until the pain exploded in a burst of light. Her coffee cup crashed to the deck, but she barely heard the thud. Neither did she feel the hot liquid on her open-toed slippers or the thump of her body hitting the redwood planks. Her mind shattered into silvery shards, each one a picture of the past—Alex aiming his Nikon at a condor landing in a stream bed. Peter playing fetch with the family dog. She saw her parents, her deceased brothers, cousins, friends, family pets.

Oh, what a glorious time!

It became more glorious still, when Alex lowered his old Nikon F, smiled and winked in that special way, then reached for her hand. Heaven was a pulse away, a last breath. She yearned to go home, but a shadow cast by giant wings blocked the light. The mirrors dulled to pewter, and she understood her glimpse of heaven was only that—a glimpse, a gift to sustain her, because her work on earth wasn't finished.

Twelve hours later she woke up in the ICU with a needle in her arm, a tube in her nose, and a clip on her finger.

"Nonnie?"

She dragged her eyelids upward and saw Kate at her bedside, grown-up Kate with her father's blue-green eyes, eyes now damp with tears. Wanting to comfort her, Leona opened her mouth to say she'd be all right. "Buh-buh-buh—"

She tried again. "Buh—" Gibberish.

Dear Lord, what's wrong? With her heart pounding, she mentally recited her name and age, address, birth date, and even her Medicare number. Next she tested her arms. She could move the left one but not the right. Her legs were in the same state of confusion.

"Buh-buh-buh!" She lay trapped in her body, paralyzed, and unable to speak.

Tears blurred her vision, but Kate's steady voice calmed her. "Nonnie, you had a stroke. We'll face it together. I promise."

"B-u-u-h."

"It's going to take time, but the doctor says you can recover." Even as a child, Kate had been optimistic to the point of pain. "You're going to need help when you go home. If you'd like, I could move in with you for a while."

No! I'd rather go to a nursing home than be a burden. Leona shook her head as hard as she could.

"I know you've always been independent." A smile tipped on Kate's lips. "I am, too."

Yes, you are.

"But right now my life's . . . confusing."

Leona hoped her eyes asked the question. *Tell me, honey. What's wrong?*

"You know Joel left."

Good riddance!

"Work isn't going well, either. Remember the Eve's Garden account?"

Of course. Eve Landon was Leona's favorite actress of all time. She also owned a famous spa, and Kate had designed the advertising. Leona would never forget the birthday when her granddaughter surprised her with Eve's autograph.

Kate squared her shoulders. "Eve put off going national until sometime next year. Without that account, there's a chance I'll be laid off. Taking a leave right now is a good idea."

Oh, honey. I'm sorry.

"So," Kate said with her typical brightness. "Moving in with you would be good for both of us."

With utter clarity, Leona recalled her glimpse of heaven and the claim she'd do anything—*anything*—for her granddaughter. God, it seemed, had taken her at her word. Before Leona went home to heaven, she had one last mission. Kate still needed her, and Leona knew exactly what she had to do. Even with her knotted tongue and limp right hand, she had to tell Kate about the condors.

1

kate darby clutched the steering wheel of her BMW with both hands. According to the state of California, San Miguel Highway was only the twenty-sixth most dangerous road in the state. That's why the county refused to pay for guardrails to protect motorists from the cliffs looming on the outer edge of the slick asphalt. October drizzle collected on the windshield, blurring the steep drops until the wipers brought the view back with startling clarity. The mountains plummeted three hundred feet to the valley floor, and the highway twisted so tightly she could see four sharp turns ahead of her.

She couldn't imagine driving this road more than occasionally, but that's what she'd be doing for the next two months, or until Leona recovered enough to live alone and go back to overseeing the *Clarion*. The stroke had occurred six long weeks ago. After a two-week stint in the hospital, Leona was transferred to Sierra Rehab for four weeks of therapy of all kinds—physical, occupational, and speech. She could feed herself now, bathe, and get around with a walker, but she still couldn't talk. The prognosis was uncertain. The doctors

11

and therapists all said the same thing. Only time would tell if she fully regained her speech, a process that could take up to a year.

In spite of the damp air, Kate lowered the side window. The hiss of rubber on the wet pavement assured her the car had good traction, though she wished she had replaced the worn tires. There simply hadn't been time. Between arranging with her boss for a leave of absence, packing her things, and visiting Leona at the rehab hospital, Kate's days were a blur. Three days from now she'd pick up Leona, but tomorrow belonged to Kate alone. She needed to unpack and buy groceries, but then she could curl up on the couch and lick the wounds left by Joel and cope with the lingering sadness of being away from Sutton Advertising. The boutique ad agency fit Kate and her talents perfectly. She was good at her job, and she loved the people, but she loved Leona more.

Sighing, she pressed the accelerator to climb a steep hill. When the tires spun helplessly on a patch of sand, adrenaline shot through her body. Local residents called the next curve the hanging hairpin. It was the highest drop on the road and had taken nine lives in ten years.

Her grandfather had taught her to drive, and now his calm instructions echoed in her memory. *"Brake going into a turn. Accelerate coming out of it."* Nervous, she steered into the hairpin with her foot on the brake. Centrifugal force pulled the car toward the cliff, but the tires held, and she confidently pressed the accelerator and rounded the bend.

A black bird standing three feet tall—a California condor—stood eating roadkill directly in front of the BMW.

The condor flapped twice, took flight, and grazed the windshield with its massive wing. A large yellow tag marked 53 in bold print slapped across Kate's field of vision, blinding her as she stomped on the brake. When the BMW fishtailed, she knew what to do—steer into a skid. But she had nowhere to go. The car was aimed toward the cliff. Frantic, she cranked the steering wheel downhill and to the left—a mistake because the right front wheel ran off the road. The car lurched to the side, throwing her off balance as the chassis sank into the shoulder, a strip of dirt about a foot wide but soft with rain.

Slowly, afraid to breathe, she eased the gearshift into Park and turned off the ignition. Silence engulfed her with the force of a dive into a swimming pool, but then the car tilted and she screamed. The new angle tugged her body forward—a death sentence if she moved. Beyond her vision, rocks careened down the slope in a rhythm as erratic and unstoppable as a heart attack.

"No," she whimpered. "*No!*"

Tentatively she dropped her gaze to the canyon below. Pine trees pointed upward like spikes, their tops a mile way. No way could she open the car door. The BMW would plummet down the slope. Neither could she reach the cell phone tucked safely in her purse, out of reach on the backseat, where she wouldn't be tempted to use it while driving. The notes of a high-pitched scream gathered in her throat—terror, hysteria, the irony of cautious Kate, a woman who didn't take chances, dangling over a cliff without her cell phone. Her ribs squeezed her lungs, and somehow she hurdled back in time to the day of her father's funeral . . . to her childhood home . . . to Leona and a flat of blue and yellow pansies.

"*It's all right, Katie girl,*" Leona had said. "*We'll plant these together.*"

The day before a car accident took his life, Peter Darby and his seven-year-old daughter had purchased flowers at the Green Thumb Nursery. She picked out the prettiest pansies, and he promised to plant them with her on Saturday. Instead, he died on a Friday afternoon in a twenty-car pile-up that made headlines on CNN. After the funeral, little Kate found the pansies wilting in the sun. She cried for a while, then put the flowers in her wagon and hauled them to the front yard to plant along the walk. Dirt was everywhere when her grandmother crouched next to her. In the first of many rescues to come, Leona helped Kate plant the flowers and clean up the mess Kate's mother didn't see at all through a haze of sedatives.

Without Leona, Kate wouldn't have survived those years. Staring into the canyon—an abyss, it seemed—Kate wished she had her grandmother's faith.

But she didn't.

Kate lived in the moment. She savored beauty where she found it, reveled in experience, and rolled with the punches.

Her friends changed with the seasons of her life—college, her first job, the big break at Sutton Advertising.

Men came and went. Joel was boyfriend number three.

Her addresses improved with her income—the latest being a tiny condo with a massive mortgage.

She took life as it came, good and bad. Why fight a string of random events? Accidents happened. Fathers died in fires, and grandmothers had strokes, also known as CVAs or cerebral vascular accidents. Sometimes condors landed in the middle of mountain roads, and cars skidded over cliffs. But why today? Leona needed her, and Kate didn't want to die. With the car teetering on the cliff, she thought of the stubborn faith that made her grandmother so strong. If Leona were in the car, she'd ask God for help. Kate didn't have that faith, but sometimes she wished she did.

Staring down at certain mayhem—injury, maybe death—she closed her eyes. "Are you real?" she whispered to Leona's God. "Because if you are, I need help."

There was no answer at all, only silence. But the BMW

stayed wedged in the mud. Was it wiser to stay still and wait for help, or to risk opening the door and jumping to safety? A shudder and a tilt made the question moot as the BMW plunged down the mountainside.

If he'd been a cautious man, Nick Sheridan would have spent the night in Valencia, a suburb on the northern edge of Los Angeles. His brother Sam had offered him the couch in the small tract home Sam shared with his wife and two young sons, but Nick resisted Sam's offer. Instead he raced his Harley up I-5 in an attempt to beat the storm. The sky opened up ten miles from the Meadows exit and he got soaked, but the adrenaline rush was worth both the chill sinking into his bones and the speeding ticket tucked in his leather jacket.

Considering Nick's former bad habits, an occasional traffic violation didn't seem so terrible. He considered it a business expense, not that he'd report it to *California Dreaming*, the travel magazine that paid him to write about everything from hiking trails to art festivals. Nick loved his work, but he hadn't always written for such a dignified publication. He was also—to his embarrassment—the author of *California for Real Men*, aka *CFRM*, a bestselling travel guide that had sold over a million copies to date and generated a popular app. Between the blockbuster sales, good investments, and his free-lance work, Nick's career made him financially comfortable. It had also made him a veteran of life in the fast lane.

A retired veteran, he reminded himself.

God was good.

God was merciful.

God had a sense of humor, because He'd taken one of the biggest sinners in California and turned him into a monk.

Nick hoped it was a temporary calling, because he hadn't

taken to celibacy like the apostle Paul. Sam, the preacher—his older brother who headed up international missions at a megachurch—was right. Nick needed a wife. But Sam had been blunt in the rest of his advice. *"I'm telling you what I tell everyone undergoing a big change. Don't make any major decisions for at least a year. You need time to shift gears."*

Sam had a point and Nick knew it. On his own he had taken the advice a step further and made a personal pledge—no dating for one year. A social sabbatical made sense for a man who did everything too fast.

Six months down. Six months to go.

But what then? He couldn't see himself among the singles at Sam's church. The women he met there were lovely, talented, and dedicated Christians, but Nick didn't fit in with all that niceness—nice barbecues, nice houses, nice everything. He'd been washed clean by the blood of Jesus, but six months ago he'd emerged from a very dark place. Sometimes the past pulled at him like gravity, and he had to fight to keep from sliding back into old habits. Those habits died hard, and some died harder than others.

He didn't drink anymore, but sometimes a cold beer sounded really good.

If he cursed, it was because he hit his thumb with a hammer.

He had always played it safe on the Internet, and he still did. No temptation there, because the porn industry disgusted him.

On the other hand, a man couldn't help but notice an attractive woman. Nick no longer viewed dating as a sport, and he was sorry he ever did, but he very much wanted to finish his sabbatical, fall in love, and settle down with the right woman.

Cold and wet, he veered on to San Miguel Highway, cranked the throttle but immediately eased off. Rain and speed didn't mix, especially on a road littered with rocks and decomposed granite. He didn't mind slowing down. He had lived in Meadows for six months now, and the drive through San Miguel Canyon still worked the same magic. His pulse slowed and his lungs filled with piney air. A deep breath scrubbed away the past, and he silently thanked God for that night on Mount Abel when he had grieved his mistakes and burned a copy of CFRM a page at a time. When the fire died to embers, Nick saw his life in the ash and called Sam.

"I'm done."

"With what?"

"Everything."

Sam had paused. *"You better explain, because 'everything' is a big word."*

Leave it to Sam to be dramatic, a side effect of taking the gospel to cannibals in New Guinea. Nick admired him for it. In a way, for a period of time Nick had been a cannibal of another kind—a man who fed off other people. He'd been a user back then, a taker. That night, his voice had cracked when he finally replied to his brother.

"Pray for me."

Nick still smiled at Sam's reaction. *"You idiot. I pray for you all the time."*

Silence.

"Pray for yourself, Nick. I'll listen."

More silence. Darkness. Then a breeze stirred the ash and a charred log glowed from the inside out. The orange sparks lit up a single moment of the endless night, but that moment changed him. With Sam on the phone, Nick cracked like an egg and spilled his guts, cursed like a sailor and cried like a little girl all at once. What a mess he'd been—and still was. Sam said Christ had died for his sins. It was that simple. Nick had believed and prayed, but Sam's next words made no sense.

"God forgives us, little brother. Now you have to forgive yourself."

Nice words, but his straight-arrow brother had no idea how it felt to get slapped with a paternity suit for a dead child—a baby girl who had endured open-heart surgery, infections, and two weeks in the NICU; a child who should not have been conceived. Nick barely remembered the Santa Cruz waitress who gave birth to the baby, but the genetic tests were a perfect match. He helped with the medical bills, then dealt with his guilt that night on Mount Abel. Those few hours changed him forever. The next morning he had ridden into Meadows, bought a half-finished log cabin, and officially become a monk.

Monkhood had some advantages. He slept when he wanted to and wrote at night, an old habit he still enjoyed; and to keep from becoming a weird recluse, he free-lanced for Leona Darby and the *Clarion*. With journalism and Christianity in common, the two of them had become good friends. The morning of the stroke, when Leona failed to show up at the office, it was Nick who found her and called 9-1-1. He often visited her in rehab and had promised to keep an eye on the house. But Leona wanted more. *And Kate,* she had scrawled on a paper tablet. *Be her friend.*

Nick had agreed, of course. But the last thing he needed in his head was the image of the pretty redhead he'd seen in photographs displayed in Leona's home and office. For now, monkhood suited his purposes.

With the Harley burbling at an easy pace, he decided to pick up tacos for dinner and then hammer out the article for *California Dreaming*. The free-lance work was a good distraction while he waited to hear from his agent about his newest manuscript—a memoir about what led to that night on Mount Abel. The income from a sale would be nice, but mostly Nick wanted to atone for *CFRM*.

He navigated the next few miles at a snail's pace, then slowed even more as he came around the hanging hairpin. What he saw put him on full alert. A quarter of the road had crumbled into a muddy slide. Nick braked to a halt, whipped off his helmet, and heard three short blasts of a horn . . . then three long ones . . . and three short ones.

SOS.

Someone had gone over the side and was alive. He snatched his phone and called the Meadows fire station. Captain Rob McAllister picked up on the second ring.

"Rob, it's Nick Sheridan. The hairpin crumbled."

"How bad?"

"It's down to one-and-a-half lanes. Someone went over the side."

"How far?"

"I can't see, but they're honking an SOS."

"We're on our way."

Nick wasn't about to wait for the rescue crew before he climbed down the canyon, but first other drivers needed to be warned. Helmet unstrapped on his head, he steered the Harley to the top of the hill, parked it across the lane and turned on the emergency flashers. He hoped no one plowed into it, but that was a risk he had to take. As he strode up the hill, the car horn continued to honk, three beeps at a time, over and over, in a cry as calm and desperate as the radio signals from the *Titanic*. He strode purposefully to the edge of the hairpin, looked down, and saw a metallic gray BMW wedged in a patch of scrub oak. The flimsy bushes made a fence of sorts, but any minute the roots could pull loose and the car would plummet another two hundred feet to the rocky bottom of the ravine.

He cupped his hands around his mouth. "Hello!"

Hooonk. Hooonk.

"Hang on," he yelled. "I'm coming down."

The horn blared again—three erratic beeps that sounded like *Yes! Yes! Yes!* He sized up the slope, didn't like what he saw, and decided to approach from farther down the road at a more horizontal angle. Staying close to the mountain, he walked several feet past the crumbled road before venturing to the cliff's edge. A slight bulge in the mountain offered the best approach, so he gingerly found footing and began the descent.

When he was halfway to the car, he called to the driver. "Can you hear me?"

"Y-y-yes."

A woman. Nick knew just about everyone in Meadows, and he didn't recognize the BMW. A visitor, he decided. Or someone speeding down an empty road the way he sometimes did. "Are you alone?"

"Yes." She sounded a bit calmer. "I'm afraid to open the door—"

"Don't."

"Are you close?"

"About thirty more feet." His boot slipped and he landed on his chest. Grunting, he maneuvered with the climbing techniques he'd learned in Yosemite for the "Daredevil" chapter of *CFRM*. His foot slipped again and knocked a rock down the slope. Female whimpering made his gut clench.

"Are you still there?" she called to him.

"Just a few feet to go."

He inched to a spot where he could see the shrubs bending with the weight of the car, their roots straining against the mud and close to breaking loose. Any minute the car could plummet to the distant bottom of the ravine. He listened for sirens but heard nothing. The rescue squad was at least five minutes away, and it would take time to rappel down the mountain. Nick glanced again at the scrub oak and got a bad feeling. He needed to get the woman out now.

"Are you hurt?" he asked.

"I'm just . . . just shaken up." An off-kilter laugh spilled through the window. "It's—it's a good car. I c-c-could do a BMW s-safety commercial."

"You could star in it," he replied lightly.

Bracing in the mud, he peered through the window and saw a woman in her twenties with blue-green eyes, ivory skin, and a swish of auburn hair. She was beautiful in a girl-next-door kind of way, and he recognized her instantly from Leona's gallery of photographs. This was Kate, Leona's granddaughter. Kate, whom he had called when he found Leona unconscious on her deck.

The woman's alto voice skittered out of her throat. "I-I'm afraid to m-m-move."

"I can see why." If he stayed calm, so would she. "We have to get you out of there."

She shook her head. "If I move, the car will f-f-fall."

"We'll work fast."

Pressed against the seat, she had one foot on the brake and was pushing as if her strength alone could hold the car in place. It couldn't. Neither could his. God alone had that power. Nick hoped He planned to be merciful today, because Leona loved Kate and needed her.

Her pale eyes flared into black disks. "Did you call 9-1-1?"

"They're on their way."

"How long?"

"Ten minutes. We can't wait." His gaze shifted to the bottom of the canyon. A few boulders jutted from the mountain, but most of the remaining drop resembled an expert-level ski slope. Nothing at all blocked the fall.

If Kate kept panting, she'd hyperventilate. And if she

thought too much, she'd be paralyzed with fear. He inched closer, braced against the slope, and kept his voice casual. "I'm going to pull you out of there."

He reached through the window and popped the door lock, praying God would keep the BMW steady for the two seconds he needed to open the door and pull her free. He hated to break her gaze, but they had one shot to get the angles right. He stepped back, gripped the door handle and prepared to grab her. The next step would be difficult. "You have to undo the seat belt."

"I-I c-can't move."

"Yes, you can."

"B-b-but—"

"Trust me, Kate. I'll won't let you fall."

"You know my name—how—"

"Later," he said. "We'll do it on the count of three."

She inched her hand to the seat-belt release button, closed her eyes, and pushed. The belt rolled smoothly into place. In the distance, a siren wailed. "Wait!" she cried. "They're coming!"

A root pushed through the crumbling earth. "There's no time."

"But—"

He gripped her wrist through the window. "One—"

"No!"

"Two."

Her fingers dug into his leather sleeve. Before he said "three," a branch snapped and the BMW started to roll.

2

Kate clawed at the man's arm
as he yanked her out of the car. If he lost his grip, she'd cartwheel down the slope like the BMW. The crunch of metal rattled in her ears; so did her screams, each one louder and more piercing than the first, until she slammed against the dirt and lost her breath. She scrambled to her knees, but the ground shifted and she splatted on her stomach. Pedaling crazily in the mud, she lost her footing completely.

"Kate! Stop fighting."

His tone stopped her cold. She couldn't breathe, couldn't move. A siren blared in the canyon, but it sounded no closer than a minute ago. Paralyzed, she stared into a pair of brown eyes so full of understanding that she didn't want to ever look away. Dark hair formed a widow's peak above brows that slashed across his high forehead, and a leather jacket fit his shoulders like body armor. Flat on his stomach but above her, he was wedged against a slight upturn in the slope and squeezing her wrist so hard his fingers were bone white. Streaks of mud covered his angular face, and his jaw sported at least three days of bristle.

23

Kate had never seen this man in her life, yet he knew her name. How? Who was he? An angel sent by her father? Of course not. Bible stories were just stories—a piece of her childhood like *Cinderella* and *Sesame Street*. No matter who he was, he held her life in his hands. A fresh scream gathered in her throat, but she swallowed it.

"That's better," he said with calm authority. "I have a good grip, but we have to work together, all right?"

"Y-y-yes."

"I'm going to pull you up. Use your feet, but don't struggle." He clamped his other hand over her wrist for a two-fisted grip. "Here we go."

Slow and steady, he pulled her toward the bulge in the mountain where tree roots gave her a place to wedge her toes. A final tug brought her over the lip of the rise, and she sprawled next to a pair of long denim-clad legs that ended in heavy motorcycle boots. Tasting mud, she wiped her face with the back of her hand and looked into the brown eyes she'd never forget. "You saved my life. I can't thank you enough. I'd still be in the car. I'd be—" *Dead . . . injured . . . trapped.*

He slid his hand from her wrist to her cold fingers. "You're safe."

"My things—"

"We can get them later," he said, as if he were inviting her to have coffee. "There's an old fire road down there."

She took a mental survey of the contents of the car—her purse and phone, clothing, her MacBook, the locket from her father, the jewelry box made by her grandfather that held little things she treasured. Some items could be replaced; others couldn't. Tears sprang to her eyes at the prospect of losing the locket, but she blinked them back. "C-can you see the car?"

"No, but it looks like the trunk popped." His gaze traveled down the canyon until he focused on something, maybe the car. What he saw made his brows snap together. "Kate?"

Her name again. "How—"

He interrupted. "How full was the gas tank?"

"I topped off in—"

Boom! An explosion blasted through the canyon. In the same breath, he pulled her against his leather jacket and rolled to the outside of the ledge to shield her from flying debris. Flames crackled in the distance. She smelled gasoline and tasted acrid smoke, but what she smelled most vividly was the leather jacket—a wall between herself, the fire, and the abyss.

Above them the siren died. Silence amplified every other sensation—the pounding of her heart, the rasp of the stranger's breath, the crackle of flames feasting on dried brush. Fresh shudders rocketed from her chest to her belly, then to her ice-cold feet. If she'd been in the car, she would have burned to death. She would have—*Stop it!* But the shaking owned her until the same hand that pulled her to safety coaxed her to hide her face in the crook of the man's neck.

His arm tightened around her middle like a seat belt. "We're safe now," he murmured. "Just stay still."

"Easier said than done," she muttered. "I c-can't s-stop shaking."

"That's normal."

Nothing seemed real—not the accident, the man, and especially not the giant bird that had caused her to swerve in the first place. A condor—what were the odds? Years ago the species had been nearly extinct when a recovery program brought it back from the brink, but the birds were still rare. Her grandfather's coverage of the early recovery efforts had earned him a Pulitzer Prize. The pictures still hung in the Clarion office, a testament to her grandfather's love of nature.

Though rattled by the accident, Kate could hardly wait to tell Leona about Condor Number 53, but first she had to get out of the canyon. She'd been safe for a full minute now, and her thoughts were beginning to land like jets arriving at LAX, one after another in a patient yet urgent pattern. Foremost in her mind was the bristled jaw pressed against her temple, the strong arms holding her tight, and the cold ground soaking through her thin sweater.

She didn't dare move, so she spoke to him with her eyes on a button on the jacket, the one over his heart. "You saved my life," she repeated. "I don't know how to thank you—"

"I'm glad I was passing by. I'm Nick Sheridan. I recognized you from pictures in Leona's office. We met on the phone—"

"You called when she had the stroke."

"That's right."

Memories assailed her—her phone ringing in a noisy restaurant, how she had complained about the unknown caller ID, then struggled to hear over the clatter of dishes and the buzz of conversation. When Nick Sheridan identified himself as Leona's friend, Kate had assumed he was middle-aged or elderly—a mistake, but neither did he remind her of Joel, who was wire thin, fashion conscious, and insanely neat. She couldn't imagine Joel climbing down a mountain to save her, needing a shave, or even getting dirty. Not that it mattered. Joel lived in New York now. People came and went from her life—everyone except Leona. That's just the way it was.

A deep voice bellowed down the mountain. "Hey, Nick!"

"Down here!" he shouted. In a normal tone, he said to her, "That's Rob McAllister. He's the fire captain."

Kate craned her neck toward the road, where flashing amber lights indicated a rescue vehicle. She couldn't see past the lip of the cliff, but a man in a dark uniform stood near the edge with his hands on his hips, assessing the situation until he narrowed his gaze to Kate and Nick. Squinting, the fireman cupped his hands around his mouth and shouted, "Anyone hurt?"

Nick's breath brushed over her ear. "How are you?"

"I'm all right," she answered. "Shaken up, but no broken bones, not even a sprain."

"Rob can send a couple men with a stretcher, or we can use harnesses and climb."

"Which is fastest?" She didn't want to spend another minute in the canyon.

"Harnesses."

"Then I'll climb."

Nick shouted back up the hill. "I'm with Kate Darby— Leona's granddaughter. Send down a couple of harnesses. We can climb out."

"Broderick's on his way," the captain replied.

The next five minutes passed in a blur. A fireman rappelled down the mountain, helped them into bright yellow harnesses and told her to let the winch do the work while she walked up the hill. The man named Broderick climbed with her to the lip of the asphalt where two other firemen lifted her to safety. One made sure she could stand on her own while the other man undid the safety harness. As soon as he finished, a third fireman wrapped her in a wool blanket that felt wonderfully warm and dry.

Captain McAllister approached from the downhill side of the road. "Miss Darby," he called in a firm voice. "Let's check you for injuries."

The fireman walked her to the rescue truck, where she sat on the top of the built-in steps. After she wiped her face and hands with a towel, the captain took her pulse and blood pressure, then checked her eyes for dilation and asked her routine questions that she answered easily. The blanket warded off some of the chill, but she could hardly wait for a hot bath at Leona's house . . . except how would she get there? And what would she wear? What about her car, her purse, her wallet, ID, credit cards, the laptop, her phone? Overwhelmed, she closed her eyes and groaned.

Captain McAllister put a large hand on her shoulder. "Your vital signs are normal, but you should be checked out at the ER. Is there someone who can take you?"

Kate shook her head. "I'm all right."

"You should still be thoroughly checked."

If she went to the hospital, they might keep her. "Really, I'm fine. The airbag didn't even deploy."

The captain patted her shoulder in a fatherly way that matched his gray hair. "You're a lucky young lady."

"Yes—" Her throat narrowed to a pinhole. If Nick Sheridan hadn't come to her rescue, she would have been burned alive. She thought of the random things she liked to do to help people—a generous tip for an exhausted waitress, helping a friend move—but nothing compared to the risk Nick had taken to save her life. The sun glared through the clouds, blinding her as she pondered the miracle she had just been handed. *Why me?* She should have died in that canyon in a random accident caused by a random bird. But condors weren't random. They were rare and special to Leona.

Rocked again by the trembling, Kate looked past Captain McAllister to the spot where roadkill testified to the reality of Condor Number 53. Kate hadn't imagined the giant bird, yet nothing seemed real—not the accident, not Nick Sheridan, who at that exact moment climbed out of the canyon, head first, then broad shoulders and long legs. He worked the latches on the harness like a pro, handed it to a fire fighter, and accepted a towel in exchange. After wiping his face and hands, he approached her with long strides that ate up the pavement.

"Hi," she said with a shy smile. "We meet again."

"How are you feeling?" A twinkle lit up his brown eyes. They weren't as dark as coffee, more like milk chocolate.

"I'm all right. Just a little . . . shaky."

Captain McAllister harrumphed. "I'm trying to convince her to go to the ER, but she won't listen."

Nick studied her for a moment. "I'll take you if you'd like."

"No. I'm fine." She fluttered her hand to prove it. "Magic Mountain could charge money for a ride like that—the Canyon Drop . . ." A ridiculous giggle came out of her mouth. Kate never giggled.

An amused smile lifted Nick's lips. "How about the Toaster Coaster, complete with exploding car?"

In spite of her terror, Kate laughed. "Or the Mudslide. Very basic."

Captain McAllister studied her with the patience of a man accustomed to seeing people cope with accidents, even tragedy. She supposed stupid jokes were better than hysterical sobbing, but her nerves were as taut as piano wires. One slip and her feelings would explode like the car. *No. Don't think about it.* She bit her lip hard to refocus her mind, a trick she had learned as a child.

Captain McAllister put away the blood pressure cuff. "How's Leona? Is she home yet?"

Kate shook her head. "I'm supposed to pick her up on Thursday. How long will the road be closed?"

"Not long," he replied. "An emergency road crew's on the way. They'll have it open in a matter of hours."

"But how?" Kate couldn't imagine it.

Nick pointed to the inside of the curve. "They'll cut the road deeper into the mountain."

Repaired or not, Kate didn't want to drive San Miguel Highway ever again. But she had to do it, and so she would.

The reality of the accident settled into her bones like a winter chill. Leona's old Subaru had a million miles on it, but Kate could drive it for now. She had to call her insurance company, but she didn't have her phone or even the number. She qualified for a rental car, but she didn't have a license. Tomorrow promised to be awful. She'd drive to Los Angeles on a back road, spend hours at the Department of Motor Vehicles, and more hours on the phone with her bank, credit-card companies—all that, while getting ready for Leona's homecoming, an effort that included cleaning, stocking the kitchen, and meeting the handyman who was installing grab bars in the bathroom so Leona wouldn't fall . . . another accident, another random event.

Dizziness sucked Kate back down the canyon. *I almost died and I'm thinking about grab bars.*

The captain's radio crackled with a call from another crew. Listening in, Kate learned the car fire was out and a wrecker was on its way from Meadows. Her possessions—some of them—had been tossed out of the car and were strewn across the mountain.

The hope of finding her purse launched her to her feet. "I want to go down there," she said to Captain McAllister.

He patted her shoulder again. "Not today, Kate. Go home and rest."

"I need my purse—"

"What's in that canyon is just stuff." He gave her a determined stare. "Trust me. It can be replaced."

But it wasn't *just stuff*. It was *her* stuff. Yes, the car was insured and so was her phone, but the locket from her father was priceless and utterly irreplaceable, a memory she sometimes held in her hands. And her ID and credit cards. If she found her purse, she wouldn't have to go to Los Angeles. Between the DMV and facing the depths of the canyon, she'd gladly choose the canyon.

Captain McAllister struck her as a "by the book" kind of man. Kate was a "by the book" kind of woman. Under normal circumstances she would have honored his advice, but today wasn't normal. Ignoring her muddy clothes and foggy brain, she lifted her chin as if she were fighting for a promotion at Sutton. "I appreciate your concern, Captain McAllister. I really do, but I have to get my purse. If there's any chance—"

Nick interrupted. "I'll go."

She opened her mouth to protest, but his offer stunned her into silence. Except for Leona, very few people had ever come to her rescue. She usually did the rescuing—first for her mom, later for college friends and boyfriends number one and two, but not Joel, who had left for New York with a casual, *"See you when I'm in town,"* as if they hadn't been together for almost year, as if she hadn't expected marriage. Kate took care of herself. She took charge in a crisis, but this wasn't a jammed photocopier or a toothache. Her *life* was in this canyon—at least remnants of it—and she wanted to see it for herself.

She faced Nick. "I'd like to go with you."

"No." That voice again—pure authority. Chin down, he matched his gaze to hers. "I can work faster alone. And the captain's right. You should take it easy."

Kate didn't like being told what to do, especially after being trapped and helpless. It was her nature to take charge, and that's what she did. Under the scratchy blanket, she squared her shoulders. "It's my car—"

Captain McAllister interrupted. "Both of you—stop. *No one* is going down there today. It's a mess and it's dangerous.

A hazmat crew needs to do some cleanup before anyone takes a hike."

Kate told herself to go with the flow and roll with the punches, but a lump refused to budge from the back of her throat. "But my things—"

Nick gave her the same strong look that had stopped her from screaming in the canyon. "I'll get them tomorrow."

"I guess, but—" She chomped on her lip to keep from crying, but her knees still buckled. Defeated, she dropped down on the step.

Captain McAllister leaned back, assessing her. "Are you sure you don't want to go the ER?"

"Positive."

As if she'd told a joke, his gray eyes twinkled. "You're as stubborn as Leona."

"I'll take that as a compliment," she replied.

"Oh, it is." The fireman chuckled. "Everyone in Meadows knows Leona. Tell her Rob and the boys say hi."

"I will."

"But Kate? Don't be too stubborn to accept help. Is there someone you can call? Someone to stay with you?"

Yes, there was. And she very much needed a friend who would listen while she talked about the condor, the fall, the rescue. "I'll call Dody Thompson." Dody was Leona's best friend. Since the stroke, she'd become Kate's friend, too.

"Good," the captain replied. "I'll drive you to Leona's as soon as we're done here. It won't be long."

"Thank you."

He left to check on the men at the other end of the roadblock, leaving her with Nick, the blanket, and a fresh attack of the shivers. "It's not that cold," she protested. "I'm just—"

"Rattled," he finished for her.

"Yes."

32

"Can you get in the house?" he asked.

A good question considering her keys were lost. "I should be fine. There's a spare key in the garage—"

"Under the flowerpot."

"You know about it?"

"Leona told me."

"You must be good friends."

"We are. I help out with the *Clarion*," he explained. "Speaking of the paper, I'll get pictures of the road."

Kate was supposed to be looking after the paper for Leona, and she had overlooked the biggest news story of the year. Embarrassed, she stood straighter and took responsibility. "I should have thought of that."

"You have other things on your mind." Nick held up his phone. "I have it covered."

"Thanks." She seasoned the inadequate word with a smile, but nothing could convey to him what she felt. She was gloriously alive because he had shown up at the exact right time and was crazy enough to climb down a cliff. He'd risked his life for her. No one had ever done anything like that. Joel wouldn't even help her paint her condo, though he was quick to want to spend the night. Suddenly her eyes burned with hot tears. She blinked them away, then raised her gaze to Nick's angular face. "How can I ever thank you—"

"You already have." He stared down at her, his gaze bright and his mouth relaxed. "Any man would have done what I did." He studied her with a tenderness she rarely saw on male faces, then handed her a blue bandanna. "Here."

She took it, wiped her eyes and succumbed to a wave of despair. Nick was wrong about *any man* coming to her aid. Joel had left her with a "see ya, babe" and a quick kiss. Her boss didn't want to lay her off, but he'd do it in a blink to protect the bottom line. The threat of losing her job loomed like the cliff that had nearly taken her life . . . *would* have taken her life if Nick hadn't been passing by. She wiped her nose with the bandanna that smelled like leather and good cologne, refrained from thanking him again, but refused to give it back when he held out his hand.

"I'll wash it for you," she said.

"Keep it." He tapped on the side of the truck and stepped back. "I'll call you tomorrow about your things."

"That would be nice." Her gaze slipped from his face to his broad chest and shoulders, then to the leather jacket marked with mud and the imprint of her body, evidence he'd held her close and kept her safe. Her turquoise sweater had a matching smudge, and she vaguely thought of the condors and what she knew from her grandfather—that young birds imprinted off older ones to learn how to survive, and that they mated for life. Beneath the streaks of dirt, a blush warmed her cheeks. She had no business thinking about muddy imprints and the mating habits of condors. She was in Meadows temporarily and had no interest in a relationship. As for commitment, she took life a day at a time because what more did anyone really have?

Focusing her thoughts on the present, she indicated his jacket with a slight smile. "The mud looks like a Rorschach test."

"So does your sweater."

"What do you see?" she joked to lighten the mood.

His eyes dipped down, then back to her face. Silence hung a moment too long, then he said, "I see mud. What about you?"

"Not bats," she said, a reference to the standard Rorschach reply. "I see a jacket that needs cleaning." *And a good-looking man.* Nick Sheridan had the posture of a soldier, the ease of a cowboy, and the daring of a pirate.

His mouth lifted into a half smile and stopped, as if he'd

stifled a reaction. Abruptly he directed his gaze to the peaks on the other side of the canyon. "I better take those pictures."

She watched him trudge up the road and around the bend, pausing occasionally to photograph the broken pavement. A few minutes later a motorcycle rumbled around the hairpin, and she looked up. There was Nick in his jacket, gauntlets, and a silver helmet he wore like a crown. The crown made him a modern-day knight in shining armor, one mounted on a black Harley with a mile of chrome. She followed him with her eyes until he passed her with a dip of his chin and a wave. Her heart gave a little flutter, but she didn't pay attention. Flutters came and went, and she'd long outgrown the childhood fantasy of being a damsel in distress. What mattered was helping Leona recover, keeping up with her career, and getting back to Los Angeles and the life she loved and already missed.

3

it didn't take long for news of the road collapse to reach Meadows. Nick had just left Kate and was about to climb on the Harley when Maggie Alvarez, assistant editor of the *Clarion*, called his cell phone. She'd heard the sirens leaving Meadows and gleaned the news on the police scanner. Could he cover the story, she asked? He told her he was already on site, and he sent the pictures from his phone so she could update the website.

With Leona in the hospital, Maggie had stepped up to keep the paper going—a challenge for a woman with two children and a husband with a demanding career of his own. Nick helped her by covering hard news in addition to his free-lance work, and he assisted with production when a deadline loomed. Advertising still had to be sold, and that job belonged to Art Davis, a retiree with a gift for gab. Eileen Holbrook was a combo bookkeeper/receptionist. Between the four of them, the *Clarion* had managed to limp to press while Leona was in the hospital.

Nick had a soft spot for the old newspaper, a weekly tab that harkened back to simpler days and fit the small-town atmosphere. After his night on Mount Abel, he had ridden into Meadows for breakfast, bought a copy of the *Clarion*, and spotted the ad for the half-finished log cabin he bought that afternoon. The living room, kitchen, and master bedroom were finished now, but the other bedrooms needed carpet and paint. Between his memoir, the *Clarion*, and *California Dreaming*, he'd been too busy to work on it.

He finished with Maggie, revved the bike, and rode close to the mountain as he passed the mudslide. When he saw Kate, he waved in the casual way motorcyclists acknowledge each other, then sped toward Meadows.

A fast ride forced him to concentrate on the road—not Kate and the Rorschach test on her sweater. Nick knew what he'd seen, what any man would see. Kate Darby had curves in all the right places. A man couldn't help a first glance, nor could he control natural interest. It was the second look that mattered, the second thought that led to mistakes. Never again would he treat women and dating casually. As Nick and the captain of the *Titanic* both knew, accidents happen. He wouldn't let Kate turn into an accident—emotionally or physically. Under normal circumstances, he'd avoid her. But these circumstances weren't normal. She was Leona's granddaughter, stranded without a car, traumatized, and . . . *admit it* . . . beautiful in his favorite way. Common sense told him to keep his distance, but both common decency and his Christian faith demanded he reach out to her. In his mind he made a checklist.

1. Check the battery in Leona's car.
2. Open the chimney flue.
3. Haul in firewood.
4. Make sure Kate had dinner.

No, not dinner. Dinner would count as a date, and Nick was dead set on keeping his one-year pledge. Other rules, though, were meant to be broken, specifically Captain McAl-lister's directive to stay out of the canyon. Nick saw no reason to wait until tomorrow to salvage Kate's things. He needed a hot shower, but after he cleaned up, he'd trade the motorcycle for his truck and take the fire road to the scene of the crash. If her purse had bounced out of the car, he'd find it. At the very least, he could collect the things from the popped trunk and take them to Leona's house. But no dinner invitation. No banter. Like a U.S. Navy Seal, he'd go in with a plan and get out fast.

Houses began to appear in the mountains above the two-lane highway. The homes were mostly log cabins, but a few cottages and old A-frames poked through the mix of pine and oak. The rustic charm gave way slowly, first to a gas sta-tion, then a convenience store with a sign shaped like a giant wagon wheel. The first time Nick cruised into Meadows, he thought he'd discovered a Hollywood set caught between a remake of *Heidi* and Clint Eastwood's *Unforgiven*. The older buildings had an alpine look—steep roofs, gingerbread trim, and colorful shutters. They harkened to the 1980s, when Meadows was home to a Santa's Village. The reindeer were gone and the buildings had lost their luster, but the Chamber of Commerce hadn't given up. The newer build-ings were western style with split-rail fences, and souvenir shops that sold cowboy hats, fool's gold, and maps to a lost gold mine.

The small town appealed to Nick for all the best reasons. People took care of each other, but there were also fights over guardrails, local politics, and environmental issues—plenty of things to talk about with locals at the coffee shop, where he frequently ate, or with Hector, the mechanic who had Harleys in his blood. He could have done without the gossip about his marital status—and Chellie Valerio, a hairdresser who boldly flirted with him. But otherwise people were friendly without being intrusive. Everyone knew he'd written a travel guide that pushed the boundaries of common sense, but no one knew about his daughter, and he wanted to keep it that way. In Meadows he was the new Nick, a better man, or at least he was trying to be.

He steered on to Falcon Drive, climbed the last three miles to his house, and pulled into the driveway. Helmet off, he blew out a breath to clear his lungs, then inhaled as deeply as he could. He was home, such as it was. A hot shower waited for him, then he'd head to San Miguel Canyon and search for Kate's belongings. When he finished, he'd call her on Leona's house phone. No dinner invitation, he reminded himself. As for working together at the Clarion, he expected Maggie to be a buffer. The friendly editor talked all the time, which meant Nick wouldn't need to say much about the paper or anything else.

He'd be friendly, yes.

Charming, no.

Attracted to her? *Oh, yeah*. He couldn't help what he felt, but he didn't have to act on it. Six months, he reminded himself. He had made a promise to God and himself, and he intended to keep it.

In typical mountain fashion, the earlier storm had knocked out power to parts of Meadows, including Leona's house at the end of Quail Court. Kate could live without electricity for a few hours, but hot water was another matter. Fortunately the gas water heater was an old model with a pilot light. She lit it, waited an hour, and indulged in a long soak. Somewhat renewed, she put on ski pants and a moss green sweater she kept at Leona's for winter visits. Her insides were still quivering and probably would for a while, but her hands were steady when she used the house phone to call Dody.

As things turned out, Dody was visiting her daughter and grandkids in Fresno. "I'll come back tomorrow if you need me," she said after Kate told her the story.

"No, don't come. I'm fine."

"Honey, are you sure?"

"Positive."

"If you need anything at all, call Nick. Did he give you his cell?"

"No."

"Well, he should have," Dody said with a hint of impatience. "If you need the number, it's in the address book in the desk."

Leona had used the same red book since moving to Meadows twenty-some years ago. It overflowed with scraps of paper, different colors of ink, and scribbled-out entries that marked changes of all kinds—moves, deaths, and friendships faded with time. Kate had moved so often she had an entire page. She wondered what Nick's entry looked like and paused to consider his friendship with Leona, a woman more than twice his age.

"Dody?"

"Yes, honey?" Dody called everyone honey.

"It seems odd that Leona and Nick are such good friends. She's seventy, and he's . . . what? Thirty?"

"Thirty-one," Dody confirmed. "He writes for the paper, which is how they met, but it wasn't long before Leona adopted him. Nick's a writer, so they have that in common. Plus he recognized your grandfather's name."

"That makes sense." Nothing made Leona happier than remembering the glory days with Grandpa Alex, especially the years he spent covering the effort to save the California condor from extinction.

"Nick's easy on the eyes," Dody said with a smile in her voice. "With Joel out of the picture—"

Kate laughed. "Forget it."

"Why?"

"Bad timing." She liked Nick well enough, but she didn't need the stress of a relationship, especially one destined to be temporary. In two months, she'd be back at Sutton, working on the new proposal for Eve Landon. Eve had loved Kate's work on the first print campaign, and Kate reveled in the entire creative process. Matching images and words to convey concepts put order in her life and satisfied her in a deep, personal way.

Dody broke into her thoughts. "I have to go, but if you need anything call Nick."

"I will."

Dody offered another dollop of sympathy, then excused herself to change her granddaughter's diaper. Someday Kate wanted to be a mother—not for a while, but sometimes she heard the tick of her biological clock, in part because of Julie. Her best friend was thirty-eight years old, married, and desperate for a baby. If the latest hormone treatments didn't work, she and her husband planned to undergo in vitro fertilization. Kate worried about Julie, and Julie worried about her. Under normal circumstances, Kate would have already sent her a text announcing her safe arrival in Meadows. Instead she called Julie from Leona's landline and left a voice mail her friend probably wouldn't check until after work.

Eager to settle in, Kate borrowed Leona's slippers and ambled down the stairs to the living room, which felt more like home than her own condo. The sliding glass door opened to a wide deck that looked up to Mount Abel, and the Ben Franklin stove looked brand-new in a fresh coat of black polish. The woodbox needed to be filled, and so did the kindling bucket. In her mind, Kate began a list of things to do before Leona's homecoming, then realized again that her own life was in the bottom of San Miguel Canyon, burnt to a crisp and mired in mud. The trembling in her middle rose like an ocean swell but mercifully receded without cresting. She couldn't afford to break down, not now. She had things to do—like call her car insurance company.

Once again she used the old plug-in on the desk next to a bookshelf. Her grandmother kept the phone specifically for power outages, a wise decision considering the number of times a year Meadows lost electricity. The mountain climate took a toll on houses and cars, but with a year-round population of four thousand, Meadows had most of the conveniences of a big city—cable, a cell tower, a branch of the county library, even its own small school district. It was also in the middle of the Los Padres National Forest and one of the prettiest spots in Southern California, a pleasure that outweighed the inconveniences.

With that positive thought in mind, Kate called 4-1-1. A fake voice connected her to CalUSA Insurance. She pressed a few prompts, and another fake voice, male this time, assured her that her call was important to them and someone would be with her in—pause—Twenty. Eight. Minutes.

"I can't believe it," she muttered.

Tethered to the wall by the phone cord, she sat at the desk and wrote out a "to do" list—a task that took less than a minute. Between the peppy music and the periodic interruption of the mechanical man telling her that he cared about her, Kate was ready to pull her hair out. Instead, she popped to her feet and perused a bookcase holding an assortment of novels, mysteries, celebrity biographies, and local history.

She skimmed the titles until her eyes locked on *California for Real Men*. The "Real Men" books had become a cultural phenomenon, and the publisher had launched a series that included New York, Florida, and Hawaii. The California book had made the rounds at Sutton about a year ago, but Kate didn't pay much attention, in part because Joel mocked the "I came, I saw, I conquered" tone as retro and unsophisticated.

This wasn't the kind of book she expected to find on her grandmother's shelf, so she opened it. A handwritten inscription read *To Leona, Don't read Chapter Fifteen—All the best, Nick Sheridan*

The same Nick who had just saved her life?

She glanced again at the cover, reread his name and flipped to the back, where the author's photograph left no doubt of the connection. His hair was shorter now, but the daring grin was unmistakable. Mouth agape, she leafed through the pages. The book covered every inch of California from Eureka to San Diego, from the Sierra Nevada mountains to the Channel Islands. In a chapter called "For Daredevils Only," he sang the praises of hang gliding at Big Sur and bull riding in Kern County. Other chapters were tamer, particularly "Golf Isn't Just for Geezers" and "Bowling Alleys a Guy Hates to Love."

The more Kate read, the more she smiled. Nick had a wicked sense of humor, and she shared his "seize the day" view of life, if not his interest in bull riding. Happily amused, she skimmed through the chapters on beach activities, roller-coaster rankings, and motorcycle hangouts until she reached Chapter Fifteen, the one he said to skip. The heading read "Hot Women, Hotter Nights." She laughed at the cheesy pickup line and wondered if the inscription to Leona was in deference to her age, or if he was a little embarrassed by the no-commitment attitude. Lots of people enjoyed that kind of social life. Kate didn't, but she went out with her friends from work because . . . well, because they were her friends.

The music on the phone stopped midnote. The connection clicked and a rep came on the line. "Thank you for calling CalUSA Insurance. Suzie speaking. How can I help you today?"

"My car—" Kate choked on the word. Suddenly she was back in the canyon, shaking from head to foot.

"Did you have an accident?" Suzie said gently.

Pull it together, Kate told herself. She set Nick's book on the desk, plopped down on the chair, and described the wreck. She wasn't sure Suzie believed her about the three-foot-tall condor, but ten minutes later Kate had a claim number.

Fortified, she hung up and decided to tackle the next item on her list: *Check the Subaru.*

She snagged the keys from a hook in the pantry and headed for the stairs that connected to the garage from the back deck. The oak tree next to the house dropped thousands of acorns every fall, and it seemed to Kate every acorn in the Los Padres National Forest was outside her door. Using her feet like brooms, she swept the acorns out of the way, listening as they clattered to the edge and fell. Between sweeps, an eerie silence echoed in her ears. Her condo was considered quiet. But quiet and silent were as different as pale pink and magenta. Lately Kate had been in a magenta kind of mood—a blend of red with a dab of blue. The color captured her emotions perfectly. She yearned to experience life in all its glory, yet she wondered every day if her own life had any real purpose.

She wished she could talk to Leona. Her grandmother dispensed nuggets of wisdom like gumballs. Kate would chew on them and feel better, but today she could only stare longingly at Mount Abel. She had never been to the top, but her grandparents had often made the drive to enjoy the incredible view. On a clear day, a person could see a hundred miles to Catalina Island. Someday Kate would go—or maybe not.

The road twisted around cliffs higher than the ones in San Miguel Canyon.

Suddenly shaky, she shifted her gaze down and eastward to the Meadows business district. The rain had washed the air to crystal clarity, but sometimes clouds settled low and blocked the view of the town. Eyes closed, she relived one of those times.

"Look, Grandpa! I could jump and the clouds would catch me."

"No, Katie. The clouds are nothing but vapor."

Her grandfather explained the science to her, but even then Kate had understood a deeper truth. Life was full of illusions. Gazing at the town now, she reluctantly thought of Joel. He'd been fascinated by heights. Or more precisely, he was fascinated by falling. She remembered how frightened she was at Yosemite when he stood at the edge of the lookout on Glacier Point, his toes queued up to the edge of the granite, his arms stretched wide and his eyes shut tight. *"Imagine, Kate, I could stand here without the railing and not fall."*

He had tried to coax her to the edge, but she refused to budge.

"Coward," he said, accusing her.

She had argued with him, but tonight she wondered if he was right. She was afraid of so many things—mountain roads, dark alleys, being late to work. Of losing Leona and having no one. Of ending up like her mother, alone and dying from a cancer that might have been stopped if Elizabeth Darby had done a monthly breast check. Kate placed her hand over heart in a pledge to be responsible, took a breath, and went to the garage to start the car.

The side door creaked as she propped it wide to let in light. In her mind she pictured her grandfather at his workbench, making a birdhouse for nuthatches, the quirky little birds that ran up and down the trunks of pine trees. Garden tools lined the back wall in a testament to Leona's passion for pretty flowers, and assorted boxes filled the corners with the clutter of a busy life.

Without thinking, she pushed the button for the automatic garage door opener. When it didn't open, she remembered the power outage and tried to open the door manually. It didn't budge, and she couldn't recall how to work the manual release. Jaw tight, she tamped down her frustration and prioritized. *Item No. 1—Avoid carbon monoxide poisoning.* That meant opening the big door before she started the car, but if the car didn't start, she didn't have to worry about the door—yet. If the car started, she could turn off the engine.

She slid into the driver's seat and turned the key.

Nothing.

Not even a click. Groaning, she rested her head on the steering wheel—a mistake because the position shot her back to San Miguel Canyon. As she straightened, tears flooded her eyes. Sick to death of fighting them, she gave in and sobbed into her hands. With chest heaving and nose plugged, she let out the anger, the fear, the utter frustration of being stripped of her phone, her money, her car—*her identity*—when she desperately needed to hold on to . . . something.

"I can't stand it!" she wailed to the empty garage. With her palms hot on her damp cheeks, she cried until she couldn't think, couldn't see, couldn't do anything but yearn to be a child again.

The crunch of tires on the dirt driveway shocked her into silence. She didn't want company—not with her eyes red and her nose plugged. Maybe it was a propane delivery, or someone turning around in the cul-de-sac. Perhaps if she stayed still, whoever it was would leave. She strained to hear the sounds on the other side of the garage door—the cut of the

engine, a car door slamming, then heavy steps on the stairs . . .
male steps. She wondered if Captain McAllister had decided
to check on her and hoped not. Whoever it was knocked on
the house door, waited, then knocked again with more force.
Kate considered confronting him, but her city instincts kicked
in. She didn't know who was out there, and she had no way
to defend herself. The hurried steps beat around the redwood
deck to the sliding glass door, then thudded down the three
stairs that led to the garage.

Knowing she was about to be discovered, she climbed out
of the car and faced the door just as daylight silhouetted a
familiar set of broad shoulders. Nick Sheridan had come to
her rescue again, and he didn't look pleased.

in the past half hour,

Kate had worried Nick once and scared him twice. The worry started in the bottom of San Miguel Canyon when he was gathering her things. Thanks to her ringing phone, he'd found her purse and used his own phone to call Leona's landline to share the good news. When she didn't answer, he figured she was resting and put the missed call out of his mind. Halfway to Leona's house, he called again. When she didn't answer a second time, he hit the gas. He didn't know Kate well, but she struck him as someone who answered the phone. The third scare rocked him when she didn't respond to his knock on the door. He imagined her dizzy, falling, hitting her head in the shower.

That's when he strode around the deck to the back of the house. The path through the acorns pointed to the garage, but why hadn't she come out when she heard the truck? It occurred to him now that she was hiding from him. Light from the window illuminated the tears in her eyes, and her cheeks were a palette of ivory, white, and hot pink.

"Hi," he said from the doorway.

"Hi."

"Are you all right?"

"I'm fine," she answered. "I came out to check the car. The battery's dead, or it's something else. I don't know."

Car trouble didn't faze Nick in the least. Kate's tears did. A year ago he would have crossed the garage and put his arm around her. He would have played the part of a knight in shining armor just to charm her. Now he wanted to do the right thing for no reason at all. He pushed the button for the garage door opener, but nothing happened.

"The power's out," she explained.

Glancing up, he walked to the overhead mechanism, raised his arm, and tugged on a short yellow rope. The lock release snapped, and he lifted the door with one swing of his arm. Cool air rushed into the garage with a burst of light that made Kate squint. The fresh air chased away the smells of grease and mulch but not her immediate need—a need Nick could meet as easily as he breathed. "I'll jump-start the car, but first I have some good news. I went into the canyon. The roof tore off the BMW, so your stuff bounced out before the fire. It's in the back of my truck."

She pressed one hand against her chest. "Did you find my purse?"

"It's on the front seat."

"I can't thank you enough."

He didn't want her to try, especially if the effort meant a hug, or if it put fresh tears in her shimmering blue eyes, eyes the color of the ocean at sunset, eyes that—*Stop it!* He gestured to his truck with his chin. "Go take a look."

She dashed past him to the pickup, stood on her toes, and peered through the tinted window at her purse. "There it is!"

He reached in front of her and opened the door. Instead of grabbing the purse, she turned and hugged him hard. She felt warm and soft in his arms, small but not weak, and as curvy as San Miguel Highway. His body roared to life with physical awareness, a dangerous reaction, because he and Kate would be working together. He eased out of the hug, then indicated the bed of the pickup with his hand. "I think I found everything."

She admired him with those blue-green eyes, then turned back to the truck and touched a box marked *Treasures*. A corner was smashed, but the flaps were in place. "This one— can I look inside?"

He set it at her feet and slit the tape with a pocketknife. Kate rummaged through crumpled newspapers, then lifted a wooden box. Standing straight, she opened the lid and visibly relaxed. "Everything's here."

He saw a condor carved on the top of the box. Like the sign in the Clarion window, the design was hand-carved with a Dremel tool. "I recognize your grandfather's work."

"He loved condors." Inhaling deeply, she hugged the box to her chest. "I swerved because I saw one eating roadkill. It scared me to death."

"Really?" Condor sightings were special and rare. He'd written an in-depth story on the endangered species for *California Dreaming*, and he covered the Save the Condor program for the *Clarion*. He knew from biologist Marcus Wilcox that Condor Number 53 had lost her transmitter and was missing. If Kate saw the bird, Marcus would want to know. "Did the bird have a tag?"

"Number 53," she confirmed.

"This is important. That bird went AWOL about three weeks ago." He took his phone out of his hip pocket and called Marcus. The call went to voice mail, so he left a message.

Kate hugged the box tighter. "I'll be glad to tell him the whole story. I still can't believe what happened."

"I'll set up a meeting." He was about to suggest a news story for the paper when her phone interrupted with a chirp.

Kate put the box back in the carton and checked her messages. "That's Julie. We look out for each other."

Sam did the same for Nick. "Why don't you call her while I haul this stuff inside?"

"I should help you."

"No."

"But—"

"No," he repeated. If she helped him, they'd laugh and joke, even flirt a little. He refused to go down that road, but then how did he treat her? Like a sister? Maybe, but he didn't have a sister. He had Sam and they ragged on each other for fun. Somehow Nick couldn't see himself challenging Kate to an arm-wrestling contest. Before she could argue with him, he played his trump card. "Call your friend. She's probably worried."

"You're right." After another grateful smile, she trotted up the stairs and went around back to the deck.

He lugged the bags and boxes into the kitchen, then tried to jump-start the Subaru. The battery wouldn't hold a charge, so he called the Meadows gas station and asked Hector to deliver a new one. As he approached the deck to update Kate, snippets of her conversation drifted to his ear. Rather than interrupt, he detoured to the woodpile. Without power, she'd need a fire for heat, so he carried up a load of split oak and dumped it in the woodbox. As he turned back to the door, his gaze landed on Leona's desk and the cover of *California for Real Men*. Kate must have spotted it on the shelf and been curious.

People either loved the book or hated it. Nick hoped Kate hated it, because he wasn't the same man who wrote it.

Pushing her out of his mind, he went to the garage to wait for Hector.

Having a friend like Julie meant the world to Kate. They finished each other's sentences, laughed at the same jokes, and rooted for each other on every front. Kate wanted to shine at Sutton and be promoted to creative director; Julie enjoyed her work as a copywriter, but more than anything, she wanted a baby. The women were on different paths, but they shared the same basic goal—to be happy.

When Julie answered her phone, Kate blurted she had almost died. Julie consoled her and listened, even when Kate said again and again that she had almost lost her life.

"Try not to think about it," Julie urged. "It's over."

"Not really."

"What do you mean?"

"It's still so real." Kate wandered to the railing and peered at the clouds lingering in the western sky. "Every time I blink, I see the condor on the road."

"It'll take time."

"I guess."

"So," Julie said with too much cheer. "Tell me about Nick. Young or old?"

"Young."

"Good-looking?"

Kate glanced toward the garage where his truck was parked close to the garage and with the hood open. He was around somewhere, so she lowered her voice. "Think tall, dark, and handsome, but don't get excited. I'm not interested in a relationship right now, and you know it. When Eve's Garden goes national, I want to be in the thick of it."

"I know, but Kate?" A familiar wistfulness echoed in Julie's voice. "Don't wait like I did. If you want kids—"

"I know."

At least once a week Julie urged her to have children before her biological clock made the choice for her. For a while Kate had thought she was ready—but not anymore. With Joel out of the picture, living a day at a time suited her just fine. After all, what did a person really have except a single moment, a single breath?

She turned her thoughts back to Julie. "So what's new with you?"

"Jeff and I saw Dr. Brady—" A fertility specialist. "We start IVF next month."

Kate's heart hitched for her friend. IVF treatments offered hope, not a guarantee. "I'm pulling for you."

"Thanks."

The rumble of an approaching truck broke the mountain quiet. Curious, she walked to the front of the house where she saw a white pickup from Meadows Automotive. Nick must have ordered a new battery. "Someone's here," she said to Julie. "I have to go."

"Call me later."

"Will do."

She detoured into the house to get her credit card, then ventured down the stairs. The driver backed away with a wave, leaving her to follow Nick as he carried the battery one-handed to the car. By the time she reached his side, he'd put the battery in place and was tightening the cables with a wrench.

"What's up?" she asked.

"The battery was shot. I asked Hector to deliver a new one and put it on the *Clarion* account."

She slipped her Visa in a pocket. "I'm amazed he delivers."

"It's a small town."

"Even so, I'm surprised." On a whim, she pinched Nick's biceps. The muscle bunched at her touch, leaving no softness at all.

His brows shot upward. "What's that about?"

"You're too good to be true," she said, feeling a bit sheepish. "I wanted to know if you're real, or if I imagined you."

"What did you decide?"

"You're real."

She expected a flippant comeback. Instead his face pulled into a scowl. She wished she hadn't been so impulsive. The touch had been unnecessary, which made it too personal. She had no interest at all in flirting with him. On the other hand, they'd be working together at the paper and she wanted to be friends. With her arm loose at her side, she moved a step away from him. "I really do owe you for all this—" She swept her hand to indicate his truck, the house. "Could I take you to dinner? Just to say thank you?"

"It's not necessary."

No, but it would have been decent of her, especially since they'd be seeing each other at the Clarion. She didn't understand his reluctance, but she accepted it. Besides, she had other things to do tonight—like wash her muddy clothes. Tomorrow she'd prepare the house for Leona's return, and on Thursday she'd pick up her grandmother from rehab. On Friday she planned to meet with Maggie about the future of the paper.

Nick closed the hood with a light slam, then walked around to the driver's seat. When he turned the key, the old Subaru purred to life.

"It sounds great," she said when he cut the engine.

Ignoring her, he picked up the wrench and rags, put them in the bed of his truck, and faced her from ten feet away. "Call if you need anything."

"I will. Thanks again."

When he climbed in the truck and slammed the door, she headed to the house feeling confused by his gruff tone. When she reached the stairs, he called to her. "Kate?"

She turned and saw him standing again with the truck door open. Maybe he'd changed his mind about dinner. She hoped so, because she was a little lonely. "Yes?"

"Just so you know," he said in a tight voice. "I'm not dating right now. If I were, I'd have said yes to dinner. It was a nice offer."

After a casual salute, he sat back in the truck and started the engine. Kate waved good-bye and watched him back out of the driveway. Alone and a little sad, she walked into the house, saw her possessions on the kitchen floor, and thought of the bandanna he gave her in the canyon. Later she'd put it in her treasure box—a souvenir from a day and a man she'd remember forever.

Leona jarred awake in her bed in Sierra Rehab, peered into the dark and struggled to calm herself. She was accustomed to the sounds of the night—rubber soles on linoleum, the nurses' soft laughter. Something else had disturbed her sleep. She listened now, heard nothing and realized her own voice had awakened her. She had dreamed she could talk.

Oh, Alex. You were there, too.

With her fingers knotting the sheet, she closed her eyes and revisited the dream. Alex was lying on a red blanket in a sea of tall grass, shielding his eyes with one hand and pointing at the sky with the other.

"Can you see it, Lee?"

"A condor," she replied. *"It's magnificent."*

"You need to tell Katie-girl about those birds."

"*I will,*" she vowed.

In the way of dreams, the condor had soared into the sun and disappeared. Somehow Leona knew the bird was Aqiwo, the female she'd seen at the San Diego Wildlife Park many years ago with Alex and Kate. *Aqiwo* meant "Path," an Americanized version of a Chumash Indian word. Leona had a particular memory of Aqiwo—a painful one. Putting that recollection aside, she focused on the other pictures in her dream. The bright sky had faded to a pewter mist that thickened into a cloud so thick she couldn't see her own hand.

Kate's voice echoed in the fog. "Nonnie, where are you?"

"I'm here," Leona cried, but the words were only in her mind. Eyes wide in the dark, she focused on Alex's reminder to tell Kate about the condors.

Leona hadn't forgotten her promise in the ICU; she just didn't know how to tell the story. Physically, she got around with a walker and sometimes a cane. Her right hand lacked the dexterity required for a keyboard, but she could grip a fat pen, brush her teeth, and manage a fork. What she couldn't do was talk. In spite of the speech therapy, her tongue behaved like a rebellious child, sticking to the roof of her mouth or wagging out of control.

Wide awake now, she pushed a button to raise the bed. As the motor hummed, she eyed the Bible on the table. The Psalms called to her, but she didn't want to turn on the light. Instead she willed her tongue to move in prayer. The stubborn thing wouldn't budge. She clenched her teeth and tried to say Jesus but only moaned.

Lord, help me. How can I reach Kate when I can't even say your name?

As a child, she had played a game with her brother. Would you rather be deaf or blind? Would you rather lose a leg or an arm? Leona had chosen being deaf and losing an arm.

The stroke forced her to play the game in real life, only she hadn't been given a choice between walking and talking. If the Lord had asked, she would have chosen words over mobility. She loved the flow of conversation. Men told jokes and talked about cars and sports, but women shared feelings; they relaxed with each other. Oh, how Leona wanted those special moments with Kate! She had so much to share . . . memories and recipes, funny stories, but mostly the miracle of the condors.

She plucked a tissue from the box and wiped her nose. Sniffing, she scolded herself for wallowing in self-pity. God had kept her alive; surely He had a plan. She looked again at the table where she saw a pitcher of water, a half-full cup, and the rubber ball she squeezed to strengthen her fingers. Next to the ball sat an empty journal given to her by her physical therapist, a pen, and her Magic Slate, a toy she used to write notes. Leona could scrawl a few words, show the slate to Kate, then lift the plastic sheet to erase the them.

Slate . . . Kate . . .

Wait! Her eyebrows arched with a tickle of enthusiasm. Only time would tell if she'd regain her speech, but she could write in a journal at her own pace. After flexing the fingers on her right hand, she positioned the notebook in her lap and picked up the pen. With the dream of Alex fresh in her mind, she began to write . . .

Dear Kate,

You need to hear a story. It's about your grandfather and me. It's also about a species that teetered on the brink of extinction and survived. Condors mate for life, and so did your grandfather and I, though we were sorely tested in ways so private I pray for the courage to tell the truth.

The story begins in 1962. I'll save you the math! I was eighteen years old, wearing my favorite yellow sundress and waiting with my parents at the San Diego naval base to meet your Uncle Frank—my brother. He was four years older and called me Baby Sister, though I was far from a baby. That day when we met his ship, I felt rather sophisticated in high heels that made my legs look a mile long. Back then, I paid attention to such things. I was enrolled in junior college and taking classes in merchandising. I wanted to be a buyer for May Company.

I also wanted a husband.

My brother saw me and waved. Frank looked wonderful, but my gaze slid like Ivory soap to the sailor next to him. Dressed in blue crackerjacks, he looked like Gene Kelly, complete with wavy dark hair and a devilish grin. Before we ever exchanged a word, he raised his camera and snapped my picture.

I tried to look bored, but he saw right through me and winked. Oh, the tingle that ran to my toes is indescribable! We were strangers, but we sparked like two halves of a severed wire.

That sailor was Alexander Herbert Darby, Frank's best friend. Of course my mother invited him to stay with us for their two-week leave. At dinner that night, I couldn't take my eyes off him. He couldn't stop looking at me either, though he tried. After all, he was a guest in our home, six years older than I, and well aware that Frank would bloody his nose if he wasn't a perfect gentleman. Life used to be like that. There were rules, not like today, where—well, you know. What I want you to know now is that I felt safe with Alex, respected, and even cherished.

My mother asked him a hundred questions, which

were the same ones on the tip of my adolescent tongue. We learned he was born in Chicago and had joined the Navy to see the world. On his first tour of duty, he talked his way into becoming a photographer's mate. He was counting the days to the end of his enlistment, when he could pursue his dream of opening his own studio.

The family dinner ended in a double date with Frank and Phyllis, the woman he eventually married. The double date turned into a "just us" date, and that turned into a kiss good-night I will never forget. Alex and I spent every spare minute together, talking late into the night, sharing secrets, and falling in love.

On his last night home, he told me he loved me. I said the words back, and he asked me to marry him. Of course I said yes. Alex had one more year in the Navy. We wrote to each other every day—passionate letters, newsy letters, letters full of promises and hope and dreams of marriage and children.

We got married three months after his discharge. You've seen the pictures of us at that little white church, surrounded by friends and looking so young. Oh, what a day!

I hope what I'm about to say isn't too personal. Forgive me, Kate, if it is. But it's important to the rest of the story. Our wedding night was everything God intended marriage to be. So was our honeymoon at Ocean Acres, a motel near Santa Barbara with cottages on the beach.

We were so much in love that we saw beauty in every grain of sand, every gull, and especially in the condor that landed on the beach to peck at a shell. Alex shot an entire roll of film before the bird flew away. Later that day we visited a local museum where we read the condor legends passed down by the Chumash Indians.

Like the Chumash, we felt blessed to see the rare bird and took that condor as a gift from God, a kind of wedding present.

Two things happened when we returned home. Alex sold the condor pictures to the Los Angeles Times, *and I came down with morning sickness. Two days before my doctor's appointment, I experienced terrible pain and went to the hospital.*

"I'm sorry, Mrs. Darby," said a doctor I didn't like. "It's a tubal pregnancy and you're bleeding. We have to operate."

"Why?" I remember asking. "Why me?"

"Sometimes things just go wrong." He assured me that another pregnancy wasn't impossible, since I still had one good Fallopian tube.

After the surgery, Alex sat on the hospital bed and held my hand. "Be brave, Lee. God will see us through."

Surely we'd have the children we desired. At that moment, I believed.

Three years later, I wasn't so sure.

5

for the first time since the stroke,
Leona woke up in her own bed . . . sort of. She owned the
twin mattress, but it was a far cry from the king-sized one she
had shared with Alex in their upstairs bedroom. She couldn't
see Mount Abel through the first-floor window, but Kate
had made the former guest room homey and bright. Family
photographs lined the bureau, and Leona's favorite knick-
knacks decorated the shelves of an antique bookcase. When
her stomach growled, she smiled. There wasn't a reason in
the world she couldn't fix herself a bowl of cereal.

She put on her glasses, gripped the walker, and headed for
the bathroom, where she inspected herself in the mirror. The
sides of her smile matched now, an improvement from the
early days of the stroke when her lower lip sagged. She had
a bad case of bedhead, but it was nothing a brush couldn't
fix. The stint in rehab had given Leona the semblance of a
life, but never again would she say to Dody, "Seventy is the
new fifty."

Being feeble annoyed her.

Being forgetful embarrassed her.

Not being able to speak tested her faith. She knew better than to ask God why; the answers awaited in eternity. But even with that assurance, she wrestled with the thoughts held captive by her inability to talk. There was so much to say, so many decisions to make—big ones that affected Kate as well as Leona. The biggest decision concerned the *Clarion*. Kate seemed to think Leona could function as owner/publisher if Maggie agreed to be editor-in-chief, but Leona had her doubts. Even before the stroke, she'd been slowing down. Secretly, she hoped Kate would take her place, but Kate lived in a different world—a faster world, a photo-shopped world where people couldn't trust their own eyes. Alex never did use a digital camera. Until the day he died, he'd shot film with a stubborn pride.

Leona shared that independent spirit, which made needing help a thorn in her side. Standing in the bathroom, she studied her wrinkled face in the mirror and wondered again about moving to one of those big senior citizen communities, the kind with everything from apartments to hospital rooms. If she moved to a place like that, she wouldn't be a burden to Kate. On the other hand, it cost a lot of money. Leona wasn't that old—she could live one year or twenty. If she went into assisted living, her savings would evaporate a month at a time. If the money ran out, what would she do?

There were no easy answers, but surely like Jeremiah said in the Bible, God knew the plans He had for her—plans for a future and a hope. She leaned on that verse the way she leaned on the walker as she entered the kitchen.

After punching the Start button on the coffeemaker, she inspected the things Kate had left out so Leona could get her own breakfast—a bowl, cereal, and a spoon. Pleased with her independence, she filled the bowl with cereal and retrieved the pint-size carton of milk from the fridge. Buying small-sized products was a tip from rehab, and it made a big difference in what she could do on her own. She liked lots of milk, so she filled the bowl nearly to the rim. When she tried to lift it, it tipped. Milk sloshed on the counter, and she realized her mistake. She could manage a few steps without her walker, but she couldn't carry the bowl to the table without spilling it.

In the spirit of doing the best she could, Leona decided to eat standing up. She managed three bites before Kate padded into the kitchen. Wearing blue pajamas decorated with white ducks, she could have been ten years old again. *Oh, Lord. Where have the years gone? Just yesterday she was a child. She needed me more than I needed her.* Leona blinked and saw a Christmas tree sparkling with a thousand lights. While Alex hummed "Jingle Bells," Peter rocked baby Kate on his hip. Oh, what a day it had been . . .

"Nonnie, what are you doing?"

"Eething blekst." *Eating breakfast.* Just like that, Leona was seventy years old again.

Kate paused at her side, looked at the spilt milk, and tipped her head. "Why are you standing up?"

"Can't sit," Leona answered. Except "sit" came out all wrong. In fact, it sounded like a four-letter word.

Kate's eyes popped wide. "Uh . . ."

"Not shhh" With her cheeks hot with embarrassment, Leona stretched her lips. "Sssss!"

Kate clapped her hand over her mouth, blinked hard, then exploded into a fit of giggles. Leona couldn't hold back either. All her life she'd objected to foul language, and here she was cussing like a sailor! She and Kate howled until tears filled their eyes, and Leona worried she'd wet her pants. When the laughter faded to hiccups, Kate hugged her tight. "I love you so much."

"Hmm-hmm-hmm." *I love you too, sweetheart.*

Leona could have held her granddaughter forever, but Kate gave her a final delicious squeeze and stepped back. "How about coffee?"

Leona hummed yes, then headed to the table.

Kate followed with the cereal bowl, then returned to the coffeemaker and filled their mugs. "The coffee smells so good. You really do make the best."

Your grandfather cleaned the coffeemaker once a week and so do I. I buy hazelnut because I like how it smells. You look beautiful, sweetheart, so beautiful . . . Oh, how Leona longed for conversation, the give-and-take that unburied memories the way ocean waves uncovered buried shells.

When Kate arrived with the coffee, Leona took a bite of the granola her granddaughter had purchased, nearly broke a tooth, and balked at the cardboard flavor. The cereal was probably good for her cholesterol, but Leona wanted her old favorite. If she didn't try to talk, she'd never get better, so she placed her front teeth on her lower lip. "Fosssss—"

Kate answered with a hum. "Let's see . . . It starts with *F*."

Leona pointed to the cereal bowl and tried again. "Fossed fakes."

A smile lit up Kate's face. "You want frosted flakes."

Yes! And get the Kellogg's brand with Tony the Tiger. Your grandfather used to imitate the way Tony talked. Oh, how he made me laugh! Leona couldn't say all that, so she nodded.

"Frosted Flakes it is," Kate replied. "When I'm done at the Clarion, I'll stop at the market. Do you need anything else?"

Only to go myself and chat with Tina at the checkout. And there's Geoff at the Acorn Nursery. He loves flowers as much as I do. And Ray at the real estate office. He has cancer and it's bad. Sighing, she settled for writing a list on the Magic Slate: Kellogg's Frosted Flakes (she underlined Kellogg's), bananas, cottage cheese, animal crackers. When she showed it to Kate, her granddaughter laughed. "I'm the one who likes animal crackers."

I know, honey. We bought those little circus boxes whenever we went to the store. Do you remember making monkey sounds?

Kate smiled. "We used to play circus. I liked the monkeys the best."

Leona drew a happy face on the slate. Kate added curly hair and puckered lips, but her own expression tensed. "Speaking of circuses, Maggie's been juggling at the Clarion and doing a great job. I'll talk to her this morning about being editor-in-chief on a permanent basis." Kate added stick arms and legs to the figure. "It won't be the same as running it yourself, but you'll still have a hand in decisions."

Leona nodded, because that's all she could do.

"We'll talk when I get back."

Talk didn't quite fit, but sometimes a person couldn't be too literal. Neither could Leona expect Kate to read her mind, and something was bothering her terribly. She wanted to thank Nick for saving Kate's life. She couldn't call him, and her fingers were still too clumsy for texting, so that left old-fashioned pen and paper. Intending to fetch the note cards in her desk, she placed one hand on her walker.

Kate popped to her feet. "Finish your cereal. I'll get what you need."

Leona pantomimed writing, then made a square with her fingers to indicate a small piece of paper.

"The little cards in the desk?"

When Leona nodded, Kate brought the box and put it in

front of her along with her pen. "I'll get dressed while you do that." A trace of confusion creased her brow. "Should I mail it?"

"Cla—Cla Bah—"

Kate made a humming sound. "Claw something?"

"Clair . . ."

"Clarion?"

Leona nodded, then concentrated on the next word. "Nick." That came out just fine, but Kate tipped her head as if she didn't understand.

"Something about Nick . . . I'm not sure what you mean."

"Bahx."

"Box," Kate confirmed. "Here's a guess. You're writing a note to Nick, and you want me to put it in his box at the Clarion."

Exactly! There was so much more Leona wanted to say. *He's handsome, isn't he? I won't play Cupid. You wouldn't like it and neither would he. Then there's his faith. You don't share it, honey. But I'm praying someday you will. I pray for you all the time. And for Nick. Oh, my stars! He reminds me of Grandpa Alex.*

Leona couldn't say any of those things, so she settled for waggling her brows to show what she thought of Nick.

Kate laughed. "Yes, he's good-looking, but don't get ideas. I'm happy to be here while you recover, but my life's in L.A. When Eve Landon goes national, I'm going to be working 24/7."

Leona gave Kate a thumbs up, but she worried about the shine in Kate's eyes. All the success in the world couldn't fill the God-size hole in her heart, but that was a lesson Kate had to learn for herself.

An hour after breakfast, Dody arrived to stay with Leona. Kate chatted for a bit, then hurried to the garage and punched the button to open the overhead door. As the panels lumbered upward, she thought of Nick and wondered if she'd see him today. It didn't matter. She had a job to do with Maggie, and that was her priority. After sliding behind the steering wheel, she adjusted the mirrors, fastened the seat belt, and backed out of the driveway. When the car jounced over the slight berm, her nerves pinged with memories of the accident. Pushing her fear aside, she gripped the steering wheel with both hands and drove exactly the speed limit to the log triplex that housed the *Clarion*.

Nostalgia washed through her as she pulled into the parking lot, and she nearly drowned in it when she saw the old sign hanging in the window. The carved wood read *The Clarion* in an old-fashioned Heidelberg font. Her grandfather had carved it himself, and it matched the newspaper's banner. Kate winced at the dated style but reveled in memories as she pushed through the door. The smells of ink and newsprint permeated the air, and her grandfather's photographs decorated the lobby walls. For just a moment, she became the child who colored at the wooden desk, long ago replaced by a gray Formica counter.

A voice came from behind a partition. "Kate? Is that you?"

"Maggie?"

"Come on back. Eileen called in sick, so I'm by myself. Wayne Hardy has me on hold."

"No problem." Kate recognized Wayne's name. He owned the grocery store and was a big advertiser.

She went to the employee mailboxes behind the counter, left the note for Nick, and checked Leona's box. Most of the mail was routine, but a postcard from the Acorn Nursery made her groan. The daffodil bulbs Leona had ordered in

August—all three hundred of them plus bone meal and two whiskey barrels—were ready for pickup. Kate had no desire to dig three hundred holes in the rock-hard earth, but she'd gladly do it for Leona. She hoped Geoff would deliver, because the barrels wouldn't fit in her car.

Wishing life were simpler, she stepped into Leona's office, where an oak desk sat next to a window looking out to the parking lot. Lilac bushes framed the glass, and a row of Jeffrey pines stood like sentries. For the hundredth time, she wished a changing of the guard wasn't necessary.

Maggie appeared in the doorway. "Sorry to keep you waiting." A petite woman in her midthirties, she wore her blond hair short and had a passion for dangly earrings. Four years ago she had started with the *Clarion* as a receptionist. Now she was indispensable. Obviously at home, she sat in her usual spot across from the desk. Kate took Leona's swivel chair, but she felt like a child in her mother's shoes. She and Maggie had spoken frequently while Leona was in rehab, but they'd agreed to postpone future plans until Leona's prognosis was clearer and she could participate. Since she still couldn't speak, Kate was forced to take the reins.

The women began to talk at the same time with Kate slightly ahead. "I'm not sure where to start—"

"Me either—"

"Leona and I can't thank you enough, but we're determined to try."

"No." Maggie held up her hand. "I love Leona. I'm just glad she's improving."

They talked about Leona's recovery, her limitations, and Kate's plan to return to Sutton in January. When the conversation lulled, Kate laced her fingers on top of the desk the way Roscoe Sutton did when he gave a performance review. "This leads to the future—"

"Yes, I—"

"Leona wants you to be editor-in-chief. It'll be more money, of course."

"I can't accept."

Kate's stomach clenched. "You can't?"

"No." Maggie shook her head, but an irrepressible smile formed on her full lips. "My husband's been promoted to regional manager. It's great for us, but it means moving to Phoenix."

"Oh, Maggie—"

"I know," she said. "The timing is awful for you and Leona. Greg leaves next week, but the kids and I are staying until winter break. If you can manage, I'd like December fifteenth to be my last day."

Losing Maggie was more than a blow. It was a death knell for the paper Leona loved. Kate leaned back in the chair, clutched the armrests, and battled waves of bone-jarring worry. The *Clarion* needed an editor, but Sutton needed Kate. And Kate needed Sutton. The creative process made her heart sing, especially when it involved someone as talented and unique as Eve Landon. Kate was already dreaming up ideas for the new campaign. She didn't know how she'd keep all the balls in the air, but she was certain Leona would give Maggie her blessing.

With more confidence than she felt, Kate offered Maggie a gracious smile. "December fifteenth is fine, but we're going to miss you terribly."

"I'm so sorry about the timing—"

"We'll be all right," Kate assured her. "If Leona were here, she'd say congratulations." She'd also declare that God had a plan, but Kate believed the planning was up to her. "How long have you known about the promotion?"

"Just a few days. I would have told you sooner, but it seemed best to wait because of the accident." Maggie blew out a breath, plainly relieved of her burden.

But the burden was now on Kate. She surveyed Leona's office as if she had never seen it before, yet the pictures on the credenza were of her own smiling face, and a poster on the wall was something she'd given to Leona—a blowup of the Eve's Garden ad from the first print campaign. It showed a woman in an evening gown, elegantly posed under the lacy branches of a willow tree. The delicate script read *Eve's Garden . . . Find the You in Beautiful.*

Maggie broke into her thoughts. "I know how much the paper means to Leona. Can you run it yourself, from Los Angeles?"

"I don't see how." Kate's days at Sutton were so full she barely had time to do laundry. Selling the *Clarion* was the only option that made sense for her personally, but it would cause the biggest heartbreak for Leona. There was also the matter of providing for her grandmother's financial future. Before Kate made any decisions at all, she needed to gather the facts. "I guess I need to crunch some numbers."

"Eileen can show you tax returns, spreadsheets—all that stuff."

"Good."

"We're in better shape than you might think," Maggie said with a note of pride. "The website reaches people with weekend cabins, and local businesses like the hard copy for tourists. We're a newspaper first, a tourist guide second; but the tourist guide is effective. It keeps us relevant and it sells ads."

Kate understood completely. "I worked here during the summer when I was in college, but it's been awhile. I need to get up to speed. Dody offered to stay with Leona when I need her, so I should be able to put in some extra time."

"Or bring Leona with you."

"I will, but later. She tires easily." Kate glanced around the office, mentally making it her own . . . at least for now. "Where do we start?"

"You know the basics." Fortunately the software was the same version from Kate's college years. She knew it well, though the *Clarion* was past due for an upgrade. The paper still ran on the same print schedule, and she recognized most of the advertisers. Maggie, Eileen, and Art worked full time, but the journalism staff was comprised of free-lancers, including Nick. When Maggie finished with the background info, they talked about the coming issue. "We're in good shape. Page one is the repair to San Miguel Highway. Nick's covering it."

"Good." Just thinking about the road made Kate dizzy.

"He's also handling the Snow Park hearing. Do you know about that?"

If Kate was going to fill in for Leona, she needed to catch up on local issues. "No. What is it?"

"It's basically restrooms and a parking lot for the city slickers who drive up for the day when it snows. It's a big story, so we're giving it all of page three."

They talked awhile longer, going over each page until Maggie asked if Kate had any questions.

"Just one." But the concern was huge. It involved the entire look of the paper, Leona's feelings, and a piece of nostalgia. "The *Clarion* banner has a proud history, but that Heidelberg font is—"

"Awful!" Maggie finished.

Kate groaned with her. "I don't think Leona will mind if I change it."

"Not at all," Maggie said lightly. "In fact, I think she's been waiting for you to offer. You know how it works. A new look signals new leadership."

Yes, but Kate wasn't about to take over the paper. She belonged in Los Angeles as plainly as Leona belonged in Meadows. Balancing their needs wouldn't be easy, but she would do her best. Without a God like the one that guided Leona, Kate's best was all she had.

6

nick scanned the graffiti inside the men's restroom at the Meadows Community Park but didn't snap a picture. Graffiti scared away tourists, and he didn't want to give glory to Colton Smith, the fifteen-year-old boy being lectured by both his mother and the deputy sheriff outside the brown stucco building. A two-inch blurb would keep the town informed without exaggerating what seemed to be an isolated incident.

From what Nick had gleaned, Colton's mother found paint cans behind Coyote Joe's Café, where she worked as a waitress. When she noticed matching paint on her son's hands, she had exacted a confession from him, spoken to Deputy Harrison, and hauled Colton to the park to take responsibility.

The three of them had been surveying the damage when Nick spotted the patrol car and stopped. But there was no real news here. Nick didn't know Colton well, just enough to say hello around town, but he understood the teenager in his own marrow. Men and boys craved adventure, even danger. That's why *California for Real Men* continued to sell well.

Nick hoped his memoir would have the same appeal,

73

because it was aimed at the same audience—couch potatoes enjoying vicarious thrills, men trapped in cubicles, even teenage troublemakers like Colton. Maybe he'd hear from his agent today. He hoped so, because the wait was driving him crazy.

But first things first. With his notepad untouched in his pocket, he approached Colton, Colton's mom—her name was Mindy—and Deputy Harrison. "I'm done here," Nick said.

Mindy knew Nick from Coyote Joe's. Instead of giving him the perky smile that usually came with a cup of coffee, she pleaded with her big hazel eyes. "Is Colton's name going to be in the paper?"

"No."

"Good." She blew a breath that lifted her wispy bangs, but Colton continued to smirk.

The gangly teenager was close to Nick in height but as thin as a post. Straight dark hair covered his ears as a protest against haircuts, but what most caught Nick's attention was the anger simmering in the boy's eyes. Rebellion oozed from every pore, at least the ones not plugged with acne.

Harrison crossed his arms and planted his feet a little wider. "So, Colton. Who's going to clean this mess up?"

The teenager gave a *"Hmm"* and then rubbed his chin. "How about the tooth fairy?"

"Colton!" Mindy squared off with him, but the fact she had to look up to her son stole some of her authority. "Be polite. You're in trouble here."

Ignoring her, Colton focused on Nick. "How about a picture? I'll pose with the paint cans."

The teenager wasn't the only person who liked a good fight. So did Nick, especially for a good cause, and Colton was definitely a good cause. Nick shoved his hands in his pockets. "So you want to be in the paper?"

"Sure, why not?"

"Clean up the mess and we'll talk about it. Until then, forget it."

When Colton replied with a snort, Deputy Harrison crossed his thick arms over his chest. "The way I see it, Colton, you have a choice. I can arrest you for vandalism, or you can re-paint the bathroom."

A glimmer of something—maybe fear—softened the hard lines around Colton's mouth. Confusion seemed to mix with the rebellion, as if he were wondering how he'd gotten into this mess.

Having been in a few messes of his own, Nick could relate. Hoping Harrison would be kind, he threw out an idea. "If Colton agrees to paint the bathroom, can he pick the color?"

The deputy's mouth lifted with the hint of a smile, but he wisely tamped it down. "He can paint it pink for all I care."

Nick and Harrison both turned to Colton, his chin jutting as if daring them to change their minds. "Any color?"

"Any color but black," the deputy replied. "We have safety concerns with lighting."

"Okay, I'll do it." A mischievous gleam lit up Colton's dark eyes, leaving the adults to wonder what atrocious color he'd choose.

Mindy gave Nick a half smile, her shoulders sagging with relief as she turned to the deputy. "We'll be here Friday. That's my next day off."

Nick made a mental note to stop by the park and maybe lend a hand. He could imagine what color Colton would pick—hot pink or egg yolk yellow, maybe purple—but who cared what color the men's room was? Nick was stifling a grin when his phone signaled a message. Hoping to hear from his agent, he stole a glance and saw a text from Kate. *Pls call ofc. Prblm w snow park story.*

He didn't expect Kate to be at the Clarion, and the Snow

Park story had legs, as journalists said. With pictures, it would fill page three. If the story fell through, they'd have a massive hole to fill. After telling Colton he'd show up on Friday, Nick headed for the newspaper office, where Leona's Subaru was parked under a pine. As he climbed out of the truck, the office door swung wide, and Maggie came out with her purse in hand.

"What's up?" he called to her.

Her mouth split into a mile-wide grin. "Greg got the promotion."

"Excellent!" Nick was friends with her husband and knew what the job meant to him. "So you're moving to Phoenix."

"I'm going to miss this place," she said wistfully. "But December fifteenth is my last day. I just told Kate, and tonight I'll visit Leona."

"It'll be rough for them." With Leona out of commission, the *Clarion* desperately needed an editor-in-chief, someone who knew the business, Meadows, and the quirks of the software program. Then there was the personality angle. The paper depended on advertising, which depended on good community relations.

Maggie jiggled her keys. "I have a meeting at school, but I'll be back in an hour."

"What about the Snow Park?"

"Kate will fill you in." Maggie glanced at the window to Leona's office, where Kate was seated at the desk with the phone to her ear. "I feel just terrible about the timing. I hope you can give her some extra help. She's going to need it."

"Of course." Working with Kate would test his pledge to the max, but what else could he do?

Maggie departed with a wave, leaving Nick to walk alone into the office. Typically he called a greeting and made himself at home. Today he felt like a guest—or maybe he *wanted* to be a guest, which struck him as cowardly. Soft footsteps tapped in the hall. Kate must have heard the door chime, and without Eileen it was up to her to greet customers. When she saw Nick, her face lit up. "That was fast."

"I got the text." Keep it businesslike, he told himself. "And I just ran into Maggie. That had to be a surprise."

"A bad one." Kate shook her head, as if she couldn't believe the news. "I was counting on Maggie to keep the paper going while Leona recovers. She's doing well, considering it's only been six weeks since the stroke. The question is where she'll be six months from now. We just don't know. . . ." She paused to take a deep breath. "The business is only part of the problem. Leona could stay in her house with a roommate, but what if she has another stroke? She could need assisted living. All I know is that it's expensive. I'm on leave from my regular job, but that's complicated, too."

Before the stroke Leona had bragged about Kate all the time. Nick knew she worked for Sutton Advertising, had a connection to Eve Landon, and loved her job. "So you're in limbo."

"Yes."

So was Nick. Until he heard from his agent, he'd be twisting in the wind. "When do you go back to Los Angeles?"

"January. What a mess—"

His ringtone cut her off. He stole a glance, saw his agent's name, and swallowed hard. "Sorry. I have to take this."

"Take your time," she said. "I'll be in Leona's office."

As she walked down the hall, Nick retreated to the conference room off the lobby and answered the call from Ted Hawser, a topnotch New York agent. "Hey, Ted," he said a little too cheerfully. "What's the good word?"

"Do you have a few minutes?"

"Sure."

"I read the manuscript last night. It's not what I expected . . ." A long pause echoed over dead air.

The dodge could mean only one thing. "You hated it."

"I don't hate anything," Ted said mildly. "This is business. Sorry, Nick. But I can't sell the story the way you're telling it."

Disappointment clunked to the pit of his stomach. Ted was a first-class agent with excellent instincts. If he didn't like the manuscript, it signaled a real problem. With his neck bent and head down, Nick paced the length of the room.

"I appreciate your honesty. So . . . why can't you sell it?"

"This isn't what your readers expect."

"It's different." *So am I.*

"Yeah." A chortle came over the phone. "Frankly, Nick, it got me thinking."

"That's good—"

"No, it's not. You turned your back on your original audience. This book isn't just different. It's in-your-face different. *CFRM* has a trendy, ribald kind of humor. The pickup lines in Chapter Fifteen are hilarious. Today's readers relate to that sort of thing. This . . . memoir, or whatever it is . . . is different."

"That's right."

"It's a little *too* different. I'm not the right agent for this kind of material. You'd be better off with someone who knows the religious market."

But Nick didn't want to focus on the religious market. He wanted to reach frustrated couch potatoes and troubled teens like Colton Smith. Had he failed to tell the story in a compelling way, or was the book just not right for Ted? It was a tough question, one he couldn't answer.

"Where do we go from here?"

"That's up to you," Ted replied. "Take a few days to think it over. If you decide to run with the new stuff, I'll pass your name on to Erica Reynolds."

Nick recognized the name of a respected agent. "I'll let you know."

He clicked off the phone, turned to a window facing a vacant field and rested his head against the glass. Rejections were part of the business and he dealt with them, but this book was different. He'd written it in two short months, working day and night because he believed with every fiber in his being that if even one man was helped by his experience, the book was worth the effort.

With Ted's rejection, what did Nick do next? Maybe he'd self-publish it. Or maybe not. Maybe the book was a bad idea. Maybe God wanted him to sell everything and be a missionary in China, except Nick understood the risk-taking facet of his personality all too well. He'd be running away from God, not to Him.

"Nick?" Kate's voice wafted from the doorway.

Turning, he threw back his shoulders and saw her leaning against the doorframe, her arms lightly crossed and concern etched on her face. "I had to get something from the counter. I couldn't help but overhear. It sounded like bad news."

He tossed off a shrug. "It was my agent. He didn't like the new book."

"That's hard," she said quietly. "I'm sorry."

"It's just business."

"Yes, but it's also personal." She let her arms drop to her sides. "When I do a presentation for a client, I put my heart and soul into it. If they hate my work, it hurts. When they love it, it's the best feeling in the world. For that moment, life makes sense and I have a purpose."

Their eyes locked and held, leaving Nick to absorb the fact she understood so clearly how he felt. He didn't want that closeness, not with his pledge in place; but he couldn't look away or dismiss her with a casual remark. Not many people understood the creative side of his personality, but Kate seemed to get it.

"That's it exactly."

"Is this book like your first one? The adventure stuff?"

"Indirectly." Becoming a Christian was the most daring thing Nick had ever done. The decision cost him friends, his professional standing, and as of this morning, his agent. He didn't want to talk about it with the rejection still stinging, but Kate's interest encouraged him. "It's about the past year—what happened after the first book."

"Some of the guys at Sutton read the first one. It was a bestseller, wasn't it?"

"Pretty much."

"It must have changed your life."

"Big time," he admitted. "But it's in the past."

"What will you do now?"

He started to say he didn't know, but the indecision made him sound weak. Only wimps gave up after one rejection, so Nick made an on-the-spot plan. He'd query agents ten at a time until he found the right person to represent the story—someone who believed in it as much as he did. "I'll look for a new agent and see what happens."

"So you're in limbo like me." She gave him a cheeky smile. "How would you like to buy a newspaper?"

"Sure. Why not?"

Her jaw dropped. "Are you serious?"

Nick had surprised himself as much he surprised Kate, but the idea appealed to him. "Maybe. I'll have to think it over, but it's a possibility."

"I'm stunned."

So was Nick. He had some financial leeway, but he couldn't coast along forever. Besides, he needed something to do. Work gave a man's life meaning, a purpose. Running the *Clarion* would cut back on his travel, but maybe it was time for a change. Thinking like an editor, he recalled Kate's text message. "We should get down to business. What's up with the Snow Park?"

"The hearing was cancelled."

"So we need to fill page three." Relieved to be done with the book discussion, he followed Kate to Leona's office. After she sat in front of the monitor, he stood behind her, one hand on the desk as he leaned forward to see the thumbnails of the newspaper pages displayed on the screen. Kate clicked on page four, then leaned back so he could review the articles. "I don't see anything we can promote. Do you?"

The stories were all routine. The annual Christmas tree thinning—an event where residents were allowed into the forest to cut down pines tagged by the Forest Service for removal—was planned for early November. A bear had been spotted at the dump. While noteworthy, the sighting was an isolated incident and not hard news. The third story covered the renewal of the school superintendent's contract for the fifth time in five years. Last, he saw a two-inch hole at the bottom of the page. "There's nothing worth moving up to page three, but we can fill the hole with a vandalism story."

"What happened?"

"Colton Smith graffitied the men's room at the park." He told her about Colton repainting the bathroom and the negotiation about the color choice. "I promised him a picture if he does a good job."

"Sure." Kate grinned. "If he goes with hot pink, it'll even be newsworthy."

She leaned back in the big chair and bumped into him. As he recovered his balance, she looked over her shoulder. "Sorry. I'm not used to this desk. At Sutton I have a cubicle with a worktable half this size."

"You must miss it."

"I do," she admitted. "But Leona needs me and so does the *Clarion*. Any ideas for page three?"

"Just one." He shifted to the chair across from her. "How about an update on the 'Save the Condor' program? Your sighting of Number 53 makes it timely."

"That sounds good. In fact, it's perfect."

"I'll call Marcus right now."

Nick reached the biologist in two rings and told him about Kate's condor sighting. The biologist's voice crackled with interest, but he couldn't talk at the moment. "Can you two come to the launch site tomorrow?"

When Nick relayed the invitation, Kate's face lit up. "I'd love to, but I have to make arrangements for Leona. Hold on while I call Dody." She picked up the office phone, reached Dody, and gave Nick a thumbs up.

"We're on," he said to Marcus. "What time?"

"Around noon."

"We'll be there."

He and Kate ended their calls in unison, looked at each other, and smiled. Nick told himself this was business—not a date—but it felt like one.

"I can't wait," she said, giving a little shiver.

He enjoyed the same pleasant anticipation, which meant he had to leave before he suggested dinner at a cozy Mexican place in Maricopa. "Anything else before I go?"

"Just one thing." Brushing past him, she walked out of the office. "Leona wrote you a note. It's in your box."

He followed her into the lobby, where she handed him a small yellow envelope. Curious, he sliced it open and read the card. *Thank you for saving Kate's life. Come and visit, okay?* This was a good time to see her, so he tucked the card in his pocket. "Leona wants me to stop by. I'll head there next."

VICTORIA BYLIN

Kate wrinkled her nose in a cute way he was beginning to recognize. "I hate to ask you for another favor, but I saw your truck out front."

"What do you need?"

"Before the stroke, Leona ordered three hundred daffodil bulbs, bone meal, and some whiskey barrels. The order is in at the Acorn, but it won't all fit in the Subaru. Would you mind picking it up?"

"I'd be glad to." Nick hauled stuff for people all the time.

"Thank you." Relief washed over her face, but her brow furrowed again. "Speaking of your truck, I'm a little nervous about the drive to the launch site."

"Because of the accident?"

Hugging herself, she gave a little shudder. "I hate mountain roads. How bad is the one we'll be taking?"

"Not bad at all." He thought a moment. "In fact, it's perfect for the bike. You might even feel more secure."

"I doubt that."

He knew something she didn't. "I'm serious. The truck has a high center of gravity and pulls against the turns. The bike hugs the road. What do you say? How about a ride on a Harley?"

"*Hmm.*"

She didn't say no, which meant she wanted to say yes but was afraid. If he provided a safety net, maybe she'd muster her courage. "If you don't like it after a couple miles, we'll go back for the truck."

She chewed her lip some more. "I want to say yes, but a motorcycle?" She shook her head.

"Have you ever been on one?"

"No. Never."

"Why not give it a try? We'll go as slow as you want."

She made another humming sound, shifted on her feet, then leveled her gaze into his. "How slow?"

"I'll keep it under fifty."

"That's too fast."

If she wanted to negotiate, so would he. "Make it forty."

"Thirty."

"Thirty-five."

Laughing, she offered a handshake. "It's a deal, but I'm holding you to thirty-five tops."

"Agreed."

He took her hand, felt the soft skin, and thought of the work required to plant three hundred daffodil bulbs. Kate had better things to do than dig like a gopher. Nick, on the other hand, needed to forget her soft skin and ponder buying the *Clarion*. Physical labor helped him to sort his thoughts; so did being outdoors under the high sky and bright sun. He didn't say a word to Kate, but when she went home, the daffodils would be in the ground waiting for spring.

7

when something heavier than a squirrel shook the tree outside her bedroom window, Kate startled awake. She was accustomed to city sounds—traffic noise, horns, even the LAPD helicopter sweeping her quiet neighborhood with a beam of light in search of a robbery suspect. At home in her condo she would have rolled over and gone back to sleep, but in Meadows the unexpected rustle of leaves signaled the arrival of an unwanted guest. A bear? Maybe.

The branch swayed again, then something thumped onto the deck. Bears occasionally wandered down the back of Mount Abel. Not often, but it happened enough for Kate to hurry down the stairs to check the kitchen window she'd left open at Leona's request. Her grandmother liked to hear the blue jays in the morning. So did Kate, but she didn't want a bear to get a whiff of leftover taco casserole and invade the kitchen.

Moving quickly through the dark, she hurried to the window above the sink and slid it shut. Still nervous, she flipped on the outside light and peered into the oak tree where three pairs of eyes stared back at her. Raccoons . . . a mother and two babies. With their backs arched, the masked marauders stared through the glass. Their bandit faces weren't so cute with their teeth showing, a reminder that danger lurked everywhere, especially in the form of handsome men who rode motorcycles.

She had to be crazy to say yes to riding the Harley, but Nick's confidence had persuaded her. So did the connection she'd felt in the conference room. He'd hidden his disappointment about the book quickly, but for a blink she'd seen his anguish.

The raccoons wore masks and so did Nick, though his mask hid a tender spot and not sharp teeth. Hugging herself, she thought of the daffodils he'd planted. When spring arrived, the driveway would be lined with flowers as yellow as the yellow brick road in the *Wizard of Oz*. Leona loved the movie and so did Kate, though she couldn't relate to Dorothy's clicking her heels and wanting to go home. For Kate, home was an address that changed with the seasons of her life. That wasn't true for Leona. For her, home meant this house, this town. When Kate told her about Nick's interest in buying the paper, Leona had looked a little sad, then given a thumbs up. If Nick agreed, several of Kate's problems would be solved.

A step at a time, she told herself.

One moment at a time . . . moments that were knit together to make a life . . . lives that somehow made a community, a world where the sun rose and set with stunning regularity. And yet each day was different—random—the colors of dawn changed, the weather changed. Today the eastern sky glowed with the intensity of ultraviolet. Beautiful and bright, it promised sunshine for the ride to see the condors, which meant there was no chance Nick would opt to take his truck.

Knowing she wouldn't be able to sleep, she hunted through

the bookcase for the album of her grandfather's photographs, the one Leona put together after he died. Kate had a copy of her own, and she never tired of browsing through the photographs and reading her grandmother's introduction.

Condor Country
By Leona Darby

Eons before human beings drove these mountain roads, condors graced the sky. In ancient times they fed on mammoths and lived free from the dangers that arrived with modern times. The Chumash Indians arrived here first. In caves west of Meadows, sand paintings tell the story of condors traveling between heaven and earth, bringing messages from the gods.

At the turn of the century, ranchers joined the parade of history. Stray cattle provided the birds with an occasional feast, but wild game felled with lead bullets turned poisonous. In the 1960s, DDT caused the shells of condor eggs to become thin and crack. Mature adults flew into power lines, poisoned themselves with antifreeze, and became a trophy bird for poachers. At the turn of the century, a hundred birds graced the sky. Five decades later, the number was down to sixty.

On a clear day in August of 1965, Alexander Darby was exploring San Miguel canyon when he spotted one of the few remaining condors. A photographer by trade, he took pictures of the bird, not knowing her destiny. That bird—identified later by the distinct pattern of her feathers—was AC-7, the last female in the wild and the bird whose DNA helped to save the species. Biologists named her Tuyu, which means *mother* in the language of the local Chumash Indians. Thus began an effort that has spanned close to fifty years and witnessed the return of the condors to the wild.

My husband dedicated his life to telling the world about these magnificent birds. The photographs are his, but the story belongs to the biologists who saved a species through hard work, knowledge, and the faith to pursue an unseen future. Ultimately, though, this tribute belongs to the California condor.

A bird that isn't pleasing to the eye yet still is beautiful.

A bird that mates for life.

A bird that faced extinction and was given new life by a power greater than itself. As Alex would say, the ultimate glory belongs to God—the original scientist, the perfect artist, our creator, and loving father.

Kate read the introduction again and stopped at the same place she always stopped. *The faith to pursue an unseen future.* Was faith what she needed to live without constant worry? The cure for the anxiety that made her insides churn? But where did faith come from? Kate couldn't turn a blind eye on reality. The paper had to be managed, maybe sold. Leona needed help. And wise or not, in a few hours she'd climb on a motorcycle and speed to a place she'd never been before. The ride, she realized, took faith—faith in Nick. Kate didn't understand God, but she would never forget the strength of Nick's grip, holding tight and keeping her from falling to the bottom of that canyon. A happy warmth wiped away the fear, and the safe feeling stayed as she enjoyed the old photographs. It lasted through breakfast with Leona, a hot shower, deciding what to wear, and Dody's arrival.

With her morning in order, Kate stepped outside to wait for Nick with her sunglasses, camera, and little purse in hand. Slowly, like the start of an earthquake, a distant rumble filled her ears. She recognized the burble of a Harley and worried.

The motorcycle sped up the hill, its engine throaty and full of power, until Nick coasted into the driveway. Still trembling, she took in the black tee shirt hugging his broad shoulders and the worn Levis that capped heavy black boots. Everything about him inspired confidence—and something else . . . a hint of those special feelings she didn't want to have for a man who lived in the woods, rode a motorcycle, and took chances. She belonged at Sutton, not here. But they were going to see the condors, and everything else about the day felt right.

He cut the engine, removed his gloves, and pried off his helmet. Unmindful of her, he smoothed his hair with his fingers, then climbed off the bike and looked up. His dark eyes focused on her face first, then skimmed her city-girl leather jacket, skinny jeans, and finally the hiking boots that somehow looked as sexy as four-inch heels.

Nick smiled. "Are you ready?"

Fear of cliffs and curves shot through her veins. "I'm . . . I'm . . ." She twittered like a chipmunk. "Maybe we should take the truck."

He watched her for a moment, perhaps gauging the inconvenience of switching vehicles, while she mulled the choice between faith in Nick and fear of the unknown. The screen door squeaked on its hinges. As she turned, the rubber tip of a cane poked through the door and tapped on the doormat. Leona shuffled outside with Dody behind her, waved at Nick, then turned to Kate and playacted a shiver of excitement.

"I'm a little scared," Kate admitted in a whisper.

Leaning heavily on the cane, Leona gripped Kate's arm as if she were small and needed help to cross the street. How many times had she encouraged Kate to stay brave and think big, to dream and trust God? Kate no longer shared her grandmother's faith, but the memories were alive, and she called on them now. "It's time to be brave, isn't it?"

After a solemn nod, Leona lowered her hand and stepped to the railing, where she waved a greeting to Nick, who called back a hearty hello. Kate kissed her grandmother's cheek, hugged Dody, and descended the stairs like a beauty queen feigning confidence. When she reached the Harley, Nick opened a storage compartment and offered her a silver helmet that matched his. "It's a beautiful day for a ride, but I'll get the truck if you'd like."

"I'm okay." She handed over her purse and camera, and he gave her the helmet. "Before we go anywhere, I want to say thank you for planting the daffodils. When I came home last night I could hardly believe it."

"Glad to help," he answered easily. "Let's put the helmet on you."

She slipped it on and fastened the clasp, but the chin strap hung loose. When she tried to tighten it, the thick fabric didn't budge.

Nick tipped his head to inspect the fit. "Let me help."

His warm fingers brushed her throat . . . once . . . twice . . . a third time before the strap tightened. A little zing went down her spine, then to her toes—both from his touch and the smoky aftershave on his smooth jaw. Why did she have to notice such things? She wanted to be Nick's friend—nothing more.

He shifted his gaze to her face. "How's that?"

"It's good."

"Too tight?"

"No, it's just right."

Without the beard scruff he belonged on the cover of *GQ* in an Armani suit, or in a courtroom fighting for justice. Or maybe on the back of a fire engine in a turnout coat. Slightly more confident, she put on her sunglasses and wondered if Sally Ride, the first female astronaut, had been nervous before lift-off.

Nick slipped on his helmet and offered his hand. "Here we go."

Kate gripped his fingers, swung her leg over the engine, and scooted onto a passenger seat that included a padded backrest and curved arms. "This feels like a couch."

"That's the idea." He swung onto the bike, pulled it upright, and started the engine. The famous Harley burble filled her ears, but it didn't rattle her bones the way she expected.

Nick looked over his shoulder. "Are you ready?"

"I'm all set."

He gave an offhand salute to Leona and Dody. Kate waved with him, then gripped the armrests and stared straight ahead as he pulled out of the driveway and coasted downhill. When they reached San Miguel Highway, he turned west. After a few miles, the pine forest gave way to rolling hills covered with dry grass. Most mountain roads hugged the side of a slope; this one twisted along the crest and offered a view that stretched north, south, east, and west. To the north Kate saw the San Joaquin Valley, checkered with green crops and fallow brown earth. The back slope of the coastal mountains rose in the distant south, a wall of sorts between the dry inland and the ocean.

Cattle grazed on a hill, all chewing in slow motion as they watched the motorcycle glide by. A line of quail waddled across the road, not bothering to hurry because Nick slowed the bike to a crawl. There wasn't a car in sight, yet Kate felt the frustration of an L.A. traffic jam. When the quail passed and Nick returned to the leisurely pace, she peeked at the speedometer. Just as he had promised, the needle was midway between thirty and forty mph.

Some of her fear melted. Not all of it, but enough to inspire her to lean forward and shout to Nick over the engine noise. "Could we go a little faster?"

He cocked his head. "Did you say faster?"

"Yes, please."

He brought the bike up to a daring forty miles an hour. "How's that?"

"It's good," she shouted. Nestling back in the seat, she drew in a breath. Somehow the speed heightened her senses. The grass smelled richer; the air sweeter. Colors shimmered in the morning light, and her face burned with sun and wind. Alive with a sensation that overcame the last of her fear, she raised her voice. "Faster!"

Nick said something she couldn't hear.

"*Faster!*" she repeated.

He answered with a nod, then worked the clutch and cranked the throttle. The engine wound up, up, up . . . until the gears shifted and they rocketed into what felt like a different dimension. Instinctively, she wrapped her arms around his waist and held tight. Shielded from the wind, she marveled at the heady rush of freedom, the excitement, and the peculiar rightness of being with a man who handled life with authority.

As the road veered west, Nick leaned into the curve. Trusting him completely, she leaned with him. A tunnel loomed in front of them. In a blink the motorcycle shot into it. Darkness blinded her and cool air slapped her cheeks, but she wasn't afraid. Nick had everything under control.

8

most people thought nick rode
the Harley for the speed, danger, and "bad boy" allure. They
were wrong. What made riding such a pleasure—an oasis of
sorts—was the intense need for control. He couldn't allow
himself to be distracted by anything, including Kate's arms
snug around his waist. The road demanded his full attention,
and he gave the asphalt the respect it required. Not even her
seat-belt-like grip could pull his thoughts from the double-
yellow line dividing the narrow highway.

In addition to controlling the bike, he needed to control
himself. No idle flirting. No leading Kate to expect more
than he had to give. This morning before leaving his house,
he had asked God to make him a slave to righteousness, to
guard his heart and eyes, and to bless Kate in unexpected
ways. Judging by her request for speed, the blessings had
begun with a lessening of her fears.

If the day went as Nick expected, they would return to
Meadows with a story for page three and his personal pledge
in place with one small modification. He and Kate would be
friends, a necessary amendment, considering they worked
together.

The miles to the Tin Canyon Wilderness Area passed quickly. When he turned on to the gravel road leading to the launch site, he called back to Kate. "How are you doing?"

"Great!" she answered. "How much farther?"

"About ten miles."

They rode in silence, with Nick dodging potholes and Kate exclaiming over the desolate beauty of empty sky and stretches of coppery earth. He agreed with her that it looked a little like Mars, but mostly he kept his eyes on the road until they reached the launch site.

A low building with solar panels provided living and office space for Marcus, other scientists, staff, and volunteers who performed a variety of tasks. A flight pen that resembled a batting cage stood tall on a low hill. It housed birds in transition from the zoo to the wild, and the biologists used it when they performed health checks. If Nick and Kate were lucky, they'd see a condor up close.

He throttled down and glided to a stop in front of the building. After removing his gloves, he climbed off the bike and offered Kate his hand. She laid her palm against his and swung her leg over the seat. In unison they slipped off their helmets and smiled at each other.

"Helmet hair," he said as he dragged a hand across his scalp.

She grinned. "Me, too."

The messy look charmed him. So did the excited grin on her face, but he knew a thing or two about women. They liked hairbrushes and lipstick, so he opened the saddlebag holding her purse. "I'll trade you the purse for the helmet and jacket."

"It's a deal."

While she brushed her hair, he set the helmets and her jacket on the concrete porch and put on the field vest he wore for adventures like this one. One pocket held a camera and a notepad. The contents of the second pocket included a knife,

Band-Aids, gloves, a water bottle, and a couple of energy bars. The boy scout in him loved this stuff.

When Kate finished with her hair, she slipped the brush in the saddlebag and removed her own camera, then faced him with her eyes aglow. "The ride was great."

"I enjoyed it, too." *We'll do it again sometime, maybe a ride up the coast. There's a good seafood place in Pismo . . .* No. Today was about friendship and a news story, not a sunset walk on the beach. Mentally, he wiped the slate clean and focused on the here-and-now. "It's a good road for the bike, one of the best in California."

"You'd know about that." A smile curved her lips, freshly pink and moist with lipstick. "With the book and all, you've been everywhere. You've done so much—"

"Too much."

He needed to set Kate straight about the allure of the old days, because his past was neither admirable nor romantic. But when? And how? Telling her about his daughter would cross the very boundary he needed to preserve—the one between casual friendship and feelings that cut deep enough to bleed. His pledge didn't end for six more months. He had to hold back, but what was best for Kate, whose eyes were shining with admiration?

Before Nick could break the mood, Marcus stepped out of the building. The biologist was in his midthirties, built like a barrel, and sporting a brown beard that matched his close-cropped hair. Dressed in a khaki shirt and green uniform pants, he resembled Smokey Bear without the hat.

Nick offered a handshake. "Hey, Marc. It's good to see you."

"Good to see you, too." The men shook, then Marcus's attention shifted to Kate. Without warning, he lifted her in a hug and spun her around. "Kate Darby, you are *awesome!*"

Nick's brows snapped together. Marcus was known to be exuberant, but a hug?

Kate wiggled out of the biologist's grasp. "I'm glad Number 53 is all right. Seeing her on the road was quite a moment."

Marcus stepped back, his expression somber now. "I'm sorry about the accident." He hooked a thumb at Nick. "This guy's a hero."

"No." Nick didn't want praise—especially from Kate, who was looking at him as if he could walk on water, even run on it. "Anyone would have helped."

"But you were the one," she said, lightly touching his arm. "You were a hero that day. I'll never forget it."

A hero with feet of clay. If they had been alone, he would have told her he was human and struggled every day to be an honorable man, that he believed in Jesus and the bloody cross and all those sticky subjects that made people cringe. He and Kate needed to have a conversation but not now, not with Marcus silently laughing at him, because the biologist saw Kate's sweetly bowed lips as plainly as Nick did.

She liked what she saw in him.

They had chemistry, sparks, attraction. Whatever a person called it, those feelings made any friendship between them complicated. For Nick, the next six months were as critical as the buildup to a NASA space mission, where every minute of preparation had a purpose, even the final ten-second countdown. He had to remember that he and Kate were just friends—nothing more. But if Marcus hugged her again, Nick would be sorely tempted to bloody his nose.

Kate prided herself on reading people's expressions, a skill she had honed in meetings at Sutton where clients masked their enthusiasm to drive down the price. If she glimpsed a client's face during that first reaction, she almost always gauged the person's thoughts correctly. Nick had blanked his expression when Marcus hugged her, but not before she saw a scowl that lasted a nanosecond. He liked her and was jealous of Marcus, though judging by his expression now—a mask of neutrality—he didn't want her to know it. Some women would have used that flash of jealousy to fire up his interest, but Kate refused to play games.

She stepped to his side, putting them shoulder to shoulder as she spoke to Marcus. "I'm thrilled to be here. My grandfather loved condors."

"He was a good man," Marcus replied. "How's Leona? I heard about the stroke."

Kate gave her standard answer. "She's recovering." Any other reply led to lengthy explanations.

"Glad to hear it." After a respectful pause, Marcus indicated a path that led to a rocky hill. "Are you ready for the ten-cent tour? It's a bit of a hike, so we'll have plenty of time for questions."

"Sounds good," Nick answered. "Where are we going?"

"To check out Tin Canyon. Two of our condors are flirting with each other. Elvis is a ten-year-old male who flew down from the program near Big Sur. He's interested in Moon Girl, and she's staked out a nest site in a cave. With a little luck, we'll see courtship behavior."

"That would be amazing." Kate tightened her grip on the camera. "My grandfather would have loved this."

"You will, too," Marcus replied. "If Elvis puts on his usual show, you'll see why he's named for the king of rock 'n' roll."

"Sounds like fun," Kate said.

"Oh, it is." The biologist waggled his brows, then made a suggestive remark.

Kate laughed, but she didn't want to encourage Marcus—

either his interest in her or the ribald joking. Apparently Nick didn't like the joking either, because he placed his hand possessively on the small of her back. The biologist stepped to Kate's other side, and the three of them headed up the path. Kate asked the question foremost in her mind.

"I'd like to know more about Number 53. Does she have a name?"

"It's *Wistoyo*, which means 'rainbow' in Chumash. And she's not Number 53. Technically she's Number 253. We drop the first digit on the tags. She's fifteen years old now and one of our veterans. We need her to find a new mate and breed, and to teach the younger birds how to survive."

"A new mate?" Nick asked.

"She was paired up with Number 174. About a year ago he perched on a power pole and was electrocuted."

Kate's thoughts drifted to her grandfather's sudden heart attack. What a loss it had been for her grandmother. "Condors mate for life, don't they?"

"Yes, but they'll find a new mate if the first one dies." Marcus kicked aside a rock. "Wistoyo was conceived at the Los Angeles Zoo, raised by foster parents, and released into the wild about six years ago. She went through aversion therapy to teach her to avoid humans, but she's still one of our more curious birds. A thousand years ago that trait would have been an asset, but today it's a flaw that could get her in trouble."

"Why?" Kate asked.

"She'll check out something she shouldn't, like old farm equipment leaking toxic fluids." Marcus heaved an exasperated sigh. "Condors and people don't mix. The same dangers that led to their near extinction are still present."

Kate knew the history of the birds as well as she knew her own family tales. In ancient times, condors ruled the skies from Oregon to Mexico, with Southern California being their primary home. As civilization encroached, new dangers entered the condor's world. Power lines, trash, antifreeze, poachers, and lead poisoning all caused their numbers to dwindle. Conservation work began in the 1960s, and the birds were added to the endangered species list in 1967, in part because of her grandfather's widely published photographs. Captive breeding began at the San Diego Zoo and fieldwork picked up, but the number of condors dropped until 1987. When there were just nine birds left in the world, the recovery team brought the last condors into captivity.

Nick glanced past her to Marcus. "Environmentally, what's the most immediate problem?"

"Lead poisoning," the biologist replied. "When hunters make a kill, they leave the entrails and sometimes whole carcasses with lead bullets and bullet fragments in place. The birds ingest the lead and become ill. If we don't intervene in time, they die."

"What do you do to prevent it?" Kate asked.

"Regular health checks. If a blood test shows lead, the bird goes to the zoo for chelation therapy."

Kate thought of Leona in the ICU after the stroke and how much she wanted to go home. "That must be hard for them."

"Yes and no," Marcus replied. "They're accustomed to being handled."

The conversation stayed on the condors, with Nick asking questions for the article and Marcus detailing condor history, which included the infamous Meadows picnic. Kate knew the story well.

When condors were re-released into the wild in the early 1990s, they were attracted to human activity. Three of them landed on Herb Watson's deck. Being hospitable, Herb fed them hot dogs. Kate smiled at the mental picture, but the reality hung over the species like a shroud. Condors lived in a fragile, dangerous world, one complicated by politics, economics, and individual beliefs about the environment.

When the trail split, Marcus led them up a hill steep enough that someone had hung a rope to use as a handhold. The path went up about thirty feet—not nearly as far as the drop in San Miguel Canyon but far enough to make Kate break out in a cold sweat.

Marcus tugged on a pair of gloves. "I'll go first. Kate, you're next, then Nick."

She faked a brave smile. "No problem."

When Marcus started to climb, Kate's mouth went dry. Her pulse rushed as if she were in the BMW, and her throat closed to a pinhole.

Nick reached into his field vest and pulled out a pair of women's gardening gloves. "For you."

"Thank you." She looked up at him, boldly because she didn't want her nerves to show. No way would she allow fear to stop her from seeing the birds.

Nick matched her gaze. "I'll be right behind you."

"No," she said. "The rope can't hold us both."

"It doesn't have to." One corner of his mouth tipped upward. "Marcus might need the rope, but I don't. I'll climb next to you."

"Thanks."

With Nick at her side, how could she not be brave? With her pulse racing, she tugged on the gloves, grasped the rope and started to climb. A few feet up, she noticed a pattern of steps and her nerves steadied. An occasional glance at Nick calmed her even more, and she reached the top with relative ease. When Nick pulled himself over the edge, the three of them walked toward a canvas tent camouflaged with a pile of brush.

"That's the blind," Marcus explained. "It has a terrific view of Tin Canyon."

When they reached the makeshift tent, Marcus pulled back the flap and Nick indicated Kate should go first. On her hands and knees, she crawled into the tiny space meant for two people at the most and scooted against the canvas wall. Nick joined her, followed by Marcus. When she bent her knee, her foot brushed Nick's boot. He pulled back, but they bumped elbows instead. Kate didn't mind the casual touch at all. They'd been closer on the motorcycle, but Nick's mouth hardened into a line. "Sorry."

"I'm fine," she assured him.

"We're in luck," Marcus said. "Moon Girl is in the cave." He pressed binoculars to his eyes, then handed them to Nick.

Nick took a quick glance and passed the binoculars to Kate, who focused on the hole in the rocks on the other side of the canyon. The high-powered lenses revealed every detail of Moon Girl's ugly wrinkled face. She wasn't beautiful at all— except to a male condor and people who cared about her—yet she displayed a graceful poise that resonated in Kate's soul.

"She's amazing." Kate handed the binoculars back to Nick. When he scanned the sky, she followed with her eyes and saw a second condor.

"Good news," Marcus announced. "That's Elvis, and he's headed this way."

Nick offered her the binoculars, but Kate didn't need them to see Elvis swoop into the canyon with something clamped in his beak. "What does he have?"

"It looks like a branch," Marcus answered. "That's a good sign."

"Why?" Nick asked for them both.

"He's courting her."

When she waddled on to the ledge outside the cave, Elvis landed next to her with his gift on proud display. Seemingly annoyed, Moon Girl hopped away from him.

101

"She's playing hard to get," Marcus said. "Watch what happens next."

Elvis spread his wings with a suddenness that made Kate gasp. When Moon Girl twisted her neck to check out the action, Elvis flapped his wings, bobbed his head, and strutted toward her. A foot in front of Moon Girl, he dropped the branch and dipped his head like an awkward teenager. Both ridiculous and majestic, passionate and pitiful, he waited for Moon Girl to decide the fate of his condor heart.

Marcus wrote something on a clipboard. "They usually don't start the courtship ritual until late November or December. Elvis is confused about the season, but he's definitely pursuing Moon Girl."

"What's she doing now?" Kate asked.

"Thinking things over." Marcus chuckled softly. "Moon Girl just might have a choice between Elvis and Number 49, a bird we named Admiral because he likes the ocean. He's older than Elvis and more dominant. He's shown interest in her, too."

Kate glanced at Nick, who was silent and snapping pictures. She didn't want to banter with Marcus about mating, especially at the risk of more tacky jokes. In a way she felt like Moon Girl, only the wrong male was dancing for her.

Marcus's cell phone went off. He answered, but the call dropped. "That was my boss. I have to get out of the canyon for decent reception."

The canvas flap swung shut. Nick inched away but not too far. Kate kept her eyes on the condors, but her heart beat with an awareness of Nick, courtship, and the human dance—one similar to the condors but with some variation. Humans didn't always mate for life, but attraction and love came from the same ingrained instincts that made her root for Elvis and Moon Girl. A wave of loneliness washed through her. As much as she loved her friends and her work, sometimes she longed for the dance, the special feelings, the mystery of falling in love.

Elvis turned his back on Moon Girl and looked over his shoulder. "What's he doing?" she asked.

Nick lowered the camera but stayed focused on the birds. "Considering the circumstances, I think he's asking her out."

"To the Road Kill Café?" A joke . . . or was it a hint? She'd be back in Los Angeles in a couple of months, but why not enjoy the time they had? She brushed Nick's elbow with hers. "I bet she'll say yes if he asks."

With a powerful flap of their wings, the condors took off from the ledge, soared down the canyon, and made a loop that brought them within twenty feet of the blind. Gasping, Kate leaned against Nick—for protection, to share the thrill—maybe because a deep, hidden part of her wanted to fly with him the way Moon Girl was flying with Elvis, wingtip to wingtip, their black feathers glistening in the sun. The sight of the pair brought tears to her eyes, though she couldn't say why.

Shaken, she looked up to Nick. He turned to her with his chin lowered and hazy amazement in his eyes. They were a breath apart, mere inches. One slight move and they'd be kissing.

9

nick blinked once,
twice, then matched his mouth to Kate's and kissed her . . .
tenderly at first, then with persuasion, and finally reluctance
because he had to break away before the kiss went places he
couldn't go.

Lord, help me. I don't want these feelings.

Silence.

Really, I don't.

But even as he prayed, his thoughts wavered between the
truth and a lie. Kissing Kate was pure joy, and not just because
of the rush in his blood. He cared about her; and because
he cared, he had to stop kissing her before he invited her to
Rosie's Cantina in Taft, his own version of the Road Kill
Café but with better food. Who really cared if they shared
a meal? What harm was there in two friends having dinner
together? And what did he do now that they had kissed? A
man and woman didn't go back to being friends after a kiss
that clanged like a big brass bell. They rang the bell again,
even louder. It was nature's way . . . and God's way but in
the right time.

Six months down. Six months to go. But instead of drawing strength from his sabbatical like he usually did, Nick wanted to bellow in frustration. Why did God give a man such strong feelings and yet expect him to deny them?

And what about Kate? As mild as the kiss had been, he was certain she heard the same clanging bell. He had to make the situation clear to her, but how did he explain his reason for backing away without telling her the truth, the whole truth and nothing but the truth about his daughter?

Fighting confusion and a whirlpool of emotion, he looked into her sparkling eyes. "Kate, I—"

"Don't say anything," she murmured. "It was just a kiss—a nice one. But still just a kiss. It doesn't have to change anything."

But it did. Nick had broken his pledge; and if he admitted the truth to God and himself, he wanted to break it again. "It changed everything," he told her.

"How so?"

Have dinner with me. But dinner meant telling her about that night on Mount Abel. He'd gladly talk about his faith, but his turnaround would sound crazy without the full story. Instead of answering her question, he dodged it with a shake of his head. "It's complicated."

"Then let's drop it," she said. "I'm just happy to be here."

The tent flap swung open, revealing Marcus in a crouch with an excited gleam in his eyes. "Did you two see that?"

Kate scooted an inch away, but her foot brushed his boot as she answered Marcus. "The birds flew right past us. What does it mean?"

"Paired flight is courtship behavior. I'd say Moon Girl is going to pick Elvis over Admiral." Marcus motioned them out of the blind. "Let's head back. I'm needed at the flight pen."

Staying low, Nick made his way out of the tent and offered

his hand to Kate. She accepted it and stood, gave his fingers a squeeze, then let go when he didn't squeeze back. After giving him a look that conveyed concern, she turned to Marcus. "What's happening at the flight pen?"

"We're doing health checks on four of the birds. The odds are pretty good one or more of them will have lead in their blood."

While Kate and Marcus put on their gloves, Nick took pictures of the cave. To get a better angle, he walked a few paces down a path hugging the side of the canyon. If a man stayed on the path, he wouldn't fall. But a step in the wrong direction, even a small one, could send him plummeting. He zoomed in on the cave, then aimed the camera into the distance. Dry reddish earth stretched for miles, but the sky radiated a deep and ceaseless blue. Tin Canyon was a simple place. It was home to an ancient species with simple needs. To eat. To breed. To survive.

Human beings had the same needs, but they also had an intelligence that set them apart from the beasts of the field. Condors acted on instinct and the drive for self-preservation. Men had the capacity to make moral choices that sometimes called for sacrifice. Silently Nick prayed he'd make the right choices for himself and Kate, then he snapped a picture of the empty plains. Humbled by the vastness, he joined Kate and Marcus for the walk to the flight pen.

While Kate and Nick were visiting the condors, Leona went with Dody to Hair We Are for a shampoo and cut. Even seventy-year-old stroke victims liked to be pampered now and then, especially when the pampering included seeing old friends. Hair We Are didn't have the ambience of a fancy spa like Eve's Garden, but Leona felt as famous as

Eve Landon when she walked into the shop and Chellie, the bleached-blond hairdresser, shrieked with delight.

Word of Leona's visit spread like wildfire. Before Chellie finished styling Leona's hair, at least ten people came to say hello. Maggie dropped by for a quick hug. So did Art with chitchat about longtime *Clarion* advertisers, and Krista Romano, the editor of the high school paper who contributed weekly articles to the *Clarion*. Poor Krista didn't know what to say to an old lady who couldn't speak, but she smiled and told Leona she was praying for her.

Dody needed her roots touched up, so Leona moved from Chellie's swivel chair to a seat under a beehive dryer. A dozen more people came to see her—the president of the Chamber of Commerce, Travis from the pizza place, realtors, clerks, even Captain McAllister from the fire department. Leona felt like royalty, but her heart ached in the face of an uncertain future. She didn't want to sell the newspaper, not even to Nick. She wished Kate were with her now. If her granddaughter experienced the love of this small town, maybe she'd change her mind about returning to Sutton. If Kate took over the paper, Leona's dream would be complete. Well, almost. More than anything, she wanted her granddaughter to know the love of God and the love of a good man—like Nick.

The afternoon invigorated Leona's spirit, but it also stretched her to the point of utter exhaustion. She perked up, though, when Nick's motorcycle rumbled into the parking lot shared by Hair We Are and the Clarion. He might have already taken Kate home, but a few moments later—long enough for them to see Maggie next door—Kate and Nick walked into the beauty shop together. With just a glance, Leona knew something was different between them. Maybe it was the way Kate's smile beamed, or how Nick placed their helmets side by side on a chair in the waiting area, though he seemed unusually somber.

"Kate!" Dody declared from Chellie's chair. "This is a surprise."

"We just got back," she called across the salon. "Maggie told us you were here."

She and Nick crossed the room to Leona. Kate greeted her with a kiss on the cheek, then stepped to the side. Nick squeezed her hand. "We saw some old friends of yours."

"Caaaahn—" *Condors.*

"That's right." he answered. "Kate will give you the details."

Chellie interrupted. "So, Nick. Did you take the Harley?"

"Yes, we did."

The slight emphasis on *we* gave Leona hope, but then she wondered if Nick was merely discouraging Chellie. Friendly but cool—that was Nick's reputation when it came to women, especially the hairdresser who flirted with him shamelessly.

Kate tilted her face up to Nick. "It seems silly for you to take me home when you have a story to write. I bet Dody will give me a ride."

"Of course," Dody answered.

"Are you sure?" Nick said to Kate.

"Positive."

Leona wished he had protested a little harder. The two of them made a striking couple, in spite of whatever differences kept them apart. Nick politely said good-bye and left. Kate sat under the dryer next to Leona and let out a happy sigh. "What a day! I never dreamed I'd enjoy a motorcycle ride."

While fluffing Dody's hair with a pick, Chellie peered over her head at Kate. "So was that a date? If it was, it's front-page news."

Kate crossed her legs with a casual air. "A date? Not even close. We work together."

"Too bad," Chellie replied. "I'm beginning to think Nick is damaged goods. You know, a ki-dult or something."

Leona poked Kate's knee to get her attention. *A what?*

"That's a kid-adult," Kate explained. "A guy who doesn't grow up. He lives with his parents and plays video games all day. That's not Nick."

Chellie reached for a can of hairspray. "He sure spends a lot of time away from Meadows. You'd think he'd be ready to settle down."

Leona wondered about that, too, but Chellie's tone rankled her. The hairdresser had no right to judge Nick. In Leona's opinion, he'd shown good judgment in avoiding Chellie.

Apparently Kate agreed, because her lips thinned to a line. "He's a working journalist. He gets paid to travel and write about it. And he's good at it. Then there's the travel book. He's had more success than most of us ever will."

Chellie gave an offhand shrug. "He'll probably never settle down."

You don't know that, Leona thought to herself.

Dody interrupted. "I want to hear about the condors. What do you say, Leona? Shall we ask Kate to tell us about her day?"

"Yes." Pleased with the clarity, she tried a second word. "Condors." Plain as day!

They chatted awhile about the birds, particularly Kate's adventure in the flight pen with a female condor named Big Bertha. Using a giant net, Kate had helped to capture Bertha for her regular health check.

"Weren't you scared?" Chellie asked.

"A little, but Nick and Marcus helped." Kate brushed a stray hair off her leg. "Mostly I felt bad for Bertha, but Marcus said she's been handled enough to know what's coming. She wasn't afraid, just annoyed."

Chellie snipped Dody's bangs. "By the way, I know about Maggie. What's going to happen when she leaves?"

A painful silence filled the small shop until Kate reached for Leona's hand and squeezed. "We don't know yet."

Dody eyeballed Kate via the mirror. "Any chance you'll stay and take your grandmother's place?"

Leona's heart burned with the same question, but she couldn't ask it without pressuring Kate. God bless Dody, who always spoke her mind.

Kate's warm fingers tightened on Leona's cool ones. "Yesterday I would have said no way, but after today I have to admit, it's a little bit tempting. I love it here."

Daring to hope, Leona put her free hand over Kate's, making a sandwich of their fingers, like when Kate was little and they played the slapping game. Today neither of them let go.

When Chellie set down the scissors, Dody inspected her new hairdo. Leona and Dody paid Chellie, then ambled to Dody's car. Kate helped Leona into the front seat, then climbed in the back. As Dody pulled out of the parking space, she spoke to Kate in her Texas drawl. "I want to hear more about Nick. You may work together, but when a man takes a gal for a ride on a Harley, it's not work for him."

"You're right," Kate said with a little laugh. "We had a wonderful time, but Nick and I are just friends."

"Freh—?" Leona had three hundred freshly planted daffodil bulbs that made her think otherwise. Nick didn't plant the bulbs for her. He'd done it for Kate.

"Yes, friends," Kate insisted.

Except Leona saw a familiar sparkle. *Oh, honey! You're blushing like you did when you were sixteen and had a crush on that forest ranger.*

"I like him," she admitted. "But we both have boundaries. We have to respect each other's choices."

"Oh, heavens!" Dody declared. "All this talk of respect is fine, but it wouldn't hurt to let Nick know you're interested. In my day, a gal put on high heels and a pretty dress to let a man know she liked him."

"He knows."

Dody paused to navigate a left turn, then heaved a sigh. "If you want my opinion, things are all mixed up now. No one knows what to do or what to expect. In our time—" she glanced at Leona to include her—"men were men and women were women."

"We still are," Kate replied. "But the rules are different."

"There *aren't* any rules," Dody protested. "That's the problem. Anything goes. People do whatever they want, and no one thinks about tomorrow, the day after, or what happens to children."

Leona hurt for her friend. Two years ago Dody's middle daughter and her husband had split up after nineteen years of marriage. They told Dody they didn't make each other happy anymore, and now her grandson divided his time between two households and a therapist's office. Before Leona's stroke, she and Dody talked about the situation all the time. When Leona patted Dody's shoulder, the touch carried the weight of those conversations.

"Thanks, Leona." Dody patted her hand in return. "Marriage has never been easy, but sometimes I think it's harder now than it was for us."

"It's not just harder," Kate insisted. "It's practically impossible. Most couples have two careers. Look at Joel and me. We didn't talk about marriage because of our work, and as things turned out, his career took him to New York. I wasn't about to follow him."

Oh, how Leona wanted to speak! Of course Kate didn't follow Joel. She didn't love him, and he didn't love her. They were part of a generation that focused on their own needs, their own happiness. Where was the concern for each other? For the marriage, children, even the future of the human species? Human beings could learn a thing or two from condors that stayed together for life and raised their chicks.

"What do you think, Leona?" Dody asked. "Was marriage easier for us?"

How could she nod yes or no to a question about a relationship every bit as complicated as the human body? Maybe more complicated, because a marriage had two brains and two hearts. Exasperated, she flung her hands in the air.

"Sometimes I feel the same way," Kate remarked. "It's all so complex."

Yes, but not for the condors.

While Kate and Dody jabbered, glancing at Leona and framing their comments to include her, she thought about Alex, their marriage, and the faith that had kept them together for forty-seven years. Marriage wasn't impossible—not with a strong faith. Not all of Leona's stories were pretty, but they all needed to be told, especially the one about an awful day in 1966.

When they arrived home, Dody left and Kate fixed a light supper. Leona claimed exhaustion and went to bed early, but she couldn't sleep. With thoughts of Kate and the condors giving her fresh energy, and maybe God blessing her with a special strength, she placed the journal in her lap and began to write . . .

Dear Kate,
This story is intensely personal, which is why I haven't shared it with anyone, not even Dody, though she'd understand. I'm telling you now because you need to know that your grandfather and I didn't have a storybook

marriage. We struggled in the way of all couples, and there was a time when the struggle swamped me. I lost my faith and nearly my husband. I wasn't just mad at God; I turned my back on Him completely. Why would He give me the desire for children and take away the ability to have them? I believed God was cruel, and I wanted nothing to do with Him.

Everything changed on a summer day in 1966. It was Saturday, and your grandfather wanted to take yet another drive in the area that's now Meadows. He was as obsessed with photographing condors as I was with having a baby, and the odds for both of us were about the same—one in a million. Only about twenty birds remained in the wild at that time, and I had visited five different doctors with the same discouraging reports. Your grandfather wanted to adopt; I didn't. Nothing mattered to me anymore, not even our marriage.

That Saturday morning, when I refused to get up for breakfast, Alex yanked the covers off the bed. "Get dressed, Lee. I've had enough of this moping. We're taking a drive."

I didn't want to go. What was the point? I couldn't laugh or even smile. Without children our house was too quiet. My friends were all mothers. I tried to embrace being an aunt to my brother's children, but jealousy ate me alive.

The first two years of infertility weren't so bad. We believed in the God who gave Isaac to Sarah and Abraham. Surely He would bless us with children of our own. But month after month, we faced the same disappointment. Bitterness grew in my heart until it choked out my love for my husband. I hope this doesn't embarrass you, Kate, but what happens in the bedroom matters. All species procreate, but human beings share a God-ordained intimacy that humbles and elevates us at the same time. That intimacy binds a man and woman like nothing else can. It builds a bridge; but it can't do its work when a husband and wife are sleeping in separate rooms.

The week before that Saturday morning was particularly bad. Our wedding anniversary had just marked another year of failure. I didn't want to go for a drive that morning, but I lacked the energy to argue. Silent, I slouched in the seat of the Chevy Impala, and we headed north on the Old Ridge Route. As Alex drove, I pretended to nap. He hummed an old song, "His Eye Is on the Sparrow," over and over, until I wanted to scream at him to stop. Finally we reached San Miguel Canyon. The highway wasn't built then, but a dirt road ran along the bottom.

After several bumpy miles, Alex stopped the car. "Let's take a walk."

"Leave me alone. I'm tired."

"Come on, Lee," he said, coaxing me. "We need to stretch."

"No."

"Fine. Suit yourself."

He snatched up his Nikon and left. I wanted to close my eyes but couldn't. Did I still love my husband? In that moment, it seemed that I didn't.

Full of bitterness, I watched Alex raise his camera to the sky and followed his aim as a giant bird glided into the canyon. He snapped pictures one after the other until the condor flew away. I, too, was riveted—both by the bird and my husband's joy. And my own anger. His dream had just come true. But what about mine? Where was God? Didn't He care?

When Alex came back to the car, he was a man on fire. "Did you see that, Lee? Did you see it?"

Sometimes joy is contagious; other times it's a slap to blistered skin. I tried to smile for him but couldn't.

He stretched his arm across the seat, almost hugging me but not quite. "Let's go a little farther."

Before I could protest, he started the car. Five hours later we reached Santa Barbara and the hotel where we had spent our wedding night. Alex checked us into one of the cottages, not the same one, but the rooms were identical.

I complained that I didn't have a nightgown.

He told me I didn't need one.

He wanted me, I could see it in his eyes. But I didn't want him. I didn't want anyone or anything except a baby. "Forget it. There's no point."

"The point, Lee, is that I want to make love to my wife. I don't care if we can't have children. Why fight what we can't change? We can adopt—"

"No!"

How dare he deny my feelings! He had a career, a vision, a dream come true in today's photographs. My dreams were dead. Breathless, I spat the words no wife should ever say in anger. "I hate my life! I want a divorce."

Your oh-so-gentle grandfather gripped my arms and pinned me in place. Nose to nose, he stared into my eyes. "Why? Because we can't have children?"

I tried to nod, but I could only stare at my feet.

Alex's grip tightened with vise-like precision. "Is that all I am to you, Lee? Someone who can give you babies?"

How could he think such a thing? I'd failed him. God had failed us both. The years of anguish congealed into a lump of sour bile. It clogged my throat and pushed tears into my eyes. Finally, I looked at him. "Of course not! I love you. I love you so much it hurts."

"Then show me."

The setting sun glared through the window. It filled the room with orange light, and for the first time ever I made love to my husband with every thought on him and not a single thought on conception and my own dreams. That night I surrendered completely to both my husband and to God, and I learned something that guides me to this day: Life and death are in God's hands, not ours.

I wish I could say Peter was conceived in that union, but he wasn't. It took three more months, and my period was six weeks late before I realized I was pregnant. By then, your grandfather's career was skyrocketing, and we belonged to a thriving church.

When Peter was born, flowers arrived at the hospital by the dozens, each bouquet a reminder of the miracle of life. I loved being a mother. I'll tell you about those days the next time. It's my favorite part of the story, but I'm tired now and need my rest.

Yawning, Leona put the journal away in her nightstand. With her head full of memories, she fell asleep with a smile on her face.

10

sweaty and itchy with sawdust, Nick pounded yet another nail into the railing of the deck that hung over the canyon in front of his house. The flooring, posts, and cap rails were in place, leaving him to cut and hammer the balusters that transformed the deck from an open-air platform to a corral. It was a fitting place for a man trapped by a promise he didn't want to keep.

Three days had passed since he kissed Kate, and he still didn't know what to do about it. Common sense told him to ask forgiveness for breaking his pledge, but God knew the truth—Nick wasn't the least bit sorry. Kneeling at the edge of the deck, with only the half-finished railing between his body and a forty-foot drop, he nailed another slat into place. The pounding jarred his teeth as the sun sank below the ridge, stealing the last rays of light and chilling the air. After one last smack of the hammer, he shoved wearily to his feet and stared across the canyon to Leona's house a mile away.

Kate was probably cooking dinner and dreaming up ideas for Sutton Advertising. If the kiss perplexed her, she was keeping those feelings to herself. Yesterday they had put the paper to bed, Maggie teaching them both the routine. Nick enjoyed every minute and had decided to make an offer on the business, one that would provide flexibility for everyone, including himself. This morning he'd sent queries to ten different agents including the woman Ted recommended, but selling a book was both a slow process and a gamble. It was just plain wise to plan for the future. The *Clarion* would never be a big money-maker, but it seemed to be financially stable, and he loved the work.

He lugged the toolbox to the garage, then toted an armload of firewood into the house. A sandwich would suffice for dinner, then maybe he'd watch a movie or read. He was about to fetch kindling when his phone jangled with Sam's ringtone.

"What's up?" Nick said to his brother.

"I need a favor."

"Sure."

"Gayle's putting together a collage of family photos." Sam's wife loved scrapbooking. "She wants a new one of you."

Nick's most recent picture was on the memory card in his camera—a photograph Marcus snapped of him with Kate in Tin Canyon, his arm draped casually around her shoulders and their heads tipped toward each other. Nick had looked at the photograph several times, felt guilty for kissing her, and had come close to pressing Delete. But what kind of silliness was that? It was just a picture and just a kiss she'd probably forgotten.

Sam's voice cut into his thoughts. "Are you there?"

"Yeah. I'm just . . . thinking."

"Did I get you at a bad time?"

"No. This is fine." Except pictures of Kate played in his mind—Kate at the condor launch site. Kate in the office, sharing French fries with him, and reveling in the challenge of a tight deadline. The scenes flashed in his mind, each one more vivid than the last, filling him with a longing for her company. Maybe she'd like to come over and watch a movie. He probably had a chick flick here somewhere . . . *No.*

"Nick?"

"Sorry. I got distracted."

"Where are you?"

"At home." He opened the pantry, saw one slice of stale bread and muttered to himself.

"Are you sure you're okay?"

No! I'm fed up and frustrated. He wanted answers about Kate and his pledge, so why was he hesitating to confide in Sam? His brother knew him better than anyone else. If anyone could understand, it was Sam. "I met someone," Nick admitted. "Her name's Kate. She's amazing." Complete transparency, he told himself. "I broke that promise I made."

"Which promise?"

"No dating." Visiting the launch site wasn't a date, but it felt like one.

"So?"

"What to do you mean *so?* You know the plan. No dating for a year. I made a promise and I broke it."

"Are you sorry?"

"Not really." He shut the pantry door. "I'm questioning why I made the stupid promise in the first place."

"Well, why did you?"

He thought for a moment. "I needed to draw a line between the past and the present, the old and the new."

"You did that." Sam's tone lightened to friendly chiding. "When we talked six months ago, I suggested you wait a year before making any big decisions. No dating was your idea. I'm not saying to throw caution to the wind, but maybe God has another plan."

"Like what?" *Join a monastery. Leave tonight for China.* He settled for wandering out to the deck and standing at the unfinished railing.

"You've been using the promise to protect yourself. Instead of hiding behind it, why not use it as a shield to safeguard Kate? The rules for dating have changed, and not for the better. It's just my opinion, but with date rape, drugs, and strangers meeting online, women are more vulnerable than ever before. Half the marriages end in divorce. Single moms have a hard time, and so do single dads. There's abortion and disease, and we haven't even touched on the emotional costs. People call that kind of lifestyle serial monogamy. It's more like serial heartbreak, if you ask me."

"I worry about her," Nick said more to himself than to Sam. "She's a lot like I used to be. I'm not sure she considers herself a Christian."

"So be her friend. But Nick?"

"Yeah?"

"Be careful. She needs to fall in love with the Lord before she falls in love with you. Because if she falls for you first, God help her. You'll let her down, and she'll have nowhere to go."

Great. More waiting. Nick wanted to bang his head against the wall. "So there's still a line, but a different one."

"That's my take on it, but there's more. Make sure Kate knows where you stand. Confusion is your enemy here—even more than temptation. She deserves to know what to expect from you. It's how you build trust."

With that bit of advice, Nick saw his next step plainly. He had to tell Kate his story. Before she could understand the man he tried to be, she needed to know the man he'd been. As soon as he finished with Sam, he'd call her. "Thanks," he said to his brother. "I'll talk to her."

"Sounds good. Don't forget to send the picture to Gayle."

When they hung up, Nick looked across the canyon to Leona's house. He was planning what to say to Kate when he smelled smoke—not the pleasant aroma of well-seasoned pine, but the oily stench from a dirty chimney. Chimney fires happened every year around this time. Someone built a fire without having last year's creosote scrubbed away, and the oily residue ignited in the pipe. On full alert, he peered into the canyon until he spotted a plume of black smoke coming from a house on the cul-de-sac directly below him.

Bang!

A fireball shot into the sky. Blood racing, he hurried inside and called the fire station. Captain McAllister answered on the first ring. "There's a fire on Tulip Lane," Nick reported as he strode to the truck. "It looks like the chimney caught."

"On our way."

Nick peeled out of the driveway and headed to the fire, both to offer help and to cover the news story. As he steered on to the cul-de-sac, the headlights swept across the front of a two-story house with a gambrel roof made of thousands of dry shingles. Chemically treated or not, they were old and a fire hazard. The electricity still worked, but smoke was billowing through the open door and the tiny cracks between the windows and walls. He parked in the driveway of a vacant cabin across the street, grabbed the flashlight in his glove box, and jogged toward the house.

"Help me!" a woman cried in the dark.

Nick aimed the light and saw Colton's mom with her two youngest children clutching her side. Her fingers were splayed over the little girl's blond head, pressing her close to shield her eyes. The boy, maybe six or so, gaped at Nick with heart-breaking helplessness.

"Nick!" she shouted. "Help me, please. Colton's still inside. He's trying to get the dog."

121

Nick knew better than to walk into a burning building. The situation was best left to the professionals, but there was no time to spare. Any minute the chimney could fail. Flames could erupt in the attic and ignite the insulation, or they'd spread to the roof and the shingles would catch. Captain McAllister would read him the riot act for what he was about to do, but there was no way Nick could wait for the fire fighters while a boy tried to save his dog.

"What part of the house is he in?" he asked Mindy.

"Second floor. Front bedroom."

Nick's long strides ate up the driveway. When he reached the door, he covered his mouth and nose with his elbow and stepped into a black hole of heat, reeking smoke, and the scream of the smoke detector. Through the haze he saw the woodburning stove and the chimney pipe glowing orange. He had minutes to find Colton, maybe seconds, before the metal pipe collapsed and the fire spread through the house.

He took the stairs two at a time. "Colton! Where are you?"

"Over here!"

Nick barreled into a small bedroom cluttered with laundry, electronics, and trash. A bunk bed was pushed against the wall, wedged in place by a desk and a chest of drawers. Colton was on his belly, reaching under the bottom bunk and straining with all his might.

"Sadie's under the bed!" he shouted over the smoke alarm.

Nick shut the door to keep the smoke out and the dog in. "Let's lift the bed."

As Colton scrambled to his feet, Nick set the flashlight on the dresser and shoved the desk out of the way. Together they maneuvered the heavy bed frame away from the wall, coughing and gagging as they worked. Sadie, a tiny pathetic thing, lay in a shivering ball of terror. While Colton snatched her into his arms, Nick grabbed the flashlight, checked the door for heat, and opened it slowly. Smoke poured through the crack, but there was no sign of fire. "Let's go," he said, taking the lead.

Halfway down the stairs, the electricity went out, and they were plunged into darkness. Cursing, Colton stopped in midstep.

Nick beamed the flashlight into the swirling smoke. "We're fine. Go ahead of me."

Colton squeezed past him, his arms tight around Sadie and his face knotted with determination. Flames rumbled in the attic near the stove, a dark harmony to the dying siren of the fire truck coming up the street and the ceaseless shriek of the smoke detector. Hacking in the rancid cloud, they hurried to Mindy and the two kids. With the youngest child now on her hip, she pulled Colton into a one-armed hug and wept.

The fire crew passed them with the hose, but flames were already gobbling a patch of the roof. The trees were several feet away, but one spark on a dry pine could mean devastation for all of Meadows. Charged with adrenaline, Nick took pictures with his phone as the fire crew hosed down the roof. The first flames hissed to silence, but orange tentacles burst through the roof five feet away.

He snapped picture after picture, coughing in the smoke and braving the heat to get as close as he dared until a wall tumbled inward and sparks flew everywhere. The fire fighters waged war with their hoses, but a second wall fell and the house imploded on itself. In a fiery plume of smoke, ash, and embers, Colton and his family lost everything except their lives.

A crowd had gathered in the driveway. He didn't pay much attention until someone approached him from behind.

"Nick?"

Turning, he saw Kate holding a camera. "News travels fast," he said to her.

"I heard the call on the scanner." She glanced at the remains of the house, charred black and glowing with embers. "What happened?"

"Chimney fire."

Behind her, Mindy and the kids were surrounded by neighbors offering hugs and blankets. They would be all right, but Kate's expression remained grim as she took in the smoking ruins. "They lost everything."

"It could have been worse. The family's safe."

She didn't seem to hear him. "The trees could have caught fire. It could have spread to other houses—"

"It didn't," he said quietly. "But it was a close call. Do you want to write the story or should I?"

"Would you mind?" She shivered in the chilly air, or maybe from the knowledge of how close this family and Meadows had come to unspeakable tragedy.

"I'd be glad to." Nick glanced at Colton, who was approaching with Sadie on the end of an impromptu leash made of rope. They'd become friends, thanks to the story Nick wrote about the graffiti incident. Instead of painting the men's room an atrocious color, the teenager had surprised everyone with a Manga-style cartoon of bears fighting wolves. If he'd meant it as a joke, the notion had backfired. The mural showed amazing talent and was the talk of the town.

"Hey," Colton said to Nick. "Thanks for what you did. I don't know what would have happened if you hadn't shown up. You saved Sadie."

"No, you did." Nick offered his hand in congratulations, then indicated Kate. "This is Kate Darby. She runs the paper."

She held out her hand. "It's nice to meet you, Colton. I

know this is a rough time, but do you think your mom's up for an interview?"

"Probably. She likes to talk when she's upset."

Colton led the way to his mother and siblings, but Kate stopped Nick with a touch on his sleeve. "Who's Sadie?"

"Colton's dog. He needed some help getting her out from under the bed."

"So you went into the house—"

"I was the first one here." He aimed his thumb up the hill where light spilled through the curtainless windows marking his cabin. "I live right there. I saw fire shoot up the chimney and called the fire station."

Kate laid her hand on his arm, lightly. "You have a knack for rescuing things—first me, now Colton and his dog."

He didn't want to be Kate's hero, and tonight was the perfect time to set her straight about a few things. "When we're done here, I'd like to talk. Can you stick around?"

"Definitely." Her face lit up. "I hope it's about buying the *Clarion*, because I get more nervous about it every day."

"It is, at least in part."

"Oh good." She hesitated. "Or maybe not. It depends on what you want to do."

"It's good," he told her. "But there's something else. Let's finish up here, then you can follow me to my place."

Just like Moon Girl had followed Elvis, Kate thought. Only instead of dancing like Elvis, Nick stood two feet away with a formal air about him. Tonight's talk would be all business, which is how he'd treated her since the kiss. That was fine, though she wished she knew why he felt compelled to remain so distant when they liked and respected each other. Stifling a sigh, she walked with him to join Colton and his family.

Nick interviewed Mindy, who put on a brave front in spite of the loss. She rented the house and had no insurance for her personal possessions.

"Do you have a place to stay?" Nick asked when he wrapped up the questions about the fire and how it started.

"I called a friend." Pale and shell-shocked, Mindy gazed helplessly down the street. "She'll be here any minute."

Aching with sympathy, Kate made up her mind to use the *Clarion* to help the family get back on its feet, maybe with an Angel Tree at Christmas, where people in Meadows could join forces and shower the family with gifts to help restart their lives.

Mindy pulled the two smallest children even closer. They hadn't budged during the conversation, but Colton had inched around to Nick's side and was facing his mom. Mindy studied him now with tears in her eyes. "I'm just glad we're all safe. But Colton—" Her voice rose to a shriek. "How could you stay inside? I love you so much . . . *You could have died!*"

"Ah, Mom." Frowning slightly, he patted the dog's head. "What was I supposed to do? Let Sadie burn to death?"

"I don't know!" Mindy wailed. "It's just too much."

"Be proud of him," Nick interrupted. "Colton took a calculated risk for something he loves. It's what men do."

Some people ran to danger; others ran from it. Kate was firmly in the second camp and understood Mindy in her marrow. Nick was in the first camp and on Colton's side. She couldn't imagine living in his skin right now, being coated with soot and reeking of smoke, but she admired him tremendously. He truly cared more about others than about himself.

A few quiet words passed between Nick and Colton, then Mindy's friend arrived with the promise of clean clothes and soft beds. Everyone said good-bye. Kate and Nick went to their respective vehicles, and she followed Nick up the hill to his house, a two-story log cabin that reminded her of a fort in a John Wayne western.

She parked behind his truck, then walked with him into a living area dominated by a river-rock fireplace, a cathedral ceiling, and massive windows overlooking a canyon. An over-sized sofa faced the hearth, oak cabinets housed electronics, and an open staircase led to a balcony in front of doors that presumably led to bedrooms. Not everything in the house was complete. The plywood floors needed hardwood or carpet, and the dining area was just drywall. The house captured Nick's personality to a T—casual yet efficient, classy but rugged in an unfinished sort of way.

"I like your house," she told him.

"Thanks. It's a work in progress." He turned up the thermostat. "It'll warm up in a few minutes." He told her to have a seat, gave her a bottled water, and excused himself to wash off the smoke and soot. While he was upstairs, Kate fingered through the magazines on the coffee table. Print journalism might be dying, but the covers of *California Dreaming* were gorgeous. She picked up an issue and skimmed an article Nick had written about a resort in Palm Springs, a place that competed with Eve's Garden. As she flipped through the pages, ideas for Eve's national campaign danced in her mind. She looked forward to returning to Sutton, but she'd miss Meadows terribly. Nick, too.

He trotted down the stairs, his hair slicked back and a fresh cotton shirt sticking to his shoulders. After fetching another bottled water from the fridge, he dropped down on the big chair at right angles to the couch, took a swig, and blew out a breath. "What a night. It's a tough way to get a front-page story."

Kate set the magazine back on the table. They talked about the fire, how best to cover it, and decided to do a secondary feature on chimney fires in general and how to prevent them. Kate loved this aspect of journalism, where reporting the news helped people avoid tragic mistakes. The Angel Tree plan appealed to Nick as much as it did to her, and they batted around ideas on how to publicize it. When the conversation lulled, she steered them to the main reason she'd come to his house. "I'm glad you're interested in buying the *Clarion*."

"I am," he replied. "But before we talk about the paper, we have something personal to sort out. I want to tell you why I don't date."

Kate's brows shot up. "I have to admit, I'm curious."

"It's a miserable story that begins with *California for Real Men*." He set the water bottle on a round coaster, being careful of the edges so it didn't tip. "You can imagine the lifestyle . . . a different city every week, a lot of drinking, hanging out at clubs."

"I understand." *Eat, drink, for tomorrow we die*. Kate gave a little shrug. "A lot of people live that way."

He looked her square in the eye. "I regret it. Big time."

"Why?"

"Because someone paid for it."

Kate could only imagine what had happened: a fatal DUI, a broken female heart, a suicide. Her imagination painted grim pictures until she finally asked, "What happened?"

He drummed his fingers on the armrest. The upholstery silenced the beat but not the tightness of his voice. "The book had been out awhile, and sometimes people recognized my name. I was doing some hang-gliding in Big Sur when I met a woman who saw life like I did at the time. She was a waitress in Santa Cruz, and we had a weekend fling. Monday came, and we said good-bye as casually as strangers on a plane. You know how that is. You talk and share stories. For that brief time, you're best friends but you expect to say good-bye."

"I understand." She had known Joel longer, but their parting had been just as predictable.

"I didn't call her, didn't text. Nothing. Frankly, I didn't like her that much. I had no idea she'd gotten pregnant until a year later when she sued for paternity."

Kate's heart ached for him. "Did you do a DNA test?"

"Of course."

So he had a child. "Oh, Nick—"

"Let me finish—"

"You're a father."

"No." His flat stare alarmed her. "The baby died. She was born with a hole in her heart. The doctors tried everything— drugs first, then surgery. She lived for twenty-six days. I never saw her, never held her. I just know she suffered."

An unwanted pregnancy . . . an accident. Kate ached for him. "I'm sure you took precautions." She meant birth control.

"Of course. But as we both know, accidents happen." He stared at the cold fireplace for the span of a breath, then turned to her, slowly, with his eyes glittering and bright. "The problem is, I can't call my daughter an accident. As short as it was, her life had a purpose. She changed me for the better."

Kate saw no benefit at all—not to the baby, the mother, or Nick. She saw only nature at work, a random meeting of cells, and misplaced guilt. Before the evening ended, she hoped Nick would set that guilt aside, because she saw no reason for a good man to punish himself simply for being human.

11

there were a lot of ways

for Nick to tell Kate about his faith. Some were direct—*I became a Christian*. Others were formal—*I accepted Jesus Christ as my Lord and Savior*. Others were a child's cry—*Jesus loves me*. They all rang true, and they all fell short. To make Kate understand, he needed to take her on the journey itself, at least in her mind. That meant starting in the attorney's office and the day he signed the settlement agreement.

"I didn't fight the paternity suit," he told her. "The DNA was definitive, and the mother just wanted help with the bills not covered by insurance. We never did speak. It wasn't until I signed the agreement that I saw the baby's name—Sophia Charlotte."

"It's pretty," Kate said.

"It is, and I had nothing to do with picking it." The name had no meaning to him, no history or family ties. "That's when I realized what I'd actually done. I'd abandoned Sophia Charlotte at conception."

Kate's brows slashed together. "But you didn't know about her."

"That's no excuse. I slept with her mother, and I know where babies come from." No way could he plead ignorance. He also knew full well that Sophia might not be his only responsibility. Someday a teenage boy as troubled as Colton could knock on his door and demand answers.

"What did you do after that?" Kate asked.

"I went numb." Inwardly he shuddered. "I could have been at the DMV for all I felt at that moment. Sophia was just a name. I honestly didn't care about anything at that point . . . except somehow I cared that I didn't care." He shook his head. "That doesn't make sense—"

"Oh, but it does!"

"Yeah?"

"It's like wanting something but not knowing what." She paused for a moment. "Somewhere deep inside, we all want joy and we're always looking for it. If we don't find it, we hurt. And when we hurt, we want to be numb."

His pulse sped up, because Kate understood the human soul the same way he did. She was seeking God, even if she didn't know it. "That says it."

"What did you do next?"

"Fired up the bike, took off up the coast. I had a vague notion of visiting Sophia's grave, but the fog rolled in near Santa Maria so I veered inland. Have you been on Highway 166?"

"It connects the San Joaquin Valley to the coast." A faint smile played on the corners of her mouth. "I remember driving it with Leona and Grandpa Alex for a trip to Pismo Beach. It was boring and scary at the same time."

"Then you know what it's like."

"It's . . . empty."

He pictured the valley as if he were on the bike, speeding past alkali-rimmed duck ponds and rusted farm equipment abandoned in parched fields. Oil derricks with pointy heads had reminded him of dead crows, and he'd seen more than one abandoned barn turning to splinters. That valley had whispered to him like a friend. *This is who you are—a dying man in a valley of dry bones.*

"Nick?"

"Sorry. I was remembering." Her voice jarred him back to the present, but his nerves prickled as if he were speeding aimlessly on the bike. "The numbness started to wear off halfway through the valley. You know the feeling when your foot's asleep and the blood rushes back?"

"Yes, of course."

"That's what it was like, except the burning was soul deep, and it didn't let up. I couldn't stand it, so I cranked the throttle full out."

Her brow furrowed. "How fast did you go?"

"Too fast." Over a hundred miles an hour, maybe faster. "I didn't slow down until I reached the west end of San Miguel Highway. The mountains offered a change of scenery, so I made the turn and ended up on Mount Abel."

"It must have been a relief."

"At first, yes."

"But not completely?"

His chair felt like the witness stand in a courtroom, where he had to tell the truth, the whole truth, and nothing but the truth, so help him God. "It was a beautiful day, so I left the bike in the campground and hiked to the summit. I figured I'd watch the sunset, then head back to L.A. But that didn't happen. I couldn't stop looking around. The sky was so blue it glowed, and the grass was neon green. Daffodils were everywhere—pure yellow like the ones I planted for Leona."

"It must have been beautiful."

"It was. But what I experienced went beyond a pretty day or a beautiful view. Everywhere I turned, I saw . . . life."

"That sounds amazing."

Slightly more relaxed, he inhaled through his nose as if smelling the mountain air. "On a clear day, you can see the ocean more than fifty miles away. I stood for a long time just watching the sun sink below the horizon. It looked like an orange cut in half, all bright and glistening, and the water . . . it shimmered like gold. What I felt can only be described as joy, yet at the same time, I felt utterly, completely insignificant."

"That's—" Kate pressed one hand to her chest. "It makes my heart hurt."

"Mine, too," he admitted. "Looking back, what I saw was a pinprick of God's glory. Without knowing it, that's when I started to pray."

His words soaked into Kate's mind, changing her perception of Nick entirely. "Are you a Christian?"

"I am now."

"Wow." She didn't know what else to say.

A half smile played on his lips. "That says it, but I didn't think *Wow* at the time. I was pretty shaken up."

"What did you do?"

"I watched the sun disappear, stared at the stars, and finally went to the campground where I found a space with some leftover firewood. Somehow I knew I couldn't leave until I figured out what had happened. My leather jacket was warm enough with a fire, so I sat on a rock and stared at the flames. If the sunset was all beauty and joy, the night was cold, empty, and dark."

"I can imagine."

"I hope not." His pupils flared into black discs. "That night was awful. I don't know how to describe the emptiness that came when the fire died, except it was like one of those old astronaut movies, where the tether breaks and a man floats away in the dark—alone, suffocating, afraid."

Kate could hardly breathe, because she knew how that astronaut felt. The moments in the BMW would haunt her forever. "How did you stand it?"

"I didn't." A twist of his mouth gave him a wry look. "I called my brother and cried like a baby. He's a minister."

"So he helped you decide about God."

"Mostly he listened. When everything was said and done, the decision was mine. I have to admit, it was hard to say the words: *Lord, forgive me for my sins.* But when I did, the weight lifted. It was all rather strange and mystical. Emotional, too." He gave a shake of his head. "All that drama isn't my style. I like to know how things work, to take them apart and put them back together, so I started reading the Bible and books by famous theologians."

That approach sounded just like Nick. "Okay," she said. "I understand you're a Christian now. But you're still human." *And lonely sometimes, like I am.*

"Yes. Definitely."

"So why not date women who share your faith?"

He paused a moment, silent, but with his thoughts showing like leaves blowing in an invisible wind. Finally he gave a last drumroll of his fingers. "Something deep and internal shifted in me that first night, but old thoughts and habits didn't just disappear. I needed to make a big change, so I took a year off to switch gears—a social sabbatical if you will. It started seven months ago."

"So no dating until—" She did a quick count. "April?"

"April ninth is the official date, but God already made His point." A self-deprecating smile softened his mouth but not the intensity of his gaze. "I've learned some things in the past few months. There's a lot to be said for building a friendship before jumping into something more complicated. I think we both know what I'm talking about."

His eyes lasered to hers, and for that moment they were back in the condor blind, lost in each other, wanting to kiss but a little afraid of the unknown. Just a few feet separated them, but a chasm of another kind opened up like a fissure in the earth. Nick had his eyes on the future; Kate lived for the moment. As a Christian he probably believed marriage was meant to last a lifetime; Kate had her doubts. She also had a career she loved—one that fulfilled her the way Nick's faith fulfilled him, though she loved Meadows, too.

The silence crackled until he broke it with a smile. "So," he said, "we're officially friends. And maybe business partners if you like my idea for the *Clarion*."

"Oh." She was still thinking about her feelings for him. Nick did that to her. He made her forget who she was. "What's your idea?"

"I'm interested in buying it, but we all need to be comfortable with the decision. What would you say to a practice run? When you go back to Sutton in January, I'll take over as editor. If it's not a good fit, I'll stick around until you find a buyer."

Kate clasped her hands over her chest and squeezed. "That would be perfect. The Eve's Garden account is on hold for a while, but I'm eager to get back. You know how it is, if you don't stay in front, you get behind. You're doing me a huge favor."

"Good," he replied. "So it's settled—"

"Not quite. You do so much, you should be on the payroll even now. Unfortunately, money's tight." Advertising was down from last year, but staff salaries still had to be paid, and Leona needed her regular draw. Kate didn't take a paycheck. She considered herself Leona's right arm, but Nick deserved an honest wage. She offered an amount she hoped wasn't insulting.

He dismissed the offer with a flick of his hand. "Let's not worry about it until January. Until then, I'll help out like I do now. I have some trips planned for *California Dreaming*, so it's better if I'm not locked into a schedule just yet."

Kate slouched contentedly against the back of the couch. "This is amazing. An hour ago I was worried sick about what to do, and now we have a plan. Thank you, Nick. You did it again."

"Did what?"

She let her eyes twinkle. "You rode to the rescue—not on a white horse or even on the Harley, but you saved me from a disaster just the same." Her heart gave a little flutter, and for a blink she longed to be the princess of her childhood dreams, not a busy woman with conflicting obligations.

"This is mutual," he said, reassuring her. "A trial period is good for me, too, especially while I query agents about the second book."

"Someone will buy it. You have a track record."

"We'll see." A frown clouded his eyes, then he swallowed hard enough for his Adam's apple to twitch. "I sent ten queries less than a week ago, and already four agents have passed. I'm disappointed, but it takes time."

"Of course, it does."

"It's a good story," he said, maybe more to himself than to her. "But it's a tough business. I'm glad to try out running a newspaper."

"I'm glad, too." Her heart stumbled with the longing to say more, to tell him she believed in him and was honored to hear about his past, but where did they go from here, except to uncharted territory? She didn't believe in forever. She wasn't sure she believed in God at all, but she knew one thing with certainty. She trusted Nick more than any man she'd ever known. The thought warmed her to her toes, but those feelings were unwise in light of his vow as well as her intention to return to Sutton.

"I better go," she said, pushing to her feet. "Dody's with Leona, and it's been a long day."

Nick stood with her and they ambled to her car, neither of them quite ready to end the evening. When they reached the Subaru, he opened the door. She started to climb in, turned to say good-bye and found herself staring into his eyes. Moonlight glinted on his angular face, deepening the shadows around his mouth and nose.

"Good night," he murmured. "Thanks for listening."

Her pulse thrummed with awareness of the half tilt of his mouth, his head above hers, the width of his shoulders. The thought of a kiss added to the rush in her blood, but mostly she cared about him—as a friend first, but somewhere deep inside, she wanted to know and be known by him. She yearned for the internal peace he'd described, but it was as elusive as a condor. Swallowing back the longing, she managed a smile. "I'm glad we're friends."

"Me, too." Bending forward, he brushed a kiss on her cheek. As tender as the caress was, it made her tingle all over.

He opened the door wider and she climbed into the car. After a final wave, she headed home, inhaling the lingering smoke from the house fire and wondering with every breath why Sutton Advertising suddenly seemed so small and far away.

12

with the golden warmth of october fading to the gray chill of November, the newspaper staff revved up for the busiest time of year. Kate spent hours designing the holiday advertising insert, pouring her talent into making it fresh and true to Meadows. Instead of the standard ads the *Clarion* had run in the past, she asked business owners to provide personal photographs and a holiday memory. With each ad she designed, she fell more in love with Meadows and the people who made it unique. Most special of all was the campaign to help the Smith family. If the initial interest was an indication, Colton and his family would be inundated with toys, clothing, gift cards, and cash.

With a happy little shiver, Kate turned her gaze from the monitor on Leona's desk to the snow-covered parking lot. It was Friday and she was alone because of last night's storm. Maggie was home with her kids for a snow day, and Eileen couldn't get out of her driveway until the plow truck arrived. If anyone showed up to work this morning, it would be Nick. Driving in the snow didn't bother him at all, but it terrified Kate. She was in the office only because the roads to Leona's house were among the first to be plowed and sanded.

138

She hoped he would arrive soon. He'd been gone all week on a story for *California Dreaming*, and she missed him, which was silly because they spoke every night on the phone. He called about the *Clarion*, but somehow she had shared everything about her life—her disappointments and dreams, even about Joel and how he'd left to work in New York. Nick understood her in a way no one else did. She couldn't imagine not being his friend, not talking to him every day and rooting for him to sell his book. When they were together, Sutton and Eve's Garden faded into a different reality.

A clump of snow plopped down from a branch, reminding her of winter and the holiday supplement. As she turned back to the computer screen, her phone trilled with "Für Elise," the ringtone she had assigned to Sutton. Expecting Julie and a report on the IVF treatments, she answered with a cheerful, "Hey, how's it going?"

"Kate?"

The voice belonged to Roscoe Sutton himself. Stunned, she spun the chair back to the desk and snatched up a pen. "Hello, Roscoe. This is a surprise."

"Am I calling too early?"

"Not at all." Her whole body tensed. Roscoe never called anyone at nine o'clock in the morning. Pen in hand and her pulse racing, she sat ready for anything. "What's up?"

"Eve Landon is with me."

Kate's jaw dropped.

"She's changed her mind about delaying that national advertising campaign. That means we need a proposal from you as soon as possible."

"That's great." Ideas tumbled through her mind—pictures of the spa, slogans, color schemes that spoke of bold elegance. But in the next minute, her stomach plummeted like a falling elevator. Leona still needed her, and she couldn't abandon the

Clarion. Swallowing hard, she stifled her confusion. "This is big news. I'm . . . excited."

"Good," Roscoe declared. "Because I need you back in the office."

Her gaze darted to the dry erase board with next week's print schedule and then to the stack of bills on her desk. The *Clarion* needed her, but the Eve's Garden account was lucrative for Roscoe and everyone involved, including herself. Money wasn't Kate's primary motivation, but she liked feeling secure and being able to help Leona.

Eve's voice warbled in the background. Roscoe mumbled something Kate couldn't make out then spoke again into the phone. "I'm putting you on speaker."

"No—"

"Eve insists. I explained you're on leave and returning in January. She knows the situation is complicated." A click followed by background noise indicated he had already put her on speaker.

Eve Landon's famous contralto came on the line. "Kate, dear. How are you?"

"Just fine." *Be professional. Stay calm.* "Congratulations on the expansion."

"It's an exciting time," Eve acknowledged. "And it's time for a serious marketing strategy. Your work on the first campaign was stellar. I still get compliments on the ads you designed, particularly that one with the willow tree."

Kate's gaze zipped to the poster of the ad on the office wall. It had been nominated for some prestigious awards and still made her puff up. "It's a personal favorite."

"Mine, too. Kate, darling, I've missed you. We work well together, don't we? I can't wait to see what you have in mind for the next step."

Kate couldn't help but preen a little. "Thank you."

"Now," Eve continued. "When can we meet?"

Kate tapped the pen on the desk in a rhythm that matched her racing heart. This was her career, a dream come true; but the joy was mixed with anxiety, and she felt strangely ambivalent. "I have to check my calendar."

Roscoe interrupted. "Monday at nine o'clock. My office."

"That's too early in the day." Sutton was a hundred miles away. She'd have to leave at dawn when the roads were still frozen. "How about eleven?"

"Fine."

Eve interrupted. "Kate, I have a commitment on Monday morning, but I'm free in the afternoon. Why don't you meet with Roscoe first, then come to the spa?"

"That would be nice." Despite the emotional havoc, Kate meant it. During last year's campaign, Eve had taken Kate under her wing and mentored her. *"If you don't love yourself, who will? Life is meant to be savored."* Eve's philosophy had appealed to Kate and it still did, but her mind flashed to Nick and his regrets. Savoring life had consequences that were sometimes unsavory.

Roscoe ended the call, leaving Kate alone in a silence so deep her breath echoed in her ears. Snow had a way of paralyzing Meadows. No cars rolled down the street, no squirrels bounced in the trees. The only noise was the low buzz of a failing fluorescent light, until her phone blasted "Für Elise" for the second time. Sure it was Roscoe, she snatched it to her ear. "We need to talk. I can't just pack up and leave—"

"We need you, Kate."

"I know, but—"

"You'll get a raise out of this. Hire someone to take care of Granny."

Kate's lips tightened at the disrespect. "Her name isn't Granny. It's Leona. And you gave me two months' leave."

"I know. I know," he grumbled. "But you know how Eve is."

"She wants her way."

"And right now she wants you on that project." Papers rattled on his desk. "Look, I've assigned Julie and Brad Martin to work up some ideas. I pitched the three of you to Eve as a team, but you're the person she knows best. And you know her. I don't have to tell you how much money is involved. I'll be straight with you, Kate. Business is down, and I'm considering layoffs. The Eve's Garden account means job security for a lot of people."

Kate thought of Tom Dawes in accounting, Maria in the mailroom, Julie and the expensive IVF treatments. Their jobs depended on her, but so did Leona. Kate couldn't be two places at once, but she could compromise if Roscoe would bend his rules about working from home. People asked for the privilege all the time, and he gave the same speech at every staff meeting. Kate knew it by heart: *"Creativity comes from rubbing two sticks together. You are a stick. You need other sticks to make fire. That's why I want you in the office."*

He didn't care what people actually did in the office. They could chat in the halls, do cartwheels, or play with the new products in what he called the playpen—a corner of the office full of beanbag furniture, Slinkys, Play-Doh and other toys. There was one rule—no phones, computers, or video games. *"This is for the right side of your brain,"* Roscoe insisted. *"That's where new ideas are born."*

Kate took a breath. "If you'll bend the rules, I'll work on the account from here."

"Ah, Kate . . ."

"I know. It's Pandora's box." If he bent the rule for her, he'd be asked to bend it for others.

"I don't like it, but Eve's pulling the strings. Until January, you can work from Meadows with one caveat."

Her brow furrowed. "What is it?"

"Come to the office once a week."

"I can't promise that, but I'll be in on Monday." She'd have to work extra hours to keep the *Clarion* on schedule, but it was doable. "We'll hash out the details then."

"All right. But Kate?"

"Yes?"

"Do yourself a favor. At least consider assisted living for your grandmother. My father had Alzheimer's. I know what you're dealing with."

"Leona's mind is fine."

"But she needs help, right?"

"Yes."

"The situation will suck the life out of you. Don't let that happen. Your grandmother wouldn't want you to sacrifice your career for her—not if she loves you."

"She does, but the situation is a little more complicated." *I've met someone. I like it here.* The admission shocked her. A month ago she wouldn't have even considered trading Sutton for the *Clarion*, yet today the tug in her heart was as real as the snow blowing off the trees.

Trembling, she managed a calm good-bye to Roscoe, then spun the chair back to the window and the snowy day. Her feelings for Nick ran counter to everything she believed about her career, the world, herself. She wasn't naïve about men and relationships, yet the girl in her longed to believe in happily-ever-after. Suddenly she wanted to run outside and make snow angels and snowmen with carrot noses. But Kate wasn't a child. She was an adult with responsibilities, goals, and dreams. Working from Meadows would put her out of the loop at Sutton, but it was the only way she could manage the *Clarion* and Eve Landon.

Which meant she'd have to roll with the punches.

And go with the flow.

Keep the balls in the air.

She yearned to talk the dilemma over with Leona but couldn't. The conversation would raise her grandmother's hopes that she'd stay in Meadows. Neither could she speak with complete openness to Nick. He was part of the equation, a bigger part than she wanted to admit. Where could she turn for advice? She knew what Leona would do—she'd ask God for help. So would Nick. Since Kate couldn't talk to the people she trusted, maybe she'd talk to God.

With eyes focused on the tallest pine, she murmured, "God, are you listening?"

Silence.

"Leona thinks you're real. So does Nick. But I can't see you, or hear you." The silence seemed even thicker. "Who *are* you?"

Nothing happened, except for a singular impression of a man on a cloud sitting behind a big desk. The nameplate read "CEO of the Universe," and the cloud was littered with notes and papers, much like the Clarion on a busy day. If the man on the cloud was God, he looked a lot like Sean Connery.

"Maybe I should send you an e-mail," she said drily.

Why not? Desperate to sort her thoughts, she turned to the computer and tapped out a memo.

Dear God, whoever you are . . .

My name is Kate Darby. We met briefly when my father died. Family members assure me that he's with you in heaven. Please tell him I remember him and miss him. I miss my mother too and hope she's happy.

I'm writing to you today for advice. As you know—that is, if you're really God—I have a decision to make. I've sorted out the pros and cons but am unable to come to a solid conclusion. Sutton or the Clarion? Los Angeles or Meadows? And then there's Nick Sheridan, a friend of yours. While I'm grateful for his friendship, I confess to being stymied by his values. Perhaps I should add one element to this personal debate: Are relationships forever or just for now?

If you have any insight into this predicament, I'd be delighted to hear from you.

Regards,

Kate Darby, Acting Editor-in-Chief, The Clarion

Lips pursed, she let out a sigh that hissed like a tire losing air. Suddenly flat in a soul-deep way, she deleted the silly memo and decided she needed hot chocolate to lift her mood. She put on her coat, hat, and gloves, stuck a five-dollar bill in her pocket, and locked the office door behind her. With light snow falling, she tromped down a path that cut across a field to a convenience store. Kicking the snow as she walked, she swung her arms and did everything she could to shake off the tension, but her breath only rasped louder in her ears. The wind whistled through the scattered pines, a lonely cry that put an ache in her chest. Snow as light as ash blew across the field, leaving behind a clean slate.

It was a beautiful scene, a beautiful day.

A lonely day . . . so lonely.

"God, are you there?" she said for the second time.

She didn't know if the CEO of the Universe was listening, but she had a sudden urge to fall backward into a drift and make a snow angel, which was exactly what she did.

Something about fresh snow dared Nick to get in his truck and drive. Breakfast at Coyote Joe's sounded good, so he headed into Meadows on a route that would take him past the Clarion. When he spotted Leona's Subaru, he veered into the parking lot with the intention of inviting Kate to have breakfast with him. Fluorescent light pressed through the window, but the door was locked and footsteps led to the back of the log building, where a vacant lot provided a short cut to a convenience store, the gas station, and the café.

Nick followed the trail around the corner and spotted Kate in the distance. He glanced down to avoid a rut in the path, and when he looked up, she was gone. Any second he expected her to appear, but she didn't. Worried, he broke into a jog. "Hey, Kate? Where are you?"

"Over here."

He swept his gaze to the right. Sagebrush had caught the blowing snow in an impromptu net, and the drift formed a sheet as blank as paper—except for Kate. Clad in a blue ski jacket and a knit cap, she was lying on her back in the middle of the drift, moving her arms and legs to make a snow angel.

"This is fun," she said.

"You scared me to death."

"Why?"

"I thought you'd fallen."

"No." Her eyes twinkled with mischief, maybe an invitation to play. "I saw the snow. It was so perfect and white, I had to touch it."

When he offered both hands to help her up, she held tight and he pulled her to her feet. The snow angel stayed behind, perfectly formed and ready to fly. "Have you been out here long?"

"Just a few minutes." Her gaze darted to the back of the office building. "My boss at Sutton called. He wants me back right now."

"That's . . . unexpected."

"I'm kind of in shock." Breathing a sigh, she kicked at the snow. "I was headed to the store for hot chocolate. Want to come?"

"Let's have breakfast instead." He hooked his arm around her waist and steered her down the untouched path. "Tell me about the call."

"How much do you know about Eve Landon?"

"The actress?"

"Yes."

"She's famous. An Oscar winner. She's made some good movies and some bad ones." She had also been married five times to men ranging from Hollywood equals to a young no-name surfer dude, who wrote a tell-all book describing her as addicted to exercise, diet pills, and plastic surgery.

"She owns a spa in Beverly Hills," Kate added.

He'd heard of it. "Eve's Garden. It's on the list for the *California Dreaming* series on wellness resorts."

"So you know something about it."

"A little."

"A year ago she did a print campaign that focused on the West Coast. I was the lead." Pride salted her voice. "At the time, Eve was opening new spas in ten cities. She planned to do a national campaign, but she changed her mind. Now she's changed it back, and she wants me on the project."

"And she's in a hurry."

"That's right."

They were close to the street now, though the line between the field and the asphalt road was invisible. Kate flicked a strand of hair away from her cheek. "I should be excited but I'm not. Leona still needs me, and I love it here. I love the *Clarion*. On the other hand, Sutton is a small agency, and I care about the people. An account like Eve's Garden is the difference between survival and going out of business."

"This is a game changer, isn't it?"

"Definitely."

They jaywalked across the empty street and passed through the double doors at Coyote Joe's. A blast of heat melted the snow in his hair, and the aroma of bacon made his stomach growl. Kate tugged off the knit cap and finger-fluffed her hair. They both shed their coats and headed for a booth in the back of the sparsely filled restaurant. Mindy handed them menus, chatted a bit, and came back with hot chocolate and black coffee.

When she left with their orders, Kate pressed back in the booth and heaved a sigh. "I envy your faith."

Nick barely masked his surprise. "You do?"

"I really do," she admitted. "You're always so steady, so grounded."

He sipped the coffee, not caring that it burned his tongue. Snow angels and faith in the same day. *Lord, be with her.* "I'm not all that grounded." A dozen speeding tickets proved it, not to mention some of the stunts in *California for Real Men.*

"Can I ask you something?"

"Of course."

"You told me about the night on Mount Abel, but how do you know—*really know*—that God is real?"

They were on a path Nick knew well. "Do you want the C. S. Lewis version, or the personal version?"

"Both."

"The C. S. Lewis version says Christ was either a liar, a lunatic, or Lord. You can't say He was simply a good and wise teacher, because His claim to be the Son of God is crazy . . . or true. I did a lot of reading after Mount Abel, and I'm convinced Jesus Christ came out of that grave alive, solely because there's no other explanation. I could go into the history, the politics, the religious conflicts, even the mindset of the disciples who had just lost a beloved leader. Either someone stole the body, or Christ came out of the grave."

"Hmm," she said.

Nick blew on the coffee, sending ripples over the hot surface before he took a swallow.

Kate warmed her hands on the mug of hot chocolate, then drummed the sides with her fingernails. "So what's the personal version?"

"My story started on Mount Abel, but it continued here in this restaurant when I stopped for breakfast and bought a copy of the *Clarion*. I saw an ad for an unfinished log cabin. It had a great view, so six hours later I made an offer." The incomplete house had perfectly matched Nick's incomplete journey. It had walls and a roof, plumbing, electricity, and appliances, but no carpet or paint, no character. The house was still a work in progress, and so was he. "It's one of the best decisions of my life."

Kate made another humming sound. "Leona would call that a 'God thing.'"

"So would I."

"What else?'

"Small things. Going to Sam's church and hearing a sermon that resonates. A Bible verse that speaks personally."

"I don't mean to take away from what you're saying, but I've had that reaction to fortune cookies."

"It's more than that."

"I'm sure it is. It's just . . . I don't get it."

He studied the tight line of her mouth, the slight narrowing of her eyes. Kate wanted something personal from God—something He'd already given. The hairs on her head were numbered; she was fearfully and wonderfully made and precious in His sight. But she didn't know it.

Praying for the right words, he approached the subject

from another angle. "Maybe this says it better. For me, being a Christian is like having a wise friend close by, someone who knows me better than I know myself."

"I want that," she said with a hint of anger. "I just don't think it's possible. I don't mean to imply your faith isn't real—"

"It's all right." He enjoyed a good debate. "Considering I just told you I have an imaginary friend, I can see why you'd feel that way."

"But God's not imaginary to you."

"No."

Mindy arrived with their meals, and they dug into omelets and waffles with the hunger that comes from tramping a quarter-mile in the snow. While they ate, Kate told him more about her friendship with Eve Landon and how the actress encouraged her to live her dreams. She was scheduled to meet with Eve on Monday, after she had a sit-down with Roscoe, her friend Julie, and a market researcher named Brad. "I like Eve a lot," Kate concluded. "But I'm dreading the drive. Do you think San Miguel Highway will be icy?"

"It's hard to say." The county plowed the road, but snow melted off the mountains during the day and froze at night. Nick didn't think twice. "I'll take you."

"It's too far."

"Where's Sutton?"

"West L.A."

"It's about a hundred miles." Some commuters drove that distance every day. "What time is the first meeting?"

"Eleven."

"I'll pick you up at eight."

Kate gazed at him from across the table with her chin tilted and her eyes shining. "Thank you, Nick. You're a good friend . . . and you're not imaginary."

"No."

150

He was definitely real, a flesh-and-blood man who experienced temptation of all different kinds. *Thank you, Lord, for your grace, because I sure need it around Kate.*

He paid the tab, and they walked hand in hand across the street to the field. When they reached the snow angel, Kate paused to look at it. Blowing snow had erased the bottom of the skirt, but the wings were still wide and reaching. Nick hoped she'd make another one, but she sighed and trudged on to the office.

13

on monday morning, the National Weather Service issued a winter storm watch for the San Miguel Mountains. If the cold front moved down from the Gulf of Alaska as expected, snow would arrive at approximately seven p.m. and reach elevations as low as three-thousand feet. Kate heard the news just as she slipped into a pair of high heels she hadn't worn in weeks. The details of the forecast were important, because the Tejon Pass on Interstate 5 topped out at 4,133 feet. If the snow level dropped as low as predicted, the interstate could close for several hours, even a couple of days.

Southern California wasn't like Colorado, where road crews and residents were equipped for blizzards. Storms of this magnitude hit the area randomly. Some years there was no snow at all. Other years, storms rolled in one after another.

As Kate listened to the forecast on the radio, her hopes sank. She and Nick had planned the day to the minute—a visit to Sutton, the meeting with Eve, an early dinner with Julie and her husband, and a stop at her condo. Today's trip already meant doing double time at the Clarion tomorrow, and a big storm demanded a new front page. Even more worrisome, Kate didn't want Leona to be alone in bad weather. She and Nick absolutely had to beat the storm back to Meadows.

Gearing up for a rush, she collected her things and went downstairs. Leona was at the kitchen table with a bowl of cereal she had fixed herself. A lot had changed in the month since Leona's homecoming. Kate still worried, but after discussing the matter with Leona, they agreed she could spend the day by herself as long as Dody called to check on her.

Leona had regained a substantial degree of physical ability, but now Kate felt paralyzed emotionally. Since Friday's breakfast with Nick, she thought often about snow angels and imaginary friends. Did a person just decide to believe in God? Was that all it took? She didn't know, but yesterday at church with Leona, she had sung "How Great Thou Art" with a new awareness. She wanted to talk to Leona about her changing perspective, but the conversation would have to wait for a more leisurely morning.

"Guh morn," Leona nodded approvingly at the fuchsia-colored business suit that nipped in at the waist. "Pretty!"

"Thank you." Kate poured coffee. "I'm worried."

"Shnow?"

"Exactly." She dropped down at the table and crossed her legs. "I'll have to skip stopping at my condo."

"Too blad."

"Promise me you'll call Dody if it starts to snow."

Leona huffed. "I'll be fine."

"But Nonnie—"

"Kaaayt, honey . . ." In a slurred but rebellious sentence, Leona insisted she was perfectly capable of turning up the furnace and heating soup for supper.

Kate stifled a sigh, but her stomach knotted with dread.

Today was stressful enough without the added concern of Leona being alone in bad weather.

A knock sounded on the door. Nick walked in, his expression troubled. "Have you heard the weather report?"

"Yes, more snow." She stood and gathered her things. "We have to get home tonight, so that means leaving L.A. by what? Three o'clock?"

"That would be smart," he replied. "You know how bad traffic is."

She could meet with Roscoe as planned, but she'd have to cancel dinner with Julie and hope Eve was on time for their two o'clock meeting. Telling herself to stay calm, she shared a glance with Nick. "I'll make calls while you drive."

"Sounds good."

She gave Leona a kiss and a hug, then walked with Nick to the truck. He helped her up, and they took off for San Miguel Highway. Covered in frozen melt-off and built on the shady side of the mountain, the road was still icy from the last storm. Nick drove without a single skid or slip, but Kate's pulse sped up with every curve. What if the truck lost traction? What if they went over the side or an oncoming car slid into them? She had no control, and neither did Nick. Not really.

They made it through San Miguel Canyon, but Kate couldn't make herself relax. Cruising down I-5, she counted the miles and the minutes. She usually enjoyed the rolling hills and the glistening blue of Pyramid Lake, but today she felt powerless and small, except for having Nick at her side.

He must have sensed her mood, because he reached across the console and squeezed her hand. "We'll leave Los Angeles whenever you say."

"I just hope Eve doesn't run late." Kate tapped her toe on the floor mat. "She's notorious for it."

"Any chance she'd move up the meeting?"

"No. She has a commitment in the morning."

"It could be tight."

"I know," she replied. "But we have to make it back. I can't leave Maggie to cover the storm *and* rework the layout. Plus we have a pile of new ads." Most of them were the result of the new banner.

Nick navigated through the San Fernando Valley, exited at Wilshire Boulevard and pulled into a six-story parking structure between two high-rises. They spiraled upward past a thousand cars, found a spot near the top, then took the elevator down to the street where cars rumbled and raced through an eight-lane intersection. The noise assaulted her ears, and the exhaust burned her nose. The rush felt like a tornado trying to lift her off her feet, so she grabbed Nick's arm and held tight.

The sudden case of nerves made no sense. She had walked from her car to the office a thousand times, always with a confident step and usually with her phone to her ear. She didn't need to look where she was going, because she knew every crack in the sidewalk. Nick tucked her against his side, but even having his arm tight around her waist failed to steady her as they waited for the traffic light to turn green.

When the signal finally changed to Walk, he matched his long steps to her shorter ones, and they crossed the street to the building that housed Sutton. The revolving door moved too fast; so did the people pushing the glass behind her, and she half-stumbled into the lobby.

Nick caught up and put his hand on her back. "City jitters?"

She groaned. "Does it show?"

"Just a little. Where are the elevators?"

She pointed to the right. "Around that corner."

He led her to the block of elevators where they waded into the crowd. When a set of doors opened, he guided her through the throng, and up they rode, stopping and starting, shifting places, saying nothing to anyone until they reached the sixteenth floor and stepped into an empty foyer. It was blessedly quiet, blessedly still.

A white marble bench sat against a white wall. Kate thought of the snowy field and the snow angel and turned to Nick. Instead of his usual cotton and denim, he was wearing slacks and a blazer that somehow turned his broad shoulders into wings as broad as the ones on the snow angel. In her mind, the snow angel flapped her wings and took off, leaving Kate in Nick's care as they walked down the corridor to a heavy walnut door.

"This is it," she said.

He turned the knob and held the door wide. Kate passed through with Nick behind her. After a quick hello to the receptionist, she led him into the heart of Sutton Advertising. Voices hummed in cubicles, and posters from past campaigns decorated the walls with ads for everything from running shoes to perfume. Floor-to-ceiling windows looked east to the Los Angeles smog and more tall buildings, not quite skyscrapers because of the threat of earthquakes, but they were imposing nonetheless. Laughter from the playpen—the place where the creatives hung out and played with products—caught Kate's attention and she turned.

"Julie!"

Forgetting Nick, she scurried across the suite. Julie met her halfway and they hugged as if it had been years, not just weeks, since Kate had taken leave. They were still babbling and hugging when she turned back to Nick and introduced him to Julie.

He offered his hand. "It's a pleasure."

While the two of them chatted, Kate checked her watch. She had a few minutes before the meeting, so the three of them ambled to the playpen. While she explained the purpose of the area to Nick, Julie signaled Tom Dawes, an accountant passing by with a bag from a donut shop. Chubby and nerdish, Tom joked more than the copywriters. Kate adored him.

He saw her and smiled wide. "Kate, it's great to see you."

"Same here." Stepping closer to Nick, she laid a hand on his arm. "Tom, this is Nick Sheridan. He's a friend from Meadows."

Tom's straight brows snapped upward. "Julie mentioned Kate knew you. You're the guy who wrote that book."

"The same."

"Cool. I went scuba diving off Catalina a few months ago. Great trip."

"It's a good spot," Nick replied. "If you're into diving, check out Anacapa Island. The marine life is incredible."

Kate glanced at Nick in surprise. A mention of *CFRM* usually put him on guard, but today he seemed pleased by Tom's interest. She wanted to listen in, but Julie nudged her elbow. "Roscoe's ready. Let's go."

Kate touched Nick's arm again. "If you need anything—"

"I'm fine." His eyes locked on to hers with a familiar confidence. "How are you? More relaxed?"

"Definitely. I just needed to get my bearings." And now she had them. Sutton was home to her, and Nick had her back. What more did she need?

Nick watched Kate disappear into Roscoe's office. She seemed to have the city jitters under control, an affliction he had experienced the first few times he'd ventured out of Meadows. Now, after six months of mountain quiet, he had the opposite reaction to noise and activity. The city invigorated him.

So did talking to Tom. It had been awhile since Nick had done a book signing or given a talk about *CFRM,* but he used to meet men like Tom all the time. They were middle-aged, worn down by life, and tired, but they were still men. They hungered for adventure and would fight bears to protect people they loved. At the same time, they were trapped by schedules and commutes, like the one he'd just made with Kate. A hundred years ago, a man could have galloped through the Mulholland Pass on a mustang with four legs instead of four tires. There was a reason car manufacturers used names like Cougar and Viper.

Most men craved adventure and purpose, and Tom was no different. The accountant eagerly shared his scuba stories and insisted on introducing Nick to his golf buddies. The time Nick spent waiting for Kate passed quickly with the men razzing each other about bad shots. No one joked about Chapter Fifteen and ways to meet women, an omission that pleased him. Maybe the good in the book outweighed the bad.

After an hour, Tom clapped him on the back. "Gotta go, man. But it was great to meet you."

"Same here," Nick replied.

"What are you working on now?"

"Another book." Never mind the three rejections he'd received this week. He just needed to find the right agent and publisher.

"I hope it's more *Real Men* stuff. How about going down in a shark cage?" Tom laughed a little maniacally. "I've always wanted to do that."

"You're crazier than I am." Even Nick had his limits. Man-eating predators? No thanks. But his new book was daring in its own way, and he hoped Tom would be curious. "The new stuff is a lot different, but it's still an adventure. My life took some crazy turns after *CFRM.*"

"Like what?"

He was never quite sure where to start. "It's about mistakes I made, things I wish I'd done differently."

"Oh." Tom's eyes glazed a bit. "So no more skydiving?"

"Not right now."

"Too bad. But I tell you what—" Tom's friendly grin lifted the mood. "Swim with sharks and I'll buy the book." He offered his hand for a shake. "I have to get to work, but it's been great talking to you."

"Likewise," Nick replied.

As Tom made his way to his office, Nick pondered the conversation. Maybe Ted Hawser was right. Maybe he should stick to the adventure stuff, even go down in that shark cage, but the idea left him cold rather than thrilled. The new book didn't interest Tom, but that didn't mean the story didn't have a purpose. If the book pointed just one person to a life of faith, it was worth the personal pain that went into the writing and the disappointment that came with the rejections. As usual, he just needed to be patient.

"Nick?"

He turned and saw Kate striding toward him, her face flushed and her eyes bright. "Let's go. With a little luck, Eve will be on time for a change."

The coming storm wouldn't wait for anyone—not even Eve Landon. Nick took Kate's hand and together they hurried to the parking structure.

14

kate ran with nick

as fast as she could in her high heels. When they reached
the truck, he helped her up, strode to the driver's side and
climbed in.

"How did it go?" he asked as he turned the ignition.

"Good, I suppose." Except she felt as jittery as she did before the meeting. "I'm the lead on the proposal, but I almost
wish Roscoe had chosen Brad."

"Why?"

"It'll be hard to juggle both Eve's Garden and the newspaper." Time was a factor, but mostly Kate struggled with a
divided heart. Every time Roscoe had asked her a question
about her work hours and setting in-house deadlines, she'd
worried about the impact on Nick and the *Clarion*. At Eve's
request, the final presentation was scheduled for February
fourteenth—a reasonable timetable if she were working at
Sutton full-time, but close to impossible with her obligations
in Meadows.

"You'll do great," Nick said, as he navigated the tight

turns in the parking garage. "You're a pro, and Eve loves your work."

"Yes, but I'm worried." The last few turns made the tires squeal. He wasn't going fast. All tires squealed on the oily concrete, but the screech unnerved her. When they reached the street, she peered at the sky through the tinted window. The dark glass made the clouds almost black, and a gust of wind caused the truck to sway. More tense than ever, she glanced at the clock on the dashboard. "I hope Eve doesn't run late."

"Me, too." Nick gave her shoulder a squeeze.

His touch calmed her, and they navigated quickly through canyons of steel and glass and out of West Los Angeles. Eventually they turned north toward Bel Air, where the road narrowed and the houses expanded into mansions. "Turn here," she said when they neared a gated driveway with two brick pillars. A brass plate displayed the words *Eve's Garden* below an intercom. Nick pressed the button and waited.

A perky female voice came over the speaker. "Welcome to Eve's Garden. May I help you?"

"Kate Darby is here to see Eve," Nick announced.

"Come on in."

The iron gate opened so slowly that Kate wanted to scream. Palm trees were swaying in the whistling wind, and the sky seemed even grayer. By the time Nick pressed the gas, Kate was ready to leap out of the truck and run to the white stucco mansion on her own two feet. Instead, she gritted her teeth until he parked in front of the heavy oak doors where a life-size marble statue paid tribute to the female body.

"I'm nervous," she admitted. "Both about Eve and getting back to Meadows."

Nick covered her hand with his. "You know what you're doing. As for getting back to Meadows, we can't control the weather."

"No." She glanced at the sky and remembered the day she made the snow angel. If God was real, maybe He'd show mercy and hold back the storm. "I just hope Eve's on time," she said again.

"Me, too."

Nick released her hand and came around the truck to open her door. As she stepped down to the pavement, the doors to the spa swung wide, and Eve appeared. Her hair shimmered between gold and platinum; her sculpted nose tipped up at a perfect angle; and her eyes sparkled with the look of perpetual surprise that came with having one's eyelids done. Eve didn't hide the plastic surgery; she flaunted it. Her war on aging had certainly been effective. She looked closer to forty than her true age of seventy.

That first glimpse of the star hit Kate the way it always did—in the solar plexus. No matter how warmly Eve treated her, Eve was still a Class A Hollywood celebrity, and Kate couldn't help being a little star-struck.

"Kate!" Eve hurried down the walkway. Dressed in khaki slacks and a pearl-white mohair sweater, she moved with her typical grace in spite of the gusting wind. "It's wonderful to see you."

"Hello, Eve."

The actress kissed Kate's cheek, then turned to Nick with an enigmatic smile. "I'm Eve Landon," she said, offering her hand.

Kate took her cue. "Eve, this is Nick Sheridan. He's a friend from Meadows." *And so much more.* She hoped Eve wouldn't ask questions about him, because she didn't know how to explain their friendship.

Nick clasped Eve's hand. "Miss Landon, it's a pleasure."

"Call me Eve," she said with a little laugh. "'Miss Landon' makes me feel like a relic from the 1950s."

"Hardly," Nick said graciously.

Smiling with delight, Eve winked at Kate. "You have good taste in *friends*."

Eve could be incorrigible when it came to men. Kate hoped she wouldn't press the issue. Not only was Kate worried sick about getting back to Meadows, she didn't want to be flirty or suggestive around Nick. "Yes, I do," she agreed in a formal tone. "Nick works with me at the *Clarion*."

Eve assessed him with a direct stare. "Will you be joining us?"

"No." He held up his hand palm out. "You and Kate have a lot to discuss, and we have a time crunch. We need to get back to Meadows before it snows. I-5 is expected to close."

Grateful to Nick for bringing up the time limit, Kate breathed a sigh of relief and faced Eve. "Could Nick wait in the library?"

"Of course." The actress led them into the lobby famous for its tranquility. White and lavender orchids filled the room, and glistening water spilled over rocks and into a stream that meandered throughout the spa. The three of them stepped into the library, where Eve used an intercom to instruct a staff member to serve Nick the spa's famous tea tray. After he assured them he was comfortable, Eve led Kate to her office, a familiar spot where they had met many times before.

When they passed through the door, Kate headed to the sitting area where a push-button fireplace displayed steady orange flames. Her favorite spa treat, a mango smoothie, waited on the mahogany table next to Eve's usual jasmine tea.

Eve indicated the leather sofa. "It's certainly a gray day. The fire is cheerful, don't you think?"

"Very." Kate focused on the flames that were so different from the fires that burned in Leona's woodstove. Leona's flames danced and changed; the logs hissed and popped, sometimes so loudly that Kate jumped. The flames in Eve's fireplace burned in a straight line and emitted a steady, undisturbed hiss. Leona's living room always smelled a bit smoky in the winter, while Eve's office smelled like purified air.

Feeling as if she had fallen into a rabbit hole, Kate sipped her smoothie. Eve dropped down next to her, set her phone on the table, lifted the teapot, and poured.

Eager to get down to business, Kate set down her glass. "So, what do you have in mind for the new marketing campaign?"

Eve lifted her teacup but didn't sip. "I know you're in a hurry, but first I want to hear about you."

"Me?"

"Yes, you."

Any other time, Kate would have welcomed Eve's interest. But not today. Not with the storm barreling toward them. Besides, what could she possibly say? *Los Angeles used to feel normal, but today it's fast and loud. I want to go home, but I don't know where home is.* No way did Kate want to reveal her weakness to Eve, though she greatly admired Eve's personal strength. No one modeled the principles of self-fulfillment better than Eve Landon.

"Kate?"

"Sorry," she murmured. "I was trying to figure out what to say. Life's been interesting lately."

Eve's eyes twinkled. "Apparently so. Tell me about Nick."

"There's nothing to tell. We're just friends."

"Oh, Kate."

"What?"

"It's obvious." Eve fluttered her hand.

"What is?"

"You like him." Eve said *like* with a waggle of her brows, making the word suggestive, when Kate saw *liking* Nick as far more than finding him attractive—which she did. Very much. But that was none of Eve's business. Kate didn't want to talk about *liking* at all, but she couldn't hide the heat of a blush. The sooner she answered Eve, the sooner they could focus on business.

"Yes, I like him," she admitted. "But we're not rushing things."

Eve tipped her head, crossed her legs, and wrapped her manicured fingers around her knees. "Kate, darling, take my advice. Love is glorious, but it comes and goes with the stages of our lives. If you're attracted to Nick, act on it. How old are you?"

"Twenty-nine."

"You're young and beautiful." In spite of her perfectly sculpted face, Eve sounded wistful. "Believe in yourself and go after what you want."

A month ago Kate would have agreed with Eve, but what did a woman do when her choices affected the hearts, minds, and lives of others? Listening to Eve, Kate felt like a marble rolling around in a box, hitting the sides and bouncing in different directions. It gave her a headache, especially when she thought of Nick, whose marble was securely glued in place. Kate envied his groundedness, but she also admired Eve.

A gust of wind dragged a tree branch across the window, scraping the glass with a reminder of the storm. "Life is definitely short," she agreed. "And I really do have to leave before rush hour."

"Of course."

Eve's phone buzzed. Shoulders rigid, she read the text and frowned. "I'm sorry, Kate. It's my daughter. I have to speak with her. She and her husband are in the middle of a messy divorce. They were in court today—"

"Call her." If Leona were on the phone, Kate would answer in a heartbeat.

Eve headed for the door with the phone raised to her ear.

"Darling, what happened? . . . Oh, no . . . He can't take the children. . . ."

The conversation faded as Eve walked away, leaving Kate alone with the whispering fire and dripping rain. She tried to shake off the grimness of Eve's tone, but her upset lingered like the scent of the jasmine tea. Another gust shook the window, this one stronger and more abrupt. Kate checked the weather app on her phone, saw the radar, and winced at the thick yellow bands off the coast of Santa Barbara. Shoulders tense, she texted Nick. *Eve stepped out. Am waiting.*

He texted back. *Want to leave?*

Not yet.

For the next thirty minutes, Kate monitored the weather while she texted. A message to Leona came back with a report of light rain and a warning to be careful. Maggie texted with a request. *If you get stuck on I-5, take pictures!*

Nick sent a warning. *I-5 predicted to close approx. 7 p.m. I'm ready when you are.*

At exactly three o'clock, Kate's fear of the storm trumped her responsibility to Sutton, and she scrawled a note to Eve, saying she needed to leave because of the weather. Eve had to understand, but what if she didn't? What if she dropped Sutton from the account? Pen in hand, Kate stared out the rain-spattered glass. How did she choose between conflicting priorities?

Eve breezed through the door, her hand fluttering an apology. "Kate, I'm so sorry. I know you have to leave."

"Yes." She shifted her weight to stand, but Eve dropped down next to her. "Stay the night. You and Nick can have the Garden House. It's my way of apologizing."

"Thank you, but no." *Absolutely, positively no.* "My grandmother's alone, and we run a newspaper. I have a deadline to meet." She desperately wanted to leave, but to protect Sutton she needed Eve's blessing. "Could we reschedule? I'd be glad to come back on Friday."

Eve paused with an air of silent disapproval. "I have commitments every day this week. I'm sorry, dear. But it's now or never."

Paralyzed with indecision, Kate wondered what Nick would do. Life didn't push him around the way it pushed Kate, though no one could predict the weather or when the roads would close, or even *if* they would close. The storm could pinball north or south, or stall off the coast. Her phone chirped with a text from Nick. *Spoke w Maggie. It's raining. No snow yet.*

Kate took the report as a sign and met Eve's stare. "That was Nick. It's not snowing yet, so let's get started."

"Are you sure?" Eve sounded concerned.

"I'm not sure of anything," Kate admitted. "But I'm here and we have work to do." With the decision made, she whipped a notepad from her purse. Eve picked up the remote for the flat screen on the wall. While the equipment booted up, Kate texted Nick that Eve was back, then turned to the screen, which displayed a marble building evocative of Greek revival architecture.

Eve gazed at it admiringly. "This is the newest spa. It's located in Atlanta."

Kate made notes as Eve narrated a slide show of the new facilities, but her thoughts ricocheted from one worry to another. Even if the interstate stayed open, she and Nick had to pass through San Miguel Canyon and the hanging hairpin. She forced herself to nod and agree with Eve's commentary, but her stomach was in knots. Rain slapped the window in waves, each gust stronger than the last.

Somehow she hid her anxiousness until Eve turned off the computer. "That's it. The buildings I've purchased are proud, elegant, and timeless. I want that impression to translate to the spas. The question is how to do it."

As badly as Kate wanted to leave, she schooled her thoughts into a quick analysis of what Eve had shown to her and described. "What do you think of tying beauty and aging together? The spas already appeal to younger women. Why not target women who are a little older?"

Eve nodded approvingly. "We really do think alike. That's exactly what I had in mind when I selected these grand old buildings. I haven't told anyone yet, but I'm starting my own line of antiaging products."

"We're definitely on the same page." Kate leapt to her feet. "I really do need to leave. I'll e-mail if I have questions."

Eve stood next to her. "Thank you, Kate. I hope you make it back to Meadows before the storm."

"So do I." She softened the words with a smile and raced to the library.

Nick saw her, tossed aside a magazine, and shot to his feet. Side by side, they raced to the truck. He wrapped his arm around her shoulders to shield her from the rain, but her insides were quaking with a nauseating mix of fear for Leona and anger at Eve. The instant she dropped down on the seat, she pressed her cold hands against her heated cheeks, but her pulse raced even faster.

"Leona shouldn't be alone," she complained as Nick started the truck. "I can't believe I let this happen. I should have walked out. I should have—"

"I-5 is still open, but it's going to be tight." He steered through the open gate, turned on the radio for weather updates, and headed for the freeway.

Warmed by the heat spilling from the vents, she stole a glance at the determined set of Nick's jaw. A warm glow swelled in her chest, and she gave silent thanks for this strong, steady man merging through traffic with the precision of a fighter pilot. She could have managed on her own, but Nick made today a thousand times easier. She liked having a friend . . . a partner. Dare she admit it? She liked being a passenger for a change.

A lump pushed into her throat, one that tasted of yearning. Eve had told her to go after what she wanted, but what Kate wanted wasn't something a person could touch or see or smell. She wanted to love and be loved, to care for people the way Nick cared for her—with respect, kindness, and attention to the most tender details of life. The ache in her chest deepened, and she imagined a hole in her heart, one that Nick filled to perfection.

The thought terrified her, because she was dangerously close to falling in love with him—to needing him. But what then? How could she manage the kaleidoscope of her life when the pieces were jagged, sharp, and constantly shifting? Tense and wary, she stared out the rain-streaked windshield, barely listening as the traffic reporter announced that I-5 was expected to close within the hour.

"Oh no," she said, her voice shaking. "Will we make it?"

"We're sure going to try." He pressed the gas pedal a little harder, and the truck surged past another vehicle.

The traffic was heavy but racing at full speed. Clutching her phone, she called Leona for an update. "What's happening?"

"Lots of Shnow. Shtay in L.A."

"No way."

"I'm fine—"

"Did you call Dody?"

Silence.

"Nonnie—call her. *Please*. I worry about you."

"I'm fine, shweetheart."

Kate chewed her lip in a fit of indecision. Leona wasn't a child. She had the right to make choices for herself, but what did Kate do with the fear sawing on her already frayed nerves? She had to get to Meadows, both for Leona's sake and her own peace of mind. If anyone could navigate the roads in a storm, it was Nick.

"All right," she said to her grandmother. "But I'm coming home. We're near Valencia. With a little luck, we'll be there soon."

She hung up with an "I love you" and tossed the phone in the console. They were just outside of Castaic, the staging area where the highway patrol formed lines of cars to be escorted over the snowy pass. She was hungry, angry, and mildly in need of a bathroom, but she didn't dare ask Nick to stop at a service station. If they missed the final escort group, they'd be stuck in Castaic for hours, maybe a couple days. Nervous, she glanced at the gas gauge and saw half a tank—enough to get home even at a crawl.

Brake lights flashed in front of them. Groaning, Nick halted behind a semi and cut the engine. "This isn't good."

"What's happening?"

"We're waiting in the escort line, but there's no guarantee the highway patrol will take another group over the summit. We'll have to wait and see."

Kate swallowed hard, tapped her toes, and watched the window fog with their breath. For twenty solid minutes they sat behind the idling semi, inhaling exhaust and staring at brake lights until the truck rolled forward.

"We're in!" Nick declared as they passed the roadblock.

They rolled forward, slowly, then at a solid twenty miles an hour. Rain pounded the roof and windshield. Unconsciously Kate drummed her fingers on the armrest until Nick covered her hand with his larger one. "I want to caution you. If San Miguel Highway isn't plowed, we'll have to wait for the county to clear it."

"Of course." At least they'd be close to home.

Abruptly the rain stopped, plunging them into a silent world of snowflakes the size of teacups. The wipers kicked the clumps off the windshield, but snow lay thick on the pavement. It would be even thicker in San Miguel Canyon because of the higher altitude. When they reached the top of the pass and the Meadows exit, Nick pulled into a brightly lit gas station.

"Pit stop," he said.

"Me, too."

While he gassed up the truck, Kate hurried to the ladies' room. When she came out, she saw Nick speaking to the clerk and joined them in time to learn that the snowplow had gone through ten minutes ago. With a little luck, they could follow it all the way to Meadows.

Nick grabbed her hand and they dashed back to his truck. The first five miles passed through a long, rolling valley. That part of the drive didn't scare Kate at all, except tonight a fierce wind hurled snow at a horizontal angle and nearly blinded them. The freshly plowed road was already white.

On her own, she would have turned back. But Nick was perfectly relaxed as they veered on to San Miguel Highway. If he could make this drive without fear, so could she. Never mind the tension in her muscles and the blinding whiteness of the storm. One curve fed into another, dipping and rising with relative ease, until they reached a twisting U-shaped dip. Nick started down the slope at a careful ten miles an hour, building up momentum that he'd use to climb the approaching hill.

They were accelerating out of the bottom of the turn when taillights appeared in front of them. The whine of spinning tires shattered the quiet, but the sedan didn't move, not even an inch, until it lost traction and started to slide backwards and straight at them, picking up speed as the front end swung to the side.

"He's going to hit us!" Kate cried.

Nick slammed the truck into Reverse and backed away. Their own tires broke loose, and they started to slide just like the car, faster and faster, picking up speed until the truck hit a snowbank and lurched—just like the BMW on the lip of the canyon.

Choking on a sob, Kate clamped her hands over her mouth. *Don't cry! Don't cry! Stay rational!*

But the sedan was sliding straight at them, sideways and crooked until it coasted to a halt at the bottom of the dip. Instead of attempting another run up the hill, the driver headed back to the interstate, passing them with a wave of apology.

Still fighting tears, Kate hiccupped with a sob. "It wasn't that bad. Not really. He wasn't going that fast But I can't—I can't—"

Nick pulled her into his arms, held her, crooned to her. "We're almost home. Hang on, okay?"

"I'm fine. Really I am. It's just—" She could fight the tears but not the truth. She was terrified. Nestling closer, she clung to Nick with all her might.

15

nick held kate tight, but his eyes stayed glued to the rearview mirror. The sedan was gone, but any minute another car could come along and lose control. He cradled her a moment longer, then kissed the top of her head. "We need to move."

She managed a brave but unsteady smile. "I'm all right. It was just a-a reaction."

He patted her shoulder, then started to rock the truck out of the snowbank. He had cat litter in the back if he needed to spread it to get traction, but the four-wheel drive did its job, and they were back on the road in a minute. They crested the hill without a single slip, but Kate couldn't seem to breathe without gulping air. He drove slowly, offering reassurances as he steered around the hanging hairpin, then the last miles to Meadows, where total darkness indicated downed power lines and a mountain-wide outage.

Some of the streets had been plowed, but the road connecting Leona's house to the main highway was still covered with snow. For once, Nick had no desire to make the first tracks. Kate had endured enough trauma for the day. She needed to feel safe and warm, and there was only one place they could go—his house. His pulse thrummed with pleasure at the thought of being with her and taking care of her, but he'd also drawn thick lines to protect himself from those fiery darts of temptation.

Tonight, what mattered more? His personal peace of mind or Kate's comfort? There wasn't a doubt in his mind that Kate's needs came first. Men protected women; they fought for them and guarded their hearts and well-being. That's what he'd do for Kate. As for his personal battle, he drew a new line for himself: No kissing and he'd sleep on the couch while she went upstairs.

Without asking her, he turned the truck around. "Leona's street is too risky. We'll go to my place."

"Thank you," she murmured, slumping weakly against the seat. "I can't stand the thought of sliding again."

He drove the plowed roads to his house, barreled through the snow covering his driveway, and parked close to the front door. "Wait here."

With the headlights illuminating the way, he trotted up the steps, went inside, and propped up a flashlight to illuminate the path to the couch. What he was about to do was necessary, considering Kate's short skirt and high heels, but it was also a little dangerous—the sort of thing that made them male and female. When he returned to the truck, her door was open and she was seated at an angle, peering down and grimacing as she planted one foot in the snow. Before she could move the other one, he scooped her into his arms, lifting her as she instinctively clung to his neck.

"Stop!" she said with a nervous laugh. "I'm too heavy."

"No, you're not." Determined not to grunt—or worse, drop her—he carried her to the couch, where they landed in a tangle of knees and elbows. He extricated himself immediately and went outside to turn off the truck. Breathing in the cold, he reminded himself of his plan and vowed to stick to it. He wished he had a guest room, but she'd have to make do with his bedroom and a pair of his sweats to sleep in. He'd doze on the couch and tend the fire, a necessity with the power out and no other heat.

With his head clear, he went back inside where Kate was ending a call to Leona. Huddled on the couch, she set down the phone and hugged herself against the chill. He lifted an afghan off the recliner and draped it over her shoulders.

"Thank you," she murmured.

"I'll have a fire going in a minute." He had set the logs in place this morning, a habit of his, so he struck a match and lit the kindling. Next he fetched the pillar candles he kept for emergencies, set them on the coffee table and lit the wicks. Straightening, he looked into Kate's eyes from across the flames. Her tears had dried, but the stress of the day was evident in the tightness of her mouth.

"Are you hungry?" he asked.

"No, but I'm still rattled." Looking at him, she patted the sofa next to her. "Sit with me."

He hesitated, then dropped down a foot away from her. Holding her would have been the most natural thing in the world. It was precisely what he wanted to do, but he had a brain as well as a body and a heart—and a soul. As long as she was safe and warm, his job was done. It was time to get back to normal, so he kept his distance. "I'm going to sleep on the couch. Why don't you head upstairs? There are sweats in the bureau—second drawer down. Help yourself to anything—"

"Nick?" Her eyes were wide again and full of angst.

"Yes?"

"I'm tired, cold, and a little afraid." Her gaze dipped to her lap and she sniffed. "Would you hold me? Just for a while?"

The candles bathed her profile in gold light, revealing all the things nature used to pull a man and woman together. Who would care if he held her close, or even if they slept on the couch in each other's arms? As long as they didn't cross a certain line, what was the big deal?

"Stay with me," she said in that wobbly voice. "I don't want to go upstairs alone. It's dark and foreign, and . . . and I've had enough for one night."

Hurting for her, he put his own needs aside and drew her into his arms. She rested her head against his chest, took a deep breath, then sighed in a way that warmed his skin through his shirt . . . the skin over his heart . . . the heart pounding with a truth he wanted to avoid but couldn't. He'd fallen in love with her—the head-over-heels, walk-on-hot-coals, talk-all-night kind of love. He was a Christian, but he was also a man who experienced temptation in all its glory. He fought the desire to kiss her with a silent cry to God, felt himself slipping, and knew he had to put air between himself and Kate before he stumbled.

He loosened his arms and slid a foot away. "You'll be more comfortable upstairs. Take the flashlight."

"I'd rather stay here." The candles burned with hot white light, illuminating her face and the loose hair brushing her shoulders. "Could we just cuddle a bit? I completely respect your faith. I'd never do anything to—to bother you."

She had to be kidding. Everything she did *bothered* him. Anger rushed through him—at himself for wanting so badly to stay and at Kate for not understanding why she needed to go upstairs alone. With his emotions boiling into a steamy mess, he cupped her face. "Kate. I can't—"

"But why?"

His throat ached with the strain of everything—wanting her, denying himself, and loving her all at once. "Do you really *not* get it?"

176

"I guess I don't."

He tunneled his fingers through her hair, tilted her face to his, and stared into her eyes. The anger and frustration melted into emotions that scoured his heart clean and left him even more determined to be the man God called him to be. "This," he murmured in a husky voice, "this is why I can't stay with you." His mouth found hers and he kissed her . . . tenderly . . . thoroughly. There were no questions in the kiss, only an answer. He had to leave because this kiss was meant to cherish her in a godly way, not tempt them beyond their ability to resist the pull of physical desire.

She kissed him back, clutching his shoulders and clinging to him, until he mustered the last of his strength and eased away with a final brush of their lips. "I'm going outside—"

"But it's cold."

"I'll be fine." He trailed his fingers down her cheek, stealing one last caress. "Now go upstairs. Please."

She nodded but just barely. Determined to stay strong, he stood and offered his hand. When she didn't take it, he kissed her forehead, put on his coat, and went outside to shovel snow from the deck, the driveway, all of Meadows if that's what it took to protect Kate and himself from regrets.

The instant Nick closed the door, Kate buried her face in her hands. With her mind in an uproar, she relived every second of the kiss—the anticipation when Nick stared into her eyes, the awareness of what he intended, the control in his touch, and most of all the authority with which he ended it. The kiss was so full of Nick she had lost herself in it completely.

"No," she murmured to the candles. "That's not right."

She wasn't lost—she was found.

In Nick's arms, she experienced a joining of hearts unlike anything she had felt in her life. A force like gravity had drawn them together, and it could only be stopped with an effort that ran counter to instinct. Joel wouldn't have made that decision; neither did her first college boyfriend, the one to whom she'd given her virginity—willingly, yes, but with enough hesitation that she still felt vaguely used. A lump pushed into her throat, because somewhere low and deep she wished Nick had been the first, and she wanted more than anything to believe that marriage really could last a lifetime.

Eve would have laughed at the dream and called her naïve. Maybe she was, but by leaving after that single, careful, purposeful kiss, Nick had shown her how a strong man loved an equally strong woman.

Except Kate wasn't strong. Not like Nick. She *tried* to be strong, but under the business suit and the professional tone, she was terrified of a world that didn't make sense. She was tired of being a marble in a box, tired of struggling to be brave and in control. As for going with the flow, she was beginning to hate that phrase. What she wanted was stability.

And confidence.

And hope.

She wanted to live the way Nick did—with the courage to face life head-on, unswayed by impulse or fear. She wanted his faith in a power greater than herself, a loving father who would take care of her.

"God," she whispered. "Are you real?"

Raising her head, she focused on the candles. The flames cast a small but steady glow, and she thought of Nick staring at a dying campfire on top of Mount Abel. Eyes wide, Kate waited for a sense of holiness or insignificance, a pinprick of God's glory. Anything to tell her God was real. But she felt nothing.

Nothing at all.

The CEO of the Universe was out to lunch or not taking calls. She considered going outside to talk to Nick but dismissed the idea. The kiss was reverberating through every cell in her body. Staring at the candles, she saw just one alternative. If she couldn't phone a friend like on that game show, she'd leave a voice mail for the CEO himself.

"Hello, God," she said in a small voice. "It's me, Kate Darby. We spoke a few days ago. I want to know if you're real."

She closed her eyes and waited. Nothing happened. She listened to the silence and smelled the candles, but there was no sense of a power greater than herself. There was nothing except an abiding sense of danger, because if God was real, her life would change the way Nick's life had changed. The candles offered a vague comfort, but it wasn't enough to slow her racing pulse. She wanted Nick. Since she couldn't be with him, she settled for the next best thing—honoring his wishes by going upstairs alone and closing the door.

With the snow falling and night pressing against the windows, Leona carried the condor journal to the kitchen table and sat down with her pen. She loved Kate very much, but she missed quiet evenings alone, where the only sounds came from the creaking floor. She would have liked a fire, but she knew her limitations and didn't try to lay kindling and logs. Instead, she bundled up in her heavy robe and sipped the hot tea she'd put in a thermal carafe before the power outage struck.

Old age came at a cost. The loss of her independence topped the list of things Leona missed, but privacy was a close second. As much as she wanted to finish the journal, she hadn't been able to write in it for several days. When Kate was at the office, Dody came to stay with her. Leona couldn't concentrate with someone else in the living room, and by the end of the day she was too tired to tell her story.

But tonight was perfect. Kate was safe with Nick, and though Leona refused to be a meddlesome old woman, she prayed every day that Kate would know the love of God and a husband, and that she'd have as many children as she wanted.

Leona knew full well God answered prayers in His own way. Sometimes the answers were painful, but sometimes the answers were yes—and not just yes but *yes*! Having waited so long for a child of her own, Leona had experienced both extremes. She knew how it felt to writhe in agony with the question *why* raw on her lips, but she had also experienced the bliss of unexpected mercy.

Tonight the in-between years were on her mind, the ones that started with Peter's birth, when condors still lived in the wild. With that thought in mind, she began to write.

Dear Kate,

I promised you I'd call Dody if you couldn't make it home, and I did. She understood completely when I told her I wanted a night to myself. She's my age, so she knows what it's like to lose your life a slice at a time. First the body becomes defiant, then the mind slows down. Young people have no idea how much effort it takes to get old.

Doctor visits.

Pills twice a day.

Planning a trip to the bathroom so I don't rush and risk a fall.

My body requires almost as much attention as an infant's. I don't enjoy feeling like a baby, but I loved being a mother. When Peter Alexander Darby came into the world on July 24, 1967, Alex and I counted his toes and marveled at his tiny fingers. We rejoiced over our son, but then the fear started. If he coughed, I raced him to the pediatrician. A bout of colic sent us to the emergency room. I slept in the nursery for six months because I was afraid Peter would stop breathing. SIDS didn't have a name then, but I knew babies died suddenly and without reason.

I worried constantly about him from the moment he was born, a natural reaction considering how long we waited and the likelihood he'd be our only child. In one breath I praised God for His kindness; in the next I feared He'd take my son away. My faith was ambivalent, to say the least. Yet once again God spoke to me through the condors.

When your father was born, the species was teetering on extinction. Environmental issues emerged in the forefront of the news, particularly DDT and how it caused eggshells to become so thin they cracked. You know the story, Kate. Over the next twenty years, your grandfather photographed every detail of the effort to save the species: the formation of a recovery team, how eggs were retrieved from the wild and incubated, the fight for genetic diversity.

The battle to preserve the species hit one snag after another until 1987, when the last condor in the wild was captured and taken to the zoo. He was Adult Condor Number 9. He made the news because he was the last, but it was AC Number 8, a female taken captive a few months earlier, that touched my heart. I knew biologists had taken eggs from her nest in the early efforts to save the species, and I wondered what she thought when that happened. She didn't understand human intervention any better than I understood God.

That point was driven home on February 1, 1994 when your father died in that awful wreck. What the Lord gave, He took away and I didn't understand at all.

I coped as well as I could, mostly for you. Your mother seemed to dissolve in front of my eyes. She was never the same—but you know that. Even at the tender age of seven, you took better care of her than she did of you.

Oh, Kate! Life can be so unfair. Not only did you lose your father, but that day you lost your childhood. In that haze of grief and despair, my faith was at its lowest ebb since that day in San Miguel Canyon some thirty years earlier.

The story doesn't end here, but it's late and I'm tired. Next time I'll tell you about that trip to the San Diego Zoo and a condor named Aqiwo. Do you remember that day? I'll never forget it, and I have a hunch you remember it, too.

With her heart suddenly heavy, Leona bowed her head and prayed for her granddaughter. She didn't know why that urge came on so strong, but it was every bit as real as the candles on the table. A long time passed before she felt calm again. At peace at last, she closed the journal, went to bed, and dreamed of Alex.

16

two weeks after the snowstorm,
Nick and Kate were working late at the Clarion office, solo-
ing on their first deadline without Maggie, who was looking
at houses in Phoenix. He was seated at a drafting-style table
and proofing the holiday insert. He thought Kate had done
a bang-up job on it, especially the Angel Tree story. The full-
page ad for the fund-raiser displayed a Christmas tree with
ornaments listing toys, clothing sizes, and household items
to replace what Colton and his family had lost. On the first
night of the Christmas Faire, Meadows residents would bring
gifts for the family to the Clarion.

Seated across from him, Kate was proofing the news sec-
tions. They had until midnight to send the file to the printer
in Bakersfield, and the paper seemed to be in good shape
until Kate startled him with a mock scream. Grabbing two
fistfuls of her hair, she did a face plant on the proof sheets.
"I can't believe this!"

"What's wrong?"

She straightened with a groan, then slumped back against
the stool. "I forgot the ad for the Craft Pavilion." The Pavilion

183

was a new account, fairly large and much needed considering the state of the *Clarion*'s finances.

"Pull the Rotary Club feature," Nick suggested. "We'll run it next week."

"Is there enough space?"

"What do you need? A quarter-page?"

"Exactly."

"It's on page twelve," he reminded her. "Take a look."

She riffled through the proof sheets, sized up the change, and gave Nick a rueful look. "It's an easy fix, but how could I forget something so important?"

"Easy." He capped his red pen. "Maggie's out of town, and you're doing double time with Sutton. I'm amazed your socks match."

"I am, too, but you know what?"

"What?"

A smile broke across her face. "I love this stuff—" she gestured at the counter littered with scraps of notepaper, colored pencils, and a pizza box. "Deadlines are kind of fun. What I don't love is being split in two."

Nick thought of the Bible story about Solomon and the two women fighting over a baby. In a very real way, Kate was the baby and Eve Landon and the *Clarion* were fighting for her time. Nick did as much as he could, but he didn't share Kate's talent for selling and designing ads. Thanks to her efforts, the holiday supplement was the biggest ever and a boon to the *Clarion*'s bottom line.

"It's temporary," he remarked. "Leona's doing well, and Dody's thinking of moving in, right?"

"Maybe."

"So in January you'll be at Sutton and back in the groove."

"Will I?"

"Be in the groove? Sure."

She glanced around the office, a forlorn expression on her face. "I just don't know anymore. I'm working like crazy on the proposal, but I love the *Clarion*, too. I used to be so certain about the future. Now I don't know where I belong, or what I believe. It's all so . . . I can't put it into words."

Nick felt a hitch in his own heart. "Are you serious about leaving Sutton?"

"Sometimes. Maybe." She gave a little laugh. "Probably not."

He wanted Kate to be happy with her choices, but he also wanted her to be at peace with God, heaven, and everything in between. Since the night of the storm, she seemed wistful and distant. The kiss had rattled him, too, but he had vowed not to repeat it. Now he wondered if the feelings between them had rocked Kate's world more than he realized. "You have a lot to consider."

"I do." She gave him a confused, woeful look. "And right now, we have a deadline to meet." She moved from the drafting table to a desk with an extra large monitor. "This won't take long. The ad's already designed. I just have to make room."

They worked side by side, trading questions and friendly banter until they were satisfied with both the regular issue of the *Clarion* and the holiday insert. Kate sent the computer file to the printer, let out a "Whoo-hoo!" and gave a little fist pump. "That's it! Our first solo issue is done."

"Good job." Nick offered his hand.

Kate gripped his fingers and held tight, watching him with a look that was more personal than business. Neither of them let go, and just like that, they were back in his living room, trapped by snow and feelings he had to deny because of his pledge and for Kate's sake. He let her go, jammed his hands in his pockets, and glanced at the clock. "Coyote Joe's is still open. Are you hungry?"

She gave a little shiver. "I'm starved, but I can't leave."

"Why not?"

"I need to work on the Eve's Garden stuff. Want to see what I have so far?"

"Sure."

They went to Kate's office, where she sat at the computer and Nick looked over her shoulder. While the file loaded, she pointed to the Eve's Garden ad displayed on the wall. "I'm aiming for something that plays off the 'Put the You in Beautiful' slogan and ties in with aging. Flowers and gardens are an obvious theme, but I'm worried that it's too obvious. I thought if I played with black and white instead of color, it might be more timeless." She clicked on a black-and-white picture of a young girl holding a white daisy.

"It's kind of blah," he said.

"You're right, but look at this one." She brought up a black-and-white photograph of an elderly woman with as many wrinkles as an English bulldog. In a wise and wonderful way, she was stunningly beautiful.

"I like that," he said to Kate.

"Me, too, but I don't think Eve will."

"Probably not." The woman in the photo looked her age.

Kate clicked through some more pictures, then showed him a list of words with the U sound in them—universal, youthful, euphoria. "I've got the pieces, but it's not gelling."

"How about *unique*?" he suggested.

"I like that a lot." She added the word to her list, then looked at him from over her shoulder. "You're good at this."

"Just with words. You're the pro when it comes to the complete package."

She studied him with the same admiring expression she wore the morning after the storm, when he drove her home, blew the snow out of Leona's driveway, and took her up on the offer of waffles for breakfast. It had been a cozy time, in spite of the lingering kiss, or maybe because of it.

He straightened his spine and stepped back. "I'll let you get to work."

Kate stood with him. "I wish I could say yes to Coyote Joe's, but I really need to make some progress here." She studied the poster on the wall, tilting her head like a curious bird. "A year ago I was so proud of that ad and what it says about personal beauty. Now it seems . . . I don't know. Just not enough."

Nick didn't know what to say. He appreciated a beautiful woman as much as any man, but in his opinion, a person's looks mattered far less than their character. Kate was still studying the poster but didn't seem to expect an answer. "I'll lock up," he said.

A smile played on her lips, then she kissed his cheek. "Thank you for everything." She looked at him as if he could walk on water. He couldn't, of course. He couldn't even sell his book. This morning he'd received his ninth rejection, a bitter pill, but one he swallowed with a vow to be patient. *Waiting* . . . it was the story of his life. After giving Kate a brotherly hug, he locked the door behind him and went alone to Coyote Joe's.

When Kate and Leona arrived at the Clarion for the first night of the Christmas Faire, dusk had already turned the sky royal blue. White lights decorated the trees as high as a cherry picker could reach, and every storefront twinkled and glowed. Decorations ranged from tacky to classic, and Kate loved them all. She especially loved what would happen later. Santa Claus would arrive on a fire engine with its lights flashing and siren blaring.

The Christmas Faire was a long-standing Meadows tradition. Started twenty years ago by the Chamber of Commerce, it lasted a full weekend and had grown from a few businesses putting up decorations to a festival of lights, music, cookies, and homemade crafts. The Christmas Faire was part of Kate's history, and she loved every bit of it.

With her arm around Leona's waist, she paused to look up and down the street. "It's beautiful, isn't it?"

"Yesh," Leona said. "All is calm. All is bright."

"I love Christmas," Kate declared with a sweep of her arm. "It's fun and pretty, and it brings out the best in people. Wait until you see the Angel Tree." Judging by the enthusiasm around town, Colton and his family were going to have a wonderful holiday. Kate had gone all out with an outfit for Mindy, toys for the little kids, and art supplies for Colton. Leona's gift to the family was a set of pots and pans, and Nick had bought Colton some clothes and a heavy jacket.

Mindy and the kids were now living in a small apartment, trying to save enough money to rent another house. Like Kate, they were caught between old circumstances and new ones. Did she still belong at Sutton? It seemed far away, but so did God. Since praying that prayer, she'd read some of Leona's Bible. The Old Testament stories scared her, particularly the ones about people whose lives were upended and changed forever, like Noah building an ark and Moses wandering in the desert. Kate feared that kind of trial, but other verses filled her with yearning. She liked one in particular—*Perfect love casts out fear*—because she knew how it felt to be afraid.

She cared deeply for Nick and wanted to share his Christian faith, but was *wanting* to believe enough? She especially wanted to believe at Christmas when the air was full of peace, love, and goodwill. With that thought in mind, she walked with Leona into the Clarion office. The warm air smelled of apple cider laced with cinnamon and cloves, and the gifts under the Angel Tree were piled even higher than this morning. Later she and Nick would deliver them to the Smith family.

Maggie hurried around the counter for a hug. "Leona! You made it!"

"I shertainly did," she said proudly. "I haven't missed a Christmas Faire in twenty years, and I'm not shtarting tonight."

While Maggie hung up Leona's coat, Kate watched the parking lot for Nick. They were working together on the Christmas Faire story, so when she saw his truck, she waved good-bye to Maggie and Leona. "We'll be back in a few hours."

"Have fun!" Leona called to her.

Beaming a smile, Kate pushed through the door and approached Nick with Merry Christmas poised on her lips. He stole the words with a brief kiss, then hugged her. "Merry Christmas."

"Merry Christmas to you, too."

Bundled in coats and hats, they joined the crowd on the street. Several times they stopped to take pictures and chat with locals and tourists alike, sharing the holiday cheer and sipping hot chocolate. Kate's favorite spot was the Kid's Corral where Chellie was painting snowflakes and candy canes on the cheeks of children as a fund-raiser for the animal shelter. There was enough snow for a snowman contest, and Nick took pictures of two brothers with a six-foot dinosaur. When they saw Mindy with her two youngest kids, Kate waved hello.

"I wonder where Colton is," Nick asked, scanning the crowd.

Kate spotted him first. "Over there."

Nick followed her gaze and they saw Colton on the other

side of the street, his hands shoved in his old coat as he talked awkwardly with a pretty girl in a red jacket and a snow-white cap.

Chuckling softly, Nick looped his arm around Kate's waist. "Let's leave him alone."

"Good idea." She smiled up at him just as he looked down, both of them touched by that first-crush feeling. Basking in it, they ambled through shops and displays until they reached a church with a living nativity scene. Mary and Joseph looked a lot like Wayne and Becky from the Meadows Market, but Kate didn't recognize the shepherds or the infant bundled in Mary's arms. While old Netta Grace played carols on her dulcimer, sheep grazed on the lawn, and a camel from a ranch that supplied animals to Hollywood gave Kate a curious look. Nearby a long-eared donkey chewed some straw.

The tableau didn't seem quite real . . . but it was. Transfixed, she took in the baby in the manger, the shepherds, Mary and Joseph, the lights in the trees, and the stars in the sky. Conscious of every prickle of cold and twinkle of light, she reached for Nick's hand. He glanced down and smiled. With their breath mingling in a frosty cloud, they traded a poignant look before returning their attention to the nativity scene.

Kate's breath snagged in her throat. *God, are you listening? Can you hear me?* Just like the first time she had asked, her pulse rushed with a yearning to belong—to be at peace with herself, Nick, and God. Trembling, she made a decision. *Wanting* to know God had to be enough, because it was the best she could do.

Before she thought too much and lost her courage, she focused on the manger and murmured out loud, "I believe." Clutching Nick's hand, she squeezed as tightly as the day he pulled her up and out of the canyon. With her heart ready to leap out of her chest, she indicated the nativity, the church, and the stars. "I believe in all of this—in God and Christmas and Jesus and—and everything."

Nick turned to her with his brows furrowed. "Kate, do you know what that means?"

"I do." At least she *thought* she did. To use a pat phrase, she had given her life to Christ. She knew about sin and salvation from going to church as a little girl, and she knew God loved her. If it wasn't enough, it was a good start.

The tightness around Nick's eyes melted into a look of joy, then he drew her close and hugged her. Warm in his arms, she savored the first notes of "O Holy Night," her favorite carol even before tonight. Somehow it sounded more alive and personal, as if it were being played just for her. The donkey brayed softly and the camel stomped its foot. With the smells of pine and hay and Nick's warm skin tickling her nose, she turned in his arms so that they were facing the manger together. "It looks the same, but somehow everything's different."

"That's the feeling exactly." A smile played on his lips. "And it's something to celebrate. I know we planned on Christmas Eve together, but how about Christmas Day, too? I want you to meet Sam and Gayle. We'll bring Leona."

"I'd like that."

Meeting Nick's family was a big step, one she welcomed, especially when he described a Christmas full of noise, food, and family—all the things Kate had missed as an only child. The future seemed as pristine as the field of snow where she had made the snow angel, and suddenly she knew what to do about Sutton. It was time to start a new life the way Noah did when he built the ark. The thought terrified her, but if God was real, she didn't have to be afraid.

She gripped Nick's fingers. "I'm quitting."

"Quitting what?"

"My job at Sutton."

"Kate—" He grasped both her hands and squeezed hard. "I want you here in Meadows. There's no doubt about it. But I know what it's like to make a big change. You should take some time. Don't rush."

"I'm not."

"But—"

A siren cut him off. Startled, they looked up the street, where a fire engine was creeping along with its lights flashing, "Ho ho ho" blaring from the PA, and Santa riding shotgun, throwing candy to people on the street as he headed to the Kids' Corral.

"Let's go!" She grabbed Nick's hand. They had pictures to take and stories to write, but mostly she wanted to savor this remarkable night.

Oh, what fun to be a child again.

To celebrate and rejoice.

To be with Nick, the most wonderful man she had ever met.

Hand in hand, they raced ahead of the fire truck to the play area. Nick positioned himself for pictures of Santa's arrival, and Kate asked kids what they wanted for Christmas. When they finished, Nick approached her with a serious look in his eyes. "What happened tonight is important. We need to talk—"

"Later, okay?" Bouncing on her toes, she planted her hands on his shoulders and kissed him. "I want to tell Leona that I'm staying in Meadows."

Nick hesitated. "Are you that sure about leaving Sutton?"

"I am." Tonight she was sure of everything.

The crowd was thinner now, and they reached the Clarion in two minutes. When they walked into the dimly lit office, they found Leona and Dody enjoying a cup of cider and gazing at the tree. At the sight of them, Leona lumbered to her feet. "It's been a wonderful evening, but I'm worn out. Dody's meeting some of the gals for coffee, but I'm not up to it. Could you take me home?"

"Of course." Kate wanted to blurt her good news, but her grandmother's needs came first. Concerned, she turned to Nick. "I know we promised Mindy we'd deliver the gifts—"

"I'll handle it," he said to her. "Colton can help."

He gave her a quick kiss, wished Leona and Dody a merry Christmas, and went to find Colton. Kate drove Leona home, waited until she was tucked into bed, then tapped on the open door. "Are you up for a little conversation?"

"Of coursh." Leona patted the mattress next to her.

Excited and a little scared, Kate perched on the edge the way she did when she was little. "Something happened tonight, and I want to tell you about it." She described the nativity and how real it seemed, the smell of the hay, and how the camel had looked at her. "You took me to church when I was little, and I believed back then. Lately, not so much." She lowered her gaze to her lap, felt the weight of mistakes and wasted time, then looked into Leona's eyes. "I don't know how to describe what I felt tonight, except to say God touched me, and I believe again."

"Oh, honey—"

"There's more." She swallowed the lump in her throat. "I'm quitting Sutton and staying in Meadows."

Leona pulled Kate into a hug. "This is what I hoped, but it's a big decision. Are you sure?"

"Positive." Nothing could dim her good mood, though the thought of calling Roscoe unnerved her.

Leona pulled out of the hug, her eyes twinkling with mischief. "Does Nick know you're staying?"

"Yes."

"And?"

"He's happy about it." A blush warmed her cheeks. "Very happy, in fact. So am I." She told Leona about the plans for Christmas Day and meeting Nick's family. "Is that okay with you?"

"It sounds perfect."

They talked about Christmas and life, men, shopping, and decorating the house until Leona's eyelids fluttered like tired butterflies. Kate kissed her good-night, then trundled upstairs and went to bed herself. She dreamed about Nick as she fell asleep, but just before dawn she jarred awake from a nightmare about Sutton, a blizzard, and speeding on a twisting mountain road.

"Oh, Lord," she murmured in the dark. "Am I making the right decision?"

As usual, nothing happened. There was only a keening emptiness in her middle, and the fervent hope God was real and wouldn't let her down.

17

on monday morning,

Kate made the coffee extra strong, mustered her courage and
called Roscoe. His assistant told her he hadn't arrived yet but
would call her back in an hour. Three cups of coffee later, her
phone rang and she jumped out of her skin. Swallowing hard,
she greeted Roscoe with a cheery hello. They chatted briefly,
then he asked when she planned to make a visit to Sutton.

"That's why I'm calling." Mentally she put on her best
business suit. "I've given this a lot of thought and—"

"Ah, Kate—"

"I'm not coming back. I'll finish the Eve's Garden proposal,
but I need to work from home like I've been doing. I'm happy
here, and—well, it's the right thing to do."

"I'm not surprised. Frankly, I saw this coming."

"You did?"

"Yes. Nick's a great guy."

"This isn't about him." She resented the notion she was
chasing after a man. She cared deeply for Nick, but she had
a life of her own.

"Whatever you say. It doesn't really matter. The bottom line is that you're throwing away your career."

"No, I'm not." She started to pace. Roscoe was like a father to her. His opinion mattered.

"I think you are. Newspapers are dying out."

"Not the *Clarion*."

"Will you earn as much as you do from Sutton, not to mention the cost of benefits like health insurance?"

"No."

"What about your condo? Aren't you underwater like everyone else?"

"Close," she admitted. She'd have to sell the place or rent it out. She also needed a car. The insurance money for the BMW had paid off the loan, and Leona's Subaru was reliable but old. Aside from the financial cost of leaving Sutton, she would miss her friends. A lump pushed into her throat, but she forced it down. If Nick could give up *California for Real Men*, she could live without Sutton. "It's the right thing to do," she insisted.

A long sigh emanated from her phone. "All right. But if things don't work out, call me. You do good work, Kate. I'll hire you back anytime."

"Thank you."

They talked briefly about Eve's Garden, with Kate assuring him she'd keep Eve happy until the account was finalized in February. After Roscoe's cold-blooded assessment, Kate needed a friend who understood her feelings, so she called Julie.

"Hey," Kate said. "You won't believe this—"

"Neither will you! I'm pregnant! I did the test this morning. It's positive, Kate! *Positive!* I want this so badly . . ." She started to cry.

So did Kate. "I'm happy for you."

196

Julie stammered about the baby and miracles, how thrilled her husband was, and her yearning to be a mom. "I'll work for a while, but when the baby comes I'm quitting. Kate, whatever you do, don't wait too long to have kids. Nick's a great guy. I saw how he looks at you."

"Oh Julie—"

"What?"

"I'm leaving Sutton." The story spilled out of her, everything from the visit to Eve's Garden to kissing Nick and finally to her new faith. When Julie offered nothing more than a few "uh-huhs" about the moment at the nativity, Kate felt self-conscious. "It must seem strange to you."

"No," Julie insisted. "Not at all. I have a cousin who's into the Christian thing. He went to India on some sort of mission trip. He had a good time."

What did Kate say to that? Her Christian faith wasn't a thing, and though she didn't exactly understand mission trips, she knew they weren't about having a good time. As for going to India, she couldn't imagine ever setting foot in Calcutta. Nick had an adventurous spirit; she didn't at all.

"Oh no." Julie groaned into the phone. "Sorry to cut this short, but I'm about to throw up. Morning sickness! Isn't that great?"

"It's awesome." Kate meant it, but she wished Julie could have been a little excited for her, too.

Lowering the phone, she wandered to the sliding glass door and looked at Mount Abel rising behind the house. Just like the living nativity, the mountain didn't seem quite real today. She had a clear view of the slope falling into the valley, but gray clouds hid the peak. She knew a narrow road twisted to the top. Nick had driven it many times, but Kate couldn't imagine braving it herself. The top of Mount Abel was suddenly as remote and terrifying as Calcutta. At the moment, so was leaving Sutton. Being a Christian wasn't as easy as she thought, but surely God wouldn't leave her to muddle through alone. He'd send help. Come to think of it, He already had. He'd sent Nick.

On Monday morning Nick went to Valencia to Christmas shop. At Toys"R"Us, he made a strafing run for gifts for his nephews. Sam would hate him for the electronic drums, but that was half the fun. Next he visited the Harley dealer and a jewelry shop, where he made purchases for Kate. He bought books for Leona, decided to give Sam and Gayle a weekend at a resort, then drove to Sam's house where his brother was expecting him.

Nick needed help. As much as he wanted Kate to quit Sutton and stay in Meadows, he couldn't stop thinking about Sam's advice to him when he was a new Christian: No big decisions for a year. If the same rule applied to Kate, what did Nick do next? He was sick and tired of waiting for his future to begin. It was time for a wife and kids, a dog . . . even a minivan.

Maybe not the minivan.

But definitely a wife. Celibacy had worked for the apostle Paul, but Nick was firmly in the "it's better to marry than to burn" camp, a point driven home every time he held Kate's hand or touched her arm, or kissed her even lightly.

Fighting his frustration, he pounded on Sam's door with his fist. Gayle opened it with a scowl that turned to a grin at the sight of him. "Nick! How are you?"

"Fine." *Sort of.*

"Come on in." She widened the door and ushered him inside. "Sam's in the garage. Can you stay for dinner?"

"I'd like that." He'd enjoy a family meal, especially since

Gayle had learned to cook from Nick and Sam's mother. "What are we having?"

"Roast beef."

His favorite, but Gayle knew that. She was the world's best sister-in-law, except for her tendency to introduce him to her single friends. She knew about his year off from dating but told him she was planning ahead. So was Nick, and Kate was the one.

He followed Gayle into the kitchen, then detoured to the garage where Sam was changing the wheels on a skateboard. When Nick entered, Sam glanced over his shoulder. His hair had some gray, and his black-framed glasses made him look owlish. Sometimes Nick thought his brother had been born wise.

"Need a hand?" Nick asked as he crossed the garage.

"I've got it." Sam went back to turning the screwdriver. "So what's up? On the phone you sounded half crazy."

"I am." Nick picked up a wrench and mindlessly spun the cylinder. "It's about Kate."

"Oh, yeah?"

He told Sam about the Christmas Faire, the living nativity, and Kate's epiphany. "I'm happy for her, but what do I do now? When I was a new Christian, you told me to wait a year before making any big decisions. I pushed that to 'no dating.' And now—" Nick clenched his teeth. "I'm really sorry I did that."

"I bet," Sam said with a laugh. "That's what you get for trying to outdo the rest of us. God made you a man, not Mr. Perfect Christian."

"What do you mean?"

"There's a big difference between 'no big decisions' and 'no dating'. The first one is just good advice. The second one is pretty extreme. As I recall, you made that rule for yourself. God didn't carve it in stone as the Eleventh Commandment."

until i found you

Sam had a point, but he didn't know how guilty Nick felt when he thought about his daughter suffering. "I had to do it."

"Okay," Sam agreed. "But it was still your choice. Maybe it's time to make a new choice."

"Like what?"

"You tell me." Sam focused back on the skateboard wheels and tightened a bolt.

Nick wished his own problems were as simple to fix as exchanging a pair of worn-out wheels for new ones. "I want to do what's best for Kate, but waiting another year—" He tossed down the wrench. "The idea stinks."

Sam laughed. "Patience isn't your strong suit."

"It never was."

The old skateboard wheels came off in Sam's hand. "You're serious about her, aren't you?"

"Very."

Sam set aside the old wheels and positioned the new ones in the same groove. When they wobbled, he pointed the screwdriver at a coffee can by Nick. "I need a washer."

While digging in the can, Nick thought of the work he'd done on his deck. Even something as small as a washer made a big difference to the stability of a railing. He wanted that stability with Kate, but he also wanted to cherish her, love her, even fight with her because that's what people did. "So what do I do?" he repeated, more frustrated than ever. "We have plans for New Year's Eve. It's business for the paper, but it could be a lot more."

"And you want to move things along."

"Yes."

"I don't blame you," Sam agreed. "And I don't think you need to worry about it. Your biggest weakness has always been going too fast, so God slowed you down. I don't know what Kate's personal character is like, but unless she has a dozen speeding tickets—"

"She doesn't. If anything, she's overly cautious."

"People learn to trust God in different ways. Maybe Kate needs to take a chance."

"Maybe," Nick agreed. "But I'm still worried. She was a Christian for five whole minutes when she decided to quit her job."

"That *is* fast."

"Especially since she loves it. I'm glad she quit, but I worry she'll regret it."

Sam spun the wheels with his hand. Without the friction of a sidewalk, they whirred for several seconds. Nick wanted that kind of friction-free life for Kate, but he knew better. Christianity wasn't a pie-in-the-sky promise of roses and vanilla moonbeams. The roses had thorns and sometimes the moon vanished. Nick knew all about the lonely times, the temptation to throw in the towel and find solace in old stupid ways. He didn't want Kate to go down that road—not ever.

Sam hung the screwdriver on the pegboard. "All you can do is pray for her . . . and for yourself, too. There aren't any rules here. I know couples who dated six weeks and stayed married for sixty years. On the flip side, a couple I married two years ago is already divorced. They did everything right— counseling, a long engagement, no sex before marriage—but they fell apart."

"Why?"

"I wish I knew."

The door to the kitchen opened, revealing Gayle with a dish towel in her hand and a scowl on her face. "Sam, I need you."

He was already crossing the garage. "What's up?"

"The sink's backed up—"

"*Again?*" He stopped and planted his hands on his hips. "What is it this time?"

"Potatoes." Her mouth thinned to a line.

Sam hung his head, then his shoulders heaved, and he looked up. "Honey, you know the sewer line is old. It can't handle sixteen pounds of potato peels."

"I didn't peel *sixteen* pounds of potatoes." Her hands landed on her hips in a pose that matched Sam's. "I peeled *five* potatoes—" She hesitated. "And some carrots . . . and two cucumbers for the salad."

"Oh, crud." Shaking his head, Sam followed Gayle.

Knowing what lay ahead, Nick collected a bucket, a pipe wrench, and rags, then joined Sam at the sink where potato peels were floating in slimy water. For the next hour, he and Sam did battle with the clogged sink. They plunged it, disassembled the trap, and tried to snake the sewer line. When all was said and done, the sink was in pieces, the clog was firmly in place, and Gayle was red-faced with embarrassment. "I know better," she said in a shaky voice. "I should have put the peels in the trash like you said. I just wasn't thinking."

Sam dragged his hand across the back of his neck. "It's an old house. I wish we could move, but—"

"No!" Gayle protested. "I love this house."

Nick knew the history. Gayle's father was an attorney with a solid six-figure income. Growing up, she had every material possession, including a new Saab for her sixteenth birthday. When she met Sam and fell in love, her lifestyle changed dramatically. Sam didn't earn a pile of money, and the family of four was crammed into an 1,100 square foot house with sewer lines doing battle with old tree roots. Something always needed fixing, but it was also a house full of love.

That love glistened in Gayle's eyes now. "Sammy, I'm so sorry."

202

When she sniffed back tears, Sam glanced helplessly around the room, then snatched a paper towel, and handed it to her. She dabbed her eyes but didn't look at him until he gripped both her hands in his and held tight. "Do you know how much I love you?"

She flung herself into his arms. "I love you too—so much."

A little choked up himself, Nick slipped unnoticed into the garage. Thanks to a clogged sink, he knew now how to be the man Kate needed. He simply had to love her more than he loved himself. He called her, smiling when she answered in a breathy voice. "Hey there."

"Hi," he replied. "I want to officially ask you about New Year's Eve. We're going to the chamber dance together, right?"

"I was counting on it."

"Good," he said. "Just so you know, this isn't business. It's a date."

18

"Kate!" Dody called

from the bottom of the stairs. "Nick's here."

"I'll be right down."

Kate did a final inspection of herself in the full-length mirror and liked what she saw. Her New Year's Eve dress was a pale aqua that matched her eyes to perfection. It was short enough to make Nick look twice, but the long sleeves and high neckline conveyed a swan-like elegance. The cut complimented her curves, but what Kate enjoyed most was the sparkle of a floating heart necklace—her Christmas present from Nick.

Fingering the gold charm, she thought of his second gift to her—a leather motorcycle jacket that fit perfectly. She loved it as much as Nick loved the Buck knife engraved with his initials. Christmas Eve had been special, but the plan for Kate and Leona to accompany Nick to Sam's house had fallen through. Leona had a bad cold and was still coughing. Kate had considered cancelling tonight's date, but her grandmother wouldn't hear of it. Instead Leona had invited Dody for a Paul Newman marathon, and they were downstairs now.

VICTORIA BYLIN

As Kate turned to check the back of the dress, she thought of last year's party at Roscoe's house. A year ago she didn't have a care in the world. Now, despite her new trust in God's providence, she worried about Leona's health, paying the bills, juggling the *Clarion*, and her final obligations to Sutton and Eve's Garden. The changes in her life were overwhelming. But Leona reminded her daily that God had created all creatures, great and small. If He could run the universe, He could handle Kate's worries. When Nick said the same thing, she believed him.

Shivering with anticipation, she touched up her lipstick, dropped the tube in her little purse, and then descended the stairs, where Nick was waiting at the bottom. His gaze traveled from her spiky heels to the shimmery dress, and finally to her face. A glint smoldered in his eyes, but the serious set of his mouth conveyed respect. A man like Nick could look without leering, a subtle difference that made her feel beautiful from the inside out.

When she reached the last step, he offered his hand. "You look amazing."

"So do you." His charcoal suit emphasized his broad shoulders and slim waist. With that "gotcha last" smile, he could have been on the cover of *GQ*.

As they turned to the living room, Leona hoisted herself to her feet. "Honey, you're beautiful."

When she teared up and couldn't speak, Dody indicated the coffee table. "Look what Nick brought us."

Kate saw three bouquets of roses—yellow, pink, and white.

Inclining his head, he murmured into her ear. "Pink for Dody, yellow for Leona . . . white for you."

Not red—the traditional color for romance. But white—the color of purity, the bridal rose. Blushing, she turned to him and smiled. "I've never received white roses before."

"Good," he replied. "There's a first time for everything."

When Dody approached with a white faux fur jacket, Nick took it and helped Kate put it on. They said their good-byes and drove away, trading glances but saying nothing, because just being together said everything. At the stop sign, Nick turned to her. "Have I told you how incredibly beautiful you are?"

Kate laughed, and they began chatting like the good friends they were. Happiness flowed from her heart like a babbling mountain stream, and she enjoyed every sight and smell, every sound, every word Nick said. She couldn't always sense God's presence, but Nick was a hundred-percent real to her. She wanted to tell him how she felt, but they were already on the long driveway that led to the Oak Glen Country Club. When they rounded the last curve, the headlights revealed the brown sedan that belonged to Ben Caldwell, a semi-hermit who opposed the condor recovery project as vocally as possible and at every opportunity.

Kate let out a groan. "Oh no. It's Ben."

His weekly letters to the editor were both a joke and a nuisance. Sometimes he ranted about the cost of the condor program, other times he used it as a springboard to predict environmental annihilation in a writing style that was wordy, pompous, and grammatically peculiar. He had very legitimate opinions, but he didn't know how to express them without rancor.

"Ben's just plain difficult," she said to Nick. "I hope he doesn't try to corner me about last week's letter."

"I won't let him." He squeezed her hand. "Everyone in Meadows has an opinion, but there's an unwritten rule for New Year's Eve, and that's no politics. If Ben needs a reminder, I'll give it to him."

At the clubhouse they were greeted by a valet. They left

their coats at the cloakroom, then walked together into the banquet hall of a club that offered golf, tennis, and equestrian trails traversing the San Andreas Fault. Silver and gold streamers, puffed-up stars, and Mylar balloons sparkled all over the room.

"Kate, darlin'!"

She turned and saw Larry Pfeiffer and his wife, a plump woman wearing what Kate knew was a mother-of-the-groom dress from her son's wedding a year ago. That was part of the fun of the Chamber dance—seeing people who normally lived in denim dressed up for a night on the town. As the four of them bantered, Geoff from the Acorn joined them. When he joked about Kate planting three hundred daffodil bulbs, she turned to Nick and smiled. "I had some help."

"Smart guy." Geoff clapped Nick on the arm. "Kate's a gem."

"I think so, too."

When his arm slipped around her waist, Kate leaned against him. Larry's wife smiled wistfully, then told her husband they should find a seat. "Let's leave the young people alone," she said with a wink.

As the Pfeiffers and Geoff wandered off, Nick steered Kate deeper into the party. "We'll avoid Ben as long as we can."

"Good."

"What would you like to drink?"

She was about to say ginger ale with a splash of grenadine when she spotted Marcus and a woman she recognized as a grad student working at the condor launch site. Kate waved, and the four of them met in the middle of the room.

Marcus shook Nick's hand, introduced Andrea, then focused on Kate. "I was hoping to see you tonight. There's news on Wistoyo."

"You found her?"

"Yes, a few days ago. She's sick."

"Oh no."

"Lead poisoning." Marcus's jaw visibly tightened. "We rushed her to the L.A. Zoo for treatment, but it's bad."

Kate hurt for the bird. "Do you think she'll make it?"

"Maybe." Marcus described finding Wistoyo collapsed by a dead steer the team had put out for food. "She let us put her in the cage without a fight. That's not a good sign."

"No," Andrea agreed. "The initial blood test showed levels close to fatal. We'll see how she responds to the treatment, then repeat it if necessary and maybe perform surgery."

"Why surgery?" Nick asked.

"To remove lead pellets from her stomach," Marcus answered. "At best, she's in for a long recovery."

When Marcus traded a somber look with Andrea, Kate slipped her hand into Nick's and held tight. Without human intervention, Wistoyo would die. The same could be said of the entire species. Just as Wistoyo had to trust the biologists without understanding the treatment, Kate needed to trust God the way a sick child trusted a parent to bring tissues and Tylenol. Such trust didn't come easily to her.

"Will you let us know how she does?" she said to Marcus.

"Definitely."

Nick motioned toward a table. "Join us."

The four of them walked to a round table near the back of the room, then Nick and Marcus left to get beverages. Kate and Andrea chatted about their dresses, shoes, and jobs the way Kate had chatted with Julie at last year's party. Feeling a bit nostalgic, she recalled everyone making crazy resolutions. She was about to tell the story to Andrea, when Ben Caldwell approached.

"Hello, Kate." Dressed in a corduroy sports coat and plaid shirt, he looked even more out of place than usual. His dark eyes glowered at her from below bushy eyebrows, daring her to ignore him.

"Hello, Ben," she replied with a chill in her voice.

He indicated one of the vacant chairs. "Is this seat taken?"

No way did Kate want to spend dinner listening to Ben pontificate about the cost of the condor program, especially with Marcus and Andrea ready to fight for their cause. She gave him a long look, then raised a brow to show she was on to his plan.

Apparently Andrea didn't know Ben, because she piped up with, "Sure, have a seat."

As he pulled out a chair, Nick arrived with her ginger ale and a small cavalry: Marcus, Chellie and her date, and Wayne and Becky from the market.

"It looks like the table's full," Kate said.

Nick set down her glass and rested his hand on the back of her chair. "Happy New Year," he said to Ben in a cool tone.

"Happy New Year," Ben replied. "I was just asking Kate if the seats were available, but I see they're taken."

"Yes."

Ben surveyed the group, honed in on Marcus, and focused back on Kate. "Looks like the condor program has the paper in its pocket. Maybe one of these days you'll report on how much money is wasted."

Nick intervened. "This isn't the time for politics."

"It's always time." The corner of Ben's mouth curled into a snarl. "Just once I'd like to see the other side printed in your paper. Do you know how much it costs to—"

Marcus put his hands on his hips. "You know what, Ben?"

"What?"

"Some of us believe in protecting the planet. The same things that kill condors hurt human beings. What do you have to say about DDT? I tell you—"

Nick interrupted. "We're going to put this on hold until later. I'll buy the beer, and you two can duke it out, but tonight we're here for a good time."

Ben smirked at him. "You're another bird lover."

"I'm a journalist." Nick lowered his chin and stared hard. "Now drop it. We're done here."

After a huff that hissed through his nose, Ben walked away. When he was out of earshot, Nick sat next to Kate. "That guy needs to learn some manners."

"Yes," she agreed. "But you were great."

"You think so?"

"Yes, very much."

"I couldn't let him ruin this evening. Not with you looking the way you do."

A half smile softened his chiseled features, a counter beat to the shameless intensity of his gaze. They were a breath apart, an inch from a stolen kiss when a waiter brought a tray of hors d'oeuvres. Kate put a few items on a plate and set it between herself and Nick.

"Want to share?"

From across the table, Marcus chuckled. "That's courtship behavior if I've ever seen it. Next thing you know, Nick'll be dancing like Elvis."

"No way," he said to the challenge.

"You don't dance?" Kate asked, a little disappointed.

"Slow dancing only," he said in a voice just for her. "I'll leave the flashy stuff to Elvis."

"That's fine by me. Men don't really like to dance, do they?"

"No," Marcus and Nick said in unison.

"But we like women." Marcus raised his glass in a toast. "Here's to courtship in all its confusing glory."

Everyone at the table clinked glasses and sipped, then Kate turned to Andrea. "Are Elvis and Moon Girl a couple yet?"

VICTORIA BYLIN

She nodded. "They've moved into the cave you saw. With a little luck, we'll have a hatchling in the spring."

The conversation settled into friendly banter and dinner was served. Kate enjoyed every minute and felt completely at home. When the band took the stage, Nick inclined his head to her ear. "Let's wait for a slow one. Just so you know, if Ben tries to cut in, I'm going to deck him."

"You wouldn't." She pulled back for a clearer view of his face and saw the forceful jut of his chin. "Or maybe you would."

"Just watch." A sparkle in his eyes indicated he was joking but only halfway. When he took her hand and caressed her knuckles, she basked in the glow of being cherished. At last the dance music shifted to something slow. Nick led her into the crowd and they swayed to the opening lyrics of "Can't Help Falling in Love," a classic by the real Elvis. With his neck bent and her face titled upward, they danced cheek to cheek until the band segued into a driving beat.

"Not my style," he said. "But if you want—"

"No."

"Let's get some air." He guided her to a wide arch leading to a glassed-in patio overlooking the golf course. It was too cold to go outside, but the moon and stars shone bright through the glass. Alone in the semidarkness, Nick drew her into his arms, moved to kiss her but stopped an inch from her lips. "We can wait until midnight—"

"No." Closing the distance, she pressed her lips to his. In that moment, all her feelings crystallized into a single unstoppable truth. She loved him. The words were exploding inside her, but she respected Nick's one-year vow. Smiling, because she was content to savor their old-fashioned courtship, she said the second best thing. "Do you know how wonderful you are?"

211

"I'm not wonderful, Kate." He stood straight, putting air between them. "I'm a hundred percent human. Without God—"

"I know," she said quickly.

"I mean it. I'm as flawed as any man. Don't put me on a pedestal."

Pedestals were for statues, not for men like Nick, who walked, talked, and breathed integrity. It was just like him to downplay his attributes. "I trust you, Nick. Completely. It's easy, because you always put others first."

"Not always."

"But you try."

He opened his mouth to protest again, but a drum roll distracted them both. The MC shouted to the crowd to get ready for midnight. Rather than go back to the ballroom, Kate and Nick gazed into each other's eyes.

"Are you ready, folks?" the MC shouted. The crowd roared, and he started to count. "Ten . . . Nine . . . Eight . . ."

Nick cupped her face in his hands.

"Seven . . . Six . . . Five . . ."

She lifted her chin, her eyes shining into his.

"Four . . . Three . . . Two . . ."

The drum roll pulsed through her body.

"One!"

At the stroke of midnight Nick brought his mouth down to hers in a soul-searing kiss. In the banquet room people cheered, balloons fell, and glitter cannons shot gold streamers into the air. The band broke into "Auld Lang Syne," and the crowd started to sing.

Nick whispered into her ear. "Happy New Year."

"Happy New Year," she repeated.

"They'll be doing a toast pretty soon. We should go back to the table." He hooked his arm around her waist and led the way to their seats. The champagne hadn't been served yet, so Kate excused herself for a trip to the ladies' room. She took care of business, applied fresh lipstick, then noticed her phone. She had three missed calls, one voice mail, and a text message. All three calls were from Leona's landline. With her heart in her throat, she opened the text message from Dody.

Call home 9-1-1.

19

shaking all over,

Kate tried to call Leona's landline. When the call failed to go through, she bolted for the lobby, found a quiet corner and tried again. The fourth ring blasted in her ear, then the answering machine picked up. A thousand horrible thoughts raced through her mind. She had to get home . . . had to get to Leona. While calling her voice mail, she hurried back to the dining room to find Nick.

He saw her approach and crossed the room to meet her. "What's wrong?"

"Dody texted me 9-1-1." Her voice quavered. "I'm checking voice mail, but it won't connect."

"Let's go."

Side by side they charged for the lobby. Nick cut through the line to retrieve their coats, then spoke to the parking valet, who ran for the truck. While they waited, Kate called Dody's cell phone. No answer. Shaking more than ever, she tapped out a text with typos saying they were headed home. Kate never sent garbled messages; she took time to fix her mistakes but not tonight.

The valet brought the truck and they sped toward Leona's house, some twenty minutes away. Kate called the house phone again, squeezed her eyes shut, and silently prayed. *Please God. Please God.*

Dody answered on the third ring. "Kate?"

"Yes. Yes. What happened?"

"Leona's conscious, but she had a fall. I called 9-1-1. The rescue squad is on the way."

Kate's throat constricted to a pinhole. "Did she have another stroke?"

"I don't know."

"Then what—"

"She was hurrying to the bathroom. She may have tripped. I don't know, and she can't tell me. I think she hit the side of the tub."

Kate thought of the rehab nurse instructing them to avoid trip hazards like throw rugs and cats. Because of that advice, they'd put indoor-outdoor carpet in Leona's bathroom. Kate had done everything possible to protect her grandmother, yet another random accident had smacked down someone she loved. Except now Kate had faith. She had to trust God knew best in spite of what seemed cruel and catastrophic.

With Nick focused on the road, she kept Dody on the phone and pressed for updates. Yes, Leona was alert. No, she couldn't speak into the phone. Yes, she was warm under a blanket. The signal was spotty in the canyon, and Dody's voice kept breaking up. Kate's only solid touch point was Nick in the driver's seat, strong and steady as the mountains passed by in a blur. With the phone against her ear, she laid her hand on his arm.

"I see lights," Dody said. "The paramedics are here."

"Go," Kate ordered. "We're just a few minutes away." She hung up and tossed the phone in the console.

Nick turned onto the road leading to Leona's house. A mile later they saw the amber lights of the rescue truck strobing through the trees. In Meadows, paramedics drove a truck equipped for rescue, not the transport of victims. To allow room for the coming ambulance, Nick parked across the street. Kate flung open the door and ran to the house, her high heels clumsy on the rough pavement. Nick caught up to her, gripped her elbow, and together they hurried into the living room where Staci, one of the paramedics, was on the radio.

Dody came out of the hallway and hugged Kate hard.

"How is she?" Kate asked

"Alert," Dody replied. "And in pain. Captain McAllister is with her."

Kate turned to Staci. "Can I see her?"

"In a few minutes. I just called for an ambulance. We don't think she needs air transport."

"That's good," Kate said, grasping at straws.

Nick put his arm around her waist, then focused on Staci. "Where are you taking her?"

"Valencia Community."

Captain McAllister called from the bathroom. "Staci, come here, please."

As Staci walked down the hall, Kate followed with Nick in her wake. They all stopped at the door, where Captain McAllister gave instructions in a low tone that Kate couldn't quite hear except for the word *arrhythmia*.

An irregular heartbeat.

Her breath caught in her throat, then burst out in ferocious gasps. If she didn't control herself, she'd hyperventilate. *Breathe! Breathe!* Nick wrapped her in his arms and held her tight, but nothing could stop the pounding in her chest. *Stay strong*, she told herself. *Go with the flow.* But the flow was a torrent threatening to drown her. *God, where are you?* She was sinking . . . sinking . . . until Nick grasped her elbow and she steadied.

Staci's voice echoed in the small room. "Base, this is Unit 34. We have a seventy-year-old woman with broken ribs, a possible shoulder fracture, atrial fibrillation, and a history of stroke. We're advising air transport. . . . Roger . . . We'll transport by ambulance to the fire station."

The fog of fear burned out of Kate's brain, not because she wasn't afraid—she was. But Leona needed her. She pulled out of Nick's arms with the intention of gathering Leona's medical info but froze when Staci's radio crackled. They all heard the dispatcher say the local ambulance was on another call.

"What's the ETA?" Staci asked.

"Ninety minutes."

Kate gasped.

"No way," Nick declared to Staci. "I don't care what your policy says. We'll use my truck."

"We've done it before," Mac called from inside the tiny room. "Get all the blankets you can."

Nick turned to Kate and gripped her arms, steadying her with a look. "I'm going to move the truck to the bottom of the stairs. You and Dody get all the blankets in the house. Stacy and Mac will do the rest."

While Kate and Dody hauled the bedding to the truck, Staci and Captain McAlister maneuvered Leona onto the stretcher and carried her outside. Relieved to see her grandmother at last, Kate ran to the gurney. "Nonnie!"

"Kay . . . Kay . . ."

She reached out to touch Leona's shoulder, but the paramedics were moving faster than she could. With calm precision, they collapsed the wheels of the gurney and slid Leona into the bed of the pickup truck, now filled with blankets. Mac made sure the stretcher wouldn't slide and stayed to ride in the back. While Nick said something to Staci, Kate hopped up next to Mac and tucked yet another blanket around Leona, who was strapped to the stretcher and perfectly still—too still. When her eyelids fluttered, Kate laid her palm on her grandmother's cold cheek. "Stay with me, Nonnie. I need you."

"Kay . . . Kay . . ." Tears flooded Leona's silvery eyes.

Kate refused to break down, but what she had to do next would torment her until they reached the helicopter, maybe forever if Leona died. "It's cold. I have to cover your face."

Leona shook her head no.

Captain McAllister intervened with a firm tone that Kate wished God would use to fix the whole messy world. "Leona," he said, in the way of a friend, "unless you want a frostbitten nose, I suggest you put up with the sheet over your face. You're going to be fine. The chopper's waiting, so let's roll."

When she nodded, Mac covered her face.

Nick draped a blanket over Kate's shoulders, then took the driver's seat. He inched over the bump between the driveway and the street, but Leona still cried out in pain. Kate clung to her grandmother's hand under the blankets, crooned to her, shivered, and battled tears of her own. Nick drove carefully, the way he drove the Harley when Kate had been afraid. She was afraid now, but she had Nick at her side . . . and God, though God seemed far away.

They reached the fire station in exactly twelve minutes. Nick parked as close to the waiting helicopter as he could and cut the engine. Staci had followed in the rescue truck. She and Mac unloaded Leona's stretcher and rolled it to the chopper. Kate ran after them but stopped when the wind from the rotor blades blew her back.

Nick grasped her arms from behind and kept her from falling. "They'll take good care of her."

"I can't bear to leave her!" There was a slim chance Kate

would be allowed to go in the helicopter, a brand-new model with room for four victims. Just last week, Nick had written a story about it and met the crew. She turned and clutched at his jacket. "I want to go with them. Will you ask?"

The noise stole his words from her ears, but he circled her waist with his arm and led her to the open door where they could see a male flight nurse securing the stretcher. Nick shouted up to him. "Do you have room for a passenger?"

The flight nurse yelled something to the pilot, who approached with his gaze on Kate first, then Nick. Recognition flashed in his eyes, and he nodded a friendly greeting.

"You're transporting Kate's grandmother," Nick shouted to him. "Can she ride along?"

The pilot shook his head. "Sorry. It's against policy."

"But you can make an exception." Nick held her even closer, fighting the cold and the wind along with the regulations. Kate knew about the exceptions. They were usually for a parent with a child, but tonight she saw no difference.

She squared her shoulders to prove to the pilot she could handle the flight. "Please. Leona's my own family."

The pilot sized her up, glanced back at Nick, and finally nodded. "Sure, why not?"

Relieved but still terrified, she gave Nick a ferocious hug. "Thank Mac and Staci for me—"

"I will."

"And hurry," she added.

"I'll be right behind you. I promise."

She slid from his arms, climbed into the chopper, and strapped herself into a padded seat. The flight nurse checked to be sure she was secure, gave a thumbs up to Nick, and closed the door. The engine whined and the blades beat the air faster, faster . . . until the helicopter lifted vertically off the ground. She imagined the snow angel flying alongside them, but the picture in her mind blew apart, and the angel disappeared. Suddenly the chopper angled downward, giving her a view of Nick holding up one arm in a kind of salute. God seemed to have forgotten her, but Nick was real and would never let her down.

He watched the helicopter fade into a circle of light, then a star, and finally to nothing but a memory. As much as he wanted to race the chopper to the hospital, Kate needed a change of clothes and her phone charger. His job tonight was to take care of her, though earlier he'd heard the hero worship in her voice and realized he had a serious problem. Kate had placed him on a pedestal, and he needed to correct that impression. But not tonight—not when she needed him so badly. He drove back to Leona's house, hauled the six blankets to the house, and dumped them on the living room floor.

Dody was in the kitchen, gulping a glass of orange juice. She looked past him to the empty doorway. "Where's Kate?"

"They let her fly with Leona. I'm going to get a few things and head to the hospital. How are you?"

"Shaky." She held out her hand to prove it. "Oh, Nick, it was terrible. I thought we'd lost her." Even with her dyed red hair, Dody looked every minute of her sixty-seven years. "It happened so fast. We were watching television, getting ready for the ball to drop in Times Square, when she headed for the bathroom. I was in here—" she indicated the kitchen. "Earlier we'd joked about toasting in the new year with Metamucil."

"That sounds like Leona."

Dody's weak smile caved into a grimace. "I heard a thump and went to check. She was in a heap on the floor, all twisted and pale. I thought—well, you know what I thought."

As anxious as Nick was to meet Kate, he couldn't leave Dody until she was more settled. "Why don't you rest while I get Kate's things?"

"I think I will."

"Can you think of anything Leona might need?"

"Her glasses. I'll get them." She took a step, swayed slightly, and gripped the counter. "I'm not as steady as I thought."

"I'll get the glasses. Where are they?"

"The bathroom."

He walked Dody to the couch and fetched Leona's glasses before bolting up the stairs to Kate's room, where a bedside lamp cast a golden glow. In a blink he took in the twin bed covered with an eyelet quilt, then a small desk littered with drawings of flowers and women of various ages—her work on the Eve's Garden account. Without the urgency, he would have enjoyed seeing this side of her. Instead, he snatched a gym bag out of the closet, stuffed it with clothes, and added the cell phone charger. On his way out he snagged her everyday purse off the knob. Whatever he missed, they could buy.

He trotted down the stairs to the living room. Dody was on the couch, her neck bent and her hands pressed to her cheeks. Either she was crying or about to faint. To avoid startling her, he slowed his pace as he approached. "How are you feeling?"

"A little better."

He set the gym bag on the floor, swallowed hard, and purged the impatience from his voice. "Do you want more juice?"

"Yes, please."

He fetched the juice and brought it to her. She sipped, then gave a painful shake of her head. "Getting old isn't for the faint of heart, I tell you."

"No."

"Go on to the hospital. I'll be fine. Just call as soon as you know something."

As much as he wanted to race out the door, he couldn't leave Dody to drive home alone when she was pale and shaking. She occasionally spent the night. Maybe this was one of those times. "Are you staying here?"

"No. I want my own bed."

"How about I drive you?" Never mind the ticking clock in his head. If Kate were here, she'd do the same thing.

Dody considered for a moment. "I'll drive myself, but would you mind following me? I'd feel a lot better."

"No problem."

She wobbled to her feet, carried the juice glass into the kitchen, rinsed it and put it in the dishwasher. Hoping to hurry her along, Nick fetched her coat and held it out, silently willing her to punch into the sleeves. Instead, she eased into the jacket, wiggled her shoulders to make it fit, then worked the zipper at an inchworm pace. By the time she put on her gloves and scarf, turned off the lights and locked the door, his jaw throbbed from gritting his teeth.

Finally they made it to her car. She'd just plopped on the driver's seat when she clapped a hand to her cheek. "Oh, I forgot something—"

"Stay here. I'll get it."

"Never mind. I was going to give you Leona's prescription bottles. Kate knows what they are."

Before Dody remembered something else, Nick closed her car door and climbed into his truck. Her house was only a couple miles away but in the opposite direction of the interstate. He followed her at what seemed like a crawl, walked her to her door, then shot out of Meadows.

He knew every inch of San Miguel Canyon and took it like a NASCAR pro. In places he crossed the double yellow line for a tighter turn, but only when he could see ahead and knew the maneuver was safe. A full hour had passed. Kate needed him, and he couldn't even call because he had her phone.

"Why?" he muttered to God. "Why let all this happen now? She's a brand-new Christian. Don't you know how fragile she is? She needs me."

A whisper of conscience told him to slow down. Ignoring it, he sped around a turn with squealing tires, saw the tail-lights of a slow-moving sedan, and braked to a crawl. The speedometer confirmed what his instincts told him. The sedan was rolling along at . . .

Twelve. Miles. An. Hour.

Fist clenched, he pounded the steering wheel. There was no way around the car until San Miguel Highway straightened through Decker Valley, five miles away. Nick did the math and groaned. Four miles meant a twenty-minute delay. Not only was he worried about Kate, he was worried that *she'd* be worried about him. He tried to pray, even for the driver of the sedan, but he could only mutter, *"Please-please-please"* while he fought four-letter words and pounded the steering wheel a second time.

Nineteen minutes later, he gunned the truck and passed the sedan. Free at last, he raced through Decker Valley, reached the interstate in record time, and merged across four lanes of light traffic. The speed limit was fifty-five, but everyone drove at least seventy. Nick hit the fast lane going seventy-five. With no one in front of him, he increased the speed to eighty, then eighty-five. On a downhill slope, the speedometer shot past ninety and topped a hundred.

Amber lights exploded in his rearview mirror. His foot flew off the accelerator but not before a siren wailed for him to pull over. He was busted—big time. And at this speed, he could be charged with reckless driving. At best he'd receive a ticket with a huge fine. At worst, the highway patrol officer would haul him off to jail and impound the truck. What a fool he'd been. What a complete, prideful, arrogant fool. Disgusted with himself, he coasted to the side of the road and pounded the steering wheel for the third and final time that night.

20

Kate swayed with the helicopter, fighting motion sickness as they zoomed through the starry night. In the distance she glimpsed the interstate slicing through the mountains. Nick would be on the highway soon, a comforting thought, but nothing could erase the fear beating in her brain as she stared at her grandmother's pale face, slack-jawed after a shot of pain medication. The flight nurse said Leona was stable, but how could anyone be stable in this crazy world? Kate silently begged God to help her grandmother, but praying seemed useless. Where was He when Leona fell? If He didn't help her then, why would He help her now?

God seemed a million miles away, but Kate recalled every detail of Nick guiding her through this awful night. With a little luck, he'd arrive at the hospital shortly after the helicopter. In the rush, she'd left her purse and phone in his truck. Until he found her, she'd be as isolated as a shooting star.

Swallowing hard, she stifled every emotion coursing through her veins. A meltdown wouldn't help anyone, least of all herself. She'd have to deal with a runny nose and a lack of tissue. The triviality of the worry calmed her. She was a competent adult, not a confused seven-year-old. She could handle whatever lay ahead, especially with Nick at her side to lend a hand.

After fifteen long minutes, the mountains gave way to a pool of city lights. The helicopter slowed again, hovered, then landed on the hospital roof. Unsteady and a little queasy, she stayed in her seat while the professionals took care of Leona. After the medical team rushed her away, a security officer helped Kate out of the chopper. She caught up to Leona, and a trauma elevator took them all to the ER, where Leona was whisked to a treatment room.

A nurse quizzed Kate about the fall and took a medical history, then a doctor arrived and performed an examination. Leona could move her fingers and toes, knew the president, was oriented to space and time, but her speech was slurred and difficult to understand. The physician ordered X rays and a CT scan. An admissions clerk took insurance information, and then an orderly wheeled Leona down the hall for tests.

More than an hour passed before a nurse directed Kate to the waiting room. "We'll call you when we have the test results."

Kate pushed through the double doors that led to a lounge crowded with people and green vinyl chairs. She had left word with the admitting clerk that Nick was family and could see Leona, but he must not have received the message. By now, he had to be worried. Nervous, she scanned the crowded room but didn't see him. Maybe he was in the men's room, or getting coffee from a vending machine. She could use a cup herself.

The adrenaline rush that started with Dody's text message was long gone, and in its place was a bone-deep exhaustion caused by more than just tonight's events. Kate was no stranger to death, loss, and the aching loneliness of being abandoned—albeit unwillingly.

Eager to find Nick and beginning to worry, she circled the entire lounge. The helicopter had left Meadows two hours ago. Even if he went back to Leona's house or stopped for gas, he should have been here by now. Something had happened. Maybe a flat tire—the roads in Meadows were littered with sharp rocks. Or maybe the truck battery died. Things like that happened on cold nights.

When he didn't come out of the men's room after five minutes, Kate went to the window facing the parking lot. An orange-and-white ambulance swept into an arrival bay. Shuddering, she thought of other ambulances, other accidents, including the one that had killed her father and the one that almost killed her. What if Nick had misjudged the hanging hairpin and gone over the side? He could be hurt and bleeding, even dead, and no one would know. On New Year's Eve drunk drivers were everywhere, including the interstate, where eighteen-wheelers rolled downhill like charging elephants.

"Stop it," she ordered herself.

Without her purse, she didn't have her cell phone or even a credit card for a pay phone. Did people still make collect calls? Could she reach an operator if she didn't have change? Kate didn't know but decided to try. Turning from the window, she spotted the security officer who had escorted her from the chopper and asked if there was a pay phone she could use for a collect call. He sympathized and gave her some change, then pointed to an alcove filled with half empty vending machines. She found the phone in the corner, punched in Nick's number, and waited. There was no answer, only the inadequate comfort of his recorded voice telling her to leave a message.

"Hey, it's me." Her voice cracked, but she steadied it. "Where are you? Leona's getting X rays. I'm in the waiting room. Find me, okay?"

She hung up clumsily and the handset clattered against the wooden shelf. She considered calling Dody collect, but she didn't know her number by heart. Behind her a child shrieked that he wanted candy. The mom told him no, and he dissolved into an exhausted, uncontrollable tantrum.

Kate fled the alcove with her ears ringing. Her feet hurt and so did her throat. She wanted her purse, her phone, a change of clothes; but most of all, she wanted Nick to stride through the door and hold her and tell her everything would be all right. What could possibly be keeping him? She grabbed at possible explanations, but each one was more frightening than the last.

Awash in fresh trembling, she returned to the waiting room and hunted for an empty chair. She spotted one but veered away from it when a man ogled her legs. People of all sorts came and went. Some were bleeding and close to panic. Others were calm in a stone-like way. All around her people were afraid and suffering, talking on phones and holding one another. Everyone had someone to be with except her. Something horrible had happened to Nick. She was sure of it. "Please, God," she whispered. "I need him."

"Kate Darby?"

The female voice came from the entrance to the treatment area. Kate shot to her feet and hurried back through the double doors, where a woman in scrubs led her to an office with a computer monitor.

"Dr. Cole will be here in a minute," the nurse said.

The single minute stretched into twenty. By the time Dr. Cole arrived, Kate had planned two funerals.

"Miss Darby?" he clarified.

"Yes."

"I have your grandmother's CT scan and X rays." He pulled out a chair and sat. "The CT scan was negative. There's no new damage to her brain, though we can't rule out a TIA. I assume you know what that is?"

"A ministroke."

"Yes." Pausing, he pushed his glasses higher on his nose. "That's the good news. The bad news is that she has a broken shoulder and four cracked ribs. I've referred her to ortho for a consult."

Kate willed herself to sit straighter in the chair. "Will she need surgery?"

"That's a question for her orthopedist." Dr. Cole scrawled something on a slip of paper and handed it to her. "His name is Dr. Arbell."

Without her purse, Kate had no place to put the paper. And without her phone, Dr. Arbell had no way to reach her. And without Nick, she had to—do what? Sleep in the ER? Call the highway patrol and ask if there had been an accident? Without Leona and Nick, she had no one. That wasn't so bad—she was used to being by herself. What hurt so much now wasn't being alone—it was expecting Nick to walk through the door and ending up frightened, phoneless, and stuck without resources. She was a helpless child again. Something she tried very hard never to be.

Dr. Cole broke into her thoughts. "We're also concerned about the cracked ribs. Patients tend to take shallow breaths to avoid the pain, which can lead to pneumonia. Mrs. Darby came in with some bronchitis, so we're doubly concerned. Considering everything, we've admitted her to the ICU. You can expect a few days here in the hospital, then a stint in rehab."

She should have been prepared—would have been prepared if she hadn't been so worried about Nick. But the news hit like a hammer blow. Not only was Leona suffering, but Kate now had another ball to keep in the air along with the ones she was already juggling. Having Leona in a rehab facility would require hours and hours of her time. The closest facility to Meadows was fifty miles away. Every visit to Leona meant two hours in the car, two hours away from the *Clarion* and the Eve's Garden proposal. Of course Nick would help—*Dear Lord, Where is he?*

Dr. Cole closed the file. "Your grandmother's in good hands. Why don't you get some sleep and come back in the morning?"

But she had nowhere to go. No phone. No money. No credit card for the hotel across the street. Her anxiety hit like a rock on a windshield. With each jolt of bad news, the spidery cracks spread in out-of-control ways, growing longer and thicker until she couldn't see past the disaster. Fighting panic, she thanked Dr. Cole in a tight voice and fled the office. With her hands buried in her coat pockets, she walked back down the corridor. Pausing at the door to the waiting room, she inhaled deeply to steady herself, threw back her shoulders, then pushed through the heavy doors to the waiting area. The crowd had thinned, but she didn't see Nick anywhere. Her hope turned to dust, drying her throat and leaving her dizzy and sick.

"Kate!" *His voice.* He'd found her.

Whirling to her left, she ran to meet him in the middle of the room. With his tie loosened and the suit coat open and crooked, he pulled her into his arms and squeezed so hard she could have lifted her feet off the floor and not fallen. They stood that way for a long time—breathing in unison, drawing strength from each other, feeling safe again. The cracks in her heart didn't disappear, but they stopped spreading. Questions and problems would come later, but for now, Kate and the people she loved were safe.

21

nick had never seen

a more haunting sight than Kate coming through the doors
to the ER. She was beautiful to him, always. But the tautness
of her face revealed a side of her he rarely saw—the terrified
child, the woman caught in the BMW. That day he had saved
her life; tonight he had failed her. By the grace of God and a
veteran CHP officer, he was here now and not in jail. Later
he'd tell her the entire embarrassing story, but not yet. His
foolishness shamed him, but mostly he needed to hold her
a little longer, a little tighter, steadying them both against
what lay ahead.

When her arms finally loosened, he asked the question that
had rattled in his mind all the way to the hospital. "Leona—
how is she?"

"She's going to be all right."

Kate relayed Dr. Cole's assessment of the CT scan and X
rays, including the plan for shoulder surgery and the likelihood Leona would spend a few weeks in rehab. The coming
days promised to be demanding, and Nick silently vowed to

do a better job of being the man Kate needed. He also wanted to see Leona for himself. "Can we visit?"

"Not now. She's resting in the ICU." Worry dimmed her eyes. "Dr. Cole told me to get some sleep and come back in the morning."

"That's a good plan." With his arm around her waist, Nick led her to the exit. "I was here about ten minutes before you came out, so I called Sam. He and Gayle are expecting us."

"It's three a.m." She shuddered a little bit. "Are you sure it's all right?"

"Positive."

She stopped a few feet shy of the door and looked back at the entrance to the treatment area. "What if something happens and I have to come back? There's a hotel across the street. Maybe I should stay there."

Nick didn't like the idea at all. He'd passed the hotel earlier and noticed torn drapes and people drinking in the parking lot. "Sam and Gayle live just a few miles away. If the hospital calls, we'll come back."

When she didn't move, he was tempted to scoop her into his arms and carry her to the truck. Instead, he cupped her waist and turned her toward him, locking eyes to make sure she knew he meant business. "Leona's in good hands. Right now, I'm worried about you. Let's go to Sam's. You can change clothes, take a nap, and eat something."

She graced him with a fragile smile. "Thank you, Nick."

"For what?"

"Taking care of me."

He intended to help her even more, starting with getting her away from the crowd in the waiting room. All around them people were fidgeting and looking at their watches and phones. The anxiety was contagious, and Kate showed all the signs of the same affliction—pale skin, dull eyes, cold fingers that trembled against his palms. With his arm tight around her waist, he guided her out to the parking lot. Yet another siren blared in the distance, and Kate shivered against him. "What a horrible night. I don't know which was worse—the helicopter ride, waiting for the test results, or worrying about you."

He pulled her close to fight back the chill and her fear, maybe his guilt. "I should have been here two hours ago."

"So what happened?"

"A little bit of everything." In painful detail, he described Dody sipping orange juice, how he'd filled the gym bag with clothes, then followed Dody to her house. When he told her about the slowpoke sedan, she groaned. "Even I don't drive twelve miles an hour."

No, but she didn't do a hundred either. His truck was in sight when he told her about the decision to make up for lost time. "Not smart. I got a speeding ticket."

"Oh no."

"It took awhile to sort out."

Oh, man, had it ever. He'd pulled over and instantly admitted guilt, but the CHP officer still ordered him out of the truck. First came the quiz—where had he been? Where was he going? Had he been drinking or doing illegal drugs? There was no evidence of substance abuse, except for the stupidity of going over a hundred miles an hour, but the officer still performed a lengthy field sobriety test. The entire time Nick had begged God for mercy.

In the end, the patrolman wrote the ticket and let him go with a stern lecture. It was a glorious moment until his phone rang five miles down the road and he knew it was Kate. His hands-free device wasn't set up, so he'd let the call go to voice mail, knowing full well she was sick with worry.

He was furious with himself for being so careless—and

embarrassed, too. He was about to open the truck door when she put her hand over his and faced him. "I feel terrible."

"Why?"

"You were rushing to get to me. How bad is the ticket?"

"Not too bad." He'd share the ugly details later. Tonight was upsetting enough for both of them.

"Oh, good." She let out a breath. "I was worried it would affect your insurance. How fast were you going?"

"It's not important. I'm here now, and that's what counts."

He pulled on the door, but she didn't move. "I want to know how fast."

"Kate—"

"Why won't you tell me?"

Suddenly she looked like Mrs. Garth, the ninth-grade social studies teacher who had sent him to detention for making smart remarks. "I was speeding," he said again. "I got a ticket and I'm sorry. End of story."

He did *not* want another lecture. The CHP officer had done a fine job of describing high-speed wrecks and dead bodies. By the time he finished, Nick had been ready to crawl under the truck.

He opened the door an inch, but Kate refused to move. "You were two hours late. How long does it take to write a speeding ticket?"

"Too long."

"Nick—"

"This isn't the time. I'm tired and so are you."

"But I want to know."

What gave her the right to hassle him? They were dating, not married. Scowling, he matched her haughty gaze with a strong one of his own. After four long seconds, she heaved a sigh. "Oh, all right." Ignoring the hand he offered to help her up, she climbed awkwardly onto the seat.

Nick shut the door forcefully but shy of a slam, then he climbed in on the driver's side. He'd left the traffic citation folded in the console, and now he saw Kate holding it up to the light and reading. He had a good mind to give her a lecture of his own—one about respecting a person's privacy. When she spotted the rate of speed, her jaw dropped and she gasped. Their gazes locked in a test of sorts—her misplaced trust versus his pride. "Well, now you know," he drawled. "I got busted big-time."

"This says you were going *a hundred and four* miles an hour!"

"It was stupid, I know."

"It's more than stupid!"

"Kate—"

"This isn't just a speeding ticket. It's for reckless driving."

"I know what it says." He was guilty and the ticket proved it, exacting the penance of a high fine, traffic court, and higher insurance rates, maybe a return to Bozo Insurance for Idiots, Teenagers, and High-Risk Drivers. Nick didn't need Kate to eviscerate him. He'd done it to himself already, and it was time to move on.

With her shoulders high and stiff, she jammed the ticket back in the console. "I can't believe it. You could have been killed, or you could have killed someone else."

"I made a mistake," he snapped back.

"But *a hundred and four* miles an hour! Not only is that crazy, it's irresponsible."

"Like I said," he ground out. "It was a mistake. Considering the circumstances, it wasn't as terrible as you think."

"Oh yes, it was!"

His jaw tightened until his teeth ached. He had tried to be her knight in shining armor, and she was treating him like a juvenile delinquent. "I'm a good driver, and you know it.

Besides, I wasn't going a hundred the whole time. It happened going downhill, and there wasn't a car in sight."

"Except the CHP officer who caught you!" She huffed at him. "And just for the record, going downhill is no excuse."

"Of course not," he lashed back. "I was driving way too fast, and do you know why? Because of *you* . . . because you were alone in an emergency room on New Year's Eve, wearing a dress that drove me *crazy* all night and shoes that should be illegal. Leona could have died, and you would have been alone in a room full of lowlifes. Of course I was speeding. I couldn't stand the thought of you being vulnerable like that!"

She gave him the Mrs. Garth look again, but her lips were trembling. "I appreciate it, Nick. I really do. But *you could have gotten yourself killed*."

"Well, I didn't."

"Everyone I care about dies," she burst out. "They crash cars and have strokes and—and they don't come home. I can't stand it." She pressed her hands to her mouth to hold back a sob, maybe a cry for help or a burst of anger.

He didn't know what she was feeling, but the tears in her eyes belied the strain of the night, maybe the strain of her whole life. No matter how fast she blinked, how tightly she pressed her hand to her mouth, she couldn't stop the terrible shaking of her shoulders. He couldn't stand to see her this way. All night she had held in her emotions and so had he, even at the dance when he'd restrained himself during their kisses, resisting the urge to move faster than was wise. As for Kate, she'd been on the ragged edge since Dody's first call.

The anger drained out of him, and compassion flooded his veins in its place. This quarrel wasn't about the ticket or speeding; it was about Kate learning to trust. She was a new Christian wrestling with faith and fear, and tonight Nick had contributed to her fear by face planting off the pedestal where she had placed him.

Inhaling slowly, he mellowed his voice. "I really am sorry. I let you down and I know it."

Stiff-lipped, she nodded but didn't speak. He wondered if she had accepted his apology or even heard it. He moved to rub her shoulder, but she slid out of reach, furiously shaking her head. He touched her anyway, massaging her tense muscles. "You've had a rough night, but it's going to be all right."

She jerked away. "Don't say things like that."

"Like what?"

"That everything will be all right. You don't know that." She was wedged against the door, trapped like an animal in a cage. "Leona could have died tonight. And you . . . you could have been killed." Her voice was a whisper now, deadly calm and determined. "I grew up without a father. My mom died when I was in college. I'm used to being alone. I can handle it. What I can't handle"—a single tear spilled down her cheek—"what I can't handle is being disappointed and left. It's just too familiar."

Everything she said was true, and there was nothing he could do about any of it. Hurting, he spoke for them both. "Sometimes life really stinks."

Nodding slowly, she gave him the saddest look he'd ever seen on her face. "I want my things."

"Your clothes?"

"Yes."

"But why?"

"I'm going to a hotel."

Nick gaped at her. "Kate, that's ridiculous."

Silent and stoic, she collected her phone and purse, climbed out, and walked to his side of the truck where he'd stashed the gym bag behind the seat. No way would he let Kate go alone to a ratty motel, but how could he stop her? She was, after all, an adult . . . and a child of God.

A child God loved.

A child He wouldn't abandon.

As abhorrent as Nick found the thought of Kate being alone, he had to leave her in God's hands, which meant respecting her wishes—but not without a fight. He got out of the truck and squared off with her. "That hotel really is a dive."

"It's fine."

"It's not. At least let me drive you someplace decent. This one's filled with drunken college kids. You won't get any rest, and frankly I'm not sure it's safe."

When her eyes flared, he knew the safety issue had grabbed her attention. But she shook her head. "I have to be close to the hospital. That's all I care about."

"Kate—"

She raised her chin. "I want my things."

No way could he let her go. But he had no choice. "Are you sure about this?"

"Yes."

"It's late. It's dark."

"I'll be fine. The hotel's just across the street, and it's well lit."

"Then I'll walk with you."

She opened her mouth to argue, then scowled and sealed her lips. The instant he pushed the seat lever, she snatched the gym bag and hobbled away on her high heels, waiflike with the heavy bag dragging on her arm.

He caught up to her in three strides, gripped the bag, and tugged to take it from her. "Let me—"

"No, I've got it."

"But it's heavy." When he pulled a little harder, she jerked it out of his grasp. The bag flew sideways and Kate lost her hold on it. Off balance, she tumbled into his arms. Her shoulders heaved once, twice; a squeak escaped from her throat, then a groan. When she flattened her hands against his chest, he expected to be pushed away. Instead she knotted her fingers in his shirt and buried her face in the crook of his neck.

"I c-c-can't take it!" she whimpered. "I just *can't!*"

He absorbed the shaking of her body, holding her tight as he stroked her back. "It's all too much, isn't it?"

"Y-y-yes . . ." She cried for a long time, clutching his lapels and dampening his shirt with her tears. Finally she wiped her mascara-smudged eyes with her wrist. "My life is falling apart, and I can't let that happen. I need a plan. Somehow I have to run the *Clarion*, finish at Sutton, and take care of Leona. I don't see how I can do it all." She swallowed hard then raised her face to his. "I really do need some time to think. Any hotel is fine. I'll rent a car."

He hated the idea. *Hated it.* "Are you sure?"

"I need to be alone. It's just how I am."

Independent.

Considerate.

Responsible.

Nick loved those things about her, but he knew that human strengths often signaled spiritual weaknesses. Independence could turn into lonely isolation. Consideration in the extreme became codependence. Being responsible was perhaps Kate's most frightening trait, because she carried the entire world on her narrow shoulders. Not only did she need God more than she needed Nick, she needed to trust God more than she trusted herself. Once again she was back in San Miguel Canyon, caught on a cliff with someone telling her to let go and trust him. Only this time it wasn't Nick. It was God.

"All right," he said. "If that's what you really want."

"It is. But you're right about the hotel across the street. Would you take me somewhere else?"

"Sure." He considered renting a room in the same place, but he didn't want to crowd her, especially when she needed the kind of security no human being could provide. He trailed a knuckle along her cheek, following the path of dried tears with a touch when he wanted to kiss them away. *Change your mind,* he pleaded silently. *Come with me. We'll face this mess together.*

Kate stared bleakly into his eyes, then laid her palm on his chest but said nothing.

Giving up, he wrapped his arm around her waist and walked her to the passenger side. Before she climbed in, she faced him with the steel spine of the old Kate, the one who wore a business suit like armor and ran the show. "You're a good man, Nick. If you could, you'd make everything right for me. I know that. But you can't. As much as you want to, you're—"

"Human," he finished for her.

She gave him another sad look. "Tonight reminded me of something I learned a long time ago. I can't depend on anyone but myself." In a voice he barely heard, she whispered, "Not you . . . maybe not even God."

He would have given anything to save Kate the pain of what she had just confessed. But he didn't have that ability. She had to come to know God's ways for herself, and she had to fight alone. All Nick could do was pray for her and stick to the speed limit as best as he could.

Leona woke up in a hard bed with her mind swaddled in fog. The misty cloud numbed her from the inside out until she opened her eyes and saw the curtain hanging from a metal track on the ceiling. The low hum of conversation filled her ears, and phones rang in the same muted tone of the phone system in the Clarion office. Confused, she blinked her way into consciousness, saw a cluster of monitors next to the bed, and realized she was in an ICU.

Oh, Lord. No . . . not again. Not another stroke.

Frantic, she recited her Medicare number. She still knew it by heart. She also knew her full name and address, her birthday, and the president of the United States. Her toes wiggled on command, and her hands clenched willingly into fists. With her tongue thick in her mouth, she tried to speak. "Help me . . . Oh, Lord. Pleash . . ."

Only a mild slur.

Still confused, she tried to pull herself up on the bed. When pain stabbed through her chest, memories of the previous night crashed down on her. Hurrying to the bathroom, falling against the side of the tub. Grimacing, she thought of the game she had played with her brother about choosing between afflictions. *Would you rather be deaf or blind?* Leona mentally added another choice. Would you rather have a stroke or broken bones? In spite of the pain, she gratefully chose the broken bones. In time, she would heal. But oh, the hassle! She hated hospitals, and she hated what her recovery would require of Kate, who barely had time to breathe.

Oh, Lord, why now?

Kate's faith was tender and new, a blossom growing on the tip of a branch. The smallest pinch could rip it from the source of life and kill it. If her faith died, she'd become hard and bitter the way Leona had when she lost her son. In the wretched days after Peter's passing, she had turned her back on a God she deemed cruel. That spiritual darkness had held her captive until yet another encounter with a condor, this time a female bird named Aqiwo.

Somehow Leona had to finish the journal for Kate. In spite of a broken shoulder and broken ribs, as soon as she could, she'd write about that long-ago day. But not tonight. Broken and battered, all she could do was pray for Kate and the trials that lay ahead.

22

In the days after leona's fall,
Kate settled into the motel where Nick had taken her that first
night. She spent most of her time at Leona's bedside, first at
the hospital and now at Casa Rosa, a nursing facility that left
a lot to be desired. She spoke with Nick on the phone every
night, or he drove down for dinner when he could get away
from the Clarion. Neither of them mentioned her meltdown,
which was fine with Kate. She didn't know what she thought
about God or faith right now.

To add to her worries, the Eve's Garden proposal was
a shambles. Julie was on medical leave with severe morning sickness, and Brad's idea of brainstorming was quoting
marketing stats. Roscoe reminded her almost daily that she
had a carved-in-stone February fourteenth deadline. That's
why she had set her phone alarm for 4:30 a.m., and why it
was screeching in her ears now. Groggy, she staggered out of
bed, popped open a diet cola for the caffeine, and stacked
the pillows against the headboard. With the computer on her
lap, she sipped the soda while the file loaded.

Without warning, the bed lurched. Earthquakes struck

California all the time. Most were small and lasted a few seconds; others lasted for minutes and destroyed skyscrapers and collapsed dams. The shaking didn't stop. It intensified to a roar, rattling windows and causing the walls to groan and sway. Forgetting the laptop, she bolted for a doorframe, the strongest part of a structure, and hung on with both hands. When the floor bucked, she slid to her bottom and protected her head with her arms.

"No!" she cried. "Please God, no!"

As suddenly as it started, the earthquake stopped. With her breath rasping, she listened to a chorus of car alarms; otherwise the morning was still again. The quake had been mild to moderate in Valencia, but the epicenter could have been anywhere—right here or in downtown Los Angeles, or most frightening of all, on the San Andreas Fault near Meadows. With her heart wedged in her throat, she turned on the television with one hand and lifted her phone to call Nick with the other.

He answered in a sleepy drawl, clearly unaffected by an earthquake. "Kate?"

"Yes." She felt silly for waking him. "You must not have felt it."

"Felt what?"

"An earthquake—"

"How bad?" He was alert now.

"Moderate here, but I just turned on the news." Los Angeles could be in ruins for all she knew. "I'm glad you're okay."

"I'm fine. No shaking here at all." There was a pause where she imagined him sitting up on the side of the bed and running his hand through his hair.

"Are you all right?" he asked.

"I'm—" she gave a nervous laugh. "I was about to say I'm a little shaken up."

"I bet. You must be quaking in your boots."

Kate groaned at the pun, but inside she smiled. "That was awful."

"Yeah."

She held his humor close to her heart, but she stopped herself from wanting to be safe in his arms. Nothing in her life was the same since Leona's fall, including her relationship with Nick. She didn't hold the speeding ticket against him. He was the same good man she loved. But she no longer understood his trust in God. If she didn't share Nick's faith, how could they be a couple? A picture formed in her mind of a Clydesdale yoked with a Shetland pony. Kate didn't want to be the pony.

Outside the last car alarm stopped, but her nerves were still wire-tight. Nick's steady voice soothed her even over the phone. "Any news yet on TV?"

She read the crawl on the screen. "Cal Tech says it was a 4.1, centered north of—oh my goodness. It was centered here."

"No wonder you felt it. You're at the epicenter."

"In more ways than one." Just like an earthquake generated aftershocks for weeks, even months, the repercussions of Leona's fall rattled daily through Kate's life, and there was no end in sight. When Leona came home, she'd need constant help. Dody was spending February in Texas with her son, which meant Kate had to hire a caregiver. The cracks in her life just kept spreading. "I hate earthquakes," she complained to Nick.

"Me, too. I'm glad you're all right."

"I am, but it never stops."

"What doesn't?"

"Life." She stared at the TV, where a camera showed a broken window at a convenience store. "A week ago I had everything under control. I could handle Sutton and the *Clarion*, but now Leona needs me, too. You're working sixteen-hour days—"

"We'll make it," he assured her. "I know it's trite, but God doesn't close a door without opening a window."

Kate answered with a skeptical hum. "Frankly, I feel like God slammed the door, nailed it shut, and boarded up the window." *And* He had turned her into a pony. "It's too much for both of us. What about *California Dreaming*? I know you were doing an article about some place in Mammoth."

"I cancelled. It's not a problem."

"It is to me." She hated the thought of Nick making sacrifices for her. Until she sorted her feelings, it seemed wrong to accept his help. "We need to hire someone fast. I'm so sorry for this—"

"Don't be." His voice took on an edge. "I'm glad to help. You know that."

"Yes, but—"

"No buts, Kate. We're in this together. And besides, there's good news on the Help Wanted front. Do you know Heather Martin?"

"A little." Kate had met her a couple of years ago. "She worked at the Clarion before going off to college."

"She's a grad student now, and she needs an internship. I hope you don't mind. I hired her on the spot."

"That's perfect."

"I thought so, too."

Relief spun through her but only for an instant. Leaning on Nick was easy . . . too easy, she reminded herself. She couldn't use him as a crutch. "I'll do as much as I can, but Roscoe's pressuring me. Leona needs me, too."

"She's the priority. How's her shoulder?"

"Good."

"And her ribs?"

246

"Not so good. She's supposed to do breathing exercises, but she hates them. The ribs hurt and so does her shoulder. She seems so old."

"Ah, Kate—"

"It's really hard. I can't bear to leave her, but the rest of my life is falling apart." *Including us.* She bit her lip hard enough to hurt, because she was afraid she'd blurt more to Nick than she wanted to admit. She missed him terribly, but she was terrified of leaning on him and being let down.

Ordering herself to stay strong, she inhaled a ragged breath. If she loosened her hold on her problems even a little bit, an aftershock would hit and the cracks in her life would spread even more. The Eve's Garden proposal would fail, Leona would die of pneumonia, and the *Clarion* would fold. Maybe not the *Clarion*, but only because of Nick. Except he'd fall in love with the college intern, marry her, and Kate would never see him again. Melodramatic or not, that's how she felt.

"You need a break," he said in that forceful way she loved. "Can you come home tonight?"

"Maybe."

"Do it. We'll have dinner together. My place. I'll cook you a steak."

After six days of hospital food and energy bars, she could practically taste the meat. If she relaxed with Nick and talked to him, maybe she could find her spiritual feet. She blinked and imagined being in his arms. "Dinner would be nice."

"Good." His smile echoed in his voice. "Hang in there, Kate. The problems won't last forever."

They said good-bye, and she went to take a shower. Fortified by Nick's words and a cup of strong coffee, she went to see how Leona had weathered the quake at Casa Rosa, which meant *Rose House* in Spanish. The garden might have lived up to the name in June, but now only thorns and withered leaves adorned the dry stems. The odors inside the building were even less rose-like. Disinfectant burned her nostrils, and a janitor passed her with a full garbage bin.

Ignoring the smells, she pasted on a smile and turned down the corridor leading to Leona's room. The aroma of bacon wafted from a food cart. Good, Kate thought. She was in time to help her grandmother eat breakfast.

"Help me. Somebody help me. They're trying to kill me!"

The shriek blasted out of Leona's open door. Yesterday the second bed had been vacant, but Leona seemed to have acquired a roommate. How long had the woman been yelling like that? And why had the staff put a dementia patient in the medical ward? Bristling, Kate picked up her pace, passing doors closed by other patients to block out the pitiful shouting.

"Help me. Somebody help me. They're trying to kill me!"

Kate ached for this suffering woman, but anxiety for Leona trumped every other concern. Rounding the corner into the room, she saw a curtain pulled around the first bed, passed by it and went straight to her grandmother.

"Kate! Oh, honey—" Leona reached out with her good arm, winced with pain, then moaned. "I can't stand another minute."

"How long has she been like this?"

"Since midnight." Leona's eyelids drooped with exhaustion, then flared wide when yet another shriek filled the room.

"Help me. Somebody help me. They're trying to kill me!"

Kate's heart broke for the poor woman, but she was seething inside. Had Leona listened to those desperate cries all night? Kate had been here a minute and was shaken to the core. "Maybe I can get her to stop."

"I doubt it."

But she had to try—both for Leona and her own conscience. She stepped around the curtain and saw a gaunt woman in a bed raised to an uncomfortably high position, her eyes vacant and searching. She raised her arms to show restraints made of soft white cotton. "Help me! Somebody help me. They're trying to kill me!"

Kate gentled her voice. "I'll call the nurse for you."

"No! She's evil." The woman pulled helplessly at the restraints. "Help me. Somebody help me!"

Kate would never understand this kind of suffering. *Why, God? Why allow this?* Incensed, she returned to Leona's bedside. "I'm sorry for her. I really am. But this is *not* acceptable. They have to move one of you to another room."

"I already asked."

Kate's brows snapped together. "They wouldn't do it?"

"The hospital's full, including the dementia unit. I thought—oh no." Leona's face knotted, then her chest heaved with a long, wet cough. Pain clawed lines into her tired face, and she moaned between hacks. When the coughing finally eased, she fell exhausted against the pillows.

Kate handed her a tissue from a nearly empty box. Leona used it and tried to drop it in the trash, but the tissue landed on the floor in a mountain of other tissues. Kate whipped her gaze back to Leona's face, studying her for signs of fever and pneumonia. Her eyes were glassy, but she'd been crying. Unsure, Kate laid her palm on her grandmother's forehead, felt cool skin but she still fretted.

Leona needed rest in order to recover. If she couldn't rest, she wouldn't heal. And if she didn't heal, she couldn't go home. And if she couldn't go home—*Stop it!* Kate bit hard on her lip to stop her runaway thoughts, but nothing could quell the anger.

She laid her hand on Leona's good arm. "I'm going to

speak to the director right now. If they can't move you to another room, we'll find another hospital."

"Oh, honey—"

She stopped Leona's protest with a kiss on the cheek and left. With her temper barely in check, she strode to the business office, where a receptionist buzzed the medical director, who greeted Kate with the plastic smile of someone well trained in the fine art of handling disgruntled people.

Twenty minutes later, Kate walked out of the director's office with a head full of steam and her phone in hand. The director had politely explained that accommodations would be made when possible, but that Leona was in a double room and difficult roommates had to be tolerated.

"Over my dead body," Kate muttered as she dropped down on a couch in the lobby.

With her fingers flying on her phone, she googled "skilled nursing facilities" until she landed on a website that stole her breath. Golden West Retirement was located a mile from her condo in West L.A., and it looked more like a Spanish hacienda than a hospital. The facility was a continuing care community, a place that offered three tiers of living—independent, assisted, and skilled nursing. As Kate read further, she realized she had visited the place when an elderly neighbor sold her condo and moved into a studio apartment there. Kate had been impressed by everything, including the staff, social activities, and the emphasis on dignity. She'd give anything to have Leona in a place like Golden West.

With her fingers crossed, she called the admissions manager and explained the situation. "I know this is short notice, but I'm desperate to move my grandmother today. I don't suppose you have an opening?"

"As a matter of fact, we do."

Kate asked questions about cost, medical care, and physical therapy. Golden West was far more expensive than Casa Rosa, but she could handle what insurance didn't cover on her old Sutton salary. Kate rarely made quick decisions, but this one was plain as day. She finished arrangements to move Leona that afternoon, then called Roscoe and explained her predicament. "I hope you meant what you said about taking me back, because I need to work full-time, at least for a while."

"Of course I meant it. When can you start?"

"How about Monday?"

"Perfect." For the first time in days, a weight lifted off her shoulders and she felt confident. "I hate what happened to Leona, but maybe this is for the best. I can get caught up on the proposal, and Leona will be in a good place."

"Do what you need to do," Roscoe replied. "I'm sorry for the circumstances but glad to have you back."

She ended the call with a sense of relief, but the calm evaporated at the thought of telling Nick about her decision. She loved him, but her weakened faith put a wedge between them. Until she could reconcile her doubts, she had to be careful of his feelings as well as her own. She'd be weak and dependent the rest of her life if she couldn't pull her own weight.

She'd explain to him tonight, but now her thoughts were on Leona and the events around the sudden move. Did she thank God for the opening at Golden West Retirement, or was it merely a coincidence? If she thanked Him, did that mean she had to thank Him for Leona's fall, or at least accept that He had allowed it? The theology was over her head, but resentment nagged at her as she walked back to Leona's room and heard the dementia patient wail yet again that someone was trying to kill her.

As much as Kate wanted to believe in God's goodness, she couldn't reconcile emotional pain with a loving God, or fear with faith. It just didn't make sense, and no one could explain it to her. Not Nick, who had been struck by mystical lightning on a mountaintop, and not Leona, who was too debilitated for a heart-to-heart. Kate was on this road by herself, and if the truth be told, she liked it that way.

23

when the phone
at the newspaper office rang at four o'clock, Nick didn't know whether to expect Kate's tired voice, someone asking about Leona's health, or another advertiser downsizing or pulling an ad completely. Winter was tough for the local businesses, including the Clarion. Eileen, the receptionist, was on another line, so he snatched the handset to his ear. "Clarion."

"Hey, Nick." It was Geoff at the Acorn. "Is Kate around?"

"She's in Valencia." He expected her to walk through the door any minute but didn't tell Geoff. Considering the week she'd endured, Kate deserved a break. A romantic evening with steaks on the grill, candlelight, and a cozy fire sounded perfect.

"Who's handling the ads?" Geoff asked.

"I am." He was a poor second to Kate, even a poor second to Art Davis, the former ad manager. Art had turned the reins over to Kate and didn't want to come back. "What can I do for you?"

"I hate to do this to you, but we're cutting back."

For the fifth time that week, Nick held in a groan at the loss of ad revenue. The Acorn was a big account with a standing half-page ad.

"Sorry to hear it. What are we looking at—a quarter-page?"

"Smaller."

"An eighth?" Advertising was the *Clarion*'s lifeblood. A winter dip was to be expected, but this dip threatened to spin into a black hole. Nick wished Kate were here. She believed in what she did and shared her enthusiasm in a way that was good for everyone concerned.

"Yes, an eighth," Geoff confirmed. "It's just until spring, but you know how things are right now."

Tight . . . very tight. Even at the Clarion. The holiday insert had been a huge success, but the windfall had gone to a much needed computer upgrade. Maggie was gone, but now they were paying Heather, and Kate had insisted Nick draw a salary. Maybe he would, maybe he wouldn't. It depended on the paper's bottom line.

He finished with Geoff, then put together the new ad for the Acorn. He did the best he could, considered asking Kate to redo it when she arrived, but squelched the idea. Nothing had been quite right between them since New Year's Eve, and he was determined to reclaim the closeness that was mired in work and worry. He'd do whatever it took to help Kate take care of Leona, though he hoped she'd come back to the paper soon. The *Clarion* needed both an editor and a strong ad manager to run efficiently. Aside from the business angle, he simply missed her.

He was proofing the new Acorn ad when his cell phone beeped. Two things caught his eye—a message from Kate and an e-mail from Erica Reynolds, the agent recommended by Ted Hawser and the last of the ten agents Nick had queried. Ted had sung Nick's praises to Erica, and she'd asked to see the full manuscript. Both nervous and pumped up, Nick opened the e-mail and started to read.

Dear Nick, Memoirs are a tough sell right now. While your experience is deeply moving, the story just isn't right for the current market. Sorry for the bad news.

Heaving a sigh, he stared blindly out the window. All rejections stung, but this one cut deeper than the others because he'd been so hopeful. What did he do now? Did he send the book to ten more agents or trash it? Somehow he'd gone from being king of the bad-boy travel guides to the unpaid acting editor of a small-town newspaper in a money slump. Between the book rejection and Geoff's call, Nick's pride had taken a beating—not a bad thing for a man with an ego a mile wide, but he hated the sense of failure. Kate wasn't the only person in need of a little TLC tonight. So was Nick. Cheered by thoughts of the coming evening, he read her text message.

Had to move Leona to new hospital. Can't make dinner. Can we meet nine-ish—your house? Have problem. Need to discuss.

"Crud," he muttered to himself.

He'd been looking forward to a relaxing evening together, and now they had another problem driving a wedge between them. A hospital move didn't happen without a reason, and Kate was driving to Meadows at night, something she avoided. The situation couldn't be good, and somehow it involved him in a way that demanded a face-to-face conversation. With his jaw tense, he texted back that nine was fine, then half slammed the phone on the desk. He'd do anything for Kate. He loved her. He wanted to tell her how he felt, set a wedding date, marry her, and have a real life.

He missed her every minute of the day.

He was also tired, lonely, worried, and sad. And a little

mad at God. Having gone through trials of his own, Nick knew what she was experiencing. She needed God more than she needed Nick, but she needed Nick, too—not as a crutch or a man on a pedestal, but as a friend and partner, someone who'd gladly share the load.

His frustration ebbed to a manageable level, though hurt and anger lurked just below the surface. Needing to burn it off, he picked up his phone and truck keys, asked Eileen to lock up, and headed for the door. He considered going for a drive, but he'd learned his lesson about the need for speed. Instead, he drove to Coyote Joe's, where he spotted Colton loitering in the parking lot. He was probably waiting for a ride home from Mindy. Even in the heavy coat Nick had put under the Angel Tree, the teenager was shivering in the cold.

Nick pulled up next to him. "Are you hungry? I'm buying."

Surprise lit Colton's dark eyes, but his scowl returned in a blink. "No, thanks."

Nick wasn't all that hungry either. "It looks like you're waiting for your mom. Do you need a ride?"

The scowl morphed into hope. "Yeah, but I have to ask her."

"So ask."

Colton was in and out of the restaurant in fifteen seconds. He hopped inside the truck, and Nick turned toward the driveway. "Where to?"

"Home," he said. "The apartments."

The run-down building housed eight families and was the closest thing Meadows had to a slum. "So you're still living there?"

"Yeah. It sucks."

Nick steered in that direction, but it felt wrong to drop Colton off and leave. The teenager looked bored to his eyeballs, a condition Nick knew well and what had led him to write both *CFRM* and the book now collecting rejections.

They were almost at the apartment building when Nick had an idea. "Have you taken Driver's Ed yet?"

"Yeah."

"Do you have your learner's permit?"

Colton gave him a sideways look. "I got it last month. Why?"

"Want to practice?"

"Practice what?"

"Driving."

Colton's face lit up. "Sure, but—"

"Let's do it." Nick veered into the school parking lot, empty now, and stopped in the middle of the asphalt striped with parking places. He and Colton switched places, Nick gave some instructions, and Colton turned the ignition and hit the gas. For the next hour they drove in circles, figure eights, and S-shapes that mimicked mountain roads. With each turn of the steering wheel, Colton's smile beamed a little brighter. Nick enjoyed it, too. Teaching Colton took his mind off both Kate and the book rejection—everything except the fun of seeing a boy get a taste of manhood. They practiced until the halogen lights popped on, then Nick told Colton to head to the apartments.

They had a bit of a scare when Colton ran a stop sign and Nick yelled, more at himself than the boy. Colton turned red and cursed, but Nick recovered quickly. "Don't sweat it," he said as Colton parked the truck. "Everyone messes up sometimes."

The teenager hesitated, then looked Nick in the eye. "What about you? Have you messed up?"

They were talking about more than driving. The question was about graffiti, growing up, and Nick's wild days. "I've messed up a lot."

He waited for Colton to continue the conversation, but the

boy donned his customary scowl, said nothing, and climbed down from the driver's seat. If he wanted to hear more, he'd have to ask. When the two of them met on the sidewalk, Nick tapped the hood of the truck. "We'll do this again. How about next week?"

"Cool." Colton headed up the cracked concrete walk but stopped halfway and turned to Nick. "Thanks. That was fun."

Nick gave a wave and watched until Colton opened a door with chipped green paint. The drapes in the window were faded and torn, but Sadie barked a greeting that made Nick smile. There was hope for boys like Colton, hope for all men, including Nick. He may have given Colton the thrill of his first driving lesson, but the teenager had returned the favor by reminding Nick why he'd written his memoir. With the driving lesson fresh on his mind, he went home and sent queries to ten more agents.

He lost all track of time until headlights flashed in the window. When the car engine stopped, he set aside the computer and went to the door, opening it as Kate reached the top step. A week ago she would have walked into his arms and hugged him. Tonight, she stopped two feet away, her posture ramrod straight and her face rigid in the glow of the porch light. There wasn't a trace of softness in her expression, only a purposeful stare that warned him not to touch her. Apparently she had come tonight to fight for something, not for the comfort he longed to give.

Hurt and irritation pulsed through him, but he pushed the reaction away with compassion. Frightened people protected themselves any way they could. They said things they didn't mean and built fortresses. Kate could have whatever she wanted from him, whatever she needed. His fear was that she would ask for nothing.

Stepping back, he opened the door wide. "Come on in."

"Thank you."

As he hung up her coat, she headed to the couch where he'd kissed her the night of the November storm. With her expression guarded, she perched on the edge of the thick cushion and laced her hands in her lap. She looked tired, worried, and small. "Are you hungry?" he asked.

She shrugged. "I'm all right."

Nick knew Kate's ways, how she answered some questions directly and dodged others with diplomatic neutrality. *I'm all right* was a dodge. A firm *no* would put distance between them, which she seemed to want; but she never ate while she drove and was probably half starved. A clear *yes* would fill her stomach, but she would have to accept food from his table, a gift from his hand. Food was complicated in a strange emotional way, so he offered something simple. "How about a bowl of soup?"

Her brows lifted hopefully. "Chicken noodle?"

"With saltines."

She followed him to the kitchen but stopped to gaze out the window that faced Mount Abel, a silhouette barely visible on a moonless night. He wondered if she could see it at all, then focused on the task of dumping the soup into the old saucepan he also used for camping. The kitchen seemed particularly Spartan. There were no canisters on the counter, no curtains on the windows. There wasn't a single feminine touch in the entire house, except for Kate's reflection in the cold, black glass. The silence between them seemed to breathe, a living wall as he poured the soup into a ceramic bowl shaped and painted like a chicken—a dubious treasure sold at Meadows craft fairs by Betty Dayton, a widow surviving on Social Security.

Kate turned to him. "It smells good."

He set the bowl and a spoon on the table, added a paper

towel for a napkin, and fetched a couple of bottles of water from the fridge. Kate saw the chicken bowl and gave in to an amused smile. "That's a Betty original."

"I have a whole set."

"So does Leona," she said. "Plus a gravy boat shaped like a turkey. That's one of the best things about Meadows."

"Soup bowls?"

"No, people helping one another." She lifted the spoon to her lips and sipped. "Thanks. This is good."

Nick set a water bottle in front of her. Rather than crowd her at the table, he leaned his hips against the countertop, twisted the cap off the second bottle, and took a long swig. She ate several bites of soup before pausing to wipe her lips with the paper towel. When she lowered it, she gave him a tentative look. "I moved Leona to a different nursing home."

"That was fast."

"It had to be. You wouldn't believe what I walked into this morning." In a calm, clear voice, she described the cries of the dementia patient, Leona's exhaustion, and the director's inability to move Leona to another room. "I couldn't leave her there."

"Of course not."

"It took some effort, but I found an opening at Golden West Retirement. It's a continuing care facility—one of those places with apartments if you can manage pretty well on your own and full nursing care if you can't. Leona's in the nursing section, but it doesn't feel at all like a hospital. There's a patio and a mulberry tree right outside a sliding glass door, and we can put pictures on the walls."

"It sounds nice."

"It is, but there's a problem."

"Money?"

"Yes and no." She pushed the bowl away. "I hope you meant

what you said about doing whatever it took to help with Leona."

"Of course, I did. I love you."

She stared at him, her expression blank until the air whooshed from her lungs. Eyes wide, she pressed the fingers of one hand to her mouth, as if she had witnessed something terrible. Nick wanted to kick himself. What kind of fool made a first declaration of love in a kitchen that smelled like canned soup? In spite of his effort to give Kate all the time she needed, he had moved too fast. It wasn't his best moment, but he'd never been more truthful. With his words now mired in silence, he realized how profoundly he meant them, and how much he wanted to hear them back.

"You can't be surprised," he said in a mild tone.

She stared into his eyes with the bleakness of a moonless night. "No. I'm not."

"I love you," he said again, prompting her to say it back, though he knew she wouldn't. A moment ticked by, then another. A log thudded in the fireplace, a sign of the dying flames and cooling embers.

Kate raised her chin, then exhaled as if she were cooling a spoonful of soup. "You know I care for you."

What did he say to lukewarm caring, except that it wasn't enough? And yet it was all she had to give, and he had vowed to go at her pace, not his. At a loss, he tightened his grip on the water bottle, crushing it before he tossed it into the trash can.

Kate pushed away from the table and stood, turned her back on him, and went to the window. She meant to hide, but the glass reflected the twist of her mouth and a sheen in her pale eyes. He thought of the Eve's Garden poster in her office and the slogan about putting the "you" in beautiful, and he wondered if she knew how beautiful she was to him.

A minute ticked by. When she turned around, her face was composed but her stance reminded him of a deer aware of a hunter. She was fearful, frozen, and ready to run. "I'm sorry, Nick. You deserve more from me. I'm just so confused."

He wasn't a hunter, so why was she afraid? He deliberately made his voice tender. "It's okay to be confused."

"No, it's not."

"Sure, it is. Everyone goes through rough times."

"I know that," she said. "But I can't stand the uncertainty. Four months ago I was at Sutton and I knew what to expect. But then everything changed. First because of you, then because of God. For the first few weeks, everything in my life fit perfectly. Then Leona fell and you weren't there. Neither was God."

"I let you down. The speeding ticket—"

"No." She shook her head. "I don't feel this way because of anything you did. And it's not because Leona fell. I know people make mistakes and bad things happen. I'm not looking for a pie-in-the-sky kind of God, but I *do* want a God I can understand, one that doesn't disappear when I need Him most."

"I understand."

"How can you? You're so sure of your faith. You never have questions or doubts."

"That's not true." No way would he let her put him back on a pedestal. "Those first months of Christianity were tough for me. I practically lived on Sam's couch, because every time I turned around, I was tempted to hit the road and do something stupid. When things are hard, I'm still tempted."

There was a trucker bar called the Black Dog Lounge down by the interstate. Nick wasn't an alcoholic and didn't miss drinking. What he missed was the mindless escape into noise, dim lights, and empty conversation. In a place like the Black

Dog, a man could forget his insignificance. As foolish as it was, that kind of escape occasionally tempted him the way graffiti tempted boys like Colton.

Kate swiped a strand of hair away from her face. "Everything is changing again, and I don't understand why. I just know that today I made a decision. It's big, and it involves you."

Whatever she had to say, he wasn't going to like it. "What is it?"

"I'm going back to Sutton."

"*Sutton?*"

"Yes."

"But why?"

"I need the money to pay for Leona's care."

"Kate—"

"There's more to it." She leaned against the windowsill, her arms stiff and bent at her sides. "Golden West is close to both Sutton and my condo. With Julie on leave, the Eve's Garden proposal is a mess. There's no one to fill in except Brad, and he's not right for this account. The *Clarion* is the only responsibility I can hand off—if you're willing to run it without me."

Nick had been afraid she'd ask him for nothing. Instead, she'd asked for the greatest gift of all—freedom. But how much freedom? Was she severing the emotional cord between them, stretching it to the point of breaking, or just putting him on hold? Somehow he managed to control his voice. "I see the practical side. What I don't understand is how you feel about it. Do you *want* to go back?"

"I want to go back to pay for Golden West and to stop the time pressure I'm under. But I hate to ask you for a favor."

"That's not what I meant."

"What?"

263

He paused to reframe the question. "Do you want to go back because you miss it?"

She didn't answer immediately. He waited, watched, and finally spoke for her. "You do, don't you?"

"Maybe . . . A little." She sighed. "I just don't know."

With her back reflecting in the window, she seemed to be walking away from Mount Abel instead of toward it. It was a fitting picture of a woman caught between opposing needs in opposing worlds. As much as Nick wanted to ride to her rescue, he couldn't do a thing to help her—except hit the brakes on his own desires and put Kate's needs before his own.

Lord, I can't do this. I can't let her go.

Except that's what he had to do. He could push for his own way, but someday Kate would resent him for holding her back. He'd be the bad guy—the hunter who shot the deer so he could mount its head on a wall. He didn't want a trophy. He wanted Kate to come to him freely. "You need to do this," he said in a tight voice. "I'll help any way I can."

"Thank you." The trace of a smile lifted her lips, but the sign of appreciation quickly faded. "I'm asking a lot of you."

"I offered. Remember?"

"Yes, but that was before . . . before we had feelings for each other." When a blush tinted her cheeks, he hoped she was reliving every kiss, every embrace. The power of attraction was on his side, and he wouldn't let her forget it. He approached her slowly, watching for a particular spark in her eyes, the look that said she wanted to be kissed. He saw the look, but Kate lowered her face to hide it. Instead of holding her the way he wanted, he clasped her stiff arms and waited.

When she looked up, her eyes had a sheen. "I'm sorry, Nick. I need time."

"It's all right."

"No, it's not. I know how I feel about you. It's more than just caring. But I don't know if I *should* feel that way. Your faith defines you. If I can't share it, I have to wonder if we belong together."

The words punched him in the gut. He loved Kate. Regardless of what she thought or believed, his feelings wouldn't change. She didn't need to be perfect for Nick to give her his heart. On the other hand, she still needed God more than she needed him. And that meant she had to seek God for herself. If Nick had a quarrel with anyone, it was with God—not Kate.

He touched her cheek. "I'm here, Kate. No pressure."

"Thank you." Another weak smile tilted her lips. "If I can be *me* for a while, maybe I can get my life under control again."

Nick almost laughed at the irony. No wonder Kate was struggling. Christianity was about *relinquishing* control of one's own self, one's will—especially when the "will" wanted to hang out at the Black Dog Lounge or to cling to pride and run from God. Suddenly he saw the crux of Kate's dilemma. She was afraid to trust, and who could blame her? Her entire life had been full of accidents. Going back to Sutton wasn't good or bad, right or wrong. It was a life choice only Kate could make. Nick could only stand at her side, encouraging her, and loving her while she made up her own mind.

"We're in this together," he promised her.

"I'm glad."

"Me, too."

When longing glistened in her eyes, he matched his mouth to hers. Her arms wrapped around him, and they kissed until she broke away to rest her head on his shoulder. "I should leave."

Knowing she was right, he helped her with her coat and

walked her to the car, wishing with every step that she'd turn around and say she'd changed her mind about returning to Sutton. But she didn't. Instead, she drove away, leaving him alone on a moonless night looking up at a mountain that seemed very far away.

24

eve landon walked
into Sutton Advertising on Valentine's Day with a bodyguard
at her side and a smile on her perfect face. A self-declared
romantic, she wore a red cashmere sweater, white slacks,
and dangling heart-shaped earrings. A necklace showed off
diamond hearts, but what most inspired Kate's admiration
was Eve's poise. The woman oozed self-assurance.

Kate, on the other hand, was a nervous wreck about today's
presentation. Where was the confident woman she used to
be—a woman who was comfortable in both her professional
and personal relationships? Nothing had been right since
she moved back into her condo. The stress of the presentation robbed her of sleep; so did the drop in advertising at
the *Clarion*.

Nick insisted he could handle the situation until she returned, but she still felt guilty. He called almost every day at
four o'clock. They bantered like the good friends they were,
but his declaration of love echoed in unexpected moments of
silence, those awkward pauses where Kate detoured around

the big messy feelings that refused to be sanitized into mere friendship.

She didn't want to be Nick's friend.

She wanted to be *the one*.

She especially wanted to be that special person today, because it was Valentine's Day. In a place like Sutton, where creative people thrived on outdoing each other, a holiday turned into a game of can-you-top-this. Giant teddy bears, balloons, custom-made candy, and exotic flowers sat proudly in several cubicles. Except for a half-eaten bag of chocolate hearts, Kate's desk was among the empty ones. She had no right to expect another declaration of love from Nick, not when she hadn't returned the first one, but she had hoped for something.

There were flowers everywhere, even on the reception desk, where Eve stopped to inhale the fragrance of a dozen red roses. Trying to appear confident, Kate approached her and offered a handshake. "Welcome to Sutton."

Ignoring Kate's outstretched hand, Eve pulled her into a hug. "Let's not be formal, dear. You and I are friends, and we both know you're a bundle of nerves."

"I am," Kate admitted with a laugh. In a few minutes she and Brad would present their plan for the national campaign. Kate had worked hard, but with the turmoil in her life she didn't trust her instincts. On the other hand, she trusted Nick and he'd come up with the U word she'd finally chosen for the slogan.

Eve lasered her with a shrewd stare. "Nerves are good. It means you care. I like that in a person."

Kate glowed with the praise, but it did nothing to ease her anxiety as they walked toward Roscoe's office, making small talk about Valentine's Day and the abundance of flowers and balloons. When they reached the open door, Eve laid her hand on Kate's arm. "Before we get started, I want you to know how much I appreciate your dedication."

"It's my job. I love it." Even with the added stress, the actual design work was an oasis for her.

"Yes," Eve agreed. "But you also have a life. How is Nick?"

"He's fine."

"Good," Eve remarked. "And your grandmother?"

"Excellent." Leona's shoulder and ribs were almost completely healed, and she was benefiting from daily therapy. "She's still at Golden West, but we moved her from the nursing section to one of the apartments." Kate didn't have to worry about Leona's being alone or getting to physical therapy or doctor's appointments, and Leona had taken full advantage of exercise classes, the book club, and shopping trips to the local mall. She also appreciated having a call button by her bed.

"I'm glad to hear it." Eve gave a mock shudder. "Aging is both a war and an art form, isn't it?"

Without knowing it, she had touched on the theme of today's presentation. Kate's jaw almost dropped at the coincidence, but she schooled her features into an enigmatic smile. There was no point in tipping her hand now. She wanted Eve to be wowed by the unexpected, not disappointed because her expectations were too high.

As they walked into the office, Kate saw Roscoe and Brad seated in the informal meeting area furnished with glass tables and leather armchairs. The men stood and greeted Eve. With her earrings flashing in the cool glow of fluorescent light, she settled into the chair with a straight-on view of the wall-mounted monitor. Roscoe's assistant delivered a refreshment tray, and the four of them talked a bit about the entire project.

The butterflies in Kate's stomach calmed but only slightly.

Finally Roscoe cued her to start. "Let's see what you've come up with."

With perspiration dampening her palms, she picked up the remote and launched the presentation. Lively music filled the room and the first of a series of full-color photographs shimmered on to the screen. It showed the profile of a teenage girl admiring a bouquet of bright Gerbera daisies. The slogan at the bottom read:

Eve's Garden
Put the You in Unique

Next came a young woman holding a single red rose, then a bride with a massive pastel bouquet. The slogan never changed, but the pictures shimmered through the stages of a woman's life.

A mother-to-be wore a leotard printed with pink and blue pom-poms.

A career woman in a tailored suit peeked over funky reading glasses to admire an exotic purple orchid.

Midlife was depicted by a grandmother, mother, and small child in a field of orange California poppies.

Last came old age. Of all the ads, this was Kate's favorite. It showed an elderly woman under the willow tree from the first Eve's Garden ad.

The slideshow closed with the women and children together in a lush garden and a final phrase that captured Eve's mission. It read,

Be You . . . Be Beautiful . . . Be Happy.

As the screen went blank, Kate held her breath in anticipation of Eve's reaction. Roscoe nodded his approval and Brad winked, but only Eve's opinion mattered. Wearing her poker face, the actress stared at Kate for several seconds. Chin high and back straight, Kate stared back until Eve broke into a wide grin and jumped to her feet. Clapping wildly, she gave a one-woman standing ovation. "Bravo, darling. Bravo! It's perfect."

Kate gave a little fist pump and shouted, "Yes!" She'd be cool and professional later. Right now, she was thrilled. For the first time in weeks, she felt like herself.

Eve sat down, crossed her long legs, and focused on Kate. "I love how you tied beauty and aging together in such an emotional way. This is perfect for the antiaging products, too. What do you think of"—she made air quotes—"'Put the You in Youthful'?"

"I like it." Kate traded a glance with Brad to include him. "We thought of a lot of 'you' words. Enthusiasm, Universal . . ."

"Rejuvenation," Brad added.

"Who thought of Unique?" Eve asked.

Kate blushed a little. "That came from Nick."

Eve gave her a knowing glance, then graced Brad with a smile. "I'm sorry to ignore you, Brad. I'm sure you helped."

"A little." He tossed off a shrug. "You'll see my role when Roscoe goes over stats and target markets."

Kate could hardly contain her excitement. With the Eve's Garden account, Sutton Advertising had a lucrative, long-term contract. Roscoe wouldn't have to consider layoffs, and Kate could return to Meadows with a clear conscience—except the moment was bittersweet. She loved moments like this one, where words, pictures, and a purpose came together in perfect harmony and in a big way.

Roscoe cleared his throat, then glanced between Brad and Kate. "We still need to go over Brad's part of the presentation, but Eve told me earlier she has to cut this short. She and I have something else to discuss, so why don't you two take a break?"

As Kate stood, Eve caught her eye. "I'd like to speak with you before I leave. Could we meet in your office?"

She nodded. "It's the third cubicle on the right." *The one without flowers or balloons.*

Kate and Brad left together. As soon as they reached the hallway, he stopped and offered his hand. "Congratulations, Kate. You get full credit."

"No, I don't. You helped and so did Julie in the beginning." And so had Nick.

"I bet you get a promotion."

"Maybe." She grinned, then realized accepting a promotion would mean living in Los Angeles permanently. It meant giving up Meadows, and in a way, the relationship she had with Nick—or didn't have. Geography wasn't the problem; people in love overcame obstacles all the time. It was a question of her heart, what she believed and loved most. She loved Nick, but she loved her work, too. Being at Sutton made her feel secure, while being with Nick seemed to demand one risk after another.

Brad clapped her on the shoulder. "Congrats again. I'm glad you came back."

"Me, too."

He walked away, and Kate headed to her cubicle. Flowers scented the air, and red, white, and pink balloons hovered in bunches everywhere she looked. Approaching her office, she spotted a new delivery. Someone in an office close to hers had received a massive bouquet of black and white balloons. She wondered if the colors were a joke, an anti-Valentine after a bad breakup. Drawing closer, she realized they were in *her* office, and a siren was going off.

The receptionist came out of the space wearing a silly grin. "Sorry, I couldn't resist."

"Resist what?"

"You'll see." Still chuckling, the girl hurried away.

Kate rounded the corner, saw the source of the commotion, and broke into a wide smile. Nick hadn't ignored Valentine's Day after all. The balloons were attached to a toy police car, a reminder of the speeding ticket and his promise to go slow with her. *Oh, Nick . . .* She'd sent him a funny little card, but she'd read a hundred mushy ones before deciding to play it safe. Suddenly melancholy, she opened the envelope that held a card with a glossy picture of a red rose. There was no printed message, only Nick's familiar handwriting.

Dear Kate,

There's no way I'm going to let Valentine's Day go by without telling you how I feel. There are no secrets between us, only things still unsaid. I respect your choices—you know that. And I've got your back here in Meadows—you know that, too. What you don't know is that I understand the need to go slow, to search, to wander in the dark, groping blindly for answers because you can't see what lies ahead. Do you remember that social sabbatical I talked about it? It ends April 9th. I really do understand the need to seek until you find. I'm not patient by nature—you know that, too. But I am in love with you, and that makes all things possible.

Love, Nick.

Tears pushed into her eyes, but she blinked them back. Was she crazy for not walking out of Sutton and straight into Nick's arms? So what if she didn't fully understand this thing called faith? No one had all the answers.

It was almost four o'clock and time for him to call. *Lord? Are you there? I can't stand this confusion!* The prayer flew through her mind like a bird crossing an empty sky, growing smaller and smaller until it disappeared from sight. That's how her relationship with God had been since New Year's Eve. Distant. Random. Faded. Aching inside, she set down the card and pressed the button on the police car to set off the siren.

"That's certainly unique."

She turned and saw Eve studying the balloons. "Are these from Nick?"

"Yes."

"Interesting color scheme. Did you two break up?"

"No. But it's complicated."

"It's only as complicated as you want it to be." Eve indicated that Kate should sit, then took the chair next to the desk. "What's the problem?"

"Problem?"

"Yes. With Nick. Why didn't he give you roses or chocolates?" Eve lowered her voice. "Or lingerie."

Eve would never understand Nick's personal choices, so Kate focused on what Eve *could* understand—the struggle to balance love and a career. "Nick's ready to settle down, but I don't know if I am. He wants . . . everything. I'm not sure how much of myself I want to give up."

"Oh, darling—" Eve gripped Kate's hand in both of hers. "A man who wants everything will destroy you. To borrow your own phrase, he'll take the 'you' out of . . . you."

Kate shook her head. "Nick's not like that."

"Are you sure?"

"Positive."

Eve lifted one of her famously arched brows. "In that case, you ought to be with him—not here at Sutton. The fact you *are* here, tells me you have doubts."

Not in Nick but in God. Kate wasn't about to share her faith crisis with Eve. The actress was famous for sampling different religions, and Kate couldn't defend herself. "I'm just trying to sort things out."

"Well, good," Eve said. "Because I have an offer for you."

"An offer?"

The actress grinned like the Cheshire cat. "Before I say anything else, I want you to know I talked to Roscoe. He expected to lose you anyway, and he knows I can do more for you than he can. He gave his blessing."

"For what?" Kate couldn't put the pieces together, and Eve's smug expression didn't offer any clues.

"Eve's Garden is expanding into EG Enterprises. I want you to be the new director of marketing."

"Are you *serious*?"

"Very."

"I can't believe it—"

"It's true. You'll be in charge of advertising for the spas, of course. In addition, we're moving into nutraceuticals, body sculpting, and a skin treatment involving a flower just discovered in the Amazon rainforest. If it's as effective as the tests suggest, it has amazing possibilities."

Kate couldn't think, couldn't breathe. "This is amazing. But—"

"But you have obligations," Eve said for her. "Every woman who's juggled a career with her personal life knows how difficult it is. No one can be in two places at once. I understand that, and I assure you I'll be flexible where your grandmother's concerned." Another twinkle flashed in her eyes. "And Nick, too."

"I just can't believe it. I don't know what to say."

"Nothing right now." Eve's voice softened, a change that lessened the drama and made her more like a mother. "Let's have dinner tonight. We'll go over the details. You can think about it over the weekend."

"I'd like that. But I have to be honest. I just can't imagine taking the job. My life is . . . Like I said, it's complicated."

Eve studied her for a moment. "We're back to Nick."

"And Leona."

Eve thought for a moment. "I have an idea. Let's make this an audition of sorts. You can test the waters while your grandmother's at Golden West. This is a big decision and you shouldn't rush into it."

Brad interrupted with a tap on the cubicle. "Roscoe broke out the champagne. Everyone's gathering in the playpen."

Kate glanced at her watch. It was four o'clock, and she wanted to thank Nick for the balloons and tell him that Eve loved the proposal. If he didn't call her, she needed to call him. "I'll be there in a minute." When Brad left, she focused on Eve. "I need to give Nick a quick call."

"Of course." Eve gave Kate's shoulder a pat and left with Brad.

Kate called Nick's cell phone. When the call went to voice mail, she called the Clarion and got voice mail again. She didn't want to leave a chirpy message, so she shot him a text. *The balloons are perfect. Thank you. More later.*

With a moment to herself, she closed her eyes and savored a heady mix of relief that the presentation was over and exhilaration that it had been so well received. Eve's offer was a dream come true, and she wanted it badly. But at what cost? It would mean leaving Meadows except for occasional weekends. Leona was recovering beautifully, but the wisdom of her living alone was questionable. And then there was Nick. She loved him and wanted to be with him, but his faith confused her. On the other hand, today's victory made her feel secure, and she wanted to cling to that good feeling.

Someone tapped on the metal post of her cubicle. She expected to see a co-worker offering congratulations. Instead, she saw Nick—handsome, tall, and strong with a resolute gleam in his patient brown eyes.

25

to nick's delight,

Kate flew out of the chair and into his arms. There was no one around, so he hugged her hard and stole a kiss, enjoying every second of the embrace. The balloons and card had been a hit, and he was glad he'd come to see her instead of returning to Meadows after delivering a few things to Leona, including a journal that was a secret gift for Kate.

The past six weeks had frustrated him on every front. The *Clarion* required his full attention, and in spite of his sales efforts, the advertising revenue was down far more than expected. He didn't have time to travel for *California Dreaming,* and five rejections had rolled in from the ten new queries he'd sent to agents. Even more frustrating, he missed Kate every minute of the day. For all his experience with women, Nick had never been in love before now. It was a little bit like having the flu. His body ached with a strange kind of fever, and he couldn't do a thing about it except wait it out.

He hoped today's presentation had knocked down the final roadblock to Kate's coming home, because holding her took away the emptiness shaped like one of his ribs. It also made the flu symptoms worse. The Lord must have enjoyed creating Eve for Adam, but the requirement to tamp down physical desire until marriage bordered on cruel. Well, not really—just at moments like this when he had to stop kissing her.

He eased back from the embrace and focused on her eyes. "I hear Eve loved the proposal. Congratulations."

"Thank you." She trailed her fingers down the long sleeve of his button-down shirt, then took both his hands in hers and squeezed. "I'm thrilled, and that's not even the biggest news."

"Oh, yeah?"

"You won't believe this." She stepped back, giving him a clear view of her glowing face. He'd thought her earlier enthusiasm was for him; now he wondered if he'd been mistaken and her excitement stemmed from something else. After letting go of him, she clasped her hands over her chest in what looked like a prayer. "Eve Landon just offered me a job as marketing director. She's expanding Eve's Garden into EG Enterprises. It's going to be huge!"

His blood congealed in his veins, making his skin cold and prickly. Just when he expected their circumstances to ease, Eve Landon had sucker-punched him. Nick had nothing against Eve's Garden, and he wanted to support Kate in every way. If that meant her having a career in Los Angeles, he could adjust—but only if her motives were right. Did she believe EG Enterprises was her destiny, even a calling to love people who were hurting, or was she clinging to past success out of fear?

"That's great," he said, trying to mean it.

"It is. But I don't see how I can take it."

The longing in her voice cut to his heart, so did the faraway look in her eyes. He didn't know exactly why Kate thought she couldn't accept Eve's offer, or what future she was imagining and if it included him or not; but he was certain she wanted the job. If she turned down this opportunity, she might regret it forever. In a way they were back in his kitchen when she asked him to run the *Clarion* while she worked at Sutton. If she accepted Eve's offer, she'd be asking him for even more, though he didn't know exactly what.

She indicated the opening to the cubicle, then held out her hand to him. "Roscoe broke out the champagne. I have to go . . . Come with me."

Nick grasped her fingers and followed, but only until they passed through the narrow opening. When they could walk side by side, he offered his arm to escort her. Smiling up at him, she slipped her fingers around his elbow and they sauntered forward together. The crowd split around them, breaking into applause as she left Nick's side and joined Roscoe. Someone put a glass of champagne in Nick's hand, and Eve Landon greeted him with a smile.

"She's remarkable, isn't she?" the actress said about Kate.

"Very," Nick agreed.

While Roscoe elaborated on Kate's accomplishments, Eve murmured to Nick, "I feel terrible. You surprised Kate for Valentine's Day, and I've already invited her to dinner to discuss business. I'd back out, but I'm leaving for Europe in the morning. You were planning a night together, and I ruined it."

Nick was planning a lifetime with Kate, not just a night. Eve might have ruined the evening, but she didn't control the future. "Kate told me about your offer."

"Oh, good!" Eve's face lit up. "I'm so glad she told you. I can't keep a secret to save my life. Would you like to join us tonight? Maybe you can convince her to give it a try."

"A try?"

"Yes." Eve tapped a finger on her champagne glass. "She's hesitant because of her grandmother—and maybe you—so I suggested a three-month trial period. I know how hard it is for a woman to juggle her personal and professional lives, but it *is* possible. I've certainly managed."

Yes, and you've been divorced five times. Nick hurt for Eve, for every person who had been wounded by life. He didn't doubt that people could combine work, home, and faith. His brother and Gayle did it as a couple, and they did it well. His concerns were all about Kate's motivation, and he had to admit, a trial period had merit.

Eve assessed him with a cool look, one that sized him up and maybe gauged his use to her. When it came to Kate, Nick could be a powerful ally or Eve's worst enemy. At the moment, neither of them knew where the other stood. When Nick said nothing, Eve raised her chin and stared at him, her gaze a bit haughty. "EG Enterprises is going to change how women see aging, and Kate's going to be part of that. A new world will open up for her."

But was it a world worth having? Nick had written an entire book about places like Eve's Garden. *California for Real Men* had given him money, some fame, and a lot of pleasure. But in the end, the experiences behind it had caused heartbreak.

When Roscoe raised a toast to Kate, the crowd clinked glasses and cheered. Nick joined in the celebration, but the champagne burned his throat. As much as he wanted Kate to return to Meadows, he had to consider another possibility. He saw Eve's offer as an apple, forbidden fruit, a temptation for Kate to be in control. But maybe the job really was a plum, something sweet, juicy, good, and desirable. Who was Nick to cast stones or make judgments?

No one.

Absolutely no one.

He was a guy who drove too fast, made mistakes, and couldn't sell his book. But he also loved Kate. He had walked away from *CFRM*, and though he still considered himself a writer, the recent rejections left him riddled with doubts about his future. He didn't want Kate to live with what ifs, especially when her faith was at a low ebb.

With the crowd cheering for her, Nick swallowed hard and made a decision. As much as he wanted Kate to refuse Eve's offer, he wouldn't press her in any way. God had given Adam and Eve a choice in the Garden of Eden, and Nick had to give Kate the same respect. For all he knew, she belonged right here in Los Angeles, a city full of saints and sinners like themselves. If Kate belonged here, maybe Nick belonged with her. He didn't want to leave Meadows, but he had to be open to the idea.

When the cheering ended, Kate bounced to his side. Eve tilted her head like a mother hen watching a chick. "Enjoy the party. I wish I could stay, but I have another appointment."

"That reminds me," Kate said. "I hate to cancel dinner, but Nick's here and—"

"He's invited," Eve said with a smile. "I'll see you at the Mediterranean Grill at eight."

Nick recognized the name of a restaurant in Beverly Hills. He had included it in *CFRM*, but he didn't belong there anymore, and he didn't belong at the meeting with Eve and Kate. "Sorry, but I can't join you ladies." He smiled a reluctant blessing down on Kate. "You can tell me about it tomorrow."

Her eyes clouded. "Are you sure?"

"Positive."

Eve dipped her chin with swanlike grace. "Thank you, Nick. I appreciate it. I was going to ask you something tonight, but I'll ask you now instead."

What more could Eve want? She had already hijacked Kate on Valentine's Day. "What can I do for you?"

"I've read your articles in *California Dreaming*. They're excellent."

"Thank you."

"Would you be interested in doing something on Eve's Garden? Be warned. If you say no, I'll have Kate use her influence to persuade you."

"There's no need to use Kate," he said. "I'd be glad to do it. Let me check with my editor and get back to you."

"Excellent." Eve clasped her hands at her waist. "I have to go, but you can arrange the details with Kate."

She hadn't accepted the job, but Eve was acting like she already owned Kate. The women hugged good-bye, then Eve shook his hand and headed for the lobby, where her bodyguard was waiting. Kate watched until she rounded the corner, then she let out a breath. "What an amazing day."

For Nick, too, though not in a good way. "We need to talk. There's a coffee place downstairs."

"I can't leave yet." She wrinkled her nose, a gesture he now recognized as guilt. "Roscoe wants to meet in about fifteen minutes. Let's go to my office."

He didn't want to be overheard. "Is there some place more private?"

"Sure," she said. "This way."

They walked down a long corridor, their hands dangling close but not touching as she led him into an empty conference room. As he pulled a seat around, Kate swiveled a chair to put them eye to eye, knee to knee. Neither spoke for several seconds. He used the pause to drink in Kate's shining face, her pretty eyes, the soft lips he wanted to kiss. She broke the tension by reaching for his hand. "I've missed you."

"I've missed you, too."

"So," she said in her business voice. "You want to talk about Eve's offer."

"Yes, I—"

"Me first." She lifted his hand slightly, taking the weight

with a determined squeeze. "Before you say a word, I want you to know how much I appreciate what you've already done. Eve's offer is a real thrill, but I can't take it, not with Leona and the *Clarion* on my plate. I won't ask you for another favor. It just wouldn't be right."

He stroked the top of her hand with this thumb, particularly her bare fourth finger. He wanted to slip an engagement ring over her knuckles and imagined doing it on April ninth, the official end of his sabbatical. He wanted Kate to be his wife. Even more, he wanted her to *want* to be with him, to make the choice with joy. But when he looked into her eyes, he saw the solemn expression of a person making a sacrifice, not the glorious smile of a woman in love.

Nick made the sacrifice for them both. "Take the job."

"What? I thought—"

"Take the job," he repeated, though his stomach soured with the champagne. "You're not asking me for a favor. I'm offering."

Drawing back, she straightened her spine. "I thought you were eager for me to come back to Meadows, not just for the paper, but so we could be together."

"I want that very much."

"Then why?"

"Because you need to do this. I walked away from *California for Real Men*, but I didn't stop being a writer. When you became a Christian, you didn't stop being you. I don't want to limit you, Kate. I want you to be everything God intends for you to be, though I have to admit—I'm being totally selfish here."

"How?" Her voice shook.

"I want you to figure out how to be *you* so that we can be *us*."

Her eyes glistened and blinked, then her lips trembled ever so slightly. "You know I love you. I couldn't say it, because—"

He didn't care why. "Say it again."

"I love you."

He raked his fingers through her hair, cupped the back of her head, and matched his mouth to hers. The kiss told her that he wanted her, loved her, believed in her. When he eased back, they were breathing in perfect time.

Kate laid her head on his shoulder. "I'm scared."

"Of what?"

"Everything," she said in a whisper. "I don't know how to live like this, how to mix the old and the new."

The black and white balloons were more fitting than he had imagined. An artist blended the two colors to make shades of gray. People compromised. But some decisions really were black and white. A person couldn't go east and west at the same time, but two people could walk side by side in the same direction. At some point, though, they had to agree which way to walk. If they couldn't and they still wanted to be together, someone had to make a sacrifice.

"Take the job," he said for the third time. "Try it out."

She lifted her head off his shoulder and stared into his eyes, her longing as evident as her earlier desire to be kissed. "Are you sure?"

"Positive."

When she flung her arms around his neck and hugged him, Nick held her tight and silently prayed for them both. It was the best weapon he had against Eve Landon and her apples.

26

a month after taking the job with Eve, Kate wrangled a Friday off and headed to Meadows. Crisp sunshine poured down from the sky, delivering a hint of warmth to the March afternoon, the first day of spring after a long wet winter. She parked in front of the newspaper office and paused, her nerves pulsing with a mix of irritation, relief, and hope. The irritation stemmed from today's mission, one given to her by Eve Landon and one she disliked.

After all Nick had done, how could she pressure him to speed up the *California Dreaming* article he'd promised to do for Eve? He was working over sixty hours a week to keep the *Clarion* afloat in the midst of a terrible advertising slump, one that refused to end. With Kate putting in equally ridiculous hours, they'd spent just one quality afternoon together—if you could call buying a car quality time. The purchase had been stressful for her even with Nick's help, but the old Subaru was a blight in the Eve's Garden parking lot, and Eve had remarked on it. Today Kate was driving a gently used red 4WD SUV that she'd bought with the Sutton bonus money.

Climbing out of the vehicle, she inhaled the clean air and savored the quiet. She loved her work, but Eve was a maelstrom of ideas and energy, a tornado in a hurricane, and she required a great deal of attention. As much as Kate disliked mentioning the *California Dreaming* article to Nick, she'd do it because it was her job, but she wouldn't do it immediately. It was Friday afternoon and she had the entire weekend to spend with him. Tingling with anticipation, she walked into the lobby.

"Surprise!" she called to Nick.

"Kate?" He strode out of the back office, his hair a little disheveled and his jaw dark with stubble. She loved that rugged look, especially when he hugged her and his whiskers tickled her cheek. After a quick kiss, she slipped out of his arms to enjoy the sight of him.

He stared back, a grin spreading across his face. "Does this mean you have the weekend off?"

"All of it. We've both been working too hard." To prove it, she trailed her fingers along his jaw. "You haven't even had time to shave."

Nick laughed. "I'm just being lazy."

"You? Never!" He was one of the hardest working people she knew, which made Eve's request even more irritating. Before Kate dumped it on him, she wanted to take some of the weight off his shoulders. "It's time I helped out around here. Let's work on the *Clarion* tonight and tomorrow, then we'll take Sunday off. If you'd like, we can go to church in the morning and then just relax."

"That sounds good." He hooked a strand of her hair behind her ear. "If the weather stays warm, we can break out the bike, maybe look for condors. By the way, I talked to Marcus earlier today."

Kate hadn't thought about the birds since working for Eve. "How's Wistoyo?"

"Much better. They hope to release her in a few weeks."

"That's great!"

Her heart gave a little leap, as if her soul were coming back to her body. Being in Meadows did that to her. So did being with Nick, but the rush of good feelings confused her. Eve said a woman could have everything she wanted, but how many balls could Kate keep in the air? And what about the balls Nick juggled in her absence? How could they be a couple with this constant battle between time, careers, and values? Kate loved him fiercely, but she was no closer to fully sharing his faith in God, or even understanding it. Maybe time with Nick would give her clarity. She hoped so, but meanwhile the *Clarion* needed attention.

Breaking away from him, she scooted to a desk with a monitor. "So fill me in. What's happening with the next issue?"

He leaned his hips against the counter, his expression grim. "It's not good. We're down to twenty pages—maybe sixteen."

"Nick, that's terrible!" The number of ads determined the size of the paper. The smaller the paper, the lower the impact. The downward spiral had to be stopped, or the *Clarion* would go out of business like dozens of other print newspapers. No way could Kate let that happen. Taking a breath, she shifted into business mode. "I know about the Acorn. Who else have we lost?"

When he raked his hand through his shaggy hair, she realized just how hard he'd been working—too hard to even get a haircut. The scruff made him handsome to her, but his voice was rough with fatigue. "I spoke with Wayne at the market ten minutes ago. They're cutting back from the double-truck to a half page."

The market's double-truck ad covered the two center pages of the paper and was the foundation of the *Clarion*'s advertising base. Wayne had run that ad in the very first issue and every paper since. The *Clarion* couldn't lose it and survive. Kate grabbed for the phone. "I'll call him right now. Cutting back in a slump is a knee-jerk reaction. It just leads to a bigger slump. Did you tell them that?"

"Of course I did." He crossed his arms over his chest, his mouth tight and his eyes slightly narrowed.

"This is terrible," she repeated. "I can't believe it. We could go out of business—"

"Yeah, I know." His voice pitched upward and came out in a near shout. "I'm doing everything I can, Kate. *Everything.*"

"I know you are." Guilt gnawed at her. Advertising was her wheelhouse and she'd left him to cope alone. Nick was a great writer, but he didn't know this side of the business at all. "I have no right to criticize. It's just—" Before she could admit to how scared she was, her phone rang. She snatched it out of her purse, saw the caller ID, and groaned. "It's Eve. I have to take it."

Nostrils flaring, he held up one hand as if ushering Eve into the room. "Sure. Go right ahead. Talk to her as long as you need."

"I'll make it quick. I promise." In spite of her taut nerves, she greeted Eve with her usual good cheer, then listened to a rambling question about the gala to celebrate the new ad campaign, an event scheduled for April eighth. Eve was worried about the catering. Kate assured her that she'd handle it. "Anything else?"

"The magazine article," Eve reminded her. "What did Nick say?"

Kate's gaze flicked guiltily to his face. "I haven't addressed it yet."

"But you will—"

"Of course." She hated being trapped between the two of them, especially with Nick watching her so closely. Facing him, she rolled her eyes to convey her frustration with Eve, then escaped into the conference room where she huddled in a corner, her back to the room as she spoke to Eve in a whisper. "I'll ask him. I promise. But not now—"

"But, darling. I need to know."

"I just walked through the door. He's—Oh." To Kate's chagrin, Nick gripped her shoulder and turned her, forcing her to look him in the eye.

Before she could say a word, he lifted the phone right out of her hand. "Hello, Eve. This is Nick. What's the problem?"

What would he think of her whispering behind his back? She loved him, but she also wanted to please Eve. Pulled in two, she listened to his side of the conversation.

"It's all arranged," he told Eve while staring hard at Kate. "I was going to tell her today. I'll be there next Friday with a photographer." He traded a few more remarks with Eve, then gave Kate the phone and walked out of the conference room without a word to put her at ease.

Nick went straight to the lobby window where he could stare at the puffy clouds while he choked back his anger. Eve's bossy tone had rankled him, but Kate's criticism for the breakdown at the *Clarion* irked him far more.

Newspapers were a little bit like condors facing extinction. They needed care and attention to survive. Nick had worked his fingers off to keep the paper going. He would have appreciated a little gratitude. He'd also received book rejection number seventeen this morning and could have used a little TLC. Instead, here he was, a has-been hack writer committed to buying a dying newspaper, and in love with a bossy woman making big money working for a whack-job Hollywood legend.

He needed to work on his attitude.

Kate stepped out of the conference room looking chagrined. "Eve's been pressuring me about the article, but I didn't want to ask you—not when you're already doing so much."

"Forget it." He could deal with Eve. It was Kate's priorities that irked him.

She plopped down at the computer. "Thanks for handling her."

"She's a pain."

"Sometimes."

Always. But that was Nick's opinion. He'd barely resisted the urge to hang up on her. Only his feelings for Kate and God's grace had kept him in control. "Don't thank me, Kate. I did it for you."

Everything was for her. They were a month into the trial period, and Nick didn't know what to think. He and Kate spoke every night, but neither of them brought up the future. He prayed for guidance, but God only whispered to keep waiting. Nick was so sick of waiting he could hardly think straight. On top of everything else, the *Clarion* was foundering like an old Spanish galleon taking on water.

But Kate was flourishing. He wanted to be happy for her, but it hurt to see her acting and sounding like Eve. *Be patient,* he told himself. This was a trial period—not forever. Surely they'd find a way to be a couple. Taking a breath, he deliberately turned off the criticism and focused on the problem at hand. "We need to talk, but right now the paper's in trouble. Let's put that fire out first. Like I said, I'm doing everything I can—"

"I know." She wrinkled her nose in that guilty way of hers, then hurried to a monitor. "Let me see what I can do over the next couple of days."

He hoped she could work wonders. He loved the *Clarion* and still wanted to own it, but the business had to be viable. "You were about to call Wayne."

"Yes."

"Do it. Maybe he'll change his mind."

With Nick listening, she called Wayne and offered him a six-month special. When the grocer agreed to it, Nick breathed a little easier and went in the back office to work on neglected news stories. Friday night passed in a blur and so did Saturday, with Kate redesigning his clumsy ads, cutting deals, and talking to people like the professional she was.

By Sunday afternoon, the *Clarion* was back up to twenty-four pages. It was too late for a motorcycle ride, so they grilled steaks at his place and watched a sunset that reminded him of the one he'd seen on Mount Abel almost a year ago. A couple of times he opened his mouth to ask her if she thought she'd stay at Eve's Garden permanently, but both times his tongue stuck to the roof of his mouth.

He and Kate kissed good-night, and she returned to Los Angeles on Monday. With the *Clarion* in good shape, Nick spent some time doing prep work for Eve's *California Dreaming* article. Early in the afternoon, he e-mailed his editor with a question. An hour later he checked for a response. Instead of hearing from the editor, he saw replies from the final three agents on his list.

He sucked in a lungful of air, held it, and blew it out as slowly as he could. This was it. The moment that would determine the future of his book, his whole career. He took another deep breath and skimmed the first e-mail. *Not right for me.*

The second one. *Sorry, I have to pass.*

The third one. *Dear Author.*

A form letter, the lowest possible kind of rejection. Shoving away from the desk, he gaped at the computer screen. He was a has-been for sure, a hack. He'd been so sure of the call to tell his story. Now what? Another ten agents? He didn't know, and his head was pounding with defeat, stinging pride, and bitter disappointment.

He couldn't think in the office with Eileen on the phone and Heather, the intern, bopping around to country music. He considered calling Kate because he needed her, but the prospect of her voice mail stung worse than a *Dear Author* rejection. He needed light and air, the freedom of the open road, so he called Colton. "How about a driving lesson?"

"Cool."

"I'll be there in five minutes." Nick picked him up in front of the apartment building but didn't get out of the driver's seat. "Me first today. You can drive back."

Colton shrugged his thin shoulders. "Whatever."

Still stinging with defeat, Nick headed past Mount Abel and toward the condor launch site, taking the curves with ease, saying nothing, barely listening as Colton yammered about a video game. When Nick grunted for the sixth time, Colton frowned. "You're in a bad mood, aren't you?"

"Yeah."

"Are you mad at your girlfriend?"

Yes, but you're fifteen and it's none of your business. The book, though, was another matter. He told Colton about the twenty rejections. "I don't know what to do next. I believe in the story, but it's just not selling."

"What's it about?"

"Christianity . . . choices. The way God changed my life."

"Oh."

Nick glanced across the truck. "Is that, 'Oh, that sounds interesting,' or 'Oh, who cares'?"

Colton gave him a superior look, one full of the impatience of a know-it-all kid. "It sounds boring. Can I drive now?"

"Not yet." *Out of the mouths of babes.* "So what's boring about it?"

"Everything." Colton tossed off another shrug. "You've done some cool stuff, but who cares about your life?"

God cares. But God already knew Nick's story. God had written it just for Nick. He was fearfully and wonderfully made, knit together in his mother's womb, born to love God, Kate, and others. The book had helped him to understand just how much God loved him. How many times had he said if the book helped just one person it was worth the effort? If it helped just one lonely man cruising through life, one idiot who'd messed up and hurt others, one hack writer who loved a woman who didn't know how to love him back?

A simple truth hit Nick between the eyes. *He* was the one person who needed the story. His memoir didn't need to be published to fulfill its purpose. It had already helped that one person—himself.

Dragging in a lungful of air, he felt the weight of the book lift from his shoulders and float away. The manuscript would always be special to him, like a diary or personal journal, but he was finished with trying to sell it. Smiling a little, he pulled into a turnout and stopped the truck. "Thanks," he said to Colton.

"For what?"

"Being honest."

"Whatever." Colton was clearly bored by talking about the boring book. "If you want to write something good, write about the end of the world. That stuff is crazy."

Apocalyptic fiction didn't interest Nick, but maybe someday he'd write a novel, a story about condors, falling in love, and finding faith.

He punched Colton's arm with his knuckles. "Your turn to drive."

They switched places and Nick offered instructions for the way home. "Here's what you need to know about mountain roads." *And life.* But he didn't say that. Colton had to figure it out for himself. "Keep your eye on the road, but don't be afraid. Brake going into a turn, but accelerate coming out of it."

Colton used the turn signal, checked for approaching cars, and pulled onto the highway. He was tentative at first, but Nick coached him until he found his groove. The miles sailed by with Nick in the passenger seat. It was a good place to be, he realized, as long as a person trusted the One doing the driving.

27

Leona glanced at the three women seated at the square table in the Golden West Retirement dining room. It was early April, and this would be one of her last meals with the friends she'd made here. Kate didn't completely approve, but Leona was going home to Meadows in a week. Her broken ribs were forgotten now, and she could breathe without coughing. Thanks to physical therapy, she could roll her shoulder and raise her arm over her head. Even the stroke symptoms were improved. She still slurred her words, but the doctor gave her the okay for daylight driving, in Meadows only.

"I'm beginning to think sheventy really is the new fifty," she said to the women at the table.

"That's because it is." Viola was a hundred and two, the oldest of the residents and a retired teacher. "Just look at you—you're a teenager compared to me."

"Me, too," Eleanor chimed in. She was eighty-nine.

"And me!" said Hattie, a sprightly eighty-five.

Viola glanced around the table, her expression both amused and conspiratorial. "I can't speak for the rest of you, but frankly, I've had enough of this crazy world. Just because we can keep a body alive doesn't mean we should."

Eleanor touched the brim of the purple hat hiding her bald head. "I'll take heaven over another round of chemo, that's for sure."

Hattie nodded gravely. "I'm forgetting more and more. The Alzheimer's—" She choked up.

Leona took Hattie's hand and squeezed. Eleanor patted her shoulder. It was a solemn moment, one typical of the camaraderie at GWR, where oldsters understood one another and cared. Silence settled over the four of them until Viola harrumphed. "Cheer up, ladies! There's no reason to mope. We all know what GWR really stands for."

Hattie and Eleanor laughed in a watery way, but Leona didn't understand. "Tell me."

Viola's eyes twinkled. "GWR stands for God's Waiting Room. We're a breath away from heaven. How wonderful is that?"

"It's glorious," Leona agreed, but she wasn't ready for eternity. She fit in here, but she had a lot of good years left. She also had to finish the condor journal for Kate, something she'd delayed because the words had refused to come to her. Content to let God determine the timing, she'd set the notebook aside. But now she felt the call in her bones to write the last entry.

When the meal ended, she retreated to her apartment and opened the journal for the last time. It would be her gift to Kate when they returned to Meadows. Pen in hand, she began to write.

Dear Kate,
   I'm about to describe the most painful time of my life—a time when I believed God had abandoned me.

The Bible says in Job that He gives and takes away, but how does a mother accept the death of her child—a child she didn't expect to have, a child so precious she thanked God every single day for the miracle of his birth?

You know the details of your father's accident—the oil tanker that jackknifed, the cars that piled into it, the explosion. I saw the report on television and instantly worried. I knew Peter's commute, the timing. When your mother called, panicked because he hadn't come home, in my heart I knew he was gone.

Alex coped by working too hard. I coped by loving you and planting a ridiculous number of flowers. Do you remember the pansies? I do. I also remember the roses and the thorns. How could God take my son? Yes, I understood the parallel. God had sacrificed His son for all humanity. But where was the good in Peter's death? I still don't see it, but I can accept that God's ways are higher than mine. When I get to heaven, I'll understand the reason why, or I simply won't need to ask. That wasn't the case in the months after the accident. Sadness and rage hardened into a knot of bitterness much like the one that grew when I thought I'd never have a child.

The next six months passed in a fog. Your mother started a new job with long hours, so you stayed with Grandpa Alex and me for the summer. When your grandfather suggested a family vacation, I said yes. We spent two days at Disneyland, another at Knott's Berry Farm, then drove to San Diego and visited the zoo. When Grandpa Alex roared like the lion, you fed him crackers. He hugged you hard and looked right at me. I could hear his thoughts. "Peter's here, Lee. He's alive in this child."

Instead of sharing that glimmer of faith, I felt the death of my son all over again. Grief is like that, Kate. It hides like a snake in the grass, striking at the most unexpected times. I usually coped with the pain by sobbing, but that day my eyes stayed dry. I wanted to go home that very moment, but your grandfather said no. He had a surprise for us.

The next day we drove north. About an hour outside of San Diego, Alex grinned. "How would you ladies like to see real wild animals?"

"Where?" you asked.

"Just a few miles up the road."

I had no idea what he had in mind.

You tapped his shoulder from the backseat. "Can we see monkeys?"

"Maybe, but they have something even better."

"What? Tell me, Grandpa."

He kept you guessing for two miles, then he looked at me. "I bet Nonnie knows."

I played along. "Dinosaurs?"

"No, but you're close. We're going to see condors."

Your grandfather explained everything. There were no birds in the wild at that time, but the recovery program was moving forward at the San Diego Wild Animal Park. Birds that once flew free over Meadows now lived in "condor-miniums," free-flight enclosures that gave them room to fly but not soar. As we approached the site, I saw real excitement in my husband's eyes. The man in charge of the program took us to a viewing area. While he talked to Alex, I peered into the flight pen and saw a condor perched on a rock, staring at the sky through the netting. I asked about her.

"That's Aqiwo," the biologist said. "Her name means

Path *in Chumash. She's one of the last birds we took out of the wild."*

"She looks sad."

"She hasn't adjusted well, but we hope that changes," he explained. *"We need every bird we can save."*

"For genetic diversity?" Alex asked.

"Exactly."

As the men talked, I stared at Aqiwo. Her eyes, shiny and black, blinked with the longing for things she couldn't have. I knew how she felt. Trapped. Alone. Cut off. Yet she had a profound purpose. Using the latest techniques, scientists would use her DNA to revive a species. She'd be a mother and never know it. Where she saw tragedy, her human captors saw a purpose.

With a great beat of her wings, Aqiwo took flight and soared straight at us until she landed on a stump just ten feet away from me. Her eyes locked with mine, and I saw her broken heart. In that moment, my bitterness dissolved. If the scientists could use this bird for great purposes, surely God had plans for me . . . plans for a future and a hope.

That happened many years ago, and I can truthfully say I've been blessed. I had a wonderful marriage to a good man. For twenty-seven years I had the best son a mother could have. Now I have you, Kate. With so few birds left at that time, the condor you saw in the canyon could easily be one of Aqiwo's descendants.

So what is the point? Simply this. The Bible says, "For now we see through a glass, darkly . . ." We don't always understand what happens to us or why, but if we could see through the lens of eternity, we'd weep with joy. Faith is what allows us to believe in the beauty behind that dark glass. It's a gift from God, not something we can conjure or create. It's a gift we choose to accept, much like a child opening a box on Christmas morning. I pray you will receive that gift and live your life to the fullest as God intended—with hope, faith, and the courage to love.

Six months ago Kate had arrived in Meadows on a day much like this one. The same sky shimmered above her, though today it was vivid blue instead of cloudy gray. The giant oak tree hadn't changed, and Mount Abel still rose majestically above the other mountains. The only difference between that October afternoon and this April morning was the vivid green of the trees and grass, and the three hundred daffodils in Leona's driveway. Winter had served its purpose.

Seated on the deck, she ran her hand over the cover of the journal in her lap. She had read it last night and didn't know what to think. The facts of the story were familiar, but Leona's anguish was a new twist. On one hand Kate found the story inspiring; on the other, it scared her to death. Until now, she had viewed her grandmother's faith as just another part of her personality, the way Kate's career was part of hers. The journal showed Leona's faith in a new light: It wasn't just a piece of her life. God seemed to have real power. Mentally Kate traveled back to her own first glimpse of Wistoyo and the prayer she whispered to Leona's God. *Are you real? Because if you are, I need help.*

Kate still needed help. But how did a person trust a God she couldn't see or hear? What-ifs plagued her. What if she left her career, went broke, and never worked again? What if she married Nick and they fell apart? Kate despised uncertainty. She preferred being in control, something Eve understood and indulged.

Kate felt confident and safe at Eve's Garden, but deep down, she hadn't changed at all. She was still afraid of mountain roads, making mistakes, being late, and losing Nick. The *Clarion* had recovered financially, and Nick had graciously written the article for *California Dreaming*, but Kate felt separate from him. Their plans for tonight's gala were typical. The event was a black-tie preview of the new advertising campaign for EG Enterprises, and Kate was responsible for overseeing it. She would have enjoyed driving back to Los Angeles with Nick, but they were going separately because she needed her own car in case Eve asked her to run a last-minute errand.

"Good morning!" Leona called from the sliding glass door. "Want some company?"

"Sure." Kate patted the chair next to her.

Leona plopped down and they inhaled in unison. The piney air was thin today, and the earth smelled new. Kate loved moments like this, when nature demanded to be noticed and pulled her into a higher state of mind. She wanted to rejoice, cry, shout, and weep all at once, just like Leona had done in the different seasons of her life. "The journal was amazing. I felt every word of it."

"I'm glad."

Kate raised her heels to the edge of the chair and hugged herself. "There's something I don't understand."

"What's that?"

"I can see God working in your life, but I don't see Him in the details of mine. I try my best, but it never seems to be enough. I love my job, but Eve can be overwhelming. I started working forty hours a week. Now it's sixty and I still can't keep up. Nick is running the *Clarion* without me, and I feel guilty."

She turned to look Leona in the eye. "I feel guilty about

you, too. I hope Dody moves in, because I don't like you living alone. What if you fall again? What if—"

"Kate?"

"What?"

"Honey, stop." Leona reached for her hand. "Even if you're here, I could have another fall or even a stroke. You can't control everything that happens."

Leona's claim fanned embers that had burned in Kate for a long time, maybe her entire life—certainly from the day her father died. The morning of the accident, he had driven her to school like always, except she forgot her lunch and had to run back to the house to get it. When they arrived at the school, she was slow to get out of the car and he'd been stern with her. If she'd been more obedient that morning, he wouldn't have been on the freeway when the oil tanker jackknifed.

She knew such thinking was grandiose. There was no real connection between her childish behavior and the accident, but there were things she *could* control—like driving the speed limit and being on time, working hard, and not expecting too much from other people. She did those things and more. So why did she feel like her life was unraveling? She made good, smart choices. She didn't expect to avoid trouble completely, but surely she could limit the intensity and number of random accidents.

"I know I'm not God," she said firmly. "But there are things I *can* control."

"True."

"Just not everything."

Leona chuckled softly. "Sometimes I think God lets us handle the small things just like we let children choose between chocolate and vanilla ice cream. But the big stuff is all His. Children are born or not. Couples split up. Careers start

303

and end. We become old and ill; we fall and get hurt. And, sadly, people die. The list goes on and on. And no matter how hard we try, we can't control any of it."

"But we control some of it," Kate argued. "For instance, healthy living reduces the risk of heart disease."

"I suppose," Leona said. "But when all is said and done, the biggest pieces of this life are beyond our understanding. In the end, we're left with a choice. We can think life is a string of random events, or we can believe God has a plan for our lives. That's the lesson of the journal."

"I can see it in your life but not in mine. You talk about trusting God, but what does faith *look* like?"

"It looks like this—" Leona swept her arm to indicate the sky and the trees, Mount Abel, and the grass on the hill. "Faith is what allows us to see the daffodil in an ugly seed, the chick in an egg. We don't understand how God works, but if we look, we see His handiwork everywhere—even in the mirror. Experience changes us, whether we want it to or not."

Kate had to agree. She wasn't the same woman who'd swerved to avoid Condor Number 53. Even that condor had a story to tell. She now had a name—Wistoyo—and she had battled lead poisoning and spent months recovering at the zoo. Kate knew from Nick that Wistoyo was at the launch site and almost ready to return to the wild.

Leona laid a gnarled hand over the journal. "You have a choice to make about working for Eve Landon."

"I do." With her shoulders straight, Kate watched a squirrel eating a nut. "I love the work, but it's hard to juggle the job with a personal life."

"How does Nick feel about it?"

"He seems okay." *But only on the outside.* Kate thought about the phone calls when she had babbled about skin cream, then asked Nick about his day. She was sorry his book didn't sell, but he assured her he was at peace with it. They talked a lot about the *Clarion*, but he didn't say much about Eve's Garden. The few times she had pushed for his opinion, he always said the same thing. *"What I think doesn't matter right now. You need to decide for yourself if the job's a good fit."* He still encouraged her, but something was amiss.

A soft hum indicated Leona's concern. "It's hard to build a relationship when you're going in different directions."

"Yes, but it can be done." Kate was on firmer ground now. "Eve's very supportive of her employees when it comes to family."

"That's a plus."

"Definitely," Kate agreed. "Working for her is a dream come true, but I worry about fitting the pieces together."

"Which ones?"

"I'm asking a lot of Nick, and Eve can be demanding. She's used to getting what she wants. I want to do more for the *Clarion*, but Eve always has an idea that can't wait. Twice I've canceled plans with Nick at the last minute."

"That's not fair to him."

"No, it isn't." Kate had apologized profusely, and he'd been understanding, but she'd heard a new distance in his voice. "He won't say it, but I wonder if Eve's whole philosophy bothers him. She talks all the time about personal power. She says it's up to each of us to make our own happiness. I don't know what to think. Sometimes Eve is the most generous person I've ever met, and other times she's just plain selfish."

Leona flicked a stray leaf off her lap. "It's complicated, isn't it? You have to balance what you believe with what Eve believes, and you and Nick need to agree on how to be a couple."

"That says it."

"Do you have any idea at all about what he thinks?"

"I just know he's been too quiet." Kate's stomach did a nervous little flip. "We've both been working long hours, but things should settle down after tonight." She glanced at the sun. Instead of enjoying the warmth, she grimaced at the tick of her mental clock. "I better go. I have a lot to do before the party."

Leona looked up as Kate stood. "I know you're planning to drive yourself, but maybe you should call Nick. Drive down together."

"I'd like that, but I can't." Tonight her job came first. "We're planning to spend tomorrow together." It was April ninth, the official end of his sabbatical, and she wanted to celebrate with him.

Leona didn't say a thing, but disappointment was evident in her slight frown. "Have a good time, honey. I'll be thinking of you both."

28

the gala was in full swing
when Nick strode through the Eve's Garden lobby and headed
to the ballroom. He maneuvered past clusters of men in tuxes
and women in long gowns, scanning the sea of faces for Kate,
the only person he truly wanted to see.

Tiny lights twinkled in every nook and cranny, and a jungle
of jasmine, jonquils, and plumeria turned the ballroom into
a scene out of *Tropical Moon*, one of Eve's most famous
movies. Tonight's gala was in honor of the expansion of EG
Enterprises, and posters of the coming ad campaign adorned
the walls. The air pulsed with music from a Caribbean steel
drum band, snippets of conversation, and the plink of glasses.

Nick knew this world well. People were elegantly dressed
and dripping with money, but they weren't any different from
the people he met writing *CFRM*, or the men who hung
out at the Black Dog Lounge on I-5. Or, for that matter, the
smiling families at Sam's church. People were just people—including Eve Landon. When he interviewed her for *California
Dreaming*, she'd been surprisingly down-to-earth. On the
other hand, he couldn't agree with her personal philosophy

of self-fulfillment. *"At Eve's Garden, we help women to love themselves and rejoice in their self-ness."*

Nick admired her spirit but not her beliefs. He'd done his share of reveling in his self-ness, and the result had been disastrous. He and Kate needed to talk—really talk—about the future. Was she at Eve's Garden because she believed God wanted her here, or was she here for the security of being the old Kate?

Nick didn't know, but he was certain of his decision to stay in the background while Kate searched for answers. He planned to stay in the background tonight, as well, at least until the party ended. After that, he wanted her to himself.

The crowd shifted and he spotted Kate across the room. Dressed in a champagne-colored gown with her shoulders bare and her hair up, she was stunningly beautiful. Knocked off his feet, he admired everything about her as he maneuvered through the crowd.

Kate didn't see him approach. She had her back to him and her eyes on an ice sculpture of the *Venus de Milo*, an ancient Greek statue that paid tribute to female beauty in the form of an armless woman. When he was a foot away, Kate turned. Her eyes widened at the sight of him, and her smile lit up the room. In a blink they were embracing.

"I've missed you," he whispered in her ear.

"I've missed you, too."

He stole a kiss, then stepped back and skimmed his eyes over the dress a second time. In his mind it shimmered to wedding white, and he imagined proposing to her. Tomorrow was April ninth, the official end of his social sabbatical and ban on big decisions, but he didn't want to propose just yet. Until they were agreed on Kate's career and the future, a little more patience was in order. Even so, they planned to spend tomorrow together, and he wanted to take her to the top of Mount Abel.

"You look amazing," he said to her.

She grinned. "So do you."

The tuxedo was new, a purchase to please Kate. If she stayed with Eve's Garden, he'd be wearing it again. Judging by the festive lights and the happy mood of the crowd, tonight's gala was a feather in her cap.

"How's it going?" he asked, glancing around.

"Eve's pleased." Kate blew out an exaggerated breath. "The caterers did a great job with the Caribbean food. The musicians were only a little late, and no one's tripped or had a heart attack. I think I can relax."

"Good. Maybe we can leave early."

She reached for his hand and squeezed. "I'd like that. You and I haven't had two minutes alone in weeks. After tonight, I want that to change."

"So do I."

They toured the room together, starting with a hello to Roscoe and his wife. Brad and his date joined them, and they chatted and joked until Kate guided him to another cluster of people who were friends of Eve. Kate performed the introductions, adding tags like "So-and-So was in such-and-such a movie." For him, she said, "This is Nick Sheridan, a good friend of mine." *Hint, ladies. He's taken.* Then she'd say, "Nick wrote *California for Real Men.*"

He wasn't proud of the book, but it no longer embarrassed him. Everyone had a past, and *CFRM* started conversations with the man he was now. Two years ago he couldn't have known that tonight he'd be in a room full of men and women deeply rooted in the lifestyle he'd left. He understood the people in this place; he loved them, hurt for them—everyone from the man who'd had too much to drink to the no-longer-young woman in a barely-there dress.

The more he and Kate mingled, the more Nick wondered

if God was nudging him to leave Meadows and return to L.A. He loved the little mountain town, but he had to be open to change just as Kate had to be open to leaving Los Angeles.

"Kate!"

They turned and he saw Eve. Dressed in a sleek black gown and pearl choker, she radiated Hollywood glamour. Nick would have admired her elegance, but her eyes shifted to Kate and narrowed in a possessive gleam. Bracing for a kidnap attempt, he murmured into Kate's ear, "I know you're working tonight, but I'd like you to myself for a while."

"Same here," she answered.

Eve air-kissed them both, then grasped Kate's hands. "I'm so glad I found you. I was beginning to think you two had run off together."

Only in Nick's dreams.

Kate's mouth pulled into a fixed smile. "We've been making the rounds."

"Good." Eve squeezed Kate's hands again, then let go. "There's someone I want you to meet. Go freshen your lipstick while I entertain Nick."

"Who am I meeting?"

"A new investor. Go on, darling. Nick and I will be right here."

Kate paused, then shrugged in a way that jiggled the little purse hanging from her shoulder. "I'll be back in a minute."

The lipstick order irked him. It seemed inordinately bossy, even for Eve, and he suspected it was a sign of things to come both tonight and for Kate in general. He'd gladly support Kate and her choices, but playing tug o' war with Eve turned Kate into a prize instead of a person.

When she was out of earshot, Eve turned to him with a smile as hard and gleaming as the pearls around her neck.

"I sent Kate to the powder room because I wanted a word with you. I love her to pieces, and I'm afraid I've taken up too much of her time. After tonight, I'm going to *insist* she stop working weekends."

The offer seemed caring, but Nick didn't trust Eve. "I'm sure Kate will enjoy the extra time."

"And you too, I hope."

"Of course."

"She's brilliant at her job," Eve said, giving a little shiver. "I'm sorry to interfere with your evening, but sometimes business comes before pleasure. If she's going to be the new vice president of EG Enterprises—"

"Vice president?" His brows snapped together.

"Oops!" Eve clapped her manicured fingers over her mouth. then flipped back her hand. "I let the cat out of the bag, didn't I?"

Questions battered Nick's brain. Eve's original offer called for a three-month trial as director of marketing. Had Kate decided to work for Eve permanently without talking to him about it? A vice presidency would launch her into the stratosphere of corporate success, maybe mark her as Eve's successor. Nick wanted Kate to live her life to the fullest, and he encouraged her to do so, but he'd never dreamed she wouldn't talk to him about the final decision. It was just plain disrespectful, especially when he'd worked so hard to support her career.

Eve's urgent murmur cut into this thoughts. "Kate doesn't know what I'm planning. Please don't say anything."

Relief washed through him, but a bad taste lingered. "So she hasn't decided to take the job permanently."

"Not yet. I was going to make the offer next week. I hope you can keep a secret better than I can!"

Nick deplored secrets—unless they involved engagement

rings or birthday parties. "That's a problem—not because I can't keep a secret, but because I won't. I don't want any deception with Kate, even for a few days."

Eve straightened her spine, putting them almost eye to eye because of her high heels. "In that case, I'll make the offer tonight. You're a good man, Nick. But you can't give her what I can."

"And what's that?"

Eve swept her arm to indicate the ballroom overflowing with important people and expensive things. "I can give her . . . everything."

"No. You can't." Nick balked at Eve's arrogance, but before he could say more, a flutter of champagne silk caught his eye. Kate met his gaze and smiled. Nick nodded, then turned back to Eve. "I want some time alone with Kate."

She laid her hand on his arm, the bloodred polish of her nails glistening in the glow of a chandelier. "You won't win, Nick. When I want something, I fight for it."

"So do I," he said evenly.

Eve slipped into the crowd, disappearing in the sea of made-up faces and glittering gowns. Nick strode toward Kate, grasped her elbow, and steered her out a glass door that led to a garden. Green floodlights tossed shadows in the junipers and ivy, and the air smelled of loamy earth. A trickling fountain made the only sound, a startling shift from the noisy party. The night air held a chill, so Nick draped his jacket over Kate's bare shoulders.

"What's going on?" she asked. "Eve wanted me to meet someone."

"That's right." Nick put steel in his voice. "But before she introduces you to Mr. Investor, I have to ask you a question."

∽∾

Kate pulled Nick's jacket tight around her shoulders. If the lingering body heat was an indication, he was smoldering inside. A hard-edged scowl had replaced his relaxed smile, and his eyes were shooting daggers. She felt a little like the woman in a knife-throwing game, pinned to a wall while her trusted partner hurled knives that would hit close to home but not wound her.

Whatever Eve had said, it wasn't the blessing on their relationship Kate had imagined when she went to the powder room—an obvious ploy so Eve could have a word with Nick. Eve liked to run the show. So did Kate, so she didn't mind. For that matter, so did Nick, and he'd just wrestled her away from Eve and the gala on a night when she needed to be in charge. Instead of keeping an eye on the waiters, musicians, and especially Eve, she was standing in a dark garden waiting for a knife to slice off her ear.

"Could this wait?" she asked.

"No."

"But, Nick, I have responsibilities." She indicated the glass wall of the ballroom. Eve stood on the other side, chatting with the man who was probably the investor. "I can't just disappear."

"Eve knows where you are."

"I should be with her. I should—"

"Kate, stop."

"But—"

"*Stop!*"

It wasn't like Nick to bark orders, and he'd picked a bad time to start. She had a good mind to march back inside, but his tone alarmed her. When Nick wanted something, he fought for it with all his might. A Shetland pony couldn't outpull a Clydesdale, so she gave up and tossed her purse on a stone bench.

"All right," she said, clutching the coat to ward off a chill. "What do you want to ask?"

He indicated the ballroom with his hand, palm up, like an emcee awarding a prize. "Why are you here?"

"At the party? It's my job—"

"Not the party. Why are you working for Eve Landon?"

Urgency tightened his vocal cords. The rasp reminded Kate of herself when she first learned of Leona's stroke. She'd been worried, afraid, and angry at circumstances she couldn't control. If Nick felt that way, she sympathized. On the other hand, she wasn't having a stroke and this conversation needed to be quick.

"I'm here because I like it. It's who I am, what I do." She paused, searching his face. "What did Eve say to you?"

"Enough to make me worry."

"About what?"

"This—" He flung his arm at the ballroom again. "I want you to be sure you're working for Eve for the right reasons."

Kate gaped at him. "And *you* know what those are?"

"I know what they're not."

"So do I." She wasn't here for money, prestige, or power. She liked her job and was happy doing it. Her career was the one area of her life where she maintained a modicum of control. "What are you accusing me of?"

"I'm not accusing you of anything."

"Then what—"

"I'm worried about you!"

She didn't understand at all. She and Nick had some schedule issues, but those could be resolved with a little compromise. She knew she'd asked a lot from him, but the sudden pressure seemed unreasonable. If he could hurl questions, so could she.

"Why are you so worked up about this? I know we haven't

had much time together, but that'll change now that the party's over. I promise."

A skeptical look crossed his face. "You can't make that promise. You don't know what Eve will ask next."

"Neither do you."

"I know this kind of life." His voice sped up. "I lived in a world just like this place. I know what happens. People go further than they ever intended. They take more, do more, need more. It's like an addiction."

Kate finally understood. Nick hated his past and wanted to protect her, but he was imposing himself on her life, pulling her away from something she loved. Well intentioned or not, she resented his interference. "You don't want me to work for Eve, do you?"

"I didn't say that."

"But that's where this is going. You think Eve's Garden is worldly. That it's wrong to emphasize beauty—"

He jammed his hands in his pants pockets. One knee jutted forward and he scowled. "You've got to be kidding."

"Well, I'm not."

Air hissed out of his nose. "Trust me, Kate. Men are visual creatures. We enjoy looking at beautiful women." He hammered his chest with his index finger. "*I* enjoy looking at beautiful women—especially you. Eve's doing men a favor. You can sell skin cream all day long, and I'll be proud of you. But you have to know *why* you're selling it. Is it because you believe in the product, or just need a job? Or do you think God put you at Eve's Garden for a purpose?"

None of those reasons resonated.

Not a one.

So why was she here—quarreling with Nick and close to tears, angry enough to scream, and hurting as if she'd been stabbed or hit by a knife hurled by a trusted partner?

Moonlight fell from the sky, casting shadows among the trees and turning Nick into a demanding stranger.

"It's not *what* you do," he insisted. "It's why. We'd have the same conversation if you wanted to go to medical school or deliver Bibles to lost tribes in the Amazon. It comes down to just one question—"

"Maybe for you!" She hated his smugness. Right now, she hated him. "I have *a lot* of questions."

"I know."

"Oh no, you don't!" How could he? He was always so sure of himself, so confident that he'd land on his feet. Trembling, she marched up to him and went toe to toe, their faces inches apart. "I don't have all the answers like you do. *I'm scared all the time.*"

He gripped her upper arms inside the tux coat. "I'm asking just one question. Is your faith in God or is it in Eve Landon?"

"It's—It's—" *Neither.* Her faith was in herself and her own abilities—in things she could see, hear, feel, and taste. Suddenly she was back on Leona's deck looking at Mount Abel, feeling the pulse of nature and full of hope and doubt and everything in between. It seemed that she could have the security of Eve's Garden and be in control, or she could have Nick, a man who forced her to travel unfamiliar roads. Those roads terrified her, because they were full of cliffs, blind curves, and obstacles like condors eating roadkill. She felt emotionally raw, laid bare, hollow, and stripped to an infant-like neediness. What was wrong with wanting to be safe and secure?

Tightening his grip, he lifted her ever so slightly. "If you believe with your whole heart that God wants you here, then take the job. *Fight for it.* But if God isn't in it, get out now. This place is an accident waiting to happen."

"So you won't support me if I stay?"

"I'll love you forever." Crushing her against his chest, he pressed her head tight against the collar of his shirt. "Nothing can change how I feel about you. *Nothing.* I'd take a bullet for you, walk on hot coals. I'll watch chick flicks and hold your purse at the mall. When babies come, I'll rub your feet, and when we're old and gray, I'll love you even more than I do now. But I can't stand here and say, 'Do whatever makes you happy,' because *happy* is temporary. I want us to have more, Kate. I want us to have joy."

She clung to him, her fingers knotted in his shirt and her nose inhaling the scent of his skin. She wanted to make the same bold declarations—to say that she'd have his babies and scratch his back, ride the Harley, and not ever nag. But she didn't have the courage to trade the world she understood for one she didn't.

His throat twitched against her temple. For another moment, he held her close. Then his arms relaxed and he stepped back, releasing her completely. "I'm going back to Meadows."

Kate held back tears. "Tonight?"

"Yes."

"But—" *We had plans. Tomorrow is special to you.* Somehow everything had changed. Not only did Kate wonder if she could ever match Nick's faith, she had fresh doubts about blending their lives into one. Even so, she couldn't bear to sever the tie with so much unsaid. "Give me a minute to explain to Eve. I'll go with you."

"No."

His response cut to her heart. "Don't leave," she pleaded. "Not like this. "

"It's necessary." He studied her for several seconds, his expression unreadable. "Eve wants to talk to you about something. You need to hear it."

"What is it?"

"It's her place to explain." He raked his hand through his hair, leaving furrows that didn't close. "We both have some thinking to do. I'm going up to Mount Abel for the weekend. I'll be at the Clarion on Monday."

With the finality of those words, the last knife missed her ear and sliced her heart in two. Fighting tears, she slipped the tuxedo coat off her shoulders and handed it to him. He stared down at the black cloth, then into her eyes. They were inches apart, but the rift between them was a mile wide. Kate craved resolution, but she couldn't sprout wings and fly across the divide. Tonight Nick had fought for her, and she'd pushed him away with both hands. If she couldn't be the woman he wanted, they didn't have a future.

"So," she said in a flinty voice. "This is it. You're leaving."

"Yes, I am." After a final lingering look, he flung his coat over his shoulder and sauntered down the path to the parking lot.

Fighting tears, anger, and a longing so deep it made her physically ill, she watched his every step until he vanished into the dark.

29

nick barely restrained himself
from burning rubber as he drove away from Eve's Garden. He'd been a breath away from pulling Kate into his arms and kissing away the nonsense. There was something to be said for staking a claim—reminding her of the elemental connection between a man and a woman, but then where would they be? She had to come to him of her own volition—fully and freely, not because of passion fueled by anger. Passion in a relationship ebbed and flowed like the tide touching the shore. Love didn't change. It was like the ocean—vast, stormy, deep, and enduring.

Nick wanted love.

And, as he told Kate, he wanted joy.

He feared now he was losing her—not to Eve Landon but to her own fear. For a moment in the garden, he'd remembered Kate trapped in the BMW and too afraid to jump. If Nick hadn't pulled her free, she would have died. In much the same way, he wanted to yank her away from Eve Landon but couldn't. This time Kate had to make the leap for herself.

"Lord, I can't stand it!" His roar reverberated in the cab

of the truck, blasting over the traffic noise and shattering the last of Nick's self-control. "She's in trouble and I can't help her. I'm losing her."

A red light stopped him from punching the gas, but he gave full voice to an obscenity. The foul word masked the searing pain in his chest where Kate had ripped out his heart. He meant what he'd said about loving her no matter what she did for a living, or where she worked; but that same love demanded that he speak the truth as he saw it. No way could he stand back and watch the woman he loved turn into Eve Landon.

But it was her choice—not his. This was between Kate and God. And that meant Nick had to set her free to choose her own path.

"No!" he shouted to God. "I can't do it!"

With rebellion hot on his tongue, he steered onto the 405. Every mile took him further from Kate and the joys he wanted to share—a home, children, a dog with a silly name. "Is that asking too much?" he muttered. "I've done everything right. A solid year of celibacy! A solid year of trusting you to make me a better man. And look where I am."

Furious.

Brokenhearted.

Terrified.

The weight on his shoulders increased with every mile, pressing down like a grindstone turning wheat into dust. Suddenly it was all too much. He was sick to death of *trying* to do the right thing, *trying* to please God, *trying* to live his faith. He was human, for crying out loud! What more did God want from him? It didn't matter anymore, because he was done fighting the good fight. He needed relief, and he knew where to find it. He hadn't gotten drunk in a year, but he sure was in the mood now. He wanted to listen to Nirvana and pound down Jack Daniels until he was drunk—not just drunk but stupid drunk.

With numbness beckoning, he sped toward the Black Dog Lounge. He was coasting down the Meadows off-ramp when his phone rang. He saw Sam's number and ignored it.

Sam called again.

Nick ignored it again but started to worry. It was late. Maybe something was terribly wrong. Maybe one of the kids had cracked his skull open and Sam needed him. Muttering to himself, he stopped at the far edge of the Black Dog parking lot and called his brother. "What's going on?"

"I know it's late," Sam said. "But I figured you'd be awake. If you're not doing anything tomorrow, how'd you like to put in a sprinkler system?"

Nick clenched his teeth so hard they throbbed. He'd been ready to go to the emergency room, maybe donate blood. Instead, Sam was babbling about landscaping. *Grass. A yard. Kids*—the kind of life Nick wanted with Kate and might never have. He couldn't stand the thought of spending tomorrow with his happy brother and his happy wife and happy kids. If Sam needed his help, the sprinkler system would have to wait. Nick pushed a polite "I can't" through his clenched teeth, but his anger leaked out in a tense sigh.

Sam paused. "You're in trouble."

"I'm fine." He'd lied, but so what?

"You don't sound fine."

Hiding from Sam was like playing hide-and-seek when they were kids. Sam knew all of Nick's favorite hiding places. "You're right. I feel like garbage. Eve Landon is about to make Kate vice president of her new corporation. Kate wants it, Sam. Badly. She's confused and God—God's not paying attention."

"You don't know that."

"I know enough."

"No, you don't. You're angry and—"

"You bet I'm angry!" He flung the truck door wide and leapt to the cracked asphalt. "I'm stinkin' furious, and you know what else? I've had it with playing by the rules. I've done everything right—*everything*. And look where it got me. Kate's about to make the biggest mistake of her life, *and I can't stop her.* I've had it, Sam—"

"Slow down—"

"No! I've had it with slowing down. I'm headed to the Black Dog and I'm going to get drunk enough to—"

"It won't help," Sam interrupted. "Remember Calexico?"

Yes, Nick remembered. He'd been a Christian for a month when grief and shame had crashed down on him. Afraid he'd slip into his old ways, he had ridden the Harley for hours, escaping into speed and noise instead of a bottle or female company. That ride ended in Calexico, a border town near Baja, where he checked into a ratty motel and finally called Sam. His brother had told him to read Psalm 139. That night, Nick had memorized it.

Where can I go from Your Spirit?

Or where can I flee from Your presence?

Now Sam was yammering again, this time about patience and hope, but Nick couldn't listen. "I have to go."

"Wait—"

He clicked off the phone, tossed it in the truck, and slammed the door. He couldn't stand his brother's advice right now. With his blood hot in his veins, he strode into a vacant lot full of weeds, cans, and broken bottles. A semi whizzed past, fouling the air with diesel as the brake hammered and the truck slowed. The yellow running lights glowed against the night, and the headlights swept through the dark while the truck navigated the on-ramp, its gears shifting and engine roaring until the red taillights disappeared over a hill.

Silence descended. There was no other traffic on the road, no one at the gas station on the corner. There was nothing except a sky lit by a thousand stars, the stinking asphalt highway, and the mountains silhouetted by the full moon. His breath rasped through his nose, a sign of physical life, though his spirit was gasping for air of a different kind. He couldn't do this—not anymore. He wanted so badly to save Kate from Eve—to be her knight in shining armor.

But he couldn't. He wasn't God.

He could only choose to trust and believe in the God who had graced him on the top of Mount Abel, the God whose name was . . .

King of Kings.

Lord of Lords.

Jesus Christ.

And the great I AM.

With those eternal words booming in his mind, Nick fell to his knees. *Faith*. It all came down to believing that God was who He said He was, and that He could be trusted even when the earthly circumstances seemed grim.

His breathing deepened, and his mind began to clear. In a way, he'd done exactly what he had warned Kate to avoid. Instead of trusting God, he'd been ready to take matters into his own hands and escape at the Black Dog Lounge. Groaning at his own sin, Nick looked again at the black velvet sky, welcomed forgiveness, and released Kate into God's hands. The weight lifted off his shoulders and his entire body relaxed. Breathing deep, he settled back into his own skin, then went to his truck and called his brother.

"Hey," Sam answered. "Are you all right?"

"Yeah. I am now."

"Good, because I was about to hunt you down. You want to talk about it?"

"No. I'm fine."

"Are you sure?"

"Positive." Nick was truly at peace. Surely the God who had saved a wretch like him would fight for a wonderful woman like Kate. "I'm headed up to Mount Abel. The reception's spotty, so don't worry about me."

"Are you sure? Being alone might not be a good idea. Gayle and the boys would love to see you—"

"Liar." Nick grinned. "You just want me to dig ditches for the sprinklers."

"Fine," Sam jabbed back. "Leave me with a mile of sprinkler pipe and no help. But, Nick, I really am worried about you."

"Don't be. I'm good."

"Are you sure, because if you're not—"

"Hey, Sam," Nick replied, laughing now. "Man up. You worry too much." With his brother sputtering at the friendly jab, Nick clicked off the phone and went home to get his camping gear.

30

the instant nick vanished from sight, Kate burst into tears. Afraid of being seen, she fled to a dark corner of the garden, hunched on a bench, and hugged herself against the chill. Rocking gently, she sobbed until her eyes burned. She desperately needed a tissue, so she opened her purse and discovered she'd forgotten the little pack she always carried. How could she not have a tissue? Kate was prepared—always. Except she hadn't been prepared for Nick's question and the pain of watching him leave.

With a fresh sob strangling her, she wiped the tears with her fingers. A tissue—if she had a tissue she could blow her nose and pull herself together. She needed to return to Eve and the ballroom, but she couldn't walk into the crowd with a ravaged face. She'd have to dash for the powder room and hope Eve didn't see her. But as she stood, the door to the ballroom opened. Backing into the shadows, she held her breath.

Footsteps tapped on the sandstone walk, came around a corner, and stopped. Eve stood in silhouette, her black dress even blacker than the night. "Kate? Are you and Nick still out here?"

As desperately as she wanted to hide, Eve was her boss and someone she admired. Pasting on a stiff smile, she stepped into the moonlight. "I'm here. Nick is gone."

Eve saw her puffy eyes, gasped, and pulled her into a hug. "Whatever he said or did, it was wrong. Just plain wrong. The man is an utter a fool, a jerk, a—"

"No! He's not."

"Oh, darling." Eve patted her back as if she were small. Instead of finding comfort, Kate felt smothered. She didn't blame Nick for her misery. He'd been honest. Now she had to be honest with herself and answer the *why* question.

Easing out of Eve's hug, she made another vain attempt to wipe her eyes. "I'm pretty upset. Would you mind if I left early?"

Eve pulled a tissue from the slit pocket in her dress and pressed it into Kate's palm. "Of course, you can leave. But before you go, we need to talk. Did Nick mention my conversation with him?"

"Not directly."

"Good." Eve grasped Kate's elbow and steered her toward the building. "What I have to say will help you understand why he left you in tears. Let's go to my office."

As they passed by the spiky junipers, Kate squeezed the tissue in her palm. Mentally she tried to prepare for what Eve would say, but her mind wandered back to Nick, to the question *why,* and to the fear lurking in her belly. If she answered that question honestly, it could change her entire life.

In the office Eve turned on a lamp, then indicated the sofa, where five months ago they had discussed the ad campaign. Smoothing the designer gown on loan from Eve, Kate lowered herself to the couch.

Eve sat next to her and kicked off her shoes. "It's been a long day, hasn't it?"

"Yes, for me, too."

Sympathy misted Eve's eyes. "Before we move on to business, I want you to know how sorry I am that you and Nick had a fight. All couples quarrel, but Kate darling—you look devastated. Do you want to talk about it?"

She longed to spill her heart, but how did she explain a man like Nick to a woman like Eve? Eve would never understand Nick's choices, and she'd scoff at the notion that joy lasted and happiness didn't. In the end, Kate settled for the obvious. "We don't see eye to eye on some things, particularly my career."

"I was afraid of this." Eve shook her head. "Some men can't handle strong women. I didn't think Nick was the type."

"He's not."

"Then what—"

"He'll support any career choice I make, as long as I know why I'm doing it."

"That's an interesting perspective," Eve remarked. "Personally, I'm less interested in *why* Eve's Garden exists than I am in *what* we accomplish. I find genuine satisfaction in helping women, and I believe you do, too."

Kate nodded, but she felt slightly dishonest. As much as she enjoyed the fun side of the spa, she didn't love it the way Eve did. Eve put her heart and soul into the beauty business. Kate's satisfaction came from the creative side of advertising.

"I'm glad we agree," Eve continued, "because working for me isn't like laying bricks. We empower women by making them feel beautiful inside and out. You have to believe in what we do to be good at it. And Kate, darling, you're amazing."

"No—"

"You're just being modest."

"That's not it." Kate had plenty of pride in her ability. What she lacked was Eve's passion for her cause. "I know

I'm good at my work. I love marketing the way you love the spa. There's something special about combining pictures and words to convey a concept in a new way, or to create a bigger idea."

"Exactly!" Eve clasped her hands in her lap. "Your work fulfills you."

"Yes . . ."

Except the affirmation sounded hollow. Kate's career made her happy, but did it give her joy? *Why did she love it?* Nick's question played through her mind, and so did a bigger question: Where did God fit in her life?

Eve inhaled deeply, her chin high and her eyes closed. When her lids fluttered open, her gaze honed to Kate's face. "We're cut from the same cloth, you and I."

Kate opened her mouth to say thank you, but the words died on her tongue. She didn't want to be cut from the same cloth as Eve. She wanted to be secure in herself, and she wanted to be with Nick. *So why was she here listening to Eve?*

The actress put on an enigmatic smile. "Kate, darling. I have a proposal for you. I don't want an answer tonight. You'll need time to consider what I'm about to say." She paused, waiting for Kate to take her cue.

"I'm listening," she replied uneasily.

"First, I want to say again that you're an amazing young woman. I've been looking for someone like you for years. When you're in my position, people approach you for selfish reasons. They want what I can give, but they lack the capacity to give back. Does that make sense?"

Kate tried to translate. "You've been disappointed."

"Yes." Eve's red lips hardened into a line. "And that's why you've become so special to me. You're dedicated, kind, and I trust you completely. And that, Kate darling, is why I want you to be my successor at EG Enterprises. Officially, you'll be vice president. Unofficially—" She pressed her hand to her chest. "Unofficially you're the daughter I wish I had."

Kate could hardly believe her ears. "I'm stunned."

The obedient child in her melted at the praise, but her heart hammered a warning. Why would Eve make such an extravagant offer? Warm air blasted from a vent, and the table lamp seemed to burn even brighter. Tonight, the actress was her most beautiful self, but Kate had seen her face bare of makeup. Without the patina of self-made beauty, Eve looked a lot like Leona—except Leona didn't need makeup or beauty to be content. Even in the throes of the stroke and broken bones, she'd been at peace. Eve, on the other hand, was on a constant hunt for satisfaction—in her career, being beautiful, and now a make-believe daughter.

Make-believe. Some fantasies were childlike and fun. Fairy tales fell into that camp. But other fantasies weren't so innocent. They whitewashed reality into a kind of lie, a deception.

A deception. A trick or a hoax.

In a moment of startling clarity, Kate understood why Nick's question mattered so much. *Why was she here?* Did she understand what working for Eve really meant, or was she believing a lie? She glanced around the room, where she had spent hours with Eve planning the future of EG Enterprises. Shelves and display cases were filled with pictures of Eve in her glory days, her awards and the trappings of success. If Eve Landon believed in nothing else, she believed in herself.

She was her own god. Or goddess.

If Kate accepted Eve's offer, Eve would pull the strings. No matter how glorious the offer seemed, Kate wouldn't be in control of her own life—not really. She could only choose whom to serve—Eve or God. In a frightening way, Eve was right about one thing: She and Kate were cut from the same cloth. Like Eve, Kate trusted in herself and her own abilities.

Blinking, she recalled the condor journal and the final exhortation to live with hope, faith, and the courage to love. Staying at Eve's Garden required none of those things. Trusting God required them all.

Oh, Lord . . . Tears flooded her eyes. *Forgive me for not trusting you and putting my faith in myself instead. I'm scared, so scared.*

Trust Me now.

The voice was in her head, but she heard it with her heart and knew exactly what she had to do. With her pulse racing, she mustered her courage and met Eve's confident stare. "I'm honored. Truly, I am. It's a generous offer, but I can't work for you anymore."

Eve straightened her spine. "I thought you were happy here."

"I am—I was," she corrected herself. "But I'm here for the wrong reasons. You believe in what you do. You believe in yourself . . ." Kate searched for words. "I'm in a very different place. Somewhere in the past six months, my entire life changed, and I just now realized it."

"Because of Nick." She spat the name.

"He started it," Kate admitted. "But just now God finished it."

Eve arched her brows with cool derision, a look she gave people who displeased her. Instead of being scared or anxious, Kate felt only compassion for a lost, lonely woman who wasn't getting any younger. Maybe someday she'd tell the actress the whole story, but right now she was desperate to find Nick. Standing, she strode to the door and opened it wide, then she turned back to Eve. "Thank you for everything you've done. I'd like to stay in touch, even be friends."

"Oh, good grief!" Eve waved her off. "You're a little fool like the rest of them. Go. Just go. There are a thousand women like you—smarter ones, prettier ones. They're just waiting for an opportunity like this."

Kate inclined her head, smiled graciously, and then bid Eve good-bye. "I wish you all the best."

With the words sweet on her tongue, she hurried down the hall to the room she'd used to dress for the gala.

Fifteen minutes later, clad in jeans and a sweater, she ran to her car, sat behind the wheel, and called Nick.

One ring.

Two rings.

His voice mail kicked on and she groaned. He should have been home by now. She called again and got voice mail for a second time. He was ignoring her, or he'd turned off his phone. Or maybe the signal was weak and he could get a text but not a call. Frantic, she typed *WAIT FOR ME!!!!*

"Please, God," she prayed out loud. "Don't let him go to Mount Abel." If he'd already left, he'd be gone until Monday. Kate couldn't imagine driving the treacherous road herself, even in her new little SUV with its brand-new tires.

Keeping one eye on her phone, she drove as fast as she dared down Sunset Boulevard, through the San Fernando Valley, and up the Santa Clarita grade through the mountains. Nick didn't call or text. All the way to Meadows she prayed he'd be at his house and not on Mount Abel, but when she pulled into his driveway, it was empty and the house was dark. He was gone—unless he'd parked in the garage. With her heart in her throat, she grabbed the flashlight in her glove box and used it to peer through a small window.

No truck.

No sign of Nick.

Only the Harley, chrome shining and waiting to be ridden another day.

Defeated, she stared across the valley to Mount Abel and

thought of all the things she feared. Mountain roads were still on the list, but Nick was on top of that mountain, and she needed to see him. Every cell in her body cried out with the news that God had touched her tonight and opened her eyes. What joy! What freedom! She wanted to shout to the world and especially to Nick. She had to get to him, but when she looked at the peak of Mount Abel, her insides twisted into a knot.

Could she trust God to get her to the top? No.

Absolutely not.

Accidents happen *all the time*.

God wasn't a genie in a bottle. He didn't run a fantasy world the way Eve did. He had created a multi-dimensional, multifaceted diamond of experience—good, bad, ugly, and beautiful. Kate couldn't trust Him to get her to the top of Mount Abel the way she wanted, but she could trust Him completely to order her steps the way He'd done for Leona. How could she not? He'd sent a condor of her own, a bird named Wistoyo.

"I'll do it," she said to God in a shaky voice. "When the sun rises, we're going to the top of that mountain."

She considered going home, but she didn't want to disturb Leona. Hoping Nick might still show up, she reclined the seat and closed her eyes. Exhaustion overcame her anxiety and she slept, but terrifying dreams played through her mind until the sun beamed through the windshield and jolted her awake.

It was time to go to the top of Mount Abel. Time to go to Nick. Like an astronaut preparing for lift-off, she checked the car's mirrors and gas gauge, fastened her seat belt, and headed for the highway she'd taken with Nick to see the condors. That day on the Harley she'd asked him to go faster, and the memory strengthened her now. With every mile, the sun rose higher, lighting the way as she searched for the Mount Abel turnoff. After several minutes, the sign appeared: Mount Abel Campground 8 miles.

Eight miles of cliffs, steep slopes, and tight turns.

With her palms damp and her stomach a mess, she turned onto the narrow road, hit a pothole, and slammed on the brakes. Alligator cracks riddled the pavement, and the double-yellow line had been scraped away by snowplows. A canyon loomed in the distance. There was no guardrail, and she'd be in the outer lane. Driving up the center of the road crossed her mind, but Mount Abel attracted amateur astronomers. It was possible she'd encounter a car coming down while she was headed up. There was no way around her fear. She could go forward or back. There was no in-between.

Butterflies swarmed in her belly, and her mouth tasted like metal. Trembling, she pressed the accelerator and rounded the first curve. Instead of potholes and chipped road paint, she saw black velvet asphalt and a glistening double-yellow line. This section of road was brand-new. She wondered why, then realized the snowplows didn't come this far up the mountain.

Hugging the yellow line, she steered around a hairpin turn and up a steep slope. The tires spun on loose dirt for a split second, but they caught before she had time to be scared. A thick mist dulled the sun, but the yellow line shone bright until the pavement leveled into a dirt road that encircled the campground.

She'd done it. With God's help, she had reached the top of Mount Abel. Laughter bubbled out of her throat, and her skin broke out in feather-light tingles. Driving slowly around the big loop, she swiveled her head from side to side in search of Nick. She spotted several tents and a big RV, but he was nowhere in sight.

Clinging to hope, she steered to the farthest edge of the campground. As the tires crunched over pine needles, the sun burst through the mist and turned the water droplets into rainbows. Beams of light crisscrossed through the trees, and diamonds shimmered everywhere. It was beautiful, but most beautiful of all was the sight of Nick's truck behind a row of pines. Kate parked next to it, climbed out, and hurried to the blue tent zipped up tight against the night. Grinning, but a little afraid because she had hurt him, she called his name.

No answer. No soft snore.

She raised her voice. "Nick? Wake up. It's me."

Silence.

Crouching, she unzipped the flap and groaned at the sight of the empty sleeping bag. Desperate to touch him in even a small way, she laid her hand on the pillow and felt a trace of warmth. He had to be nearby, but where? She'd passed the restroom facilities earlier. If he'd gone for a shower, she would have seen him by now. No way could she sit idly and wait for him to return from a hike, not when he could be gone for hours.

Standing straight, she scanned the campground until her gaze landed on an arrow-shaped sign that read, Summit 1/4 mile. Praying he'd be there, she took off at a jog.

nick dropped down on the bench at the summit of Mount Abel, rubbed an ache out of his neck, and inhaled as deeply as he could. When he had visited this spot a year ago, a pinprick of glory had ended in a spiritual blood transfusion. He was a different man now. But he was still a hundred percent human, and today he was bleeding inside. Sleep had deserted him last night, but there was comfort in prayer and peace in spite of the fear that Kate would choose to stay at Eve's Garden.

A painful peace . . . but still it was peace.

Closing his eyes, he raised his face to the sky and soaked in the first traces of the day's warmth. He needed this moment like he needed air, but the beat of footsteps coming up the trail broke his concentration. Scowling, he opened his eyes and peered through a screen of sage to a bend in the narrow path. A flash of auburn hair caught his eye, so did a turquoise sweater like one Kate often wore to the office. There was no way the hiker could be Kate. She'd never make that treacherous drive.

He didn't want company, so he stood to leave. As he turned,

the woman rounded the last bend and looked up. Huffing and puffing, with her eyes riveted to his and her cheeks flushed pink with exertion, she grinned at him.

He had to be dreaming. *"Kate?"*

"I found you!" In spite of the thin air, her voice was exultant and she jogged even faster up the hill. Nick peered down at the top of her head, his mouth slightly agape, and his feet glued in place by the shock. He'd prayed hard last night, but he had never imagined Kate's finding him on top of Mount Abel.

She climbed the six concrete steps to the observation pad, hunched with her hands on her knees, and sucked air like a distance runner. "I'm so glad . . . you're here."

He drank in the sight of her messy hair and glowing face, but what did it mean? Was she here to fling herself into his arms because she'd answered the *why* question, or was this the start of another negotiation? He didn't know what to think until she straightened her spine. As their eyes met, a smile broke across her face with the force of a cloudless dawn. Her entire countenance was full of joy and life, triumph and love.

The glow spilled on to Nick, and he started to grin. This wasn't the opening salvo in a new argument. Kate had made that terrifying drive for just one reason. She loved him enough to face her greatest fear. He longed to pull her into his arms, but this was her victory lap, and he wanted to savor the moment with her. There was a time to rush, and a time to go slow. It was up to Kate to set the pace.

"So," he said in an overly casual tone, "what's up?"

Airy laughter rippled from her lips. Still breathing hard, she straightened. "Not a whole lot. How about you?"

He shrugged. "Just marking the biggest day of my life. You know how it is. There are days you'll never forget, the ones where you make a decision, or you change your mind about something. Or you meet someone you're destined to be with forever, and somehow you know it."

Her eyes twinkled into his. "I've had a few of those. Like when you see a condor and swerve off a cliff. Or when you think you're going to die and you ask God if He's real. Or when a stranger shows up and you see his face and you want"—she blinked away the sheen of tears—"you want so badly to believe in love and forever, that God is real, and that there aren't any accidents, not really."

He reached for her hand. "I take it this is one of those days."

"It is." She raised her chin. "Eve offered me the vice presidency. I turned it down. In fact, I quit my job entirely. I couldn't wait to tell you, but you weren't home. You were already gone, so . . . so here I am." She gave a little shrug, swallowed hard, and waited for him, just as he'd been waiting for her.

The vulnerable look zinged straight to his heart. This was indeed a day they would never forget. Loving her more than ever, he hauled her into his arms, matched his mouth to hers, and branded them both with a deep kiss.

When she came up for air, he pressed her head to his shoulder. "I thought I'd lost you."

"Never."

Their breathing synchronized, and they stood strong and steady in each other's arms until he recalled the road to the campground. Shuddering, he stroked her back. "It took real courage to make that drive."

"It *was* awful," she admitted. "It was even harder than walking out on Eve, but I had to see you. You were right. I was there for the wrong reasons."

He guided her down to the stone bench, where they sat

hip to hip, her hand on his knee and his arm snug around her waist. "Tell me everything."

She laid her head on his shoulder and took a deep breath. "After Leona's fall, I was confused and hurt. I thought God had disappeared, so I went back to taking control of my own life. I know God gives us free will and all that, but last night in Eve's office I finally understood something. The first choice we make is where to put our faith. Do we put it in God, ourselves, or other people? Do we trust Him to order our lives, or do we believe that all this—" sitting straight, she gestured at the mountains and sky with her hand—"that all this happened by accident?"

He turned his head so he could see into her eyes. "And what did you decide?"

"I decided Eve's a mess, and I don't want to be like her. Being in charge of my own life didn't go well, not at all. I almost lost you—" Choking up, she cupped his jaw with her warm fingers, rubbing slightly to feel the bristle. "I hurt you last night. I'm so sorry. I just didn't know."

He silenced her with a kiss. "Eve's a mess, but so am I."

"I don't think so—"

"I am." He meant it. "No pedestals, Kate. Especially not after last night. When I left you in that garden, I lost it. If Sam hadn't called about a stupid sprinkler system, I'd be camped out at the Black Dog Lounge. I couldn't stand the thought of losing you."

"You didn't." She hugged him hard.

"I'm human, Kate. So human it scares me to admit how much I love you."

"I love you, too."

A breeze rustled through the pines. Birds chirped all around them, and a feather-white mist swirled in the valley below. He and Kate were specks beneath a sky so blue they had to squint. A jetliner vectored north. In the distance, the Pacific stretched to the ends of the earth. Today was the official end of his sabbatical, and Kate was at peace with God and herself. Nick couldn't think of a more fitting time or place to ask her to be his wife.

Drawing her tight against his side, he soaked in the warmth of her body, inhaled the scent of her, then drew back enough to focus on her delicate profile. When he was sure he'd never forget a single detail of this extraordinary morning, he stood and took her hand in his. Gazing into her eyes, he hoped the right words would come, because he hadn't planned this moment. There would be no speech, no ring, nothing but the awareness that he was asking her to take another leap of faith. Not all marriages lasted, but all things were possible with God.

As her brows arched, Nick dropped to one knee. "Marry me, Kate. Be my wife."

Instead of squealing with joy and shouting yes, she pressed her free hand to her lips. The silence terrified him until she slid to her knees so they were face-to-face, kneeling before God and each other. The pose acknowledged that they were both specks on a mountain—mere human beings who loved God first, then each other.

Tears glistened in her eyes. "Yes . . . Yes, I'd be honored to be your wife."

He stood, then lifted her with his hands strong on hers. They stayed still for a moment, their gazes locked until he kissed her. Kate pressed tight against him, and they rejoiced together in the glory of what lay ahead—the joys and surprises, the triumphs and adventures, and the bittersweet knowledge that every road had bumps and tight turns, cliffs, and occasional potholes.

Nick didn't know how long it took to organize a wedding,

but he hoped it wasn't a year or even six months. Pulling back from the kiss, he whispered into her ear. "How long?"

"For what?"

"To plan the wedding."

She eased out of his embrace but held both his hands. "Would you mind terribly if we kept it small?"

"Not a bit." If it was up to him, they'd elope tonight.

"Good," she said, bouncing on her toes. "Because what I really want is a small wedding on Leona's deck with just family, a few friends, and Sam performing the ceremony. How about next Saturday?"

Nick's brows shot up. "In seven days?"

"Yes."

Grinning crazily, he picked her up and spun her around. To think they'd be married in just one week. Rejoicing, he threw back his head and laughed at God's always impeccable timing. "You know me," he said to Kate. "The faster, the better."

Epilogue

the morning after taking wedding vows on Leona's deck, Kate awoke in her husband's arms. Staring into Nick's sleepy eyes, she debated what to do. There were two things on her mind. The first was gloriously private. The other was about the invitation they'd received from Marcus Wilcox. Wistoyo was being released back into the wild today, and Marcus had invited Nick, Kate, and Leona to witness her liberation. Even though the event was the first day of their honeymoon, Kate and Nick had insisted Leona accompany them. To Kate's surprise, her grandmother said no.

"You don't want an old woman tagging along. Besides, Wistoyo is your bird, not mine."

Seeing Wistoyo struck Kate as the perfect way to start their honeymoon trip to a resort near Monterey. It had taken a few miracles to arrange a wedding in just seven days, but the pieces came together exactly how she envisioned. She skipped the traditional gown, choosing instead a short white dress with a poufy skirt and jeweled belt. The diamond wedding set on her finger was stunning, and Sam had performed the traditional ceremony with humor, wisdom, and appropriate gravity.

Just when she thought the day couldn't get any better, Nick had whispered in her ear that it was time to leave. Alone at last, he carried her over the threshold into his house—their house now. What a beautiful night . . . and today promised yet more blessings.

After breakfast, Nick packed the Harley and they headed to the condor launch site. Just for fun, Kate yelled, "Faster!" He cranked the throttle, and they arrived with a rumble in a cloud of dust.

Just like before, Marcus greeted them and pointed the way to the blind where they had watched Elvis dance for Moon Girl. They climbed side by side up the mountain, only this time Nick made an appreciative remark about her tight jeans and she teased him back. Voices drifted up from the canyon. Reaching for Nick's hand, Kate looked down at the field workers carrying a cage to a dry streambed.

"It's almost time," she said eagerly.

Nick handed her the binoculars. "Wistoyo's been cooped up for months. I bet she can hardly wait."

A lump pushed into Kate's throat, because she knew how Wistoyo felt. Kate, too, had been in a cage of sorts and was savoring her new freedom. When she turned to Nick, he took her hand. They exchanged a long look that said *I love you* without words and *I want you* without guilt. Then he kissed her lips to seal the promise.

In unison they turned back to the ravine. Below them, Marcus opened the door to Wistoyo's cage. The massive bird stuck her head out, glanced around, strutted forward, and spread her wings to reveal the yellow tag identifying her as Condor Number 53. She flapped those giant wings once, twice, then soared out of the canyon. She rose higher, higher still, until she caught a thermal. Gliding with no effort of her own, she circled above them, widening the loop with every pass until she broke free and flew north, farther and farther, until she was nothing but a speck. And then she was gone.

Kate lowered the binoculars and squeezed Nick's hand. Someday she'd write about this moment in a condor journal of her own—a book for their children and grandchildren. She'd tell those generations all about the birds, how she'd met a strong man and learned to fly free at his side.

With a heart full of joy, she thanked God for His grace, His love, and the pinprick of glory named Wistoyo.

Victoria Bylin is a romance writer known for her realistic and relatable characters. Her books have finaled in multiple contests, including the Carol Awards, the RITAs, and *RT Magazine's* Reviewers Choice Award. A native of California, she and her husband now make their home in Lexington, Kentucky, where their family and their crazy Jack Russell terrier keep them on the go. Learn more at her website: www.victoriabylin.com.

If you enjoyed *Until I Found You*, you may also like...

After his spontaneous marriage to Celia Park, bull rider Ty Porter quickly realized that he wasn't ready to be anybody's husband. Five years later, when he comes face-to-face with Celia—and the son he never knew he had—can he prove to her that theirs can still be the love of a lifetime?

Meant to Be Mine by Becky Wade
beckywade.com

Blake Hunziker has finally returned home to Whisper Shore, and he's planning to stay. Local inn owner Autumn Kingsley, on the other hand, can't wait to escape. When the two of them strike a deal to help each other out, will they get what they're looking for... or something else entirely?

Here to Stay by Melissa Tagg
melissatagg.com

On the trail of a missing friend, reporter Darcy St. James is shocked to find Gage McKenna—handsome and unforgettable as ever—on board the cruise ship she's investigating. She'll have to enlist Gage's help when it becomes clear that one disappearance is just the tip of the iceberg.

Stranded by Dani Pettrey
ALASKAN COURAGE #3, danipettrey.com

BETHANYHOUSE

Stay up-to-date on your favorite books and authors with our free e-newsletters. Sign up today at bethanyhouse.com.

Find us on Facebook. facebook.com/bethanyhousepublishers

Free exclusive resources for your book group! bethanyhouse.com/anopenbook

You may also enjoy…

On the set of a docudrama in Wildwood, Texas, Allie Kirkland is unnerved to discover strange connections between herself and a teacher who disappeared over a century ago. Is history about to repeat itself?

Wildwood Creek by Lisa Wingate
lisawingate.com

After her Olympic dreams are shattered, can Sabrina Rice help a troubled teen runner find hope for the future in a life that's spiraling out of control?

Chasing Hope by Kathryn Cushman

When Addie Cramer and Jonathan Mosier fall head over heels for each other, can their love finally end the feud between their two families?

Adoring Addie by Leslie Gould
THE COURTSHIPS OF LANCASTER COUNTY #2
lesliegould.com

BETHANYHOUSE

Stay up-to-date on your favorite books and authors with our free e-newsletters. Sign up today at bethanyhouse.com.

Find us on Facebook. facebook.com/bethanyhousepublishers

Free exclusive resources for your book group! bethanyhouse.com/anopenbook